THE LONG-RANGE WAR

(A LEARNING EXPERIENCE, BOOK V)

CHRISTOPHER G. NUTTALL

The characters and events portrayed in this book are fictitious. Any similarity to real persons, living or dead, is coincidental and not intended by the author.

Text copyright © 2018 Christopher G. Nuttall

All rights reserved.

Printed in the United States of America.

No part of this book may be reproduced, or stored in a retrieval system, or transmitted in any form or by any means, electronic, mechanical, photocopying, recording, or other-wise, without express written permission of the publisher.

ISBN-13: 978-1724215598
ISBN-10: 1724215590

Cover by Alexander Chau
www.alexanderchau.co.uk

Book One: A Learning Experience
Book Two: Hard Lessons
Book Three: The Black Sheep
Book Four: The Long Road Home
Book Five: The Long-Range War

http://www.chrishanger.net
http://chrishanger.wordpress.com/
http://www.facebook.com/ChristopherGNuttall

All Comments Welcome!

AUTHOR'S NOTE

The Long-Range War features characters from *Hard Lessons* and *The Black Sheep* and takes place roughly five months after *The Long Road Home*. A recap of the previous four books has been included as an appendix at the back of this book.

As always, if you enjoyed reading, please leave a review.

CGN.

PROLOGUE

"Signal the fleet," Empress Neola ordered. "The first divisions are to begin the attack."

She ignored her flunkies as they scurried to do her bidding, instead lifting her eyes to the massive display. Hundreds of thousands of starships were floating near the gravity point, slowly readying themselves to jump the hundreds of light years to Hudson in a single second. Five-mile-long superdreadnaughts and battleships to tiny destroyers and frigates, the latter crewed by client races...ready to go to war. As she watched, the first flotillas moved forward and into the gravity point, flickering out of existence and vanishing. Neola tensed, despite herself. She was all too aware, despite the optimistic reports from her scouts, that the advance elements might well meet a hostile reception. There had been human ships based at Hudson until recently.

But it doesn't matter, she told herself. The humans had superior firepower, but she had superior numbers. *Vastly* superior numbers. *That's why I sent the potentially disloyal elements into the fire first.*

She kept her face completely expressionless as the second and third divisions rumbled towards the gravity point. It had taken years, far longer than she would have liked, to start reactivating the reserve. The gerontocrats who'd ruled the Tokomak for thousands of years couldn't react quickly to *anything*, even a threat to their existence. They'd refused to believe that a race as young as *humanity* could threaten their enforcers, let alone themselves; they'd found it easier to blame Neola for incompetence than stretch their minds to encompass a younger race that posed a real threat. She supposed she should be grateful. They hadn't had the imagination to comprehend that *she* might pose a threat too. They'd expected her to sit tight and wait, for years if necessary, until they decided how they were going to slap her wrist. She was only a handful of centuries old, after all. There was no need for any *real* punishment.

And now they're safely restrained, she thought, feeling a flicker of glee. They *really* hadn't thought she could launch a coup. The idea was unthinkable until she'd actually *done* it. *They can't stand in the way any longer.*

Neola sobered as the third division of starships blinked and vanished. The gerontocrats hadn't bothered to keep the reserve up to date. It hadn't mattered, not when the pace of innovation had slowed down to a trickle. A starship built a thousand years ago was no less capable than one that had been completed only last week. But things were different now. The humans had proved themselves to be revoltingly ingenious and some of the other younger races were starting to follow in their footsteps. It was vitally important, if Tokomak supremacy was to be maintained, that the humans be enslaved or exterminated as quickly as possible. They were giving the other races ideas.

Her eyes found a cluster of icons moving into attack position and narrowed sharply. The squadron commanders were young, only a few hundred years old. They'd had nothing to look forward to, but a long slow climb up the ladder…until now. She'd shown them that someone could overthrow the established order and take power for themselves, she'd shown them—inadvertently—how she herself could be overthrown. She wondered, grimly, which one would have the imagination to make a bid for power. The gerontocrats would take years to plan a coup, more than long enough for her to nip it in the bud, but someone from her own generation might move faster. No, *would* move faster. Neola knew she wasn't the only one to have been impatient, over the last few centuries. The people she'd promoted—for having a certain level of imagination, for being able to think outside the rules and regulations they'd enforced on the known galaxy—were the ones most likely to be dangerous to her. Their ambitions would not be satisfied with anything less than absolute power.

It was, she acknowledged privately, a deadly balancing act. She *needed* people who could think outside the box...and there were very few of them, even amongst the young. Fleet operations had been so bound by formality over the last thousand years or so that too many officers simply didn't know how to cope, when presented with an emergency. Their fleet exercises had been carefully scripted, with the winners and losers known in advance. But she couldn't expect the humans to be *conventional*. Unconventional tactics were their only hope of surviving long enough to win the day.

She watched another set of icons vanish and smiled to herself. The humans were good, but they weren't *gods*. They'd be crushed by overwhelming firepower, even if her trap failed completely. If she had to fly her fleet all the way to Earth and turn the planet into a radioactive wasteland, she could do it. She *would* do it. If worse came to worst, she told herself time and time again, the Tokomak could trade hundreds of starships for a single human ship. She would still come out ahead.

A blue icon appeared, near the gravity point. Neola allowed her smile to widen. Local space on the other side was clear, then. Very few races would challenge a Tokomak ship, even one that was completely alone, but it was well to be sure. Her intelligence staff had reported all sorts of rumours making their way through the empire, from vast defeats that had never happened to talk of mutiny and revolution. She was all too aware that the staff might not be picking up everything, no matter what they claimed. The underground knew how to hide itself. It would have been exterminated by now otherwise.

"Hudson has been secured, Your Excellency," the communications officer reported. "There was little resistance."

"Very good," Neola said. She hadn't *expected* resistance, but who knew? The humans had been making inroads on Hudson—and hundreds of other worlds—for years. "Take the remainder of the fleet through the gravity point."

"As you command, Your Excellency."

• • •

"It's like a bloody nightmare."

"Keep your eyes on your console," Captain-Commodore Jenny Longlegs advised, dryly. Lieutenant Fraser had served long enough to remain calm, even if hell itself was pouring out of the gravity point. "Do we have an accurate ship count yet?"

"No, Captain," Lieutenant Fraser said. "But definitely upwards of five *thousand* starships."

Jenny sucked in her breath as more and more icons appeared on the display. The gravity point was disgorging a veritable *river* of starships. SUS *Schlieffen*, her cruiser, was more advanced than any of the superdreadnaughts and battleships forming into rows and advancing towards the planet, but Jenny doubted they'd survive long against such firepower. She prayed, silently, that the cloaking device held. The Tokomak weren't trying to hide. Their sensors were sweeping space so thoroughly that they'd probably know the exact location of every speck of dust by the time they headed to the next gravity point. She might have to order her ship to back off before the Tokomak had a chance to spot her. They'd risked everything to grab SUS *Odyssey*. She was fairly sure they'd be just as interested in grabbing *Schlieffen*.

"They're forming up," Fraser reported. "One flotilla is headed directly for the planet, another is heading for Point Four."

The shortest route to Earth, Jenny thought. It would still take months for the enemy fleet to reach the planet, and she had her doubts about their logistics, but there was no doubting the Tokomak's willingness to expend starships to crush their enemies. Half the ships on the display would be crewed by client races, utterly expendable as far as their masters were concerned. *They're on their way.*

She studied the display for a long moment, noting just how many ships had started to blur together into a haze of sensor distortion. Tokomak ECM was inferior to its human counterpart—the Tokomak hadn't faced any pressure to improve or die for thousands of years—but quantity had a quality all of its own. Her passive sensors were having fits trying to keep track of each and every enemy starship. She had the nasty feeling that there were *more* enemy ships in the system than her sensors could detect. They might well be using their own ECM—and cloaking devices—to hide part of their fleet.

Although they'd be taking a risk, she thought. *With so many ships in such a confined region of space, the odds of a collision are non-zero.*

She dismissed the thought with a flicker of irritation. The Tokomak probably wouldn't *care* if two of their ships collided, even if they were battleships. They had *thousands* of active starships and *tens* of thousands of starships in the reserves. *Schlieffen* could expend all her missiles, with each hit a guaranteed kill, and still lose. Quantity *definitely* had a quality all of its own.

"Captain," Lieutenant Hammond said. "I have a direct laser link to *Sweden*. She's requesting instructions."

Jenny nodded, slowly. "Copy our sensor records to her," she said. *Sweden* had held her position close to Point Four, ready to nip through before the Tokomak arrived and sealed the gravity point. *Schlieffen* would continue to monitor the enemy fleet from a safe distance, if indeed there was such a thing. "And then inform her CO that he is to run straight to Earth. Tell him..."

She sucked in her breath as she looked back at the display. The torrent of starships hadn't stopped. *Hundreds* of superdreadnaughts were gliding through the gravity point, their weapons charged and their sensors searching for trouble. Whoever was in charge over there was no slouch. Normally, the Tokomak were careful not to put too much strain on their sensor systems. But then, who would dare to attack them? Their defeat in the Battle of Earth, seven years ago, had been the first battle they'd lost in nearly a thousand years.

And every ship they lost represented less than a percentage point of a percentage point of their overall numbers, she reminded herself. *They could lose a thousand starships and never notice the loss.*

"Tell him to warn everyone," she finished. "The Tokomak are coming."

CHAPTER ONE

Hameeda walked down the long corridor, alone.

It felt as if she was walking for miles, even though she *knew* the corridor was only a few short metres from one airlock to the other. She couldn't help feeling nervous as she made her slow way towards the second airlock, despite all her preparations. It felt as if she was on the cusp of apotheosis or nemesis, the crowning height of her career or a disaster that would ensure she never served in space again. Her heart thumped so loudly in her chest that she was glad she was alone. Anyone escorting her wouldn't need enhanced hearing to pick out her heartbeat.

She stopped outside the second airlock and took a long breath. Her CO had told her, an hour ago, that it wasn't too late to back out. She didn't *have* to go through with the bonding. No one would fault her for changing her mind, even now. The vast resources that had been expended on preparing her for the process would be better wasted, then expended on someone who didn't want to go through with it. Hameeda understood their concerns—and her mother's fears, during their last call—but she had no intention of backing out. The old fogies, the ones so old they remembered living on Earth, simply didn't have the imagination of the spaceborn. *They* feared technology even as it had given them a chance to reshape both their former homeworld and the galaxy itself. Hameeda and her generation embraced the promise of technology, without fear. The future was within their grasp.

And we must make sure we have a future, she thought. *Because there are always those ready to take it from us.*

It wasn't a pleasant thought. Her mother had been a refugee from Afghanistan, from a life so *alien* that Hameeda had problems grasping that it had ever existed. The mere *concept* of being forced into eternal servitude, simply for being born female, was difficult to grasp. How could someone be so uncivilised? And yet, after her mother had told her yet another horror story, Hameeda had looked it up. If anything, her mother had understated the case. Earth was an uncivilised world. They fought over nothing, even when they could reach out and claim the stars themselves. Their mere existence was a reminder that the human race could sink back into the mud.

Her reflection looked back at her. Hameeda had kept her mother's dark hair, darker eyes and tinted skin, even as she'd spliced more and more enhancements into her genome. She was stronger, faster and fitter than any groundpounder, more than capable of holding her own in a fight. But she felt hesitant now. If something went wrong, if one of the doubters had been right all along…she'd be dead before she knew it. But life was risk. Safety was an illusion. And she knew better than to feel otherwise.

Hameeda took another breath, then pressed her hand against the sensor. There was a long moment as the security systems checked and rechecked her identity, then the airlock hissed open, revealing a vast hanger. Hameeda suddenly felt very small indeed. The LinkShip floated in the centre of the chamber, dwarfing her. It was tiny, compared to a regular starship; it was barely sixty metres from bow to stern. And yet, it was also the most advanced starship in the galaxy. Her FTL and realspace drives were the fastest known to exist, faster even than a courier boat. It had taken *years* to turn the concept into reality. Hameeda had spent almost as long training to serve as its—*her*—commanding officer.

She drank in the sight for a long moment, her eyes wandering over the dark hull. The LinkShip looked like a giant almond, its weapons and defences carefully worked into the material so they didn't spoil the ship's lines. Hameeda wasn't sure how she felt about that, even though she admired the elegance. An observer would not have to look *inside* the ship to know she was a distinctly non-standard vessel. And yet, it was a step towards a human aesthetic that was obviously different from the galactic standard. Too many races, even the ones that had been walking the stars when humanity had been crawling in the mud, used modified Tokomak designs. Humanity had to be different.

Bracing herself, she activated her command implants and sent a command into the computer network. The world seemed to shimmer around her. Hameeda closed her eyes for a long moment as the teleport field made her entire body tingle, then opened them again. She was standing in the LinkShip's command centre, alone. Her lips curved into a smile. The old fogies distrusted teleporters, asking all sorts of questions about souls and other unquantifiable issues none of the spaceborn understood. To them, teleporting was normal. Hameeda had been having her molecules broken down into energy and put back together again since she was a child. It was normally very safe.

Unless there's a jamming field, she reminded herself, as she rested her hands on her hips. *Or a delay that causes the energy pattern to start to degrade.*

She pushed the thought out of her head as she surveyed the command centre. It looked bland and boring, compared to a starship's bridge, but it was *hers*. A single chair, sited in the exact centre of the chamber; a helmet, primed to make the first connection between Hameeda and the ship's datanet. There were no consoles, no display...there *were* emergency control systems, in another compartment, but very little effort had been wasted on them. Anything that broke through the LinkShip's defences would almost certainly be enough to destroy the ship, or—at the very least—render it completely beyond repair. Hameeda had been told, time and time again, that there would be very little hope of long-term survival. Once the Tokomak realised what the LinkShips were, they would do everything in their power to destroy them. Their mere existence was an affront to the laws the Tokomak had written for the entire galaxy.

And they may have had good reason to ban direct organic-computer interaction, Hameeda thought, as she sat down on the chair. *We simply don't know their reasoning.*

She shook her head. The Tokomak had banned a *lot* of things, without bothering to explain their reasoning. Some of them made sense, she supposed; others appeared to have been banned without a valid reason. And still others appeared thoroughly pointless. She had no idea why they'd put a ban on interspecies relationships. It wasn't as if they'd had to bother.

The air suddenly felt tense as she reached for the helmet. If she put it on, if she allowed her implants to make contact with the datanet, she would be bound to the LinkShip for the rest of her life. She wouldn't be able to leave, not without breaking the connection. The scientists had sworn blind that there *would* be a way, eventually, to freeze the ship's mentality to give her some downtime, but for the moment she was committing herself to remain on the ship permanently. Hameeda had no qualms about living on a starship—and she had no particular interest in returning to the carefree days of her youth—yet she knew it was one hell of a commitment. She would practically be a prisoner...

A prisoner with a starship and freedom to fly, she thought. She'd be a naval officer for decades, of course, but afterwards...she'd be free. *I wonder where I'll go.*

She took a long breath, then pulled the helmet over her head. Her implants activated a second later, providing the datacores with a string of coded identifications that even *she* found hard to follow. She was dimly aware of classified systems steadily coming online, each one checking and rechecking the codes before slotting itself into the datanet. The sheer immensity of the LinkShip scared her, despite all her preparation. She'd put herself *en rapport* with an AI two weeks ago, but that had been different. She hadn't been trying to bond with that AI.

The datanet came to life. "Are you ready to proceed?"

Hameeda blinked, surprised despite herself. It was talking...of *course* it was talking. Even a very basic system, a restricted intelligence, had simple conversational overlays, linked to a self-learning system that allowed it to evolve as it went along. She'd heard of RIs that had somehow managed to bootstrap themselves into true AIs, despite their programming. The old fogies had found that more than a little alarming, but Hameeda and her generation rather approved. Their creations had started to evolve.

"Yes," she said. She made it as clear as she could. "Proceed."

For a heartbeat, nothing happened. She had a moment to wonder if something had gone wrong, either with the technology or the command codes, before her mind was suddenly linked to something much greater. Her thoughts expanded with terrifying speed, reaching out to merge with the LinkShip's datanet. She was suddenly *very* aware of everything from the drives, slowly readying themselves to push the LinkShip out of the hangar and into open space, to the weapons systems, currently powered down but ready for immediate activation if she had to go to war. She was linked to the ship...no, she *was* the ship. It was practically her body.

Wow, she thought, as a torrent of data poured into her brain. The ship's sensors were sucking in data from all over the station. She could see *everything*. The images were so sharp that she could even see a handful of warships holding position outside the station, watching and waiting. She felt a stab of bitter annoyance as she remembered why those starships were there. The naysayers had insisted, pointing out that the LinkShip might go insane. *And they were wrong.*

She powered up the drives slowly, watching as power ran through the tiny starship. It really *was* a miracle of science. She'd known that all along, of course, but she hadn't *really* understood it until she'd actually *touched* the datanet. They'd miniaturised all sorts of systems in order to cram them into her hull, despite the risk. Warning icons flashed up in her mind as she checked the self-repair functions, pointing out their limitations. The naysayers had had a point about *them*, she reflected ruefully. A single hit might well be enough to cripple the LinkShip beyond repair.

Then we will have to be sure not to be hit, she thought, as she accessed the hangar datanet and opened the hatch. *Luckily, we're the fastest thing in space.*

The LinkShip practically *lunged* forward as she gunned the drive, throwing itself into the inky darkness of space. Hameeda felt her mind split in two, one half thinking it was still human while the other half thought it was a starship. Space was both incredibly dangerous, lethal even to an enhanced human, and her natural habitat. Her mind expanded, once again: the station, the starships, a handful of test beacons…she was suddenly very aware of their exact locations. Subroutines within her mind assessed their positions, calculated their trajectories and analysed their threat potential. She would be safe enough, her mentality concluded, as long as she kept her distance.

But they would also be safe from me, she thought, as she circled the station. She felt like a child purchasing her first in-orbit buggy. No, like a child who had moved from a buggy to a marine assault shuttle with nothing in-between. The sheer *potency* of the LinkShip frightened her as much as it thrilled her. *I'd have to close the range if I wanted to fight them.*

A voice popped into her awareness. "LinkShip Alpha, please engage the first set of beacons."

Hameeda smiled to herself as she swung the LinkShip around, bringing the weapons online. LinkShip Alpha. She was going to have to think of a better name. Perhaps something defiant, something that fitted humanity…or perhaps something that would make children smile, when they read her name in their history books. A subroutine went to work, considering possible names, even as she refocused her mind on her targets. The first set of beacons were not designed to be hard to hit.

Baby steps, she told herself, as she started her attack run. Her phasers jabbed out, time and time again. The beacons vanished with terrifying speed. She reminded herself, sharply, that the beacons were practically *begging* to be killed. The next set of targets would be a great deal harder. *You have to learn to walk before you can run.*

But she *wanted* to run. Her mind had blurred so much into the ship that she was no longer truly certain where she ended and the ship began. Indeed, her mentality had imprinted itself upon the datanet. Her lips twitched in annoyance. The Solar Union might have been reluctant to build a ship that was commanded by an AI, but it had no qualms—or at least fewer qualms—about designing a ship to draw from a human mind. There was a part of her that simply wanted to throw caution to the winds and run as fast as she could, crossing the entire solar system in a split second. But her duty held her firmly in place.

Hameeda put the thought aside for later consideration as she moved the LinkShip through its paces, systematically taking out target after target. The tests grew more complicated as she progressed, from targets that were hidden behind stealth coatings and cloaking devices to targets that actually shot back. She discovered that the LinkShip was perfectly capable of engaging targets while dodging incoming fire, although it lacked hammers and other heavy missiles. But with a little twiddling, she could turn the drive into a makeshift hammer. Who knew what would happen then?

I might get caught in the blast, she told herself. It was the sort of trick that worked in *Stellar Star* movies, but was completely useless in the real world. *I'd have to be well away before the explosion hit.*

Another voice entered her awareness as she completed the final set of tests. "Permission to come aboard?"

It took her a moment to draw her mind back to the here and now. Admiral Keith Glass wanted to board. She accessed the teleport system, synchronised with the station and yanked him onto the LinkShip, deliberately materialising him in the command centre. The process was easy, with the ship's datanet handling the transfer, but a chill ran down her spine as she realised just how many buffers Glass's pattern has passed through. Perhaps the old fogies were right to be concerned about teleporting. He appeared in front of her, his face darkening as he looked at her. It was harder than Hameeda had expected to disengage herself from the helmet and stand. Her legs felt wobbly. Her uniform was damp with sweat.

The datalink is still engaged, she thought. She might have disengaged from the helmet, but she was still linked to the ship. *I can never leave again.*

"An interesting set of tests," Glass observed. He was studying her, his eyes—older than the rest of him—clearly concerned. "How are you feeling?"

"Different," Hameeda admitted. Her throat felt parched, despite her enhancements. She was going to have to work on taking care of her body while she was directly connected to the ship. It would probably require a whole new set of subroutines. "It's nothing like flying a regular starship."

"One would hope so," Glass agreed. He was old enough to remember when the most advanced spacecraft on Earth were rockets. "How well does it—does *she*—stack up against enemy systems?"

"She's very agile," Hameeda said. "And she combines speed and hitting power with stealth. I think they'll have some problems hitting me."

"So the simulations say," Glass said. "And yourself? How are you feeling?"

Hameeda took a moment to allow her intellect to roam over the entire ship before she answered. "It will be different," she said. The LinkShip was large enough to accommodate her and a few guests—indeed, her quarters were larger than the average admiral's quarters—but she had a feeling it wouldn't be long before the crew compartments started to feel small. "I will cope."

Glass smiled, humourlessly. "I'm glad to hear it," he said. "And so will the beancounters."

"Until you tell them you intend to produce ten more," Hameeda said, wryly. "They'll throw a fit."

She had to smile at the thought. The Solar Union could have produced ten cruisers for the cost of a single LinkShip, although she suspected that costs would be going down now the design was finalized. It wasn't a small amount. The Solar Union was immensely rich, compared to many of the other younger races, but the cost was still notable. If the first LinkShip didn't pay off, in everything from tactical advantages to new technology, it was unlikely a second would be built. Her ship *had* to be a success if she didn't want to remain unique.

"Let me worry about that," Glass said. "Are you ready for deployment?"

Hameeda blinked. "Sir...?"

"The war may be about to resume," Glass said. He looked faintly meditative for a second. "I believe that an ultimatum has already been received. So far, it's been hushed up, but that won't last."

"No, sir," Hameeda said, doubtfully. On one hand, she understood the principles of operational security; on the other, she—like most of her generation—believed that governments should not be allowed to classify anything. Secrecy always led to tyranny. It was a contradiction she'd never been able to resolve. "When do you expect me to be deployed?"

"Not long," Glass said. He clapped her on the shoulder. "You'd better start planning to be gone within a week."

Hameeda stared. "A week?"

"It's nowhere near long enough for a proper shakedown," Glass said. "But tell me...are there any problems?"

"No, sir," Hameeda said, after a moment. "But if something makes itself apparent during the deployment..."

"You'll cope with it," Glass told her. "Word is, Captain, that this time it's serious. And we have to be ready."

"Yes, sir," Hameeda said. "We *will* be ready."

CHAPTER TWO

Admiral Hoshiko Sashimi Stuart forced herself to look confident as she strode into the small briefing room, her aide—Captain Yolanda Miguel—dogging her heels. Only a handful of people were waiting for her, but they were amongst the most powerful and influential people in the Solar Union. President Allen Ross, Admiral Mongo Stuart, Director Kevin Stuart and, perhaps most influential of all, Steven Stuart himself. Hoshiko's grandfather held no formal title, not since he'd purchased a starship and set out to explore the universe, but there were millions of people who practically worshipped him. He could be President—again—if he wished, whatever the law said. Hoshiko would have been surprised if Ross hadn't been more than a little discomforted by *the* Founding Father's presence.

It wasn't a thought she liked. She'd gone to some lengths to get away from her heritage as one of *the* Stuarts, to the point where she'd played up the Japanese side of her ancestry as much as possible. Indeed, to be fair to the old men, they hadn't given her or any of her relatives an unfair advantage as they climbed the ladder to command rank. Hoshiko knew better than to expect her elderly relatives to save her from the consequences of her own decisions. But, at the same time, others *had* given her an advantage. She'd welcomed the mission to the Martina Sector simply because it separated her from her relatives. The crews who'd been sent with her didn't care about her family or anything else, save for her competence.

And at least I proved my competence, she thought, as her implants reported a number of privacy fields coming to life. *They cannot doubt me now.*

"Admiral Stuart," President Ross said. "Please, be seated. We're quite informal here."

"Thank you, Mr. President," Hoshiko said.

She nodded for Yolanda to take a seat beside her, then sat herself. She'd always felt an odd kinship to the other woman, even though they had little in common. Yolanda had been born on Earth and escaped to the Solar Union in her late teens, while Hoshiko was a third-generation Solarian. And yet, they both had Japanese ancestry. It mattered very little in the Solar Union, but it meant something to Hoshiko. She'd studied her family's past purely because it was different. No one wrote detailed biographical studies of the Sashimi Family, even though Mariko Sashimi had been the original First Lady. Hoshiko had always wondered if there was a reason her grandmother had been practically written out of the history books.

The President smiled at her, although it didn't quite touch his eyes. "Kevin?"

Kevin Stuart leaned forward. Hoshiko studied her great-uncle with interest. Like most of his generation, he'd frozen his aging at a point that made him look around forty, but his eyes looked old. He was in his second century and everyone knew it.

"We *finally* received the official ultimatum," he said. "It was surprisingly short and concise for something from the Tokomak, a *mere* ten thousand words. Boiled down to the bare essentials, it basically tells us to surrender unconditionally or die."

"How surprisingly practical of them," Mongo growled.

Hoshiko nodded, shortly. It was a mystery to her how such an *ossified* government could survive for thousands of years without being overthrown, but the Tokomak had somehow managed to make it work.

It helped, she supposed, that they had the respect of most of the other Galactics. The elder races simply didn't want to rock the boat.

"We also received an update from the Hudson picket, shortly afterwards," Kevin added, tapping the console. A starchart appeared, hovering over the table. "The Tokomak are coming. Our most pessimistic estimate says their fleet will arrive at Sol within nine months."

"If they keep coming, without bothering to stop," Hoshiko said. She'd been in the navy long enough to know that deploying thousands of ships over thousands of light years required bases and service facilities. She suspected it would take the juggernaut over a year to reach its target, particularly if the Tokomak smashed the remainder of the Galactic Alliance on the way. But that wouldn't stop their fleet from being effective when it arrived. "Do we not think they'll take bases along the way?"

"We assume so," Kevin said. "But we don't *know*."

"There have already been leaks," Ross said. The President's voice was tightly composed, but Hoshiko could hear annoyance under his words. "We need to present a plan before the debate *really* gets going."

"Quite," Steven said. "Hoshiko, I believe you *have* a plan?"

"Yes, sir," Hoshiko said. She took a datachip from her pocket and slotted it into the terminal, then entered her security code. "We spent the last six months drawing up a basic contingency plan. It will not take long to update it for the current situation."

Although we thought we'd have more time, she added silently. Whoever was running the Tokomak these days clearly didn't believe in letting the grass grow under his feet. She felt a flicker of admiration, mingled with concern. Anyone who could push the *Tokomak* bureaucracy into acting quickly, by their standards, was clearly a formidable opponent. *The enemy is already breathing down our necks.*

A new starchart, covered with tactical icons, appeared in front of them. "There are three gravity point chains that can be used to deploy a fleet from Tokomak itself to Sol," she said, without preamble. "Based on the report from Hudson, I'd say they were planning to use the Apsidal

Chain, a string of nine gravity points that literally cut *years* off the transit time. This gives us an opportunity to take the fight to them."

"They might be using the other two chains as well," Ross pointed out.

"They might," Hoshiko agreed, "but they would be *very* aware of the dangers of trying to make such a plan work, to say nothing of the damage to their economy if they block transit through all *three* chains. I'd be very surprised if they weren't sealing off the Apsidal Chain as they move down it. They have to be aware that we had ships at Hudson."

She took a long breath. The plan had been drawn up by a planning cell, under her direct command. It hadn't been shared with the Admiralty, let alone the Senate or the Special Security Council. She'd watched it take shape and form, even though she'd been aware that the enemy might do something—anything—to turn the plan into so much wasted effort. War was a democracy, she reminded herself. The enemy got a vote.

"They will have to funnel ships through the gravity points, which will create a series of bottlenecks," she said. "That will give us an opportunity to bring our concentred strength to bear against isolated enemy detachments. A full-scale gravity point assault, sir, is hugely costly to the attackers. I believe the attackers would require a ten-to-one advantage to break through the defences and secure the system."

Which is why it took so long for a galactic hegemony to arise, she thought, remembering her history lessons. *The Tokomak didn't take control until they found a way to bypass the gravity points.*

"The plan is basically simple," she continued. "The Offensive Fleet will depart, within the week, and secure control of Apsidal itself. We *should* be able to beat the enemy fleet to the nexus if we move now. We take control of the system, land troops on the planet and prepare to bleed the enemy white when they start moving through the gravity point. They'll have some real problems if they want to take the system without suffering immense casualties."

"And if you're wrong?" Mongo asked. "What happens if they get there first?"

"We harry them as best as we can, while setting up ambushes further down the chain," Hoshiko said, bluntly. The Tokomak would have more options for outflanking her if they reached Apsidal first. If *she* were in command of the enemy fleet, she would have put securing Apsidal right on the top of the list. "We don't want to waste ships and men trying to mount a gravity point assault ourselves."

She contemplated the possibilities for a long moment. The planners had made it clear that Apsidal *had* to be taken and held. Giving the Tokomak a chance to flood the sector with warships would be disastrous in so many different ways. They'd have the opportunity to batter their way to Earth, but also the chance to intimidate wavering members of the Galactic Alliance into returning to their side. Hoshiko wouldn't blame the younger races for rethinking their positions, if the Tokomak put a gun to their heads. They resented the dominance of the elder races, but they also knew they couldn't stand up to their elders in an even fight. Their technology, even with human assistance, wasn't enough to turn any engagement into an even fight.

"Apsidal itself may be wavering," she added. "If we arrived in sufficient force, we might be able to convince the planet to switch sides."

"And it wouldn't matter if it remained loyal," Kevin pointed out. "They wouldn't be able to interfere once you controlled the outer system."

"Yes, sir," Hoshiko said. Apsidal was heavily defended—the Tokomak had invested in securing all of the known gravity point nexuses—but the planetary defences couldn't hit anything beyond the high orbitals. She could lay siege to the planet, if she wished, or simply ignore it. "There is good reason, however, to think that most of the population will switch sides."

Mongo coughed. "We will see what happens when we arrive," he said, gruffly. "They told us the Iraqis would welcome us as liberators too."

"We can promise the locals a better deal," Kevin countered.

"Which we may not be in a position to enforce," Mongo warned. "If the locals switch sides—and then we lose control of the system—Apsidal is doomed. The Tokomak will probably bombard the planet into submission, then take direct control of whatever is left.

"Yes, sir," Hoshiko said. She'd read the reports from Hudson and the Harmonies. The Tokomak had been securing the gravity points for the last few years. They'd been quite relaxed about them, in the past, but clearly *that* had changed too. They might just have realised that they were in a fight for their very existence. "We have no reason to doubt it."

"And nor do they," Mongo said. "It might be better to give the locals plausible deniability."

"If we can," Kevin said. "Do you know how many underground groups have requested our support over the last six months?"

"Yeah," Mongo said. "And do *you* know how many of those groups will survive if the Tokomak take the gloves off?"

Steven cleared his throat, loudly. "I believe we're getting off-topic," he said. "Admiral"—his eyes rested on Hoshiko—"do you believe the plan is workable?"

"I believe it offers us our best chance to survive," Hoshiko said. "If we allow them to bring their fleet to Sol, sir, we will be unable to keep them from devastating the entire system. They won't remain focused on Earth, not this time. They'll concentrate on wrecking the solar system from one end to the other. We'll hurt them badly, sir, but they can afford to take it. They can trade a thousand ships for every one of ours and still come out ahead."

She nodded at the starchart. "We can bleed them badly at Apsidal, without exposing too many of our ships to their fire. And we can *keep* hurting them, keep their fleet off-balance, until we bleed them dry. It may be our only chance for survival. The Tokomak are out for blood."

"Yes," Kevin agreed. "We have good reason to believe that surrenders are *not* going to be accepted, at least in our case. The Tokomak want us exterminated. We're simply too disruptive, too bad an example to the younger races. We cannot hope that they will allow some of us to live."

"There *is* the long-range colonisation project," Steven said.

"We assume they will have the time they need to settle an isolated system and rebuild," Mongo said. "But how many things could go wrong?"

Hoshiko nodded. The idea of sending a colony ship a *very* long way from Sol—and the Tokomak—was a good one, but Mongo was right. Too many things could go wrong. The ship could run into a powerful and hostile alien race, or have technical problems that would wreck the ship thousands of light years from any help, or have problems finding a suitable star system to settle. And if the Tokomak suspected that a colony ship *had* been dispatched into the unexplored regions, they'd spare no effort to find it. If humanity had shaken their empire to the core in less than sixty years, what might happen if an isolated colony had a couple of hundred years to rebuild? Hoshiko had been told, once, that humanity would have been able to stomp the Tokomak flat if they'd been allowed a hundred years or so for research and development. She wasn't sure if that was true, but it didn't matter. The Tokomak might believe it.

Ross frowned. "How many ships do you intend to assign to the operation?"

"As many as possible," Hoshiko said. "I'd like to have the first, second and third fleets, for starters. And then reserve ships too. I'd also like to take the prefabricated fortresses from Varner, if they can be collected in time. We need to mass as much firepower as possible on the gravity points."

"You're talking about stripping the Solar Union of two-thirds of its mobile firepower," Ross pointed out. "*That* won't go down well in the Senate. There's always some hysterical personage who'll start insisting that we'll all be murdered in our beds."

"The more things change," Steven commented, "the more they stay the same."

"Human nature doesn't change." Ross sounded amused. "And no one has any doubt that we'll be slaughtered if the Tokomak invade the system."

"Then it would be better to keep the Tokomak away from the system," Mongo said, dryly. "I think we should be able to guarantee Sol's security against any real threat, at least until the Tokomak arrive. The real problem will be escorting convoys to the Grand Alliance. We might have to call on our allies to provide protection."

"They should be able to handle it," Ross said. "But they're scared too."

"If we can block the Tokomak at Apsidal, their worlds should be safe," Hoshiko said. Her lips twisted into something a charitable man might call a smile. "And if we fail, their worlds are doomed anyway."

"I think we'll be a *little* more diplomatic when we discuss the matter with them," Ross said, dryly. "Gentlemen? Do you have any thoughts?"

"Boldness is our only hope," Steven said. "If we sit here and wait to be hit, we'll lose. We cannot hope to survive the first blow, just to make a crystal-clear case that we were attacked."

"And we don't *have* to make such a case," Mongo teased him. "Everyone *knows* the Tokomak are out to destroy us. We all knew that it was only a matter of time before they dispatched another fleet to Sol. Show the records from Hudson to the people, Mr. President, and you'll have all the support you could possibly need."

"Let us hope so," Ross said. "Admiral, when would you intend to depart?"

"As soon as possible," Hoshiko said. She hastily assessed the situation. "Realistically, we'd be looking at a week to two weeks. The fleet is maintained in a constant state of readiness, but we'd have to load up the fleet train and, if necessary, recall and requisition freighters from their other duties."

"The merchant spacers will love *that*," Kevin muttered.

"They'll understand the urgent need for transport," Steven said, briskly. "My ship can be amongst those requisitioned. The real problem lies in the damage this will do to our economy."

"Better to be poorer for a while than dead," Mongo said. "We can rebuild afterwards, if there is an afterwards."

"Yes, sir," Hoshiko said. "We can still support the fleet and, right now, that's all that matters."

"True," Kevin agreed.

Ross tapped the table for attention. "I'll make a formal request for war powers this afternoon, then," he said. "The Senate will be meeting in emergency session, where they'll see the recordings from Hudson for the first time. Admiral, start preparing to mobilise as soon as you return to your ship. I have no doubt the Senate will agree to grant war powers."

"Yes, Mr. President," Hoshiko said. She kept her doubts to herself. "I have to say, though, that we have to keep our intentions secret. The Tokomak must not be...*ah*, encouraged—to speed up their plans. We must assume that they're keeping a close eye on us."

"Insofar as they can," Kevin said. "We did manage to turn a couple of alien spies into assets."

"We can't assume they're the only ones," Hoshiko reminded him, dryly. She couldn't understand why some humans might betray their own race, but she couldn't deny that it had happened. There were enough humans amongst the stars, descendents of men and women taken from Earth centuries ago, for her to believe that the Tokomak might be able to turn them into spies. "It's important that we don't give them any hint of our plans."

"I'll see to that," Ross said. "Only the Oversight Committee will know the full plan."

"Thank you, Mr. President," Hoshiko said. There would be no way to conceal the mobilisation, but no one outside a handful of people would know the fleet's intended destination. "As long as we have the advantage of surprise, we should be able to take Apsidal before they realise what we're planning."

Steven met her eyes. "And if they get there first?"

"We'll have to improvise," Hoshiko told him. "We *have* to bleed their fleet white before it reaches Earth."

CHAPTER THREE

Captain Martin Luther Douglas couldn't help swaggering a little as he strode into the briefing room, followed by two of his subordinates. Special Forces Recon were the best of the best, heirs to traditions that stretched all the way back to the Navy SEALS, the Special Air Service and a dozen other special forces outfits from Old Earth. Martin knew, without false modesty, that he and his men were perhaps the finest fighting force in the galaxy, capable of everything from stealthy insertions into enemy territory to training and supporting insurgent forces on alien worlds. Indeed, their last deployment had been to a world—Earth itself—that was both familiar and disconcertingly alien. It had been shitty when Martin had left, six years ago, but it had somehow managed to grow worse. He hadn't enjoyed the deployment.

He took a seat at the front of the room, crossed his legs and settled down to wait. No one stood on formality in Special Forces Recon, not when they'd all seen the elephant time and time again. Senior officers had nothing to prove to their juniors. Anyone who made it through Selection—and survived his first deployment—was an outstanding soldier. Martin had been told that he'd be jumped up two ranks if he went back to the regular forces. It hadn't interested him.

Major Griffin entered the room and strode to the podium. He was a tall man, his brown hair cut close to his scalp. Griffin wasn't as heavily muscled as some of the men in the room, but it didn't matter. Martin had been on deployments under Griffin's command. He knew from experience that Griffin was a good leader as well as a soldier. Martin envied the man's children, even though there was a risk their father would never come home. What would *he* have become, he'd wondered more than once, if he'd had a *real* father in his life? But a boy who grew up in the ghetto would be lucky if he had *any* positive role model to emulate.

"Gentlemen and ladies," Major Griffin said. "We're going into lockdown after this briefing, so remember the rules. Anything you write, and I mean *anything*, will be scrutinised before it reaches its destination."

Martin nodded, although it was irritating. There was only one person outside the Special Forces Recon he wanted to contact and *she* had a security clearance that left his in the dust. But he understood the precautions. Special Forces Recon couldn't do half of its work if *everyone* knew what they were doing. He'd just have to be careful what he put in the letter, when he wrote to Yolanda. The lockdown wouldn't let them actually speak face-to-face.

And we can't even mention going into lockdown, he thought, crossly. *That'll get scrubbed by the censors too.*

"We will be deploying in less than a week," Major Griffin informed them. "Ideally, we'll be transferred to a MEU in a day or two, where we will wait for everyone else to catch up with us. I trust this won't be a problem?"

Martin shook his head. Special Forces Recon was designed for immediate deployment, if necessary. They were supposed to be able to reach any point within the Solar System in less than a day. Having a couple of days to make preparations was unusual. It suggested a long-term deployment rather than an emergency that had popped up out of nowhere. But it felt a little odd. He wondered, idly, what had happened. The Solar Marines normally handled long-term deployments.

"Our destination is a system called Apsidal," Major Griffin said. The name meant nothing to Martin. "Apsidal is a gravity point nexus, with no less than five known gravity points within the system. *Our* interest lies in

Apsidal-VI, the centre of civilisation for the sector. All you need to know, right now, is that it's ruled by a planetary oligarchy that spends most of its time sucking up to our enemies."

His lips quirked. "Believe me, you will have plenty of time to read the background files during the voyage."

If you give us time, Martin thought. They'd be spending most of the voyage training, of that he was sure. Downtime was relatively rare, even during leave. He'd been unable to go on a long vacation for fear he might be recalled at any moment. *You'll be pitting us against the marines to test their skills, will you not?*

"Ideally, we will be able to secure the system—and the planet—without difficulty," Major Griffin added. "If not, depending on the exact situation, our task will be to either take the planet itself, neutralising its defences along the way, or provide support to local insurgents. I don't think I need to remind you, particularly after the incident in San Francisco, that the latter will be extremely difficult. There are no hints, in any of the briefing notes, that there are any alternate power structures on the planet."

Which means the different insurgent groups may hate each other as much as they hate the oligarchy, Martin thought. He hadn't been in San Francisco when the shit hit the fan, but he'd heard the stories. One group of insurgents had been more interested in slaughtering its rivals than actually rebuilding the country. *We may find ourselves caught in the middle.*

"A further complication is that the enemy may attempt to kick us out of the system, once we secure it," Major Griffin warned. "I'm sure you can tell what that may mean for our deployment. We might find ourselves trapped on the planet, with no way out."

Martin nodded, curtly. It wasn't a pleasant thought. On Earth, they'd been able to teleport out if things *really* went wrong. On Apsidal, that wouldn't be an option if there were no ships in teleport range. The Tokomak knew how to jam teleport signals, too. It wasn't that hard with the right equipment. They'd have no trouble trapping the troops on Apsidal until they were ready to deal with them.

"If that happens, our objective will be to harass the enemy as much as possible, ideally with help from the locals," Major Griffin warned. "But the odds of survival will be very low."

"Never tell me the odds," someone said from the rear.

Sergeant Pickering cleared his throat. "How much will we stand out on Apsidal?"

"The planet does have a number of humans, according to the last census," Major Griffin said. "But we must assume that we have all been targeted for extermination."

Martin winced. He'd met enough aliens to know that they came in all shapes and sizes, but it would be a rare alien who mistook a human for a member of another race. It was vaguely possible, he supposed, that an alien might not know what a human looked like…he shook his head. It wasn't something they dared count upon, when the shit hit the fan. The Tokomak probably would make sure that *everyone* knew what a human looked like. All humans probably looked alike to the aliens, but they still looked *human*.

"Maybe we should disguise ourselves as Klingons," he offered. "It wouldn't be as if anyone would be *sure* the Klingons don't exist."

"It might come to that," Major Griffin said. "For the moment, we'll hope for the best and prepare for the worst. I trust you have all brushed up on your Galactic Standard?"

Martin nodded. Languages had never been his talent, even though he'd grown up in a place where people spoke a mishmash of three *different* languages, but he'd learned hard lessons since joining the Solar Marines. Nearly everyone who wanted to work with aliens, or travel outside the Solar Union, spoke Galactic Standard. The Tokomak-created language was staggeringly inflexible—it didn't allow its speakers to make up new words, let alone borrow them from other languages—but it was practically universal. Aliens who couldn't pronounce the words could still understand it.

"Very good," Major Griffin said. He raised his voice, slightly. "Senior officers, report back here at 1800. Everyone else, prepare for transfer to the MEU. Bear in mind that we might be leaving in a hurry. Dismissed."

Martin stood and hurried for the door. He *was* a senior officer, at least as Special Forces Recon reckoned it. He'd have to be back in an hour, when the clock reached 1800. He stepped through the hatch and walked down the corridor to the barracks, exchanging salutes with the guards as they passed. There was no reason to fear attack, not in the very heart of the Solar Union, but they'd been taught to be careful anyway. Martin had slept in places where there had been a very good chance he wouldn't wake up, if his men hadn't been on guard. He stepped through the hatch and nodded to the officer on watch. The remainder of the squad were catching up on their sleep.

"When they awake, tell them to prepare for deployment," he ordered the officer. It would be cruel to wake his men now. They'd just completed an extensive series of exercises. "We may be leaving as soon as this evening."

"Yes, sir."

Martin nodded, then walked to his bunk. Rank didn't have many privileges, not in Special Forces Recon. The bunk was identical to the other bunks, right down to the bland sheet and blankets. He opened the drawer under the bunk and frowned, just for a second, as he realised just how little he really owned. A handful of datachips and a reader—he spent most of his off-duty time reading when he wasn't with Yolanda—and very little else. He'd been taught to travel light, but…he reached for his carryall, placed the reader and the chips at the bottom and then started to find his clothes. He would be expected to carry at least two complete sets of everything with him, but experience had taught him that he needed to take more. It was astonishing how easily something could get messed up.

I'll have to write to Yolanda, he told himself, as he finished packing. It had only taken a few minutes. *Tell her I won't be able to meet her this weekend.*

The thought cost him a pang, even though he was used to it by now. Their relationship was a long-distance relationship—it could hardly be anything else—but there were times when he wished he could be closer to her. He was old enough to father children and responsible enough to bring them up…wasn't he? The Solar Union wasn't the ghetto. No one *here* would abandon a child they'd sired, not unless they gave the baby up for adoption. Martin had no idea who'd fathered *him*, so many years ago, but he was sure he'd do a better job at raising *his* children. He could hardly do a worse one...

We have time, he told himself, firmly. *We could have children a hundred years from now, if we wished.*

He sighed. In truth, he didn't want to give up his career...he didn't even want to take a break long enough to raise the children. And yet, Yolanda didn't want to give up her career either. She might reach flag rank, if she was offered a command of her own...Martin didn't blame her for wanting to stick with it. *He* could take a break, if he wished, and then return to the military, but Yolanda would find it harder. Starship technology and tactics would advance in her absence, leaving her hopelessly out of date.

Shaking his head, he put the carryall on top of the bunk and reached for the military-issue reader. A warning about the lockdown blinked up, the moment he touched the screen. Martin rolled his eyes—there wasn't a man or woman on the base who'd risk the lives of his or her fellows by talking out of turn—and then accessed the files. Unsurprisingly, a detailed briefing on Apsidal was at the top. It didn't take long to realise that it had been drafted by a Tokomak. The writer never used one word when he could use a hundred. Martin smiled—he knew exactly what sort of reaction *he'd* get if he wrote his reports in such a verbose manner—and settled down to read. Apsidal sounded fascinating, despite the writer's best efforts. He was almost looking forward to the deployment when the bleeper rang. It was time to go back to the briefing room.

He caught Sergeant Howe's attention as he sat upright. "Get everyone packed and ready, once they awake," he ordered. "And make sure they know about the lockdown."

"Yes, sir."

Martin felt his cheeks heat as he headed out the door, silently grateful that his dark skin concealed his embarrassment. Sergeant Howe had been in the military longer than Martin had been alive, first on Earth and then in the Solar Union. He'd outrank Martin if he'd decided to move to officer track, rather than stay as a sergeant. He knew what he was doing, but Martin had nagged him...he sighed, again, as he walked down the corridor. There were times when he felt very young and very inexperienced, despite having been in the military for years. The old men had been serving for decades. Some had even been serving for centuries.

And would I want to stay in the military for centuries, he asked himself, *or would I go looking for something else?*

He pushed the thought aside as he walked into the briefing room. Major Griffin was at the front, talking to a portly officer in naval uniform. Martin didn't recognise him. The other officers assembled quickly, chatting quietly amongst themselves. Martin joined in, sharing his impressions of Apsidal. Their destination might be a nice place to visit, but it was going to be utter hell if they had to fight. The megacities alone would be nightmares if they had to be stormed block by block.

We won't have to do it, he told himself. Much of Apsidal, just like much of every other planet, was largely irrelevant to a spacefaring race. There was no need to fight their way across the entire surface, not when mere control of the high orbitals would be enough to keep Apsidal under firm control. *All we have to do is capture the planetary defences—or destroy them.*

"We'll be transferring to the MEU tonight, at 2100," Major Griffin said. "I trust your squads are ready?"

There was a brief murmur of assent. It would be a rush, particularly for the delta squads, but they'd cope. They'd been trained to expect the deployment order to arrive at any time. There would be some grumbling, of course, but nothing he couldn't handle. Anyone who couldn't take the pace had transferred back to the regular forces long ago.

"Very good," Major Griffin said. "Are there any questions before we proceed?"

"Just one," Captain Hawke said. "Are we going to war against Apsidal— or the Tokomak? I heard a rumour..."

"The rumour is true," Major Griffin said, flatly. "The Tokomak are coming."

Martin swallowed. He'd been a newly-minted Solar Marine when the Tokomak had attacked the Solar System for the first time. They'd won, but at a staggering cost. It was chilling to realise that the Tokomak had barely noticed the losses. It reminded Martin of a brief deployment to some hellhole on Earth, where the locals had used human wave attacks in a desperate bid to shut down the spaceport. The marines had gunned them down in their thousands, but they'd just kept coming. Martin had had nightmares about *that* for months afterwards. How could anyone put so little value on their own lives that they'd charge gun emplacements with nothing but raw courage? And why would they keep following the leaders who hurled them into the fire?

I should have been paying more attention to rumours, he thought, grimly. *I might have realised that we'd be deployed...*

"Our job is to stop them in their tracks," Major Griffin added. "And *we* will be playing an important role in the operation."

He paused for a moment, then started the briefing in earnest. Martin listened carefully, recording the discussion for future reference. Major Griffin was remarkably concise, but he had a lot of subjects to cover. Martin suspected that most of them were above his pay grade, yet it was hard to be sure. If he was unlucky, he might wind up in command of the forces deployed to Apsidal. It wouldn't be the first time a lower-ranking officer had found himself suddenly thrown into command when his superiors had been killed.

And the Tokomak have even less regard for the lives of their client races than ourselves, he reminded himself. *They'll throw millions of their slaves into the fire just to get at us.*

"I expect each and every one of you to comport yourself in a manner befitting Special Forces Recon," Major Griffin finished. "If we are lucky, we won't have to fight...but if we *do* have to fight, we'll give them hell."

"And try not to damage too much of the planet's infrastructure while you're at it," the unnamed naval officer said. "Apsidal might be very useful in the right hands."

"But very dangerous in the wrong hands," Major Griffin said. "We have to prepare for the worst."

Martin nodded to himself, feeling the same mixture of anticipation and trepidation before going on deployment. They were going to war, they were going to fight the enemy...he knew better, these days, than to think that war was glorious, but he still felt a thrill when he considered the challenge. Going up against the Tokomak on their own ground...

Not quite their own ground, he reminded himself, firmly. *But close enough for the moment.*

"Have your men ready for transfer at 2100," Major Griffin said. "Dismissed."

CHAPTER FOUR

"Welcome onboard, Admiral," Captain Robin Lifar said. "*Defiant* is at your service."

"Thank you," Hoshiko said. "It's a pleasure to finally come onboard."

She smiled as they shook hands. There was little ceremony for an admiral boarding her flagship, not in the Solar Navy. The officers who'd written the regulations had always been a little suspicious of superior officers, even though they'd *become* superior officers. Hoshiko understood their reasoning better than she cared to admit. The old wet-navies had had quite a problem with senior officers lacking practical experience of military affairs. That wasn't a problem in the Solar Navy. One simply couldn't progress past a certain level without genuine experience.

"Your staff have already arrived and are setting up in the CIC suite," Lifar said, as he led Hoshiko down the corridor. "They've been preparing on the assumption that the people will vote for war."

"They don't have a choice," Hoshiko said. Life amongst the asteroids had bred a hard degree of common sense into the population. They knew, at a very basic level, that even the most advanced technology in the galaxy couldn't keep them safe forever. "The vote will take place soon."

"Yes, Admiral," Lifar said. "But what if they vote *against* war?"

Hoshiko considered it for a moment. The constitution was clear. War—active war—could only be declared with the consent of the people.

She understood the logic, given how governments on Earth had used war-making powers to expand their post-war powers. But the constitution was not a suicide pact. If the people voted against war...

They'll get war anyway, when the enemy fleet enters the system, she thought, morbidly. *But by then it might be too late.*

She followed him into the CIC and looked up at the display. *Defiant* was surrounded by nearly five hundred starships, nearly all of them new-build warships. The remainder were heavily-modified Galactic starships or freighters, the latter crammed with supplies and prefabricated components. Logistics was going to be a nightmare, even with the AIs to help keep the situation under control. And yet...she felt a thrill as she surveyed the fleet. It was already the most powerful fleet humanity had ever assembled, save for Home Fleet itself, and it was still growing.

And it's mine, she thought. Command of an entire fleet was the very peak of her career. She might be promoted still further, but she'd never have so much direct authority again. Even Mongo Stuart himself, her great-uncle, didn't have so much power at his fingertips. *This is all mine.*

She sat down and nodded to Yolanda. "Status report?"

"A third of our strength has already arrived, Admiral, and the last update from Sparta claimed that the reminder will arrive within the next two days." Yolanda spoke from memory, rather than checking a datapad. "I've had the command staff running tactical simulations, but I have to report that managing so many ships will not be easy. We don't have time for proper exercises."

"We'll have to work our way through hundreds of simulations," Hoshiko said. It was annoying. The simulations were good, but she knew that they couldn't match *real* live-fire exercises. No matter how much care and attention the programmers invested in their creatures, they always left out *something*. "And we will have time to carry out *some* exercises if we get to Apsidal first."

She considered it for a moment, cursing the enemy under her breath. There should have been more *time*, damn it! They should have had *years* to prepare, instead of a desperate rush to get forces to Apsidal before it was too late. She was uncomfortably aware that it might *already* be too late. If *she* was in command of the enemy fleet, she would have seized Apsidal by now and turned it into a fortress. Who knew *what* the enemy commander would do?

"Once the remainder of the fleet arrives, assign fleet control groups to the flagships and then run intensive datanet exercises," she added. "We might as well do what we can to prevent disaster."

"Aye, Admiral," Yolanda said.

Hoshiko stood and started to pace. "Is there any other news?"

"Locally, the first LinkShip has been assigned to the fleet," Yolanda said. "There's a classified briefing waiting in your private datanode. The security level is too high for me to access. There have also been a number of freighter captains offering their services, above and beyond the requisitions. I've asked them to report to Sparta."

"Good thinking," Hoshiko said. "And internationally?"

"The ambassadors from the Galactic Alliance have volunteered to provide ships, but so far none of those ships have actually materialised," Yolanda told her. "Their homeworlds might have other ideas."

"Unsurprising," Hoshiko said. She'd helped create the Galactic Alliance, but she was all too aware of its weaknesses. The Tokomak could simply intimidate most of the members into sullen submission. "We'll plan on the assumption that they're not going to send help."

"Aye, Admiral," Yolanda said. "And if they *do* send help?"

"We'll slot them into our command network somewhere," Hoshiko told her. Practically, it would be a headache, but diplomatically there was little choice. The Solar Union was first amongst equals, as far as the Galactic Alliance was concerned; it wasn't in a position to simply order its alien allies to do as they were told. "We'll deal with that when—if—it happens."

She turned to look at the display, silently assessing the fleet as it took shape. The most powerful fleet humanity had ever assembled, yet tiny compared to the juggernaut bearing down on Sol. Would it be enough to win? Or would humanity be finally doomed? Some remnants would survive, she knew, but nothing would ever be the same again. The Tokomak certainly wouldn't let down their guard in a hurry.

And they're more patient than us, she told herself. *It might be centuries before they relax.*

"Keep an eye on the vote," she ordered, finally. "I want to know when the results are called."

"Aye, Admiral," Yolanda said.

"If there are any other issues, alert me at once," Hoshiko said. "I'll be in my cabin."

"Aye, Admiral."

Hoshiko nodded, then stepped through the hatch into her cabin. It felt uncomfortably large, even though it was tiny compared to her suite on the family asteroid. She could hold a private meeting in her sitting room, if she wished, or share her bed and bathroom with someone...she shook her head in annoyance, dismissing the thought. There wasn't *time* for a romantic partner, not even a quick roll in the hay. She wouldn't have time until the war was finally over.

She snorted, rudely. Her mother had asked her, point-blank, when she intended to do her duty to the family and have kids. Hoshiko had pointed out, in response, that she had plenty of time to have children before it was too late—and besides, she had a career. *And* she'd made sure to have some of her eggs stored, just in case. Her mother could find a suitable sperm donor, if Hoshiko died in the line of duty. Something of her daughter would survive.

Her bags were already resting on the deck. Hoshiko checked them quickly, then sat down at the desk. The terminal lit up at once, informing her that there were hundreds of messages in her inbox. Hoshiko glanced at the headers, decided that most of them were pointless and sighed, again. Too many people thought she had nothing better to do than answer their queries immediately.

Shaking her head, she brought up the classified report on the LinkShip project and began to read it carefully. Very carefully. She didn't have the groundpounder fear of linking herself to a computer, even an AI, but she had to admit that the scientists really *had* pushed the limits about as far as they would go. A human-machine interface was one thing, yet this...the pilot and the ship were practically one entity. Hoshiko had no idea how the concept would work in practice. Ideally, she would have preferred to test the LinkShip thoroughly *before* sending it into a war zone.

We have no choice, she told herself, firmly. *We are at war. And we are massively outnumbered. If we don't come up with some advanced weapons, something to even the odds, we're screwed.*

She took a moment to reflect on what the Tokomak would do to the Solar Union. They'd smash every asteroid, bombard every world...they'd bombard Earth, even though it was a blatantly uncivilised hellhole these days. Even letting them anywhere near the sector would be a grave mistake. They'd lay waste to the Galactic Alliance even if they couldn't touch Sol herself. The war had barely begun and humanity had its back pressed firmly against the wall.

We need every weapon we can muster, she thought, coldly. *And if that means taking risks...well, we'll have to take them.*

・・・

Hameeda sucked in her breath as the fleet came into view. It was massively impressive, even to her; hundreds of warships and freighters, assembled in something that might—charitably—be called a formation. A Tokomak fleet commander would have had a heart attack if his fleet had been assembled so poorly—the Tokomak insisted that fleets had to fly in precise formation at all times—but it was unlikely that any such commander had ever seen real combat. A loose formation would be far more agile if the shit hit the fan.

She slowed the LinkShip, falling neatly into position behind the cruisers. They were powerful ships, perhaps the most powerful ships of their size in the entire galaxy, but they would have great difficulty hitting her. Simulations ran through her mind, suggesting that she could carry out a whole series of attack manoeuvres against the cruisers without running a serious risk, although she knew better than to take that for granted. The cruisers were linked together into a formidable fighting force. They'd be able to fill space with energy blasts and missiles if they wished.

I really do have to think of a name for the ship, she thought, as she sent her IFF to the flagship. *Calling the ship by my own name does seem rather pretentious.*

She leaned back in her chair, waiting for a response. Admiral Stuart would have been briefed on the LinkShip now, she thought. The Admiral's file downloaded into her head, confirming that Hoshiko Stuart was one of *those* Stuarts...and, more importantly, that she was spaceborn. She wouldn't have any qualms about the LinkShips. Hameeda read the file carefully, then disconnected from the helmet and stood. Her body felt weak, even though she'd only been in direct rapport for...she frowned as she checked her implants. They insisted she'd been in rapport for hours, but it felt like only a few minutes. She summoned an energy drink from the nearest dispenser and took a long swallow. It tasted foul, but it helped snap her awake.

An alert popped up in front of her. Admiral Stuart was trying to contact her.

"Put her through," she said. Or thought. She wasn't sure herself. "I'll speak to her in here."

Admiral Stuart's image materialised in front of her. Hameeda studied her with ill-concealed interest. She looked young, surprisingly slight for a spaceborn; her face was pale, with almond eyes that reflected her family's genetic heritage. Hameeda felt an odd flicker of kinship, remembering just how much of her mother's looks *she'd* kept when she reached adulthood. She'd been mature enough to realise that endlessly reshaping her body to fit the latest fashions was stupid by the time she'd reached adulthood. Some of her childhood friends had never quite realised it.

"Admiral," she said. "I'm sorry I can't report to you in person."

"I quite understand," Admiral Stuart said. She had a Solarian accent, without any hints of Old Earth. "I read the briefing notes very carefully, Captain. Do you have anything to add to them?"

"Not yet," Hameeda said. "If I discover any limitations, or inaccuracies written into the paperwork, you'll be the first to know."

Admiral Stuart's eyes narrowed. "And do you believe there *are*...limitations or inaccuracies?"

Hameeda took a breath. "With all due respect, Admiral, we're breaking new ground here. The neural link itself is remarkable, but it isn't the *only* thing. There are dozens of pieces of technology worked into the LinkShip which are either completely new or extensive revamps of last-generation tech. We will not know *quite* what is wrong, if anything, until we test the ship extensively."

"Very good," Admiral Stuart said, finally. "Now, the paperwork said nothing about how you should be deployed. What do you recommend?"

"The simplest mission is scouting," Hameeda said, after a moment. "My stealth systems are remarkably good. I can pass through a typical gravity point, I believe, without being detected. They'd have to sweep the area *thoroughly* to catch me."

"I believe they've already started securing the gravity points closer to Tokomak itself," Admiral Stuart said. "Could you get through one of *those*?"

"Perhaps," Hameeda said. "The real problem would be the gravity fluctuation caused by the transit. I would find it a great deal easier to sneak into a planet's high orbitals."

"You might have your chance," Admiral Stuart told her. "Anything else?"

"I can handle hit-and-run attacks," Hameeda said. "However, I should warn you that this ship does not have the killing power of a cruiser."

"So the reports said," Admiral Stuart said. "We will, of course, discuss it at a later date."

"Of course, Admiral."

"We should be departing in a week, two weeks at most," Admiral Stuart added. "I'll make sure to meet with you personally before we go."

Her image vanished. Hameeda frowned, sitting back in her chair. Admiral Stuart sounded doubtful…not, she supposed, that she could really blame the older woman. Everyone had read *Superiority*, after all. A star empire had become so intent on developing and deploying the latest advanced weapons—all of which had really been quite advanced—that they'd overlooked their glaring weaknesses until it was too late. The Solar Union was in the same boat, with the added disadvantage that victory with conventional weapons was extremely unlikely. They were so badly outnumbered that they *had* to push for the most advanced weapons possible.

And we have imaginations, she thought, remembering Admiral Webster's briefings. *The Tokomak forgot how to imagine a long time ago.*

A servitor drone appeared, carrying a bowl of soup and a mug of coffee. Hameeda felt a flicker of annoyance, just for a second. She'd programmed the datanet's subroutines to look after her, with a level of intrusion that would be unthinkable outside a prison, and it was quite insistent. She didn't *feel* like eating, but…she took the bowl and spoon anyway. The subroutine would keep nagging her until she gave in.

Which is why no one wanted to buy a House RI, she thought, wryly. *Being nagged by your parents or your partner is one thing, but being nagged by a machine is far worse.*

She sipped the soup carefully, forcing her body to relax. It was hard to realise, sometimes, that she'd had a life before bonding herself to the ship, even though it had only been two days. She'd grown so used to it that her former life felt more like a recorded memory than anything else. And yet, and yet…

I have to take care of myself, she told herself. She could get some rest, now, while the remainder of the fleet assembled. She'd be fresh when the time came to jump into FTL and head to their destination. *The ship is useless without me.*

...

Hoshiko broke the connection with a strong sense of unease. She hadn't been quite sure what to expect from a person who'd linked themselves—permanently—to a starship computer, even though the briefing notes had insisted that the process wasn't fatal. Hameeda—there was no surname listed in the files, suggesting she was a second-gen who wanted to cut all ties to Old Earth—had come across as a strange mixture of arrogant and scatter-brained. Hoshiko had met more than her fair share of aliens, entities who weren't human and didn't think as humans did, but Hameeda had still struck her as *odd*. But then, anyone who wanted to accept a life sentence on a starship had to be a little bit odd. Hoshiko had loved her first command, but she hadn't wanted to stay on the ship for the rest of her life.

But it might be better than the alternative, she thought, making a mental note to obtain the remaining files. She was Hameeda's commanding officer. She had every right to demand the files. *And a LinkShip is surprisingly comfortable for its size.*

Her intercom bleeped. "Admiral?"

"Yes, Yolanda?" Hoshiko glanced towards the closed hatch. It wouldn't have been *hard* for Yolanda to walk into her cabin. Bad news? Or just another case of the younger woman's shyness. She'd never be a commanding officer unless she overcame it. "Go ahead."

"The vote was just taken," Yolanda said. "Nine-tenths of the electorate voted in favour of war. The Senate has authorised us to depart on our planned date."

Hoshiko frowned. She'd expected all, but a few crackpots to support the war. Very few of the voters would *want* the war, yet...they'd understand it had to be fought. But then, few forces in the universe were as powerful as self-delusion. Hoshiko had seen vast fleets, in the course of her career, and even she had difficulty grasping the size of the juggernaut bearing down on Earth.

"Very good," she said, banishing the thought. They had a chance to turn back the tide and that was all that mattered. "Signal the fleet. We're going to war."

CHAPTER FIVE

Hurry up and wait, Martin thought, as he tossed his carryall into the locker. *Hurry up and wait and be told that your destination has changed four times before you even reach the fleet.*

He told himself, firmly, that he shouldn't be so annoyed. The Solar Union had *never* deployed over a thousand warships outside the Sol System in its entire history. *Millions* of men and women were being deployed, from starship crews to groundpounders and maintenance staff. They should be grateful there hadn't been more confusion. But it was still a little irritating.

"The lads are finding their bunks now," Sergeant Howe said. The flagship, in common with all capital ships, seemed to begrudge setting *any* space aside for the marines. Marine Country was a tiny set of compartments, barely large enough for a couple of SF units. "You'll be delighted to know you have an office."

Martin snorted. "If I ever have a chance to use it," he said. He'd never actually *had* an office before, although he'd sometimes had to make use of secure briefing rooms. Special Forces units were not encouraged to grow attached to any particular base. They had to be ready to pack up and leave on a moment's notice. "Leave it empty, for the moment."

"Yes, sir," Howe said. He sounded vastly amused. "And you have a visitor. She's waiting at the hatch."

"I have a visitor?" Martin frowned. He had very few friends outside the marines. Had one of them been assigned to *Defiant*? "Who?"

"Go see, sir," Howe said. "You won't regret it."

Martin eyed him warningly, then shrugged and strode up towards the hatch at the end of the compartment. By tradition, Marine Country was practically a foreign embassy. Spacers were not allowed to enter, not without permission. The ship's captain could enter, of course—the captain had boundless authority over his ship—but even he would hesitate to enter unless it was urgent. Marines and spacers simply didn't mix. Countless bar fights during shore leave proved it.

The hatch hissed open at his approach, revealing a pale dark-haired girl. Martin felt his mouth drop open in surprise, then ran forward and gave Yolanda a tight hug. She'd said she had a new assignment, when she'd written to him, but it had never occurred to him that she might be on *Defiant*. They hadn't served together—or at least on the same ship—since their first deployment.

She kissed him quickly, then stepped back, her eyes flickering around nervously. They weren't in the same chain of command, which would have made their relationship illegal, but people would still talk. Martin wondered, idly, what they'd make of it. Would they tease Yolanda for dating a marine? Or him, for dating a spacer? Or would they suggest that Yolanda had somehow gotten his unit assigned to *Defiant* so she could be with her lover?

"It's good to see you again," she said. "I thought...I thought you'd be on *Chesty*."

"They reassigned us here, eventually," Martin said, trying to keep the annoyance out of his voice. He was tempted to suggest that they seek privacy, although he knew he had to go back to his berth fairly quickly. "What happened?"

"A handful of units were added to our order of battle," Yolanda told him. "And they had to remain concentrated. We couldn't split them up and scatter them over the warships."

"Ah, newer units," Martin said. "Are they fit to fight?"

"So we have been told," Yolanda said. Her almond eyes crinkled with amusement. "I thought *you* were the ground-combat expert."

Martin shook his head. "Talk to the oldsters," he said. "The *really* old guys. They've forgotten more than I'll ever know."

"You'll be old too, one day," Yolanda said. "And then you'll look back on this day and laugh."

"Maybe," Martin said. He'd never sought higher rank—Special Forces was simply more *challenging* than flying a desk—but there were times when he wondered. If the senior officers were constantly rejuvenated, to the point where old age wouldn't force them to retire, would they retire at all? And what would that mean for younger officers who wanted to rise to the very top? "Or maybe I'll die on the mission."

Yolanda looked reproving. "Don't even joke about it."

Martin shook his head. Yolanda had a million-ton starship wrapped around her. *Defiant* could shrug off nuclear and antimatter blasts that would devastate entire planets. But a marine on the ground, even one wearing a battlesuit, was fragile in a way no spacer could understand. Martin had seen too many people die on combat deployments. There were limits to how far his life could be protected and he knew it. A single superheated plasma burst would be enough to burn through his suit and kill him.

And if we go without the suits, we'll be even more fragile, he reminded himself. *We're not invincible...*

"We'll see what happens," he said, neutrally. "I...I didn't realise you'd been assigned to *Defiant*."

"Admiral Stuart has been assigned to *Defiant*," Yolanda said. "And where she goes, I go."

"Ouch," Martin said. Following a senior officer around, acting as a combination of secretary, tactical officer and sounding board, was pretty close to his idea of hell. He'd enjoyed shadowing Major Tracy, back before he'd transferred to Special Forces, but it wasn't something he wanted to do for the rest of his life. Or even for a year. "Is she a good boss?"

"She could be worse," Yolanda said. "And I only have six months left before I get reassigned."

"Unless it gets extended," Martin pointed out. There hadn't been any discussions about how long the deployment would actually *last*, but he'd be surprised if it was less than a year or two. Yolanda might find herself stuck until the fleet returned to Earth. "You might have to roll with it."

"Probably," Yolanda said. She sounded as if she didn't particularly care. Martin admired her ability to make the best of a maddening assignment. *She* didn't have the opportunity to go to the shooting range and burn off her frustrations on a handful of holographic targets. "Needs must, when the devil vomits on your toenails."

Martin laughed, remembering the days they'd watched the entire series of movies, one after the other. They'd been hellishly unrealistic—he dreaded to think what his CO would say if he proposed arming marines with *swords* on a modern battlefield—but funny. And gruesome. It was almost a shame that the *real* universe was not quite as fantastic.

But it does have thousands of aliens who want to kill us, he thought. *So it isn't really that different after all.*

Yolanda's wristcom bleeped. "I have to get back to the CIC," she said, glancing at it. "I should be free tonight, if you want to sneak through the tubes to my cabin."

"As long as the admiral doesn't want you," Martin said. He considered it, briefly. The marines were meant to settle in, before they started training the following morning. It wasn't as if he had to babysit, but still...sneaking off to spend the night with his girlfriend would set a bad example. "I'll let you know. I have to put everyone to bed first."

"I understand," Yolanda said. She leaned forward and kissed him again. "See you soon."

She turned and walked away. Martin watched her go, feeling a surge of pure affection. They were so different, in so many ways, and yet they *clicked*. She wasn't the sort of girl he would have been encouraged to like, let alone love, on Earth...no, he wouldn't have been encouraged to love *anyone* on Earth. Love was a weakness...

Back to work, he told himself, firmly. *You can meet up with her later.*

...

"Admiral?"

Hoshiko looked up from the latest report. "Yes, Yolanda?"

"The final fleet units have arrived," Yolanda told her. She stood at the hatch, as if she were reluctant to enter the office. "The datanet has been updated. All ships are signalling that they are ready to depart."

"Very good," Hoshiko said. She deactivated the terminal, banishing the report and its contents to the back of her mind. There were too many bureaucrats who'd fallen into the habit of assuming that their work was so important that it had to be sent straight to the fleet commander. It was probably time for a cull. "Are there any other updates?"

"The reporters have been embarked on *Daredevil*," Yolanda said. "Half of them have filed requests to be transferred to *Defiant*."

"Stall them," Hoshiko ordered. The Solar Union's newshounds weren't as bad as the media groupies from the bad old days on Earth—she'd heard the old sweats calling the reporters everything from liars to traitors—but they were still annoying. "They can find what they need from the unclassified sections of the datanet."

She rolled her eyes at the thought. There was very little in her life that was *interesting*, although that hadn't stopped the newshounds from digging into her past and interviewing her childhood friends for signs of future greatness. Who'd have thought that building a treehouse on the family asteroid was a sign of leadership ability? Her siblings had taken a gleeful delight in forwarding copies of *that* article to her.

"Aye, Admiral," Yolanda said. She cleared her throat nervously, a sure sign she was about to disagree with the boss. "They *do* have clearance to attend intership conferences."

"Which they can do holographically," Hoshiko said, shortly. The Admiralty might have pressed her to remember that the newshounds had to be kept onside, but that didn't mean she had to give them everything they wanted. Besides, it wasn't as if they'd get very far by pressing an anti-war narrative. They'd be more likely to lose followers so rapidly that their reliability ratings dropped to nothing. "And if they request any private interviews, tell them I'll be busy for the next few months."

"Aye, Admiral," Yolanda said. She glanced at the datapad in her hand. "The logistics and support units are in place, ready to follow the fleet. They assure me that they have everything they need."

"It won't be enough," Hoshiko predicted, grimly. Consumption rates were *always* higher than predicted. Thankfully, between the generally-sensible officers in command and the mobile factory ships, it shouldn't be a problem. "Were there any troubles getting the final tranche of industrial workers assigned to the fleet?"

"No, Admiral," Yolanda said. "There *may* be some long-term problems back home, but…they're here."

"I imagine enemy missile strikes will cause some long-term problems too," Hoshiko said, dryly. The Solar Union simply didn't have enough industrial workers. She'd heard that more and more were being trained up, but it would be a while before the first newcomers entered service. "Are there any other issues that should be brought to my attention?"

"No, Admiral," Yolanda said. "The fleet is ready to depart."

Hoshiko stood and walked around the desk. Yolanda stepped to one side to allow Hoshiko to precede her out of the office and into the CIC. The display was glowing with thousands of icons, ranging from powerful warships to escorts and support vessels. She couldn't help feeling awed, even though she'd seen it time and time again. It was the largest fleet humanity had ever assembled, perhaps the most *powerful* fleet in the history of the entire galaxy, and it was *hers*. No naval officer in human history, save perhaps Admiral Jellicoe, had ever had so much weight on their shoulders. She was truly the only officer who could lose the war in a single day.

And Jellicoe wasn't staring down the barrels of racial extinction, Hoshiko thought. The Druavroks had wanted to kill all humans, but the Tokomak were worse. She had no doubt that the human race was fighting for its very survival. *The worst that could have happened to Jellicoe was watching his beloved country being occupied by the Kaiser. I might have to watch as the Solar Union is wiped from existence.*

She shook her head. No, she'd be dead by then. The Tokomak would hardly let her live long enough to see her solar system being destroyed. She wondered, morbidly, if they knew the fleet was on its way. All traffic in and out of the Sol System had been halted once the vote had taken place, but she was all too aware that *someone* might have sneaked out of the system to alert the enemy. The Tokomak had allies, lots of them. She wouldn't be too surprised to hear that some of the Galactic Alliance races were preparing fallback plans.

Her eyes found the LinkShip, holding station next to *Defiant*. She wished she'd had enough time to *visit* the ship, both to satisfy her curiosity and to keep an eye on the pilot. Hameeda—*Captain* Hameeda, Hoshiko supposed—had very strong stability and reliability ratings, but *no one* had permanently linked themselves to a datanet before. There was simply no way to tell what the long-term effects might be. In hindsight, perhaps it would have been wiser to assign someone to the LinkShip, even over Hameeda's protests. But Hameeda had seemed to think she'd be better on her own.

That will have to change, Hoshiko thought. *A human connection might be good for her.*

She cursed the scientists under her breath as she took her chair. They'd insisted that Hameeda had to make her own choices, at least until the fleet went into battle. But Hoshiko couldn't help thinking that it was a mistake. There *had* been people who'd sunk into VR fantasies to the point where they thought the fantasy was *real*. Hoshiko could understand the urge to pretend that one was more important than one was, or lived a more exciting life, but she distrusted it. A person born in the Solar Union could go far, if he or she was prepared to make the sacrifice. Their lives were what they made of them.

And Hameeda could sink so far into the datanet that she might never come out, she told herself. *Who knows what will happen then?*

"Admiral," Yolanda said. "System Command has sent us a message, wishing us good luck."

"In other words, they expect us to get moving," Hoshiko said, wryly. It was the sort of departure that should be feted with flags flying and bands playing, but they *were* on the very edge of the system, as far as they could go without leaving the system limits completely. "Contact the fleet. Inform them that we will depart in"—she made a show of looking at the chronometer—"ten minutes."

"Aye, Admiral."

Hoshiko felt the ship's drives change, just slightly, as the FTL nodes came online. *Defiant* was the latest generation of cruiser technology, designed to be able to slip in and out of FTL with over two-thirds of her FTL nodes non-functional. It made her feel slightly different from *Jackie Fisher*, Hoshiko's old command, but it gave her a tactical flexibility that more than made up for the additional expense. *And* when—not if—the Tokomak designed gravity traps of their own, *Defiant* would have a good chance of remaining in FTL long enough to get out of the trap and make her escape.

Although it will cost us nearly every node we have, Hoshiko said. Crashing into a gravity shadow was every spacer's nightmare. The scientists hadn't been clear on what would happen if *Defiant* hit a *natural* gravity well, like a planet, but Hoshiko doubted it was anything *good*. The odds of survival would be very low. *It might be better to let them yank us out of FTL and punch our way out.*

"The fleet's responded, Admiral," Yolanda said. "They're ready to go."

"Copy our final records to System Command," Hoshiko ordered, "and empty the message buffers."

"Aye, Admiral," Yolanda said. Her hands danced across her console. "Done."

Hoshiko concealed a smile. The censors were going to have a tedious time, digging through the datapackets to make sure that someone on the ship hadn't told his family anything that the enemy could use against them. Hoshiko doubted the Tokomak could or would spy on private communications, but it was well to be careful. Someone in the media might pick up on something important and relay it to his followers, unaware that the Tokomak were listening too. There were enough people who believed that information wanted to be free—and rebelled against any form of government censorship—for her to expect common sense to prevail.

And it will be a long time before anyone on the fleet sees their family again, she thought, morbidly. Yolanda was really quite lucky to have her *boyfriend* on the ship. *We won't be back for a year or so.*

She took one final look at the in-system display, her eyes seeking out the cluster of asteroids that comprised the core of the Solar Union, then took a long breath. "Order the fleet to enter FTL," she said. "Now."

"Aye, Admiral," Yolanda said. "FTL in five..."

Hoshiko braced herself as the display went blank, half-expecting to feel her stomach twisting out of shape. But there was almost nothing, beyond a slight queasy sensation that vanished almost as soon as she noticed it. Her lips curved into a smile. The Tokomak had never bothered to make the transition into FTL easier on the ship's passengers. She rather suspected they didn't feel it themselves. But humanity had found a way...

"The fleet has entered FTL," Yolanda informed her. "The gravity-pulse network has been established. Datalinks are being established now."

"Very good," Hoshiko said. She stood. "Once the network is up and running, prime the ships for an exercise. We have two months to go and I want to be ready."

"Aye, Admiral."

CHAPTER SIX

If Martin had been forced to be honest, as the days turned into weeks and the weeks turned into months, there were some advantages to being stationed on *Defiant*. Quite apart from being able to see Yolanda, whenever they could find a mutually-convenient time to meet, it allowed them to practice everything from boarding and counter-boarding actions to infiltration, subversion and sabotage. His squad racked up thousands of kills in the simulators, constantly pushing the limits as far as they would go, while testing their skills against a series of elaborate traps. The ship's engineers seemed delighted to have the chance to design death traps for the marines, even if they *did* seem more like something from a TV show than anything they might expect to encounter in real life.

The Tokomak simply want us dead, he thought. *They don't want us to suffer.*

He paused, considering. *No*, he added, grimly. *They don't care if we suffer.*

It wasn't a pleasant thought. He'd met too many humans who were sadists, who got off on hurting people. The gangbangers who ruled the streets where he was born had never been content with merely *killing* their enemies, not when they could make them suffer first; later, as his career expanded, he'd met people who killed women for being raped or brutally beat little girls into a pulp for daring to seek an education. It was shameful, somehow, to think that aliens might be more human than some *humans*.

The human capacity for torturing its own kind was unmatched throughout the galaxy.

The Tokomak have a superiority complex large enough to blot out the galaxy, he thought, *and they'll do whatever it takes to stay on top, but they're not monsters.*

He pushed the thought aside, forcing himself to start working through yet another after-action report. One *disadvantage* of being on *Defiant* was that he had to write the wretched things himself. Technically, he then had to *read* them to himself—as a couple of jokers in the squad had gleefully pointed out—but he'd decided that there was no point in following regulations *too* closely. They'd been written on the assumption that the writer and the reader would be two different people.

We've tested ourselves inside and outside the starship, he told himself, *and worked our way through all kinds of simulated environments. What else do we have to do?*

He sighed as he finished the report. The squad was at risk of losing its edge, if it didn't get to see *real* action soon. Space was dangerous—and going outside in FTL could be literally *maddening*—but people weren't *really* shooting at them. Even highly-experienced men could start treating simulations with contempt, when they knew there was no real danger beyond being chewed out by the CO. There wasn't even the risk of being mocked by the rest of the ground forces for *losing*.

"We might have a moment to go to one of the MEUs," he muttered, crossly. "A chance to drill with some of the others would let us burn off a lot of steam."

Shaking his head, he turned to the next set of briefing notes. Apsidal had been settled long enough to have a sizable tourist industry, putting out everything from travel brochures and guides to detailed maps that were strikingly informative. Clearly, no one on Apsidal had ever thought twice about the wisdom of putting so much information on the planetary datanet. A handful of notes from Solar Intelligence confirmed that much of the data had been verified, right down to the locations of the planet's military bases. It looked as if no one on Apsidal had considered the possibility of being attacked either.

He smiled, sardonically. The Tokomak Empire was older, far older, than all of humanity's recorded history. And, in all of that time, it had never encountered a serious challenge. From the discovery of FTL to First Contact, the Tokomak and their allies—their subordinates—had been effectively unchallengeable. No wonder they'd let everything from research and development to basic defences slide. There was no point in pushing the limits when one was quite happy where one was. They wouldn't want to accidentally develop something that might disrupt their entire economic base.

A shame we don't know where we'll be landing, he thought, as he surveyed the detailed maps and their accompanying notes. General Edward Romford and his staff had been tight-lipped about the landing zones, suggesting they hadn't made any concrete plans. There was no way to be *entirely* sure what they'd encounter when they landed on Apsidal. *It could be anywhere.*

He sucked in his breath. There were, if the notes were to be believed, over fifty *billion* intelligent life forms on Apsidal. Solar Intelligence had added a suggestion that the official figures, pushed by the planetary government, were actually too low. Martin could believe it. The Galactics liked to think their societies ran like clockwork, but there were entire sections that existed outside official notice. Every major Galactic world had an underclass made up of immigrants from junior and servile races that existed off the books. Apsidal was no different, according to the notes. There was a good chance that the underclass would welcome the invasion. They might see it as a chance to improve their lot.

Poor bastards, Martin thought. His ancestors had had a hard time, first at the hands of slaveowners and then at the hands of well-meaning do-gooders, but both they and their oppressors had been human. It was far worse for the junior races. They would *never* be allowed to rise to power, not when it was clear they weren't *senior*. *Perhaps we can give them a chance to be better.*

He sighed, inwardly. It was going to be utter hell. Apsidal was covered in cities—the planet itself was practically one whole city—and surrounded by a ring. Martin felt his stomach twist as he considered the possibilities. It was the sort of environment that limited their advantages, while minimising *enemy* disadvantages. And the places they'd have to take were places the enemy would know to defend.

And they'll have plenty of warning, Martin thought. Operations on Earth had spoilt him. The opposition, as brutal as it had been, had been primitive. The marines had got the drop on them, time and time again. But the Galactics had advanced technology and knew how to use it. *They'll see us coming from light-years away.*

His wristcom bleeped. "Hi," Yolanda said. "Are you going to be free in an hour?"

"Well, *technically* I'm supposed to be napping," Martin said, although he doubted that his squad were in their bunks. He'd discovered, to his private amusement, that most of the squad had found partners amongst the spacers. He wouldn't make an issue of it, as long as it didn't interfere with their work. "But I suppose I could be, if you asked nicely."

Yolanda snorted. "Get up here," she said. "I've only got a few hours before I'm due back on duty."

Martin nodded, sympathetically. Admiral Stuart was working Yolanda to the bone, although—as Yolanda had assured him—she was pushing herself hard too. Martin understood, better than he cared to admit. Commanding thousands of soldiers was hard enough, but Admiral Stuart was commanding the largest fleet in human history. Merely getting so many warships going in the same direction was a challenge. They were learning by doing, with a powerful enemy waiting at the far end. Soon, they'd find out how well they'd done.

Particularly if we get there first, Martin thought. Space combat wasn't his forte, but he'd discussed it with Yolanda often enough. If the fleet got to Apsidal first, they could hold the gravity points against all comers. The Tokomak would have to decide between expending enough warships to make even *them* blanch or finding another way to Sol. Either way, the Solar Union would have more time to prepare. *We could turn the system into a bastion of humanist thought—and a new world for the Galactic Alliance—if we get there first.*

"I'm on my way," he said. "See you in a moment."

• • •

Hameeda resisted—barely—the urge to swear at the cooker as she carefully worked her way through the recipe. It wasn't as if she *needed* to cook for herself, was it? The LinkShip had everything from food processors to servos and gravity manipulation. She could assign a subroutine to cook dinner, if she didn't content herself with eating something from the processor. The processed food actually tasted good. She'd met a few perfectionists who insisted that food processors simply couldn't substitute for real food, but Hameeda had never been able to tell the difference. Her mother had taught her to be glad that she had enough to eat every day.

This is supposed to be good for you, she told herself firmly, as she dumped the cooked chicken into a bowl and followed up with mayonnaise, lemon juice, chopped celery and spring onions. The ship's stores were *crammed* with good food, almost all of it natural. She was meant to be comfortable, apparently. *It's just a shame you're eating alone.*

She sighed, hearing her mother's voice in her thoughts. Her mother had never *quite* adapted to processed food, although she'd eaten it without qualms. She'd believed that good cooking was meant to be shared with one's family, an attitude that Hameeda had absorbed without quite meaning to. She didn't *have* a husband, let alone children. And now, it was unlikely she'd ever have either. She could never leave the LinkShip. The ship was a constant presence in her head.

Hameeda poured the mixture into a cooking tray, sprinkled crushed crisps on top and then placed it in the cooker, setting an automatic timer as soon as she closed the hatch. The recipe was yet another fusion, a mixture of foods from a dozen different traditions that had been blended together in the Solar Union, but that didn't stop it being tasty. She rather suspected she was going to get sick of her limited collection of recipes, sooner or later; her mother had attempted to teach her how to cook, torturing both of them until they mutually decided it was pointless. Hameeda could follow a recipe, but she lacked the talent to determine how the ingredients could be changed to enhance the taste.

The datanet broadened around her, alerting her to an incoming hologram. Hameeda sighed again—there was only one person who'd be contacting her—and allowed it into the kitchen as the timer rang. Admiral Stuart's image materialised behind her, her expression—seen through the ship's sensors—mildly surprised. No doubt she hadn't realised Hameeda was cooking.

But she's getting an excellent look at my ass, Hameeda thought. The joke was pathetic, but she had to fight to keep from giggling anyway. Maybe she *had* been alone for too long. The datanet was an extension of her, not a separate person in its own right. *It's lucky I remembered to dress today.*

It was hard, so hard, to keep from giggling. Mooning one's commanding officer was *probably* on the list of court-martial offences, but she doubted it would be written up like that. Conduct unbecoming an officer, probably. The thought nearly set her off again. Once, as a teenager, she'd absent-mindedly invited her mother to enter the room where she and her boyfriend were making out. Her mother's reaction had been memorable. Admiral Stuart's reaction would be worse.

She sobered as she pulled the hot tray out of the cooker and placed it neatly on the cooling rack. The recipe was a particularly unforgiving one, she recalled. Letting it cook for too long was guaranteed to result in an inedible mess. It wouldn't be a waste—she could simply pour the horrid stuff into the recycler—but it would be frustrating to have gone to so much effort for nothing.

"Admiral," she said, turning. Her shipsuit was relatively modest. "I'd offer to share, but..."

"I quite understand," Admiral Stuart said. Holographic etiquette mandated a certain level of pretence that the image was real, but there were limits. "You may eat while we talk."

I could put the food in stasis, Hameeda thought, crossly. *Why have you contacted me, again?*

"Thank you," she said, instead. She helped herself to a generous portion, then sat down at the table. "What can I do for you?"

"I wanted to assess how you're coping with your isolation," Admiral Stuart said. "It's been six weeks."

Hameeda nodded, tersely. Her mind seemed to have split into two tracks. One track was perfectly aware of just how long they'd spent in FTL, right down to the nanosecond; the other track seemed to have long-since lost track of time. She'd been so closely linked to the datanet that hours had felt like minutes. And, when she hadn't been using the neural link—or sleeping—she'd been immersing herself in entertainment files. They'd been quite a few television series that she'd wanted to binge-watch, but she hadn't had the time.

"I have learned how to cope," she said, stiffly. She wasn't about to admit that she'd also accessed a number of pornographic files. "The secret, it would seem, is to keep myself occupied."

She took a bite of her food, savouring the taste. It was a little sharper than she remembered—she made a mental note to use less lemon juice next time—but edible. Definitely edible. It was almost a shame there was no one to share it with. Perhaps she'd invite the admiral to dinner, when they were out of FTL. Or someone else...there were millions of people in the fleet. She had to know *one* of them from her previous career. She'd almost welcome Girard Burke if he showed up in the fleet lists. He might have been an asshole, back at the academy, but he'd probably grown up since...

Unless his father really did give him a post in his shipping company, Hameeda thought. Matt Burke wasn't super-rich, not like some of the Stuarts and the others who'd gotten in on the ground floor, but he was well on his way. *He was looking for experienced officers, wasn't he?*

"A good answer," Admiral Stuart said. Hameeda dragged her mind back to the matter at hand. "And are you coping well with your isolation?"

"I'm never truly alone in the datanet," Hameeda assured her. "And I look forward to showing you exactly what I can do."

"Good," Admiral Stuart said. Her lips curved into a predatory expression. "Because I have a job for you."

• • •

"FTL drives deactivating…now," Yolanda said. A dull shudder ran through the ship. The display filled up with red icons, tactical alerts flashing brightly before the icons slowly turned green. "Local space is clear, Admiral. No encroachments."

"Good," Hoshiko said. She'd selected their destination at random, keeping it to herself until the fleet was well away from Earth. A Tokomak spy would have been hard pressed to beat them to Garza, let alone to Apsidal, but there was no point in taking chances. The enemy had already proven that they were willing to move fast when necessary. "FTL sensors?"

"Just routine traffic, heading in and out of the gravity point," Yolanda said. The display updated rapidly, showing a number of starships in FTL. Infoboxes beside the icons insisted that they were freighters. "There's no sign we've been detected."

Hoshiko nodded, although she wasn't convinced. Garza was a barren little system, without even a single asteroid as far as the Galactics could tell, but it *did* have a gravity point that connected directly to Apsidal. She'd brought the fleet out of FTL well clear of any sensors that might be mounted near the gravity point, yet there was always the possibility of the Tokomak expanding their sensor network. If they were careful, they could shoot an alert up the chain without tipping her off. A lone starship in the right place might force her to throw all her plans out the airlock.

A good thing my plans aren't too solid, she told herself. She'd drawn up a wide range of contingency plans, but she hadn't allowed herself to get too attached to any of them. It was an easy way to get blindsided by something she hadn't seen coming. *We can adapt to what we find at our destination.*

She cleared her throat. "Contact the LinkShip," she said. "Inform Captain Hameeda that she is cleared to begin Operation Snoop."

"Aye, Admiral," Yolanda said.

Hoshiko sat back in her chair. It had been easier, a great deal easier, when she hadn't been responsible for *quite* so many ships and spacers. If the Druavrok War had gone badly wrong, if her entire force had been annihilated, it wouldn't have been disastrous. The Solar Union would barely have noticed the loss of nine cruisers. But here…she'd been trusted with nearly two-thirds of humanity's *entire* deployable force. If something went wrong…

And I don't know if I can trust the LinkShip either, she thought. Hameeda was…odd, in ways that were hard to put into words. There were times when she was strictly professional and times when she seemed to forget who and what she was. *If her mind wanders at the wrong time, if she doesn't come back…*

She pasted a calm expression on her face and watched, grimly, as the LinkShip vanished from the display. At least the stealth functions were working. The Tokomak—or whoever was waiting at the far end—should have no clue the LinkShip was there. But if Hameeda did something erratic, in the middle of enemy territory, who knew *what* would happen next?

Wait, she told herself, firmly. *There's nothing else to do.*

CHAPTER SEVEN

The trouble with analysing the Tokomak, Hameeda had once been told, was that so little of their society made *sense*. On one hand, they'd taken control of much of the known galaxy through a technological breakthrough that had given them a decisive advantage; on the other, they showed little interest in pursuing technological research and development past a certain point, even though there was considerable room for improvement. The scientists had insisted, for example, that faster stardrives were theoretically possible, but the Tokomak—who'd had a thousand-year head start—hadn't spent much time and energy improving their drives. They hadn't even found ways to baffle the gravimetric emissions that betrayed a starship's course and speed to long-range sensors.

They're alien, she reminded herself, thoughtfully. *They don't have to think like us.*

The scientists had split into two camps, both firmly convinced that they were right. One group held that the Tokomak were simply too satisfied with what they had to change, a problem made worse by their gerontocratic society. Who knew what new inventions would rock the boat until it capsized? But the other group argued that the Tokomak had secretly continued to develop new technologies, technologies they hadn't shared with the rest of the galaxy. They'd want an ace in the hole for the time their power was seriously challenged…

We might be about to find out, Hameeda thought. *Will they see me coming?*

She could *feel* the gravity pulses fluctuating around the ship, only to be fed back into the FTL field rather than being allowed to break free. The technology was expensive and incredibly complex, and she'd been warned not to depend on it too much, but it seemed to be working perfectly. A sense of satisfaction, even *anticipation*, ran through the datanet. Everyone knew that sneaking up on a settled star system was impossible. Everyone knew...

They'll be suspicious of incoming freighters, now they've seen us use them to tow warships through FTL, Hameeda reminded herself. *But they won't see even a hint of my presence.*

She tensed as the FTL field slowly unravelled, sending her slipping back into realspace. Her awareness filled with contacts, all potentially unfriendly. Garza was surprisingly *useful*, for such a barren system. The Galactics didn't need inhabited planets to use the system as a way to cut weeks or months off travel times. Hell, the sheer emptiness of the system was a plus in their eyes. There were no pesky locals to charge transit fees.

Her awareness expanded, confirming that a single station held position on the near side of the gravity point. It was a very basic design, surprisingly primitive for such an important transit point. A handful of interlocking rings linked together by spokes radiating out of a central nexus, a couple of industrial nodes hovering below the station; docking ports crammed with dozens of freighters. She wondered, as she noted the presence of a handful of automated weapons platforms, just who'd built the station. It looked to be the work of a servile race, rather than one of the Galactics.

No one realised just how important this chain was going to become, she told herself. The Galactics still had problems wrapping their heads around the concept of *humanity* posing a threat. *They probably assigned the task to a slave race and didn't bother to set up defences when they realised they might have to defend the system.*

She turned her attention away from the station and studied the gravity point. It was invisible to the naked eye, although she had no trouble tracking the stream of starships flickering in and out of existence and using them to pinpoint the gravity point's exact location. Her gravimetric sensors picked up a twist in the local space-time fabric…she wondered, suddenly, how the first spacefarers had stumbled across the very first gravity point. They'd had to be quite *close* to detect the point, even with modern sensors. Every tactician feared the discovery of a previously-unknown gravity point in their backyard. Sol had been surveyed thoroughly over the past fifty years, with sensors of increasing range and power, and nothing had been found…but there was still that quiet nagging doubt. Space could be full of undetected gravity points, just waiting for someone to find and exploit them.

But most of the models suggest that gravity points are quite rare, she reminded herself, as she patiently tracked starships using the gravity point. *If there was one closer to Sol than Varner, we would have found it by now.*

She dismissed the thought and bent her mind towards getting through the gravity point without being detected. The transits appeared to be under tight control, with a five-minute gap between one starship jumping to Apsidal and another appearing in Garza. Hameeda guessed, based on past experience, that the locals were staggering the transits to minimise the risk of a collision. The odds of two starships actually *colliding* were higher near the gravity points than anywhere else. She directed the LinkShip forward as another freighter headed towards the gravity point, silently assessing the timing. She'd have to be very careful. If she interpenetrated with the freighter, both ships would be utterly destroyed.

They're moving fast, she told herself, firmly. A shiver ran down her spine anyway. The slightest error in timing would be disastrous. Admiral Stuart would never know what had killed her scout. *I have to follow at just the right speed.*

Her awareness focused on the freighter as it reached the gravity point, paused…and vanished. Hameeda followed, triggering the jump pulse as soon as she was on the gravity point. The universe seemed to blink, just for a second—there was a sense that she existed and yet she didn't, followed by a falling sensation that made her stomach churn—and then reformed. The freighter was already moving away from the gravity point, exchanging IFF signals with a pair of battlestations. Another freighter was heading *towards* the gravity point, blithely unaware of the cloaked LinkShip. Hameeda hastily triggered her drives, slipping after the freighter. The battlestations didn't seem to have realised that someone else had slipped through the gravity point.

Hameeda cursed under her breath as more and more data flowed into her sensors. The battlestations were new—at least, they hadn't been there when *Odyssey* had passed through the system—and they weren't alone. Three squadrons of warships, Tokomak warships, were holding position near the stations, their weapons at the ready. Hameeda had no idea if they knew the fleet was on the way or not, but it didn't matter. They were ready to mount a conventional gravity point defence at any moment.

Taking them by surprise will be difficult, Hameeda thought. *They'll have plenty of time to go on the alert before we can move through the gravity point and attack.*

She considered their options for a long moment. The LinkShip could get through the gravity point without being detected, but the remainder of Admiral Stuart's fleet didn't have that advantage. Hameeda could give the enemy a nasty surprise, if she attacked their rear, yet it wouldn't be enough to take them all out. She put a handful of subroutines to work, considering the possibilities, then glided smoothly away from the gravity point. Admiral Stuart wanted her to survey the entire system.

Apsidal was, she conceded ruefully, an impressive system. It had been settled for thousands of years, more than long enough for every world and most of the asteroids to be settled or exploited. Thousands of freighters moved through the system, making their way towards the gravity points or Apsidal itself; dozens of warships patrolled the system, as if they were expecting trouble at any moment. She wasn't surprised to discover that there were four battlestations guarding the gravity point to Mokpo. The Tokomak would almost certainly be funnelling ships through the naval base at N-Gann, three transits up the chain. They wouldn't want anyone interfering with *that*.

They haven't managed to get the majority of their fleet here, she noted, as she steered around the gravity point. There were another five squadrons of starships on guard duty, but they were a mere handful compared to the enemy fleet. She guessed they'd been hastily rushed to Apsidal from N-Gann once the enemy had started putting their plan together. *But they're doing everything in their power to make it work.*

A chill ran down her spine. Her subroutines were silently calculating the possibilities, throwing up a dozen different simulations. None of them were very cheerful. She'd been told, time and time again, that the enemy could trade a hundred starships for every *human* ship and come out ahead, but she hadn't really believed it. Now...*now* she believed it. The Tokomak ruled a massive empire, with the resources to match, while humanity had a pitiful handful of colonies and a tiny number of allies. How could they hope to prevail?

Advanced technology and better tactics, she told herself, setting her course towards the planet itself. *We can make them bleed until they think better of it.*

She allowed herself a moment of frustration. She'd seen the projections. If they'd had fifty more years to prepare, fifty years to build up the fleet, the Tokomak wouldn't have stood a chance. Advanced weapons, advanced drives...perhaps even an FTL communications system...humanity's tech advantage would have been too great for them to overcome. They would have been tribal warriors, blissfully unaware of machine guns until they charged their enemies and were mown down in their thousands. But instead, the Tokomak had started the war too soon. She couldn't help wondering if that was deliberate.

Apsidal slowly grew in her awareness until it dominated her mind. The world was nothing *but* city. It was surrounded by a giant ring—she thought it looked like a donut—that was connected to the surface by six orbital towers. She wasn't sure if she should be impressed by the sheer *size* of the construction or horrified by the risk. If the ring shattered and fell out of orbit, the entire planet would be rendered uninhabitable. Billions of lives would be lost, billions more would be forced to flee. Her awareness passed over the multitude of orbital defence platforms, industrial nodes and fabricators. Apsidal was an industrial powerhouse and it showed. She suspected the entire system was slowly being turned into a support base for the Tokomak war machine.

Good thing we're about to come take the system away, she thought, as more and more data flowed into her sensors for later analysis. There were surprisingly few radio transmissions. Apsidal seemed to be less *chatty* than Earth, even though the entire population of Sol would have vanished without trace on the ancient world. Perhaps they used lasers, or hardwired connectors, or...perhaps they weren't allowed to talk. Restrictive societies did everything in their power to keep their people from talking freely. *They wouldn't want someone to start plotting a revolt.*

She watched Apsidal for nearly an hour, studying the planetary defences carefully, then started to inspect the remainder of the system. A couple of other worlds—they looked to have been very similar to Mars, once upon a time—had high populations too, although they didn't seem to be particularly industrialised. The gas giants were surrounded by so many cloudscoops that it looked as if they were on the verge of being drained dry. Her lips twitched in amusement. Gas giants were so incredibly vast that it would take thousands of years to literally siphon away *every* last bit of gas. She'd once read a proposal to put FTL drives on a planet and turn it into a giant starship, but the drives would have to be gigantic and the power requirements incomprehensibly high. She doubted it would ever be anything other than a theory.

Although it would have its amusing side, she thought, wryly. *What would the Tokomak think if we start hurling planets at them?*

She dismissed the thought as she turned back towards the gravity point. There was no clue that anyone had seen her, but it looked as though the pace of starships through the gravity point was starting to pick up. The gap between starship transits had narrowed to three minutes. Hameeda paused, well clear of the gravity point, and watched the battlestations suspiciously. Were they trying to make life difficult for her? Or were they merely trying to get more starships through the gravity point? There was no way to be sure.

Not that it matters, she told herself. *Whatever they have in mind, it has been quite effective in slowing me down.*

She waited as long as she dared—nearly an hour—but the transit pace didn't change. Her sensors picked up a handful of transmissions between the battlestations and transiting freighters, yet none of them seemed particularly suspicious. She considered waiting longer, but she knew the admiral was depending on her. Gritting her teeth, she followed the next freighter towards the gravity point and transited back to Garza. Her awareness filled with new freighters. An entire convoy of ships was waiting to make the jump.

Crap, she thought, as she hastily moved out of the way. *What are they doing here?*

More data flowed into her sensors. Analysis subroutines scanned the data and offered tentative conclusions. It looked as though one of the *really* big interstellar corporations had dispatched a convoy to Garza. No *wonder* the battlestations had allowed the transit rate to speed up. The Galactic corporations were even less understanding of interstellar realities than their human counterparts. They'd be more annoyed about bureaucratic regulations slowing down the convoy, even if the regulations were—for once—quite sensible—than the risk of losing a handful of ships. She was surprised they hadn't demanded that their ships were allowed to jump through in pairs.

Perhaps the crews refused, she thought. A *human*-run corporation would know better than to issue orders that would be disobeyed, but would the Galactics? *They* seemed to believe they could bend the universe to their will. *Any trained spacer would know that the odds of surviving a multiple jump are poor. Who'd sign up for the chance to commit suicide?*

She slipped back into FTL and headed away from the gravity point, heading back to the fleet. The mission had been a success by any reasonable definition, although she was sure the admiral wouldn't be pleased. She'd have to decide between forcing the system, which would give the Tokomak a chance to bleed her before their main fleet even arrived, or pulling back and picketing Garza instead. *That* would be a serious problem. The Tokomak could simply bypass the system and, by using one of the other gravity points, head straight for Earth.

Mission elapsed time, thirty-two hours, she thought, as she removed her helmet and forced herself to stand. Her body was covered in sweat. *It didn't feel anything like so long.*

She staggered into the shower, signalling the automated systems to turn on the water, and sighed in relief as warm water cascaded down. It was all she could do to slowly undress and dump her shipsuit in the basket for cleaning. Her fingers felt brittle, as if she'd forgotten how to use them. She could direct the ship's waldos to do anything—or use precisely-modulated gravity fields to do more delicate work—but it was all she could do force her fingers to work properly. Perhaps she was just too tired.

Maybe I should put myself in a sensory tank, she considered, as she used a ship's field to dry herself. A new shipsuit floated into the compartment and hovered in the air, waiting for her to put it on. *My body would be held in suspension while I controlled the ship.*

Hameeda sighed. She doubted she'd be allowed to do anything of the sort. The scientists had considered it important that she remembered she was human, even though she'd bonded herself to a datanet. No partner, male or female, would ever be so intimate with her. They would never share her thoughts. And they would go, in time, while the datanet would remain.

A chime ran through the ship. They were dropping out of FTL. Hameeda hastily grabbed the clean shipsuit and put it on, then ordered the datanet to transmit everything they'd detected to the flagship. Admiral Stuart's intelligence staff would want to go through everything, even though the analysis subroutines had already drawn a number of conclusions. Hameeda wondered, idly, if they were testing her and her ship as much as they were planning an assault on the enemy position. The Solar Union wouldn't commit to building a whole *fleet* of LinkShips unless they were certain the concept was workable.

Admiral Stuart's hologram requested permission to enter the ship. Hameeda granted it with a sigh. She wasn't in the mood for talking. Her body felt drained, even though her implants had taken care of her while she'd been *en rapport* with the datanet. She needed a solid eight hours sleep before she could consider herself fit for duty. But she was starting to think she wasn't going to get it.

"Captain," Admiral Stuart said. "Good work."

"Thank you," Hameeda said. A cruiser or destroyer could have scouted the system, but not sneaked through the gravity point. The admiral would have had to send a modified freighter if she hadn't had the LinkShip, raising the spectre of the ship being inspected before it was allowed to proceed into the system. "I trust the data is useful."

"It has some worrying implications," Admiral Stuart said. "But yes, it has helped us plan our assault."

Hameeda nodded. "When are we going to move?"

"As soon as the towlines are connected," Admiral Stuart said. "Are you up for a return visit?"

"I need some sleep," Hameeda admitted. "But I will be ready soon."

"Then get some rest now," Admiral Stuart ordered. "You need it. And Captain..."

"Yes, Admiral?"

"Well done."

CHAPTER EIGHT

"Admiral," Yolanda said. "The towlines are connected. We are ready to depart on your command."

Hoshiko nodded. If there was one thing she'd learnt in her career, particularly during her assignment to the Martina Sector, it was that it was better to move as fast as possible once one had decided to use force. The Galactics tended to be slower than humanity at reacting to bad news—although *that* was starting to change—but it was dangerous to give them time to go on alert and rally their forces. Better to hit them as hard as possible, then press the advantage before they had a chance to get back on their feet.

And most of my officers agreed, she thought, crossly. She wasn't used to being *diplomatic* when it came to issuing orders, let alone debating tactics, and she was still annoyed that some of her subordinates seemed to expect her to consult them before she made up her mind. But then, they *had* been independent commanders before their squadrons had been folded into her fleet. She wouldn't have been too happy if someone had done that to *her* ships. *We have to take the offensive.*

"Remind the officers that it is *important* that we secure the gravity point as quickly as possible," Hoshiko said. "The enemy freighters aren't important as long as we block their path to the gravity point."

"Aye, Admiral."

Hoshiko took a breath. "Pass fleet command to Commodore Harding, then order the freighters to take us into FTL," she added. "It's time."

A jerk ran through the starship, followed by a queasy sensation that refused to fade. Hoshiko gritted her teeth, telling herself—firmly—that the sensation would be gone in less than twenty minutes, when they dropped out of FTL. The freighter towing *Defiant* through FTL didn't have a modern drive. Her designers had copied the Tokomak design, ensuring that no watching sensors noted anything odd about her. She certainly didn't *look* like a human-designed ship, not from a distance. Hoshiko could put up with her inefficiencies for *that*.

They also designed their ships for easy conversion, she reminded herself. *A ship designed for humans would be incomparably vast for some races and incredibly cramped for others.*

She put the thought aside as the timer started to count down the seconds to emergence. The watching sensors would see them coming, of course, but all they would see were a handful of freighters. They *wouldn't* see the warships behind them until it was far too late. And yet, if the station reacted quickly, they *could* get a drone through the gravity point before Hoshiko could move to stop them. Too many things could go wrong.

Stop doubting, she thought. *You're committed now.*

She leaned back in her chair and concentrated on projecting an impression of being calm and composed. Her staff were moving with cool professionalism, but there was a sharp edge in the air that she knew all too well. It was the first time they were going into battle against a *real* enemy, rather than computer-generated simulations; it was the first time they were at real risk of dying, if something went badly wrong. Hoshiko had come to terms with her own mortality long ago, back when she'd gone to the academy, but she knew that others refused to believe they *could* die until it was too late. She wondered, suddenly, how many of her staff had uploaded brainprints into computer matrixes, trying to ensure that something of themselves would live on. It struck Hoshiko as silly, but the younger generation saw no difference between a biological person and a brainprint.

There were even people who claimed that, one day, everyone would live in computers.

"Two minutes to emergence, Admiral," Yolanda said.

"Prepare to engage," Hoshiko ordered. "Stand by to engage."

She braced herself. Commodore Harding would be following their progress. He'd take the remainder of the fleet into FTL the moment he saw them vanish from his sensors. Her reinforcements would arrive within twenty minutes. And yet, she was worried. She knew, all too well, just how many things could go wrong. There was too much complexity worked into her battle plan for her to have much faith in it.

A shudder ran through the ship. The display blanked, then filled with fearsome speed. A station, hundreds of freighters and a gravity point...just as the LinkShip had reported. The station's automated defences started to come online, only to be blown away as Hoshiko's ships opened fire. A freighter that had been inching towards the gravity point veered away, snapping into FTL with commendable speed. Hoshiko made a silent bet with herself, as other freighters vanished too, that their commanders were from the younger races. They tended to react quicker.

"Seize the gravity point," she snapped. "And signal the remaining freighters to stand down or be destroyed."

The squadron lunged forward, just as a freighter appeared in the gravity point. It had no time to react before a missile struck her amidships and blew her into an expanding ball of superheated plasma. Hoshiko felt a flicker of pity, combined with a grim awareness that they *couldn't* risk letting the defences on the far side be alerted. And yet, the sudden pause in transits from Garza would alarm them. *Someone* would poke their head through soon enough to see what had happened. And when *they* didn't return...

"Admiral, the station is surrendering," Yolanda said. "The remainder of the freighters are running."

"Noted," Hoshiko said. The station was a fourth-order concern at the moment. It had no defences, nothing to keep her from blowing it to dust if the whim struck her. "Is the squadron ready to deploy assault pods?"

"Yes, Admiral," Yolanda said. "The squadron is standing by."

Hoshiko sucked in her breath. Admiral Webster and his team, most of whom had been science-fiction writers before science-fiction had been outdated by real-life alien contact and space war, had devised a relatively simple approach to assaulting gravity points. Indeed, it was so simple that she was surprised the Tokomak or one of their rivals hadn't invented it themselves, although their technology had been rather more primitive in those days. The assault pods were really nothing more than missile pods with a single-use jump drive attached, allowing them to make transit through a gravity point. A number would interpenetrate and be destroyed, of course, but they were expendable. Hoshiko had no qualms about using them to save lives.

"Signal all ships," she ordered. "Launch the assault pods."

Defiant shuddered as she emptied her external racks. The other ships followed suit, hurling the assault pods towards the gravity point. Hoshiko leaned forward, watching avidly, as the assault pods reached the gravity point and started to vanish. There was no attempt at stealth—the scientists had warned that there was no way to keep the enemy from detecting them—but it might take the Tokomak several minutes to react. They simply wouldn't know what the pods *were* until they released their deadly contents.

And there will be hundreds of missiles suddenly bearing down on their targets, Hoshiko thought. *That will make their lives more interesting.*

She glanced at the timer, then nodded. "Order the squadron to advance, as planned," she said. The long-range sensors were showing the remainder of the fleet, ten minutes away. "Take us through the gravity point in quick succession."

"Aye, Admiral."

Hoshiko smiled, grimly, as *Defiant* transited into Apsidal. The display blurred, then cleared, revealing that the assault pods had done better than expected. Two of the enemy battlestations were gone, while the third was badly damaged. The enemy fleet had taken a beating, although—as it had been further from the gravity point—it had had more time to bring up its point defence. She was mildly surprised the ships hadn't simply dropped into FTL and put an impossible distance between themselves and the missiles. Perhaps they simply hadn't been keeping their drives at the ready.

"Station Three is disabled, Admiral," Yolanda said. "However, she is still capable of engaging targets."

"Deploy two hammers to take her out," Hoshiko ordered. The black hole-tipped missiles *could* be countered, or simply avoided, but the station was too badly damaged to do either. "And then prepare for engagement."

The enemy fleet was reforming rapidly. Hoshiko frowned as she watched. The Tokomak had always been good at *looking* good, but now they were *being* good. Whoever was in command on Tokomak itself—now—had forced her spacers to forget scripted exercises and work their way through problems that included a number of nasty surprises. The survivors would be just as good as their human counterparts, if they'd been cured of their superiority complex. Merely being Tokomak wasn't enough to win anymore.

"They're preparing to engage, Admiral," Yolanda warned. "I suspect they're planning a missile duel."

"Perhaps," Hoshiko said. The Tokomak outnumbered her—twenty-five starships to eighteen—but they had to be aware that her ships outgunned them. Unless they hadn't been warned about the hammers, or the other advanced weapons at her command. "Or they may be trying to lure us away from the gravity point."

She nodded to herself as the enemy starships suddenly sparkled with red icons. They'd opened fire, with conventional missiles. *That* made sense, she supposed. As long as she was sitting on top of the gravity point, she couldn't take her ships into FTL and simply outrun the missiles. And they knew it. They could be trying to keep her pinned down while they summoned reinforcements. Recapturing the gravity point was their first priority, now. She'd read their tactical manuals.

Not that it matters, she thought. *Commodore Harding has more than enough assault pods to force his way through the gravity point if they manage to recapture it.*

"Contact the squadron," she ordered, as the red icons drew closer. "The battle line will advance and engage the enemy."

She smiled, coldly. The enemy wanted a missile duel? She saw no reason to indulge them, not when it would give them an advantage. They could simply flee at any moment, if there was a risk of her actually *winning*. This way, she could not only test their weapons and defences, but force them to flee or fight on her terms. She wondered, as her ships started to move, which choice they'd make. There was no way even the *Tokomak* could keep word of the battle from getting out. A defeat now might undermine their prestige to the point that their slave races started to rebel. Hell, some of the older races might start looking for a way to switch sides.

The Tokomak didn't show any visible reaction as her ships inched away from the gravity point, heading straight towards the wall of incoming missiles. Hoshiko's ships deployed deception drones and ECM, but they were largely ineffective. She frowned, noting just how few missiles had been diverted from their targets. Had the Tokomak improved their systems to the point where her deception was simply laughable? Or had they merely gotten hard locks on her ships, allowing them to ignore the sensor ghosts and engage the real targets?

"Point defence is engaging now," Yolanda said. "Captains Young and Harrington are requesting permission to return fire."

"Let us close the range first," Hoshiko ordered. The Tokomak still had the option of running, although she suspected they'd trade blows with their human counterparts first. They *really* didn't want to be seen as cowards. "We'll open fire when we're within sprint-mode range."

The Tokomak fired again. There were fewer missiles this time, Hoshiko noted. Their ships must have been equipped with external racks. *That* was odd. The Tokomak hadn't had the concept, as far as Solar Intelligence had been able to determine. Their ships certainly hadn't been designed to carry external racks. But there was nothing particularly difficult about the concept. A Tokomak agent must have seen a human ship with external racks, perhaps during one of the post-Battle of Earth skirmishes, and sent a warning up the chain. She wondered, wryly, if some Tokomak engineer had claimed credit for the idea. They wouldn't want to admit that they'd stolen the concept off the despised human race.

"Entering sprint-mode range," Yolanda said, tersely. "Admiral."

Hoshiko nodded. "Signal the squadron," she said. "Fire at will."

Defiant shuddered as she unleashed her first barrage. Hoshiko leaned forward, watching the display as the missiles raced towards their targets. The Tokomak might *just* have enough time to spin up their drives and jump into FTL if they moved now...her lips curved into a smile as she realised they'd reacted too late. Their point defence went to life, blowing hundreds of missiles out of space, but hundreds more made it through the defences and slammed home. One by one, the enemy ships died.

"Their point defence has improved," Hoshiko commented. "I wonder how much further they can go."

Her lips twitched. She wondered how many of the reporters, particularly the ones who'd never been stationed on a warship before, would realise that the enemy point defence *had* improved. Hoshiko's ships had given the Tokomak one hell of a beating. A couple of enemy ships had managed to survive long enough to slip into FTL, but the remainder had been blown away with almost contemptuous ease. There would be no stopping the Galactics from telling and retelling the story of how an outnumbered squadron of primitive aliens from the edge of explored space slaughtered a Tokomak fleet.

And yet, if we hadn't fired so many missiles, we wouldn't have been able to smother their defences, she thought. Something would have to be done about the improved enemy point defence. *They might even have held us off long enough to get more ships out of the cauldron.*

"Admiral, the remainder of the fleet is making transit," Yolanda said. "Commodore Harding is asking for orders."

Hoshiko smiled. "We proceed as planned," she said. "Detail two squadrons to watch the Garza Point, then assemble the remainder of the fleet for the advance on Mokpo Point."

She took a breath. "Launch long-range probes towards the planet," she added. "By the time we turn our attention to Apsidal, I want to know precisely how they're planning to welcome us."

"Aye, Admiral," Yolanda said. "Do you want to demand surrender?"

"Not yet," Hoshiko said. There was no way to know if the enemy—either the forces defending the Mokpo Point or Apsidal itself—had any idea what had happened to the Garza Point, although they had to know that *something* had happened. It wouldn't last. The escaped ships had raced straight to the Mokpo Point. "We need to be a little bit more intimidating first."

She studied the display for a long moment, watching as starship after starship transited through the gravity point in a never-ending stream. Her forces were building up rapidly, yet there were far more starships waiting on the far side of the gravity point. She smiled, coldly, as she realised just how many problems the Tokomak would have getting through the gravity point, once she was sitting on top of it. They might outnumber her fifty-to-one—a conservative estimate—but their numbers would mean nothing if they could only come at her one by one.

They'll have sent a warning up the chain by the time I get to the gravity point, she told herself. There was no way to avoid it, unless she got very lucky. The enemy CO *might* want to avoid blame for the disaster—the Tokomak appeared to see failure as a sign of inferior breeding, if the xeno-specialists could be trusted—but surely he'd put his duty ahead of his personal future. *Not that he has a future.*

"Hundreds of freighters are leaving the system," Yolanda commented. The long-range sensors were picking up thousands of starships in transit. "Hundreds more are still coming this way."

"They don't know what's happened here," Hoshiko said. She had a feeling that they were going to be seeing *that* a lot, at least until word spread. Starships in transit wouldn't know that anything had happened until they dropped out of FTL. Hopefully, the civil affairs teams would be able to take advantage of their surprise to establish a few new trading links. "We'll see less traffic once they know the truth."

She shrugged. "Damage reports?"

"None, Admiral," Yolanda said. Data flowed up in front of her. "The point defence datanet worked as predicted. No enemy missile made it through to strike our shields. However, we have expended our external racks."

"Have them reloaded, once the ammunition ships come through the gravity point," Hoshiko ordered. She wanted at least a third of her fleet on hand when she advanced on the Mokpo Point. The LinkShip would have to take a look at Mokpo once Apsidal was secure. Solar Intelligence hadn't reported any fortifications in Mokpo, but their data was months—if not years—out of date. "And then prepare the fleet to advance."

"Aye, Admiral."

Hoshiko leaned back in her chair, studying the system display. Apsidal *was* an impressive system, far more industrialised than anything she'd seen in the Martina Sector. And yet, she could see weaknesses too. The industry was concentrated around the planet itself, rather than scattered across the system. Anyone who took the planet—and she intended to take the planet—would take the industry too. Once the governors on the planet's fabricators were removed, Apsidal would be more than capable of supporting her fleet indefinitely.

Don't count your chickens before they're hatched, she reminded herself. Her grandmother had used to say that, citing the days when she'd lived on a ranch. *Something could still go wrong.*

"Admiral," Yolanda said. She turned to face her commanding officer. "The fleet is ready to advance."

"Then set course for the Mokpo Point," Hoshiko added. "It's time to finish this."

CHAPTER NINE

Admiral Yosho, Tokomak Navy, was not having a very good day.

He'd seen the assignment to Apsidal as a blessing, at first. He was only a few hundred years old, too young for any *serious* posting, but the Empress had had faith in him. She'd directed him to take command of the system and its defences, then prepare it to support her fleet as it advanced towards Earth. Yosho had had some difficulty coming to accept that such an insignificant world could pose a major threat, but he knew better than to argue. Empress Neola was dangerously unpredictable.

And everything had been going well, until the humans had arrived.

They'd timed it well, he conceded ruefully. He'd assumed he'd have plenty of time to reinforce the Garza Point if a threat happened to materialise—assuming, of course, that the humans didn't simply stare helplessly at the juggernaut bearing down on them until it was too late—but the invaders had overrun the point before he'd even known the system was under attack. Worse, if his long-range sensors were to be believed, the humans had arrived in considerable force. Retaking the Garza Point was likely to be impossible until the main fleet arrived, which wasn't going to happen for weeks. Even holding the Mokpo Point was going to be difficult.

This is going to destroy my career, he thought, morbidly. The irony would have made him laugh, if it had happened to anyone else. Under the old system, even a tactical ignoramus was assured of promotion...eventually. But now, with merit being considered instead of age, he'd be lucky if he wasn't summarily sacked. His family would disown him rather than admit they had a failure in their midst. *What do I do?*

"Admiral," his tactical officer said. "The human fleet will enter engagement range in fifty minutes."

"Send an alert up the chain, then move as many freighters through the gravity point as possible before the humans arrive," Yosho ordered, curtly. There was no point in leaving more ships to be captured or destroyed. The freighters waiting on the far side would have to be told to flee. "And then put our defences on full alert."

He scowled. The human commander was being kind enough to give him time to concentrate his forces, but it didn't matter. His fleet simply wasn't strong enough to do more than bleed the enemy before it was pushed aside. He briefly considered ordering his warships through the gravity point and making a stand on the far side, before dismissing the idea. The battlestations couldn't make the jump and he couldn't abandon them, not without being branded a coward as well as a failure. His only hope of saving his reputation—and his family's reputation—lay in making a stand and dying bravely.

And they can't replace their losses anything like as fast as we can, he thought. The Empress was bringing more and more ships out of storage and preparing them for war. There was no way the humans could hope to produce enough ships to match the sheer *size* of the Tokomak fleet. *Every ship I kill now will weaken them for the later battle.*

He allowed himself a flicker of dull admiration for the humans, although it wasn't something he would ever admit aloud. They hadn't been in space for a century and yet they'd already developed more advanced weapons than anyone else, although they'd had help. If they'd had to invent everything from scratch, the Empress had pointed out more than once, they'd have taken far longer. And yet…the fleet advancing steadily towards him was impressive. The humans seemed to have solved the command and control problems that plagued any fleet larger than a few hundred ships. He wondered, vaguely, how they did it.

They probably gave their commanders more authority, he thought. He'd served long enough under the gerontocrats to know that questioning orders was a career-ending blunder. The senior officer gave the orders and everyone else did what they were told. *But if they subdivided their fleet into smaller sections, they might...*

"Admiral, the fleet is ready to engage the enemy," the tactical officer said. "All weapons and defences are online."

"Good," Yosho said. The distraction was almost a relief. "Order all stations to open fire the moment the enemy comes within range."

...

"The situation on the planet itself is confused," Yolanda said, "but a number of asteroids are signalling us. They're asking if they can join the Galactic Alliance."

Hoshiko frowned. The intelligence staff had tracked everything from riots to outright revolutions, spreading across the system in the wake of their arrival, but there was no way to be *entirely* sure what was going on. She'd known that Apsidal was unstable—a relatively small ruling class lording it over a giant underclass—yet the revolutions might be put down before she could take control of the high orbitals. Or, if they succeeded, destroy installations and industries she needed to preserve.

"We have to secure the system first," she said, studying the display. The Mokpo Point was growing larger on the display, surrounded by a small galaxy of red icons. It looked as though the Tokomak were preparing to make a stand. And, on the other side...who knew *what* was on the other side? The Tokomak could funnel an endless stream of reinforcements into the system if their main fleet had arrived in Mokpo. "Tell them...tell them to wait."

She sighed, inwardly. She didn't blame the locals for wanting to revolt, or taking advantage of the fleet's arrival to rise up, but it was a nuisance. If they slaughtered their overlords, the Tokomak would turn it into propaganda; if they were slaughtered themselves, the Tokomak would probably *also* turn it into propaganda. They'd want to make it clear to their allies that they were fighting for their lives, while suggesting to their enemies that the human race couldn't protect them. The fact that the human race hadn't encouraged the uprisings would be left unmentioned.

And they're not even tactically advantageous, unless they manage to capture the high orbitals for us, she thought. *But the Tokomak would be fools to allow a sizable number of potential rebels onto their battlestations.*

"Admiral, the enemy are locking weapons on us," Yolanda said. "They're preparing to fire."

"Target the battlestations with hammers, then target the starships with conventional missiles," Hoshiko ordered. The Tokomak had clearly learnt *something* from the previous engagements. Their starships were altering position constantly, seemingly at random. There was little hope of hitting one of *them* with a hammer missile. "And deploy enhanced countermeasures."

"Aye, Admiral," Yolanda said. "Should we deploy the Storm Shadows?"

Hoshiko hesitated. The new weapons *would* help her win the engagement, quickly and decisively. It was a tempting thought. She didn't have *time* for a long engagement. But the Tokomak would have observers watching the battle, lurking near the gravity point. Anything she deployed now would be carefully noted and reported up the chain for analysis. The advantage might be lost by the time she encountered the main fleet.

"No," she said. "We'll hold them in reserve."

Her heart jumped as the display suddenly blossomed into red light. The Tokomak weren't holding anything back. Hundreds of thousands of missiles were rocketing through space, heading directly towards her fleet. Combat instincts urged her to jump into FTL and flee, even though they were just a *little* too close to the gravity point. She watched, grimly, as the enemy attack took shape and form. It looked like an uncontrolled and uncontrollable swarm, but she knew better. They'd enhanced their coordination over the last few years. They might well have duplicated Admiral Webster's command missiles too.

We gave them the idea, she thought. *What other tricks have they managed to copy?*

"Fire," she ordered, putting the thought aside. The Tokomak were already firing a second barrage. "And deploy additional ECM."

"Aye, Admiral."

The wave of human missiles passed through the wave of alien missiles and continued towards its targets. Hoshiko watched them hungrily, trusting her subordinates to handle the point defence. They didn't need micromanagement. They'd drilled so extensively that they could handle it in their sleep. The Tokomak had drilled too, she realised. Their point defence looked to have significantly improved in the last few years.

We probably removed some of their more thick-headed officers for them, she thought. The irony of actually doing the Tokomak a favour by kicking their ass irritated her more than she cared to admit. She had no idea what had happened on the alien homeworld, but it was clear that the new regime was going to be far more dangerous in the long run. *The survivors learnt from the shock of defeat.*

"Admiral, they're launching a new type of missile," Yolanda said. "They're...they're aimed at the hammers."

Hoshiko blinked. The hammers didn't mount conventional drives. Instead, they carried a powerful gravity well generator that produced a small black hole, which dragged the generator after it on an endless charge through space until the hammer hit something hard enough to destroy it. There was no point in trying to engage them with countermissiles or point defence because the black hole would swallow anything aimed at the missile. No force shield could stop them. The only real defence was to get out of the way.

"Redirect the recon drones to watch the results," she ordered, curtly. The Tokomak had seen hammers in action. If they'd come up with a countermeasure...it didn't bode well for the future. "And direct what they see to the analysis deck."

Her eyes narrowed. The countermissiles looked more like conventional antiship missiles than standard antimissile missiles. Her mind raced. It was rare for *anyone* to use antimissile missiles. Energy weapons were generally far more efficient. But the Tokomak had something in mind...

The first countermissile approached the hammer...and exploded. Hoshiko blinked as the live feed from a handful of seeker heads and recon drones cut off abruptly. The hammer was gone, the remnants of the black hole already fading out of existence. Space didn't *like* being twisted into a pretzel. Hoshiko had heard people speculate that twisting the fabric of space-time would eventually start tearing holes in it, although most scientists were dismissive of the concept. Black holes were not gateways to other dimensions. They were merely massive gravity wells that sucked in and compressed everything, even light.

"Antimatter," Yolanda said. She sounded shaken. "Those missiles are crammed with antimatter!"

Hoshiko swallowed a thoroughly undignified curse. She'd never consider the Tokomak unimaginative again. They'd come up with a neat countermeasure, one that was already proving all too effective. The antimatter blast had been large enough to destroy the gravity generator and take out the hammer. It had its downside—the blast had probably also damaged their sensors—but they'd had no choice. The hammers would have smashed their battlestations if they'd been allowed to plunge into their targets.

"Clever," she said. Only a handful of her missiles had survived long enough to reach their targets and strike home. "Fire the second salvo."

Yolanda looked up. "Including the hammers?"

Hoshiko considered it for a moment. She had, for once, an abundance of hammers. And yet, she couldn't afford to waste them. How many antimatter missiles did the enemy have? The Tokomak didn't normally store large quantities of antimatter on their battlestations, fearing a containment breach, but times were far from normal. The facilities at Apsidal could certainly produce vast quantities of antimatter at a moment's notice.

"No," she said, reluctantly. "Conventional missiles."

"Aye, Admiral," Yolanda said. Her hands danced across her console. "Missiles firing...now."

Hoshiko nodded, then turned her attention to the display. The human datanet had updated rapidly as the sensors picked apart the alien point defence network, locating weak points and directing missiles to take advantage of them. It looked as though the Tokomak were still using a strictly-hierarchical system, with orders coming down from a handful of flagships, rather than a more decentralised system. The datanet took full advantage, pointing the first clusters of missiles straight towards the flagships. Hoshiko smiled, grimly, as the enemy command network began to fall apart. The system simply wasn't designed to designate another flagship in a hurry.

They haven't changed that much, then, she thought. Cut off from the network, each enemy ship was effectively fighting alone. *They don't give their subordinate officers much independence.*

She pushed the thought aside for later consideration, then looked at Yolanda. "It's time to finish this," she said. "Order the fleet to advance."

• • •

At least we proved we could stop their gravity-well missiles, Yosho thought. It was a satisfying thought, even though damage was mounting rapidly. The humans were knocking down his point defence networks almost as fast as he could put them together. His station was tough, designed to soak up blows that would destroy a starship, but its shields were already fluctuating rapidly under the constant bombardment. *They know their weapons are not invincible any more.*

He smiled, holding onto his chair as another impact ran through the giant fortress. The damage control teams were working hard—he'd drilled them extensively, just to make it clear that *nothing* could be taken for granted any longer—but it was only a matter of time. His fleet was being systematically smashed to rubble. The only consolation was that he'd hurt the humans too.

"Order the remainder of the fleet to escape through the gravity point," he said. There was no point in letting them be destroyed, now the point defence network had been knocked offline completely. "And then divert all power to weapons and shields."

Another impact ran through the station. He muttered an ancient curse under his breath, knowing that he was about to die. The humans had been hurt, but...but not enough. And yet, he'd achieved one objective. He'd warned them that the Tokomak were no longer limited to technology that had been old when they had been crawling in the mud. They would be just a *little* bit unsure, now, of what to expect. And it would make them hesitant to advance further up the chain.

And the main fleet is at N-Gann, he thought. *The Empress is closer than the barbarians think.*

Leaning back in his chair, he watched the missiles fly...and waited patiently for the end.

• • •

"The enemy fleet is retreating," Yolanda said. "They're heading through the gravity point."

"And waiting for us on the far side, no doubt," Hoshiko said. She was surprised the Tokomak hadn't attempted to retreat earlier. There was no saving the fortresses, but the starships could have lived to fight another day. "Redirect as many missiles as possible to take them out before they can escape."

"Aye, Admiral."

Hoshiko nodded, then directed her attention back to the battlestations. One of them had been battered into uselessness, but the other four were still firing. The Tokomak had designed them to take a beating. Their shields were failing badly, allowing her missiles to slam into their hulls, but they were surviving. She allowed herself a moment of droll admiration. The Tokomak designers had done a very good job.

And they're buying time, she thought. Who knew how close the enemy fleet truly was? *And we don't have time to waste.*

"Target the remaining fortresses with hammers," she said, shortly. The fortresses had been battered so badly that it was unlikely they could see the hammers coming, let alone launch countermissiles in time to save themselves. Even if they could, she doubted they would prove effective. "Fire."

"Aye, Admiral," Yolanda said. She keyed her console. "Firing...now."

Hoshiko leaned forward, watching as the four streaks of light sliced through space and slammed into the giant fortresses, crashing through their shields and armour as if they were nothing more than paper. They were so massive that even the hammers couldn't destroy them with a single blow, but their fire slackened rapidly and died. One fortress vanished in a fireball—Hoshiko guessed an antimatter chamber must have lost containment—while the remaining three crumpled. There was no hope of further resistance.

She sucked in a breath. "Deploy Task Forces 3.4 and 3.5 to hold the gravity point," she ordered. "Inform Commodore Yu that the lockdown contingency is now in effect. He is to hold the gravity point unless confronted by superior force."

"Aye, Admiral."

Hoshiko nodded. Commodore Yu would do what he could, but if the Tokomak arrived in force in the next couple of days her fleet would have extreme difficulty holding the system. She keyed her console, ordering the steady stream of reinforcements from the Garza Point to make their way directly to the Mokpo Point. Yu would need the reinforcements.

She took a breath. "Damage report?"

"We lost five cruisers and one destroyer," Yolanda said. "Seven other ships took varying degrees of damage; *Houston* is probably beyond immediate repair, but the others claim they can be brought back to full readiness in less than a day."

Hoshiko allowed herself a moment of relief. She'd expected worse, far worse. The enemy had pulled off a couple of surprises of their own, both unanticipated. She didn't like the degree of imagination they were showing. It wasn't much, by human standards, but it was more than she'd expected from them. The Tokomak had spent the last thousand years trying to keep the galaxy from changing. They hadn't encouraged their people to be imaginative.

"Direct *Houston* to return to the Garza Point and link up with the mobile repair ships," Hoshiko ordered. If *Houston* could be repaired, she would be. If not…she'd have to be abandoned and her crew placed in the personnel pool for redeployment. "And then contact the remainder of the fleet. It's time to hit the planet."

CHAPTER TEN

"Now, *that* is impressive," Trooper Rowe breathed.

"Quiet," Martin snapped. They were in open space, with nothing but their battlesuits for protection. If they were detected, they'd be killed. "Maintain radio silence."

It *was* an impressive sight, he had to admit. The Apsidal Ring was *immense*, wrapped around the entire planet like a giant donut. His mind refused to grasp the sheer *size* of the ring. It was so big that he could see it with the naked eye, even though they were thousands of miles away. There were countries on Earth that were smaller than the Apsidal Ring. It grew bigger and bigger as they approached, practically blocking out the planet below. He wondered, grimly, just how the locals coped with a permanent shadow. The ring was large enough to block out the sun.

The Solar Union never built anything so large, he thought. There had been plans for starships large enough to pass for cities, but none of them had ever made it off the drawing board. The Solar Union had no interest in building planetary rings, let alone Ringworlds or Dyson Spheres. *And how are we meant to capture it?*

Alerts flashed up in front of his eyes as they fell towards their target. The planet was at war with itself, the underclass rising up to wage war on their betters. Some of them were screaming for human help, others were trying to surrender in exchange for protection...the briefing had made it clear that nothing could be trusted. Martin understood, all too well. The locals would have countless grudges to pay off, which would make peacekeeping difficult, while their former masters would expect humanity to put them back on top. And even if they didn't, the locals would fear betrayal. They might fret that humanity would become nothing more than a new set of masters.

He gritted his teeth as his suit reported plasma bursts in space. The planetary defences were engaging the fleet, despite the war on the ground. Perhaps there *wasn't* a war on the ground, perhaps...it didn't seem likely, but it wouldn't be the first time someone had tried to lure the marines into a trap. He checked the live feed from the fleet and frowned. The planetary defence centres—and smaller bases mounted on the ring—were firing on the fleet. It wouldn't be long before the fleet would have to engage with heavy weapons.

Unless the rebels can take the PDCs, he thought. He doubted it was possible, unless the defenders were mind-numbingly incompetent. *Perhaps they'll smuggle nukes under the PDCs and blow them to hell.*

He pushed the thought out of his mind as his suit twisted. His perspective twisted too—he was rising up towards the ring, he was falling down towards the ring—making his head spin for a long chilling moment. And then the ring grew larger and larger, tiny blisters on its surface becoming skyscraper-sized constructions that looked strikingly unfriendly. The ring had looked pretty, from thousands of miles away, but up close it was ugly as hell. There was something about it that looked unfinished, as if construction had stopped halfway. The reports had suggested that large chunks of its interior had never really been used.

They have more land surface than they know what to do with, he thought, as the marines landed neatly on the metal terrain. It was just like standing on a planetary surface, right down to the gravity. He could delude himself that he wasn't in space, if he wished. *I wonder why they didn't turn it into living space.*

He checked the latest updates, then led the way towards the nearest airlock. If intelligence was right, there was a control centre only a few miles into the ring. If not...they'd still be in an excellent position to block the orbital towers and open the path to the planet below. The Tokomak wouldn't take the risk of firing on the ring itself, even if the humans took complete control. They'd have to come up and fight to recapture it.

A sense of unreality settled over him as they jogged across the ring. He felt like an ant crawling across something incomprehensibly vast. Giant structures poked out of the ring and reached up towards the sky, their purpose a complete unknown; freighters and interplanetary transports hung in the sky, so close he could make them out with the naked eye. He'd been in alien environments before, real and simulated, and he could honestly say that *this* was the strangest environment he'd ever seen. He felt tiny. It defied belief that a relative handful of marines—or even the entire division—could capture the ring.

We never realise just how big space truly is until we see it, he thought, recalling basic training. The Drill Instructors had taken pains to point out that something that looked easy on paper might be very difficult in real life. Marines had often found themselves fighting bitterly to take and retake a relatively small patch of ground. REMFs might wonder why it took so long to travel a single mile, but the truth was that the plans never accounted for the enemy. *And the only territory we control is the territory under our guns.*

A flash of light caught his attention as they reached the hatch. He glanced up, noting a pair of freighters slowly slipping away from the ring, then opened the hatch. The airlock inside was huge, as if the inhabitants were giants. It wasn't uncommon on multiracial structures, he knew from experience, but it still made him feel uneasy. He couldn't help feeling relieved when they made it through the inner airlock and into the ring itself. It was still vast, still incomprehensibly alien, but at least it wasn't discomfiting.

"Deploy snoops," he ordered, as his suit checked their position against the map. "And follow me."

The interior of the ring was oddly unfinished too, as if the Galactics had decided there was no point in trying to make it look habitable. It reminded him of a warehouse he'd once worked, before the gangbangers had forced the owners to close down and move away. Perhaps it *was* a warehouse. The spacers would want places to store their goods while waiting for a starship or transhipment down to the planet. There might be other, more developed, sections of the ring a few thousand miles away.

They flew on, using the suits' antigravity field to fly through the corridors at breakneck speed. Everything seemed to be larger, even the elevator shafts. They passed through giant compartments that might have been warehouses—or football fields—without seeing a single inhabitant. Even the snoops had found nothing. It made him wonder if the Tokomak had had time to evacuate the entire section. He was almost relieved when they approached the command centre and ran into resistance.

They don't look prepared for us, he thought, as plasma bolts sizzled through the air. They were handheld burners, not heavy weapons. His suit could take a number of hits without losing integrity. *What happened to their heavy weapons?*

He assessed the situation quickly. The enemy commander didn't strike him as a professional soldier, but he hadn't done a bad job. He'd put his forces, such as they were, in a bottleneck, forcing Martin to come to him if he wanted to break through to the command centre. There was no way to know, either, what might be holding back, waiting for Martin to commit himself. The snoops were encountering jamming fields and counter-drones as they tried to probe their way towards the command centre. For all he knew, the enemy commander could have put his expendable forces on the front line while conserving his *real* forces for the counterattack.

Not that it matters, he thought. *We could take out the entire ring if we wanted.*

"We'll clear the way with plasma grenades," he said. "Sergeant…"

His suit flashed up an alert. Someone was trying to call him.

Martin blinked. "A Galactic?"

He hesitated, suddenly unsure of himself. The message was coming from the command centre, although it wasn't coming over the ring's communications network. And that meant...what? A rebel? A spy? Or someone who wanted to make contact without having it recorded? He wondered, briefly, if he should relay the message to Major Griffin, but the major was on the other side of the planet. Martin was the man on the spot.

"Put it through," he ordered.

A sibilant voice, like a child with a lisp, echoed over the communications network. "Is this the human commander?"

Martin shivered. The voice was indisputably alien. "Yes."

"We will surrender, in exchange for protection," the voice said. "The"—the next word was unfamiliar to Martin—"are at the airlocks."

Martin hesitated, taking a moment to run the message through the suit's translator. There was no exact translation, but it came across roughly as *shit-scum*. Martin cursed under his breath, realising just what sort of headache they'd stumbled into. The Tokomak had to have cleared the entire sector when they'd realised the system was under attack, only to discover that their panic had inspired the underclass to rise up against them. They no longer looked invincible...

"Order your defenders to stand down," he said, finally. He had orders to accept surrenders if they were offered. "Turn over all command keys to us, open your datanets and give us full cooperation in taking control. And, in exchange for that, we will grant you protection."

There was a long pause. Martin forced himself to wait, despite a grim awareness that they might be running out of time. The Tokomak might just be stalling, hoping to find some way to retake the advantage. And yet...the enemy fire slackened and died. An uneasy silence fell over the chamber.

"We accept your terms," the sibilant voice said.

Martin exchanged glances with Sergeant Howe, then slowly walked down the corridor. A small collection of aliens stood at the far end, their weapons lying in a heap on the ground. It was a multi-species group, with at least five different alien races represented. Martin was surprised to see that not all of them were Galactics, although he supposed he should have expected it. There were always members of the junior races who were willing to collaborate with their masters, even at the expense of their own kind. Humans had collaborated too.

He detailed two of his men to watch the prisoners, then stepped into the command centre itself. It looked weirdly like a circular throne room, with the commander—a Tokomak—seated in the exact centre, allowing him to look down on everyone else. Most of the senior officers were Tokomak, save for a couple of Harmonies. Martin eyed the latter two suspiciously. The Harmonies had a reputation for backstabbing since they'd lured *Odyssey* to their system and tried to capture her.

The commander stood and held out a set of code-keys. Martin took them, realising that it was a gesture of surrender as much as anything else, then nodded to his men to take control of the system. The Galactics had locked their computers, but the code-keys unlocked them instantly. Martin allowed his suit to access the network and scan for potential trouble while the prisoners were removed to somewhere a little safer. It wasn't particularly surprising to discover that their captives hadn't had control of the *entire* ring. *That* rested in the planetary governor's hands.

"Shit," Sergeant Howe muttered. "Look at that."

Martin looked at the monitor. A swarm of aliens was pressing against a set of heavy airlocks while, behind them, a handful of more organised rebels were approaching with cutting tools. There were thousands of rebels in that one sector alone. No *wonder* the Tokomak had surrendered so quickly. They'd known there was no hope of saving themselves if the rebels overwhelmed the defences. Their plasma burners wouldn't last forever.

He forced himself to think. The snoops were still reporting no contacts, outside the command centre itself, which meant…he poked the system until it threw up a location. He'd half-hoped the rebels might be hundreds of miles away, but they were on the other side of the main airlock, far too close for comfort. And he couldn't think of any way to stop them without deadly force. A stun bolt that would put a member of one species out of commission would either kill—or merely irritate—another.

"Close the hatches between the main airlock and here," he ordered. It wouldn't slow the rebels down for long, but it would buy him some time. "And then deploy half the troop to...to here."

He tapped a location on the map, cursing under his breath. Mobs simply didn't listen to reason. Human mobs didn't, in any case, and he doubted it would be different for the aliens. And that meant...he was going to have to use force, if reason wasn't enough. There was no way he could get the prisoners out of the ring before it was too late...and besides, even if he could, he couldn't allow the rebels to tear the command centre to bits. They *needed* that orbital tower to get troops down to the surface.

"Request additional troops from the fleet," he said, although he doubted that reinforcements would get to the ring in time to be useful. There was so much electromagnetic disruption in the high orbitals that no one would risk teleporting. "And then take command here. I'll be at the front."

He ignored the sergeant's protest and headed down towards the blockade, trying desperately to think of a peaceful solution. But he'd seen enough riots—at refugee camps, at detention centres—to know that there probably wasn't one. Their suits carried non-lethal weapons, but with aliens involved...it was hard to be sure what was truly non-lethal. His mind ran around and around in circles. They might have to hurt the people they'd come to help.

The hatch burst open. A torrent of aliens poured in. Martin felt a flicker of pity for the ones at the front, the ones who were being pushed forward and would be trampled if they fell. One of his brothers had died in a protest march, years ago. He'd fallen, according to the official report, and been crushed to death. Martin hadn't believed the report, not then. It had been easier to blame everything on everyone but his brother. And yet, Charlie had always been talking about violence...

"ATTENTION," he said, using the suit's speakers to amplify his voice. The aliens recoiled as the sound blasted into their ears. It would be acutely painful for a human. He tried not to think about what it might do to them. "THIS SECTOR HAS BEEN SECURED BY THE GALACTIC ALLIANCE. IT IS NOW UNDER OUR PROTECTION. YOU NEED TO RETURN TO YOUR QUARTERS AND *WAIT*."

The alien mass seemed to waver. Martin noted over a dozen different kinds of aliens in the mix, all of them from servile races. He thought some of his ancestors would approve of them trying to free themselves, even though their revolution would have ended very badly if the human ships had been driven out of the system. But he couldn't allow the aliens to ransack the sector. The engineers were already reporting that the orbital elevators could be put back into service, with a little work, or the tubes opened up to allow a rapid and sheltered descent to the planet. His reinforcements would probably pause long enough to say *hello* and then hurry down to the surface. He wanted—he needed—to go with them.

"YOU WILL HAVE THE SYSTEM, ONCE WE HAVE LIBERATED IT," he told them. "BUT, FOR THE MOMENT, YOU NEED TO STAY OUT OF OUR WAY."

"Send out the childless ones," a voice called. The speaker looked rather like an oversized chicken, although the nasty-looking beak and unpleasant glint in his eye robbed his appearance of any humour. "Let us peck them to death!"

The mob roared with agreement, although they didn't try to move forward. Martin didn't know why. They might not trust the humans to deal with the prisoners properly…or they might think that nothing short of pecking them to death themselves would satisfy their lust for revenge. Martin didn't really blame them. Slaves sometimes *needed* to watch their former masters *burn*. But he had his orders.

"RETURN TO YOUR QUARTERS," he ordered. "I WON'T ASK AGAIN."

There was a long, chilling pause. Martin braced himself, trying to guess what the mob would do. It seemed to be a universal law that a mob's intelligence was inversely proportional to the number of people in it. And all it would take to start a riot—and a slaughter—would be one idiot saying the wrong thing. He looked at the mass of aliens, silently urging them to go home and wait...

And then, slowly, they turned away.

Martin let out a sigh of relief. There hadn't been any real danger to him, as far as he could tell, but he hadn't *wanted* to kill thousands of aliens. He'd wanted...

"Let them go," he ordered, quietly. They'd have to set up forcefields, just in case the mob decided it had been given a raw deal and returned. "Sergeant, do we have any update on those reinforcements?"

"They're coming down the pipeline now," Howe said. "They'll be here in a couple of minutes. But they're going on to the planetary surface."

"Lucky bastards," Martin said. He ignored the sergeant's snort. "I wish I was going down too."

"Cheer up, sir," Howe said. "There will be plenty of other tempting opportunities to commit suicide in the future."

CHAPTER ELEVEN

"DC Four is still holding out," Yolanda reported. "But the majority of the planet is quiet."

"For a given value of quiet," Hoshiko said.

She shook her head in disbelief. The planetary government had surrendered, once the Apsidal Ring had been captured, but there were countless riots and purges breaking out on the planet's surface. Hoshiko hadn't seen anything like it, even during the aftermath of the Druavrok War. The former slaves were turning on their masters with a brutality unmatched since the collapse of the United States. Appeals from orbit for patience and restraint had simply been ignored. The slaves wanted their pound of flesh and no one, not even humanity, could deny them.

"How's the refugee situation coming along?"

"We have most of the former masters and their dependents on their way to the orbital towers and the ring now," Yolanda said, checking her records. "Civil Affairs thinks we will be dealing with millions of refugees, eventually. The slaves aren't being very discriminating, Admiral. They're attacking *every* Galactic on the surface."

"We'll save as many as we can," Hoshiko said. Providing protection was part of the terms of surrender, but there were limits. She wasn't going to risk an open confrontation with the rebels, not when she might need them later. "Getting them further away is going to be a major headache."

"The logistics will be impossible, despite the ships we've seized," Yolanda said. "It would take every ship in the fleet *years* to move the refugees to the next star system. And there are no facilities at Mokpo to house them."

Hoshiko nodded, curtly. Something would have to be done, but what? She couldn't afford to leave the refugees on the ring indefinitely. If nothing else, their mere presence posed a security threat. The Galactics weren't very good at acting on their own initiative, without orders from higher up the food chain, but it would only take one of them to start real trouble at the worst possible time. The marines were already badly overstretched.

And that PDC is still holding out, she thought, sourly. The planetary government had ordered the PDC to surrender, but the CO had refused. And his forcefield was strong enough to keep her from simply dropping rocks on his head. The force she'd need to crack the field would do unacceptable damage to the surrounding area. *We might be able to starve them out, but it would take years.*

Yolanda looked up. "Major Singh had an idea, Admiral."

Hoshiko lifted her eyebrows. Major Singh was an engineering officer, not someone in the chain of command. She'd assigned him to inspect the orbital towers and the ring itself, both to see if it was still stable after the battle and to decide if it was worth duplicating. She had no idea if the Solar Union would be genuinely interested in building rings of its own, but she could see the advantages. Apsidal moved millions of tons of freight—and millions of people—between the surface and the ring every day. There was no way teleporting could move so much material without unacceptable energy costs.

"What?"

"He thought we could disconnect the ring from the orbital towers, then push it away from the planet and turn it into a giant space station," Yolanda said. "The refugees would then be safe, without interfering with anyone else."

Hoshiko had to fight to keep from giggling. Major Singh didn't think *small*. It made her wonder if he'd join the Extreme Construction Society, once he served his time in the navy and returned to civilian life. She'd seen some of their plans. They made *Dyson Spheres* look small. She couldn't imagine any responsible government agreeing to waste resources on what was effectively a giant vanity project for the entire human race.

"I think it would be too risky," she said, finally. "And it would piss off the provisional government. Speaking of which...?"

Yolanda picked up the unspoken question. "The various rebel groups are pulling together now," she said. "They've promised they'll appoint a representative soon."

"We'll see," Hoshiko said. In her experience, provisional governments took years to form and rarely wielded much authority, at least at first. "They might not hold together for long."

She sighed. The rebels had been held together by an overpowering threat. They'd known, after centuries of having their cells broken open and countless members dispatched to penal colonies that were effectively death sentences, that they *had* to remain united against the planetary government. But now they'd won—or at least they'd been liberated—and all the issues that had been buried under the urgent need to fight would come bubbling to the surface. Who would rule Apsidal? And *how* would it be ruled? Would the different races manage to live together? Or would they break up into different factions and start fighting?

Her lips twitched. *The only people we hate more than the Romans are the fucking Judean People's Front.*

She smiled, remembering Movie Night when she'd been a child and her parents had been introducing her to the classics, then pushed the thought aside as she turned her attention to the reports. The Mokpo Point was now heavily guarded, with a number of prefabricated fortresses being hastily assembled and manned to provide additional cover. Hoshiko would have preferred to rely on a mobile defence, but she had to admit the fortresses could soak up a hell of a lot of incoming fire. The Tokomak fortresses had proved that during the first engagement. It wouldn't be too long before the Tokomak copied the assault pods and put them into production.

They have an industrial base at N-Gann, devoted to supporting their fleet, she thought, grimly. *They can just start churning out assault pods there and funnelling them up the chain towards us.*

It was a worrying thought. The one thing the planetary government had been unable or unwilling to do was tell her when the main enemy fleet was supposed to arrive. They knew it was coming—they'd said as much, when she'd asked—but they didn't know *when*. Hoshiko had no idea if they were telling the truth or not, although she suspected they were genuinely ignorant. The Tokomak CO wouldn't have given them a precise time. There was a good chance the fleet would be delayed, simply by having to funnel thousands of starships through the gravity points one by one. It was something she hadn't really appreciated until she'd had to take her own fleet through the gravity points.

She shook her head, again. So far, everything had gone according to plan. She'd secured the system, landed troops on the planet's surface and begun the immense task of turning the planet's industries into a support base for her fleet. Given a few weeks, they'd start churning out vast quantities of everything from missiles to mines. Minefields were normally useless in interstellar war, but not when the enemy *had* to come through the gravity points. It was clear why it had taken so long for a genuine interstellar hegemony to arise. Waging interstellar war through the gravity points alone was immensely costly for the attacker, while giving the defender nearly every possible advantage. It made her wonder why anyone had bothered.

"Admiral, we just received a message from the surface," Yolanda said. "The provisional government has finally appointed a speaker. He's requesting a meeting with you at your earliest convenience."

Hoshiko glanced at the status board, already knowing what she'd see. There was nothing that required her attention. Her subordinates were handling everything. They didn't need her peering over their shoulders and making unhelpful remarks. She sighed, then stood. She'd have to wear her dress uniform for the diplomatic meeting. It would probably be lost on the aliens—they paid as little attention to human dress codes as humans paid to theirs—but not on the folks back home. *Someone* would probably make a terrible fuss if she wasn't dressed to the nines.

Stupid, she thought. *The aliens wouldn't care if I was stark naked.*

"Arrange to have him teleported up in thirty minutes and escorted to the briefing room," she said, as she turned to the hatch. "The marines are to keep a sharp eye on him."

"Aye, Admiral."

Hoshiko changed rapidly, inspected her appearance in the reflector field and walked back into the briefing room. The Galactics were stiffly formal in all diplomatic discussions—although even *they* had to make allowances for different species having different ideas—but she had no idea how the rebels would act. Did they have anyone trained in diplomacy? If they did, did they *trust* that person? Or would they be rough and crude and desperately posturing to hide their essential weakness? Hoshiko wished, suddenly, that the fleet had brought someone from the Diplomatic Corps. But the planners had insisted on having a ready-made excuse to disown any agreements she made, if they considered it necessary.

Weasels, she thought, with a twinge of disgust. *As if I'd give away Sol during the opening talks.*

The hatch opened, revealing a giant alien. Hoshiko held up one hand in the approved greeting, then nodded her head. The alien looked like a giant chicken, but somehow there was nothing *amusing* about its appearance. She'd met members of the avian race before, during the Druavrok War. They were a servile race, as far as the Galactics were concerned; they tended to be used as low-level bureaucrats to keep the system operating smoothly. And yet, she'd met enough of them to know they hated their masters as thoroughly as most of the other servile races. She wasn't surprised to know that one of them had been leading a rebel cell. They were *very* good organisers.

And genderless, she reminded herself. *They can both lay eggs and fertilise them.*

"I greet you," she said, in careful Galactic. The hatch hissed closed as the alien advanced forward. "And I welcome you to my ship."

The alien's beak opened. "I greet you," it said. Up close, it smelt faintly rank. There was something sinister about its voice. "We thank you for your assistance in freeing our world."

Hoshiko nodded, but the alien wasn't finished. "We also demand that you hand over the"—Hoshiko didn't know the next word, but it didn't sound pleasant—"for judgement, particularly those who are also us."

The ones who stayed loyal, Hoshiko thought. There had been members of the speaker's species who'd been taken into custody, simply for staying with their masters. She wondered, idly, why they'd stayed loyal. Did they think their masters would be back on top soon? Or were they too frightened to move against them? *But we gave them our protection.*

"We gave them our protection, in exchange for their surrender," she said, putting the thought into words. "If we hadn't done that, speaker, it would have been far harder to liberate the planet."

The speaker's beady eyes seemed to spin in their sockets. "They are ours to judge, particularly the traitors," it said. "We must pass sentence on them."

"We have to honour the terms of surrender," Hoshiko told him, flatly. "Now, can we discuss…?"

"We also demand that you evacuate them from the ring," the speaker said, as if she hadn't spoken. "That ring is ours."

"We will remove them when we can figure out a way to do it," Hoshiko said. "Would you be willing to grant them safety on the planet's surface?"

"It is *our* world," the speaker said. He made a loud whistling sound. "We do not want it…*contaminated*."

Hoshiko cleared her throat. "The matter is now closed," she said, firmly. "Are you willing to assist us in our war?"

The alien eyed her, then twitched its beak. "Yes," it said. "It will be a war of revenge. We will assist you in burning the monsters from the skies."

It looked at her, sharply. "And we demand that you turn the industries over to us at once," it added. "They are *ours*."

"We will discuss that once you have a provisional government," Hoshiko said. Technically, *she* was the legal ruler of the system. It was her fleet that controlled the high orbitals and asserted authority. But the Solar Union had no real interest in annexing Apsidal. There was nothing to be gained by trying. "You also need to think about who runs those industries and why."

"They are ours," the alien repeated. "And we will fight for them."

"You will have to," Hoshiko said. "The Tokomak have already dispatched a fleet to recapture Apsidal. Will you work with us to keep the system?"

The speaker twitched, again. "Do we have a choice?"

"No," Hoshiko said. The provisional government might be able to declare neutrality, but she doubted it would stick. Even if its own people didn't demand that they fight, the Tokomak would be unlikely to let the murder of so many Galactics go unpunished. The best Apsidal could hope for would be orbital bombardment and they knew it. "You have to fight with us or fight alone."

The discussion raged backwards and forwards for nearly an hour before she could pronounce herself satisfied. It hadn't been a pleasant discussion, even though both sides had been in conceptual agreement. The speaker seemed unsure if his system had merely traded hands or if it had been truly liberated. Hoshiko didn't really blame him for being confused. Apsidal—or, rather, the gravity points—were important enough that *no one* would simply give them up without a fight. He'd come to the meeting expecting Hoshiko to dictate terms to him. He certainly hadn't expected her to promise to hand the gravity points over as soon as the enemy fleet was defeated.

She watched the alien go, with the first draft of a treaty, then sat down and forced herself to relax. Matters could have gone a great deal worse. Hell, there'd been times when she *had* been tempted to dictate terms. But they'd found some kind of resolution...she hoped. It helped that they had a common enemy. Afterwards...who knew what was going to happen?

Her wristcom bleeped. "Admiral, Commodore Yu has signalled that the first level of defences are now in place," Yolanda said. "His crews need their rest."

Hoshiko laughed. The prefabricated fortresses had been designed to be put together in a hurry—and her crews had practiced, time and time again, before they left Sol—but she was still impressed they'd been put together so quickly. Commodore Yu's men, knowing what was at stake, had worked double and even triple shifts to get it done. They would *definitely* need a rest.

"Very good," she said. The construction crews would have to be put down for medals. She'd see to it personally. "Has anything poked through from the other side?"

"No, Admiral," Hoshiko said. "Traffic appears to have dried up completely."

That will cause some problems, Hoshiko thought, wryly. The Galactic economy wasn't *dependent* on the Apsidal Chain, but losing control of the gravity point nexus would have to hurt. Freighters that didn't reach their destinations on time would cause all sorts of knock-on effects. Her intelligence staff had attempted to model the likely outcome, but they'd eventually been forced to admit that there were too many variables to make any projections that were any better than guesswork. *And if it does hurt the bastards, it will make them all the more determined to recover this system.*

She stood, brushing down her uniform. A faint smell hung in the air, fading slowly. She took a breath, then headed for the hatch. The recyclers would purify the air. She smiled, humourlessly, at the thought. There was a reason why multi-species starships were rare. Issues that were meaningless on planetary surfaces became deadly serious in confined spaces.

Even the Galactics were reluctant to have members of two different species serving together.

"Contact the LinkShip," she ordered, as she walked back to her cabin. "I want a direct link to her captain."

"Aye, Admiral," Yolanda said.

Hoshiko wished for a shower, but she didn't have time. Instead, she sat down at her desk as soon as she entered her cabin and activated the holographic implant. The world went dark, just for a second. And then she was standing in the LinkShip. It felt almost as if she had teleported, although she was only a holographic projection. She had no more substance than a ghost.

And walking around like this can be dangerous, she reminded herself. The holographic implant was designed to read her intentions and feed them to the hologram, but there had been times—when she'd started using the system—that she'd walked her corporal body into walls because her mind had been hundreds of miles away. Her image had been walking, but so had her body. *I have to be careful.*

She turned, slowly. Hameeda was sitting in a chair, reading a physical book. A Heinlein, Hoshiko noted. *Starship Troopers*. There were a dozen cantons that took the book as gospel and based themselves on its teachings. She hadn't thought Hameeda came from one of them.

"Admiral," Hameeda said. She was wearing a black shirt and slacks, rather than her uniform. It made her look unprofessional, but at least she didn't look as if she was steadily wasting away. "Congratulations on your victory."

"It wouldn't have been possible without you," Hoshiko told her. It was true. "And I have another job for you."

Hameeda stood. "Probing Mokpo?"

"Yes," Hoshiko said. "This time, though, the enemy will be on the alert. They'll be watching for *someone* coming through the gravity point."

"I understand," Hameeda said. She ran her hands through her uncombed hair. "But even their *best* sensors won't spot me."

"I hope you're right," Hoshiko said. She'd served long enough to know that overconfidence could be disastrous. Hameeda had done well, but the defenders had had no reason to expect attack. This time, it would be different. "Good luck."

CHAPTER TWELVE

Hameeda was not about to admit it, certainly not to Admiral Stuart, but she couldn't help feeling a flicker of trepidation as the LinkShip slowly approached the Mokpo Point. The admiral had been right about one thing, at least: *this* time, the Tokomak would be expecting trouble. They might not have realised quite *how* Apsidal had been surveyed, before the fleet burst in through the gravity point, but they'd probably know that it *had* been surveyed. It was very likely that they would be watching the gravity point like hawks.

And there's a second problem, she thought, as she opened her awareness to peer through the ship's sensors. *I might be fired upon by my own side.*

The gravity point was surrounded with automated weapons platforms, prefabricated fortresses and—keeping a slight distance back—hundreds of starships. Minefields lurked on the edge of the gravity point, waiting for someone to poke their head into the occupied system; gunboats prowled; single-shot energy and missile platforms watched for a clear shot at their enemies. The classic gravity point defence doctrine had been modified, in light of the assault pods. It was only a matter of time until the Tokomak developed assault pods and put them into mass production.

A shiver ran down her spine. It was all too likely that one of those platforms would see her coming through the gravity point and open fire on her, before she had a chance to identify herself. And if that happened…

she shuddered at the thought. The LinkShip was tough, with far stronger shields than any regular ship her size, but it couldn't take so many hits indefinitely. If she was mistaken for an enemy ship...she pushed the thought aside. She had to take the risk. She owed it to the men and women who'd died taking Apsidal.

"Send the last copy of our records to *Defiant*," she ordered, verbalising the command. "And then, take us forward."

She allowed her mind to blur into the datanet as they made their way through the minefield. This time, at least, she could use an IFF code without being immediately located and blown out of space, although she wasn't *entirely* confident it would work. The mines were mass-produced pieces of crap, little more than nuclear warheads with basic sensors attached. There was no *guarantee* that they wouldn't go after her, IFF or no IFF. She rather suspected that the minefields would be removed quickly, when the main offensive began, but it didn't matter. Their true function was to buy time for the *real* defenders to come to life. No military force could remain alert indefinitely, even with automated systems and AIs.

The gravity point loomed up in front of her, barely visible even to gravimetric sensors. Her records noted that the Tokomak had been lucky. They'd found the Mokpo System first and stumbled through into Apsidal, rather than the other way round. The gravity point was too weak to be detected at a distance. They'd have to stumble across it if they hadn't found the other side first. She'd heard that the Galactics insisted that all starships had to keep their gravimetric sensors active at all times. Now, she thought she understood why.

Here we go, Hameeda thought.

She triggered the jump drive. The universe blinked, just long enough for her to be aware of it before the stars—different stars—snapped back into existence. Alerts flashed up in front of her, pointing to a dozen starships sitting some distance from the gravity point. They seemed to be watchful, but not at battlestations. She puzzled over their stance for a moment, then decided they were trying not to place unnecessary wear and tear on their systems. Losing Apsidal had to have been a shock, particularly as the nearest naval base was two weeks away. It was almost certain that N-Gann still didn't know what had happened.

It's certain, unless they invented an FTL communicator, Hameeda reminded herself. *Even a fast courier boat won't have reached N-Gann by now.*

She flinched as she sensed a handful of enemy ships heading towards her. Shuttles...no, gunboats. They were patrolling the gravity point, their sensors sweeping constantly for trouble. Hameeda moved away, as stealthily as she could. The gunboats weren't designed for anything more complex than patrol duties, and she knew she could wipe them out in seconds, but their big sisters would have plenty of time to power up their weapons and come after the intruder. It was an unusual tactic for the Tokomak...

No, it isn't, she thought, as the pieces fell into place. *That's a deployment designed to counter assault pods.*

She felt a flicker of uneasy admiration for whoever had thought of the tactic. A cluster of assault pods, transiting the gravity point, would need a handful of seconds to re-orient themselves, pick their targets and launch their missiles. The gunboats would have time—a few seconds, but time enough for automated systems—to open fire on the pods before they could fire themselves. It was clever, for the Tokomak. They'd certainly never faced pods until two days ago and they'd already devised a countermeasure.

Crafty bastards, she thought. *That's going to hurt us if we need to mount another gravity point assault.*

The LinkShip slipped steadily away from the gravity point, its sensors drawing in information from all over the system. Mokpo itself was a planet that would have been an industrial powerhouse, if it hadn't been unlucky enough to be right next door to Apsidal. The planet's energy emissions were strong, suggesting a vibrant industrial base, but nowhere near as strong as she would have expected. The remainder of the system didn't seem to have been developed at all. Apsidal appeared to have claimed all of the investment for the sector—and then, probably, used political pressure to keep other worlds from rising up to challenge its dominance. It struck her as quite likely. Perhaps, just perhaps, humanity would find allies on Mokpo.

If we win the war, she reminded herself. *No one likes a loser.*

There were only two gravity points within the system, one leading to Apsidal and the other to GS-3532. The latter was so useless that neither the Tokomak nor anyone else had bothered to give the system a name. It would have been completely ignored if it hadn't had a second gravity point of its own, leading further up the chain towards N-Gann. The last set of reports insisted that the second gravity point hadn't had any defences and it looked as if *that* hadn't changed. She couldn't detect any fortresses—and only a pair of starships—keeping an eye on the gravity point.

They must be assuming that we won't be mounting any offenses up the chain, Hameeda thought, wryly. The Tokomak were probably right, although it was also possible that they simply hadn't realised they *needed* to fortify the system. They'd been so insistent on leaving the gravity points undefended—to keep anyone else from turning the defences against them—that they were being forced to rush to fortify the chokepoints. *We might be able to take advantage of that, if we wanted to push up the chain.*

She directed a pair of subroutines to consider the possibilities as she directed the LinkShip to move away from the gravity point. It was tempting, very tempting, to poke her head into GS-3532 and see what was waiting for her there, but she knew better. Admiral Stuart was relying on her to remain alive—or, at least, to report back before she put her life on the line again. Instead, she set course towards the planet and settled down to wait. There was no point in pushing the limits *just* yet.

A stream of possible scenarios flowed through her mind. One subroutine insisted that there was a good chance of bleeding the Tokomak, if they made a stand in Mokpo or even GS-3532. Another pointed out that neither system was as central as Apsidal and trying to defend them might force Admiral Stuart to spread her fleet out too much. The enemy would certainly be *trying* to bring their main body to bear against the human ships. Giving them a free shot at a small deployment seemed a bad idea.

She dismissed the subroutines—deciding what to do next was not her responsibility—and waited as the planet slowly came into range. Mokpo had a ring of its own, although it was nowhere near as big as the Apsidal Ring. Hameeda studied it for a long moment, noting that despite its smaller size it still had plenty of accommodation for warehouses and transients, then turned her attention to the planet itself. Mokpo looked *nicer* than Apsidal, even though it was nowhere near as wealthy. For one thing, the land surface actually looked *green*.

Not that it matters, she told herself, as her sensors made a careful note of where the planetary defences were located. *I won't ever be able to take shore leave again.*

The thought stabbed into her mind, shaking her concentration. She'd known that she was confining herself to the LinkShip for the rest of her life, she'd known she going to be trapped, she'd known…but she hadn't really believed it. She hadn't really grasped what her commitment entailed, not at an emotional level. And now…she could be surrounded by holograms of everything from Norwegian mountains to the Arizonian Grand Canyon, but she'd never see them with her own eyes. She could send drones, or surveillance devices, or anything…anything, save for going down herself and taking a look. And…

Hameeda drew a shaky breath, ordering the ship to move away from the planet as fast as possible. She was going to be alone, in a very real sense, until the day she died. She was surrounded by entertainment—there were enough eBooks and movies and VR simulations in the library to keep a small army entertained for thousands of years—but she was going to be alone. No lover would stay on the ship for the rest of her life. No…

She disconnected from the datanet, trusting in the automated systems to keep them undetected. Even then, even without the helmet, there was still a steady trickle of data at the back of her mind. She didn't even have to *ask* to be bombarded with information, everything from the local situation—a flight of enemy gunboats two million miles away—to power curves and other engineering details that were better left in automated hands. The LinkShip would be at the back of her mind for the rest of her life.

Damn it, she thought, as she walked through the ship on shaky legs. She loved it. The LinkShip was pretty much the single most advanced piece of technology in the entire known universe. And yet, it was also a prison. *Her* prison. *What now?*

The datanet offered a series of suggestions, everything from getting a few hours of sleep to inviting someone she knew over for a few hours of guilt-free fun. She glared at the bulkheads, dismissing the list with a wave of her hand. The datanet was trying to help, she knew, but it couldn't help with the *real* problem. She was part of the ship, to all intents and purposes, and the link couldn't be cut. It couldn't even be placed in stasis...

Alerts flashed through her mind. She'd been detected! How? She swung around and ran towards the chair, cursing as more information came through the neural link. A flight of enemy gunboats had appeared from nowhere...had they been under stealth themselves? Gunboats were even smaller than the LinkShip, barely larger than cargo shuttles. They couldn't mount cloaking devices, not unless the Tokomak had had a major breakthrough. Given everything else that had happened in the last few days, she wouldn't necessarily dismiss the idea out of hand.

There must have been a stealthed platform nearby, she thought, as she threw herself into the chair and jammed the helmet onto her head. The datalink sharpened rapidly, allowing her to see the gunboats as they swept into attack formation. *And the platform directed them onto me.*

She felt her teeth draw back into a snarl as she dropped the cloaking device and brought her weapons online. There was no point in trying to hide now—and besides, she *wanted* to take her ship into battle. She'd run thousands of simulations, pitting the LinkShip against foes both real and fictional—she'd particularly enjoyed doing the Trench Run and blowing the Death Star out of space time and time again—but this was *real*. She spun around, ignoring harshly worded commands to stand down and surrender *at once*. This was *very* real.

The gunboats opened fire with plasma guns and phasers. They were no threat to the LinkShip's shields—her forcefields were tougher than anything smaller than a heavy cruiser—but she evaded them anyway. The datalink hummed in her mind, pushing her into more and more complex evasive patterns that left the enemy unable to score a single hit. They bunched up, seemingly very aware that they'd bitten off more than they could chew. Hameeda opened fire a second later. All nine phaser bursts struck their targets and vaporised them.

Warning, the datanet stated. *Enemy cruiser inbound.*

Hameeda nodded. The light cruiser was a more significant threat than the gunboats, if she let the ship get into range. She could turn and flee, leaving the cruiser eating her dust; she could even play chicken, charging at the enemy ship and veering away at the last possible moment before collision. *That* would give the enemy a fright. Or she could press her advantage and take the cruiser out. It was a potential threat to the human fleet, when—if—it entered the system.

But that would give them too much information about me, she thought, soberly. She didn't *want* to think about it. She wanted to go on the offensive. *The next set of starships I encounter will be prepared for me.*

She opened her awareness, scanning the entire system. Four starships were rocketing towards her in FTL, but the remainder of the system was quiet. Someone must have sent an alert back to the planet, one that hadn't reached the gravity point yet. Those two ships hadn't moved, as far as she could tell. They certainly hadn't dropped into FTL. Her lips curved into something that could charitably be called a smile. In theory, there was no way she could take five cruisers in a straight-up engagement; in practice, she had advantages they'd never heard of. And yet...

The simulations tempted her. Their missiles weren't going to be able to score a hit. Her ECM would keep their energy weapons from hitting her too. She could get in close and land a series of blows, then retreat before they managed to break through the jamming and target her. And she could keep doing it until they broke off or died. As long as she was careful, she'd have nothing to fear.

No, she told herself, firmly. Simulations were far from perfect. A single hit would be enough to take her out of the game permanently. She couldn't afford the risk. *It's time to go.*

The LinkShip rotated, then rocketed away from the cruiser. Hameeda activated the cloaking device as soon as she was outside active sensor range, allowing the cruiser to get just a hint of her course before she vanished completely. They'd expect her to change course, she knew, but it hardly mattered. She slipped into FTL and headed straight to the gravity point, returning to normal space as she approached. The guardships hadn't heard a peep from the planet. She moved past their defences, sneaked past the gunboats and slipped into the gravity point. A moment later, she was back in Apsidal.

Success, she thought, as she started transmitting her IFF code. There was a nasty moment when she was *sure* she was about to be blasted by her own side, then the automated defences stood down without firing a single shot. *I made it.*

She chuckled, despite herself, as she glided away from the gravity point, her sensors seeking out *Defiant*. Admiral Stuart's flagship was amongst the rest of the fleet, preparing to either repel a gravity point assault or launch one of her own. Hameeda smiled, again. The fleet could take Mokpo any time it liked, clearing out the Tokomak before they could muster any real resistance. But keeping it was quite another thing.

"Transmit the full report to the flagship," she ordered, as she disconnected the helmet once again. Oddly, despite her earlier fears, she felt happy. She'd *enjoyed* destroying the gunboats and taunting the other ships, even though she knew she was going to be chewed out for it. The Tokomak hadn't seen *everything* she could do, but they'd seen enough. "And then run me a bath."

She headed down to the ship's bathroom, feeling tired and sweaty and yet—somehow—invigorated. She'd done something worthwhile, hadn't she? The information she'd gathered would help Admiral Stuart plan her offensive, if she decided to push into Mokpo; Hameeda had no doubt that it wouldn't be long before the LinkShip was sent to GS-3532 and even Winglet. It was unlikely she'd be allowed to cross the gulf between Winglet and N-Gann, but it hardly mattered. She'd have plenty of opportunity to hurt the enemy.

And do it in luxury too, she thought, as she undressed and climbed into the bath. She was mildly surprised the admiral hadn't called, but she *was* a very busy woman. *There are midshipwomen who'd kill for a proper bathroom in their ships.*

Smiling, she leaned back into the water and closed her eyes.

CHAPTER THIRTEEN

"It looks like the Dark Lord Shadye's fortress," Trooper Rowe breathed, as the PDC came into view. "You know, from the movies. All it needs is a giant glowing eye on top of it."

"We could take out the Dark Lord's fortress with a single KEW," Trooper Cuthbert pointed out, sardonically. "*This* place is a little tougher."

Martin kept his face expressionless as he surveyed the PDC. It *did* look like a fortress from a movie, although he wasn't sure if it was from a fantasy movie or one of those grimdark universes that had been all the rage for a few short years. It was a towering construction, bristling with plasma weapons so large they dwarfed an assault shuttle, glowing with eerie light as the forcefield protecting the PDC from a KEW strike interacted with the alien atmosphere. Lightning crackled around the upper reaches of the structure, as if an evil magician was indeed practicing his spells.

"It is impressive," he said, finally. The PDC was *still* refusing to surrender, despite the remainder of the planetary government having given up the ghost. He'd heard rumours that the enemy fleet was only a few days away and *that* was why the PDC had refused to surrender. "But we have work to do."

He looked around as he led the way towards the command post. The alien environment was weird, simply because it was in permanent semi-darkness. It was meant to be morning, but it felt more like twilight. The

Apsidal Ring hung high overhead, a dark line blotting out the sun and throwing the world into shadow. It wasn't as dark as he'd thought, when he'd first seen the briefing notes, but it was weird. The alien constructions nearby—he thought they were homes and offices—only made it worse. There was something about them that was subtly *wrong*. The absence of any visible inhabitants was the icing on the cake.

But then, anyone with any sense will have vacated the area long ago, even though we ordered them to stay put, he thought, morbidly. *They know this place is going to become a battleground soon enough.*

Major Griffin had set up his headquarters in what Martin *thought* might have been an alien house, once upon a time. The furniture had been pushed to one side and a handful of portable chairs and tables had been brought into the room, while a small collection of terminals had been pressed against the wall. He hoped there were no prying alien sensors looking for hints of human presence anywhere nearby. The terminals were shielded, ensuring they couldn't be detected from a distance, but the radio microbursts were all too easy to detect. They might be shelled at any moment if the aliens realised where they were.

"Captain Douglas," Major Griffin said. "Congratulations on your victory."

"It was a small one," Martin said, modestly. "They surrendered when they saw the mob coming."

"But still a victory," Major Griffin assured him. He tapped the map on the desk. "Right now, we have an uneasy stalemate with that thing"—he jerked a finger in the direction of the PDC—"and that isn't going to change in a hurry. We can't get to them and they can't break out."

"So we put a nuke under the PDC and blow them to hell," Martin said.

"So far, we haven't been able to get under the complex," Major Griffin said. "And, judging by the ones that *did* surrender, it might be hard to actually destroy it. The lower levels are quite heavily armoured too."

He shrugged. "Hopefully, they'll surrender once they see the main fleet being smashed," he added. "However, for the moment, I have another role for you. I want you and your men to patrol the area and become accustomed to it."

Martin nodded in understanding. They *were* an elite unit, but they'd never served on Apsidal before. It was better to learn the lay of the land now, before they had to fight to defend it. A sense of precisely how Apsidal *worked* would be very useful when the Tokomak arrived. He hoped the fleet would smash them, as planned, but he knew better than to assume the good guys would always win. God was on the side of the big battalions and the Tokomak had some very big battalions indeed.

"Very good, sir," he said.

"You may be going back to the ring soon," Major Griffin added. "This might be your only chance to explore Apsidal itself."

"Yes, sir," Martin said. Apsidal was no bigger than Earth, although the orbital towers and the ring gave it a staggering amount of living space. There was no way he could see the entire planet, even if he devoted the remainder of his life to the task. The space-born might think that planets were small, but the groundpounders knew better. "Do you have a local sitrep?"

"In the datanet, but it changes frequently," Major Griffin said. "Take nothing for granted."

"Yes, sir," Martin said.

He went outside, conferred briefly with Sergeant Howe, then downloaded the sitrep from the datanet. It was strikingly familiar, reminding him of operations on Earth. The former authority had collapsed, the new authority had very little actual *authority* and entire districts were being taken over by gangs and small groups of rebels who were practically identical to criminals. So far, no one had actually shot at the human troops, but Martin was grimly aware that it was just a matter of time. Their presence was welcome now, yet it wouldn't be long before the locals started to resent it. They hadn't freed themselves, after all.

We should have kept the battlesuits, he thought, as the squad formed up for the patrol. *But some dickhead thought we'd look more friendly if we wore BDUs.*

The temperature began to rise, despite the semi-darkness, as they made their way away from the base. His eyes adapted rapidly, thanks to his enhancements, but there were still pools of shadow that worried him. *Anything* could be lurking in there. The squad started off laughing and joking, but silence gradually fell as the alienness of their surroundings penetrated their good humour. Martin had to keep himself from resting his finger on the trigger, even though it was bad weapons discipline and against regulations to boot. There was something about the environment that nagged at his mind.

There were no lights in the alien buildings, no suggestion of habitation. And yet, the sitrep insisted that the area was inhabited. It had been an upscale housing estate, if the reports were to be trusted; a gated community, insofar as the aliens had such things. The lords and masters of the planet—rather, the subordinates of their subordinates—had lived here, while using everyone below them as slaves. It reminded him of Chicago, before the collapse had finally begun. The people who lived in the fancy homes had claimed they wanted to help the poor, but instead they'd only made matters worse.

The Tokomak weren't lying about their intentions, at least, Martin thought. *They didn't claim they were helping when they took over the entire known galaxy.*

Here and there, he started to see signs of movement. Faces at windows, brief glimpses of alien life before they vanished again; brief flickers of light from inside houses, drawing his attention before they were turned off. His sensors reported a faint increase in communications traffic, although it was all very low-level. He didn't find it reassuring. There were plenty of things he could do with low-level communications that would *really* fuck up someone's day.

"All the houses look the same," Sergeant Howe said. His voice was quiet, but Martin tensed anyway. "Look at them. They're practically identical."

Martin nodded. The alien houses looked *odd*, just different enough to be uncanny, but the sergeant was right. They had started out exactly the same and they hadn't really changed, even as their inhabitants moved in. There didn't seem to be any customisation, none of the individuality he'd seen in the Solar Union. Perhaps the aliens didn't see any value in customising their houses. Or perhaps their housing association didn't let them. He'd heard enough grumbles from people who didn't know how lucky they were to know that housing associations could turn dictatorial very quickly.

A flicker of light danced through the sky, high above him. He looked up in time to see it strike the distant orbital tower and vanish into the tower's forcefields. Lightning, he realised dumbly. The orbital tower seemed to be surrounded by dark clouds, as if they and their lightning were drawn to the massive structure. He wondered, morbidly, if the tower was truly safe. The Tokomak were safety freaks, determined to remove as much risk as possible, but there were limits. Even a hundred miles from the tower, it was still an awe-inspiring construction. It would have been a marvel even without the ring blocking out the sun.

He looked back down as his head started to spin. The tower was just too large. And the ring was unimaginable. It was easy to believe that the sky was falling, that the tower was on the verge of collapse...he pushed the thought aside angrily, reminding himself that he'd fought battles on the hulls of giant space stations. But none of them had been so large. He looked ahead and saw a fence, blocking the road. On the other side, there was a horde of silent aliens, all from the servile races. They were staring into the gated community...and waiting.

They could take down the fence at any moment, Martin thought, as the squad slowly altered course to follow the fence around the compound. *It wouldn't be that hard to simply push it down.*

He tensed as he felt the watching eyes tracking him. Crowds were always dangerously unpredictable. It would only take one person throwing a rock to start a riot—or worse—and they weren't wearing their battlesuits. He cursed the idiot who'd insisted on going in BDUs—they might as well have gone naked—and keyed his communicator, reporting back to Major Griffin. The QRF on standby near the Command Post would have battlesuits. They could tear their way through a thousand unarmoured aliens without having to worry about their safety.

The crowd made no move, but it was still a relief when the patrol route turned away from the fence and back into the estate. Here, the houses were smaller and darker, although with more signs of life. Servant homes? Or… or what? He couldn't imagine the Tokomak—or any of the Galactics—choosing to live in such tiny homes. There were some Galactics who would have seen them as cruel and unusual punishment. And yet…he'd known people who'd been prepared to live in shoeboxes, as long as it put them in the *right* catchment area or simply kept them away from the ghettos. He hadn't understood what had driven them until it was too late.

A scream split the air. He hit the communicator, tapping out an emergency signal, then led his men around the corner. A young alien—a child, he thought—was running from a mob of older aliens. It was hard to be sure, but he thought the child was a Galactic…and the others were from the servile races. They were carrying knives and a handful of other makeshift weapons, waving them around threateningly. And they didn't stop when they saw the marines.

Martin levelled his rifle. "Stop," he snapped. "Stop or I shoot!"

The child kept running, right into the marines, but the others skidded to a halt. They were aliens, their faces weird and wonderful, yet Martin could read them. They were torn between charging the marines, trying to drag them down before they could be shot, or turning and running for their lives. If they'd been human, Martin would have said they'd been hyped up on something. He'd seen enough human insurgents using drugs to boost their stamina—and reduce their intelligence—to know it made it impossible to reason with them.

He cursed under his breath. The last thing he wanted—that his *superiors* wanted—was an *incident*. He didn't blame the servile races for wanting to kill their masters, and it was clear they weren't drawing lines between adults and children, but he couldn't allow them to run wild. The gated community was under human protection. And yet, he didn't want to kill the rioters. There had to be another way to stop them.

"Return to your homes," he ordered. "Or I will use deadly force."

The aliens stood there for a moment, glaring at him. They were a mixed group, with no less than four different species represented. Unless they were from a race with profound sexual dimorphism... He'd heard there were Galactics who thought that all humans looked alike and couldn't even tell the difference between male and female, simply because their males looked very different from their females. But he didn't recall meeting any of these aliens before. They'd been left out of the briefing notes.

A flicker of motion caught his attention, a half-second before the alien threw a chopping knife at him. Martin cursed as it stabbed into his shoulder, the pain unbearable for an endless moment in time before the nerve-blockers went to work. His left arm was no longer working; cursing, he dropped the rifle and scrabbled for the pistol on his belt. His men were already firing, putting the remaining aliens down. They were dead before Martin had managed to draw his pistol.

"Fuck," he muttered. He'd been hurt before, and it wouldn't take the medics long to fix him up, but being hit with a chopping knife was a new low. "Ouch. Damn it!"

A crashing sound echoed from behind him. The fence had been taken down. Martin exchanged looks with Sergeant Howe, then snapped out a command to run. They were far too exposed in the open air. The alien child was right behind them, his eyes fearful. Martin put his gun back in the holster, scooped the alien up and followed his men. Behind him, he heard the sound of aliens shouting for blood.

His communicator bleeped. "Help is on the way," Major Griffin said. "Hold on."

Martin nodded, although the sound of pursuit was growing louder. He glanced back and saw flames rising in the distance. It looked as though the houses were getting torched, one by one. He hoped their inhabitants had the sense to flee. They wouldn't have a hope of escape if they stayed in their homes. The flames were already spreading. Someone had probably splashed inflammatory liquid on the buildings before they lit the match or threw the makeshift bomb or whatever. The rebels had had plenty of time to plan their uprising before the human fleet had arrived and thrown all their plans out of alignment.

The child tightened his grip on Martin's shoulder, a surprisingly tight grip for a child so young. Martin eyed him for a moment, wondering what species he was and what his parents had been doing on Apsidal. There were some aliens who had a very careless attitude to children and barely mourned their deaths, while others wrapped their children in cotton wool and treated them like little dolls. Martin snorted at the thought—it would have been nice to be pampered, but it wouldn't have prepared him for adulthood—and then glanced behind him as he heard the roar growing louder. The mob had seen them.

"Run," he snapped.

They picked up speed, hightailing it back to the edge of the estate. A pair of skimmers swept overhead, plasma bolts already raining down. Someone had clearly decided to take the gloves off and give the rioters a thumping, even though it wouldn't do wonders for relationships with the provisional government. Martin didn't blame whoever had made that call. The provisional government seemed to have very little real power. Hell, the only thing that seemed to bind it together was Admiral Stuart pretending to take them seriously.

He handed the child over to the Civil Affairs specialists at the Command Post, once they passed through the defence lines, then sat down beside an alien building and took off his helmet. He could hear shooting in the distance, although it sounded as though things were quietening down a little. *That* wouldn't last for long. Aliens might not be humans, but there were times when he couldn't tell the difference. Certain things were universal and one of them was that certain communities reacted badly to outsiders coming in and poking around.

A hand fell on his shoulder. "Long day?"

He looked up at Major Griffin. "Yes, sir."

"Things will get easier," Major Griffin assured him. "And then we'll be moved to somewhere harder."

Martin shrugged. He wouldn't mind a battlefield with clear lines between friends and enemies, even if they were outnumbered ten to one. There was a certain *simplicity* about battlefields he'd always appreciated, despite the risk of dying horribly. The fighters didn't have to worry about figuring out who was on your side, who could be convinced to be on your side, who wanted to stay out of the fighting and who simply wanted to kill you. An insurgency was always a nightmare because someone could move from category to category at will.

"Yes, sir," he said, finally.

"Good man," Major Griffin said. His voice hardened, just slightly. "Now, you appear to be wearing an axe in your shoulder. As interesting as this fashion statement is, might I suggest you get it removed?"

Martin glanced at the knife. "Yes, sir," he said, unwilling to admit that he'd forgotten it was there. Between the drugs and his enhancements, he'd been almost normal. "And the child? The alien I brought in?"

"You'll have to check with the CA lot," Major Griffin said. "But get that knife out first."

"Yes, sir," Martin said.

CHAPTER FOURTEEN

The really annoying thing about commanding so many starships, Hoshiko had decided before the fleet had even left Sol, was that she was obliged to allow a degree of debate, even democracy, when it came to deciding their next move. She could not simply draw up a plan—more accurately, have her staff draw up a plan—and then put it into action without delay. No, she had to call a holoconference, present her plan and wait for her senior officers to have their say. It had been a great deal simpler, she felt, when she'd only been commanding a single squadron.

"There is a great deal to be gained by occupying Mokpo, at least the system itself," Hoshiko told them, for what felt like the tenth time. "We would not only be able to wreck their industrial base, but create a firebreak for when their fleet starts filtering down from N-Gann."

She paused to hammer the point home. "We won't be trying to defend the gravity points with the same forces we've stationed here," she added, sharply. "We'll just harass them as they make their way towards us. And *that* will give us more time to prepare."

The holographic heads nodded in unison. Hoshiko sighed, inwardly. Her most pessimistic estimates suggested that N-Gann *still* hadn't heard that Apsidal had fallen—assuming a message had been sent on a least-time course, they wouldn't hear anything for another week—but there was no way to be *sure*. The Tokomak had already proven that they *could* be imaginative…and they'd had thousands of years to research gravity technology. Hoshiko could easily believe that they'd advanced far beyond the technology they'd supplied to the other Galactics, let alone the younger races. They might have something utterly devastating up their sleeves.

"The assault force will commence the offensive in one hour," she said, once the chatter was finally over. "And then I'll dispatch scouts further up the chain to N-Gann. We *might* be able to get some warning when they finally start to move."

She nodded politely to her officers, then closed the connection. What *was* it about a large group of senior officers? They were perfectly capable of showing initiative on their own, but as a group they seemed to become risk-averse. It wasn't as if humanity could sit around and wait to be hit. Hoshiko had watched the simulations, time and time again. The Tokomak juggernaut would smash the Solar Union into rubble if they were given time to get their forces into place.

Perhaps they're just scared of being blamed, she thought, as she walked into the CIC. She'd had complete authority in her little squadron—the buck had stopped with her and she knew it—but here there was a degree of shared responsibility. She couldn't wait for the day she could go back to commanding a smaller formation, where everything was clear-cut. *Losing four squadrons of cruisers would be embarrassing.*

She pushed the thought aside as she took her chair. "Yolanda, are the advance forces in position to attack?"

"Yes, Admiral," Yolanda said. "They're ready to jump on your signal."

Hoshiko took a moment to survey the gravity point. Nine fortresses, surrounded by a cloud of automated weapons platforms and gunboats; five hundred starships, with the remainder of the fleet sitting in reserve. And layer after layer of mines. Hoshiko had little hope that *they* would kill more than a handful of enemy ships, but it would buy time for the defenders to go on the alert. It was just a shame there was little point in positioning mines right on *top* of the gravity point. The first set of interpenetrations would sweep the remainder of the mines out of existence.

We could lose every ship in the assault force and still hold the gravity point against any rational enemy, she thought, grimly. *But the Tokomak have ships to burn.*

She took a long breath. "Begin the assault."

The first cluster of assault pods moved onto the gravity point and vanished. Hoshiko's tactical staff had programmed them with the data from the LinkShip, but they'd warned that the missiles might not be able to lock onto the defenders before it was too late. The enemy gunboats would take out quite a few pods—perhaps all of them—before they were able to open fire. It was frustrating to face an enemy who was alternatively imaginative and unimaginative. There was no way to guess what the bastards would do next.

The best swordsman in the world doesn't fear the second-best swordsman, she reminded herself, as the next wave of assault pods vanished. *He fears the worst, because he doesn't know what the idiot will do.*

She looked at Yolanda's back. "Order the first assault waves to make transit."

"Aye, Admiral."

Hoshiko felt a pang of guilt as the first squadron entered the gravity point in a tight stream, each ship blinking out of existence a second before the next. The stream was carefully coordinated to cut the gap between transits down to a minimum, without running the risk of interpenetration, but she was all too aware that too much could go wrong. *She* should be on those ships, sharing the risk. But she was the fleet commander. It had been all she could do to wrangle a place on the assault fleet.

Apparently, there's no authority attached to this position, she thought, wryly. *Who knew?*

She watched the display, silently counting down the seconds. The first assault force had included a pair of courier boats, both under strict orders to take stock of the situation and return through the gravity point, but it was quite possible that the entire force had been annihilated. Who knew *what* the enemy might have done in the last couple of days? They had enough ships in Mokpo to mount a defence, if they chose to stand and fight...

A courier boat blinked into existence on the display. Hoshiko let out a sigh of relief. The attack force hadn't been destroyed, thankfully. She leaned forward to study the live feed from the courier boat as it uploaded its records into the fleet datanet, silently matching what it had seen to the LinkShip's report. The enemy had positioned additional ships near the gravity point, but fewer than she'd expected. They might not have realised that the LinkShip had come through the gravity point.

Although they might have reason to suspect something, she thought, crossly. The intelligence staff had given her an earful about the LinkShip being detected, demanding that she chew the pilot out immediately. Hoshiko had told them to let *her* handle military affairs. *The LinkShip had to come through the gravity point or FTL. Either way, she wasn't detected.*

"Order the second assault wave to make transit," she said. "And then we will make transit ourselves."

"Aye, Admiral," Yolanda said.

A dull quiver ran through *Defiant* as she made her slow way towards the gravity point and vanished. Hoshiko braced herself, expecting to see anything from incoming missiles to an expanding cloud of debris when the display rebooted. A handful of alien ships popped into view, trading missile fire with the first wave as they headed away from the gravity point and into deep space. They'd clearly decided there was nothing to be gained from trying to mount a suicidal defence.

"The enemy ships are dropping into FTL," Yolanda said. "They're heading for the next gravity point."

And not the planet, Hoshiko thought. She'd expected the local starships to defend their homeworld. *Why don't they want to link up with the planet's defences?*

"Detail one squadron of cruisers to watch the gravity point," she said, finally. It was unlikely that the enemy was planning an ambush—and growing unlikelier by the minute, as her shell of recon drones expanded to cover a greater and greater volume of space—but it was well to be careful. "The remainder of the fleet will advance to the second gravity point."

She studied the system carefully as the fleet moved into formation, readying itself for the jump to FTL. Mokpo had a lot to recommend it, under other circumstances; she'd have seriously considered trying to make contact with any rebel groups that might be on the planet's surface if she hadn't *known* she couldn't hold the system indefinitely. Even if she had been prepared to make such a commitment, it would have stretched her forces too thin. The whimsical nature of the gravity points would even have allowed the Tokomak to perform an end run around Mokpo and hit Apsidal from another direction. It would have added more time to their transit to Earth, but she doubted it would bother them that much. They'd be preserving vast numbers of ships for the final battle.

"Take us into FTL," she ordered, once the fleet was ready. "And take us out at the designated arrival point."

"Aye, Admiral."

Hoshiko smiled, coldly, as the fleet advanced on its target. If she was lucky, if she was really lucky, she'd have a chance to pick off the enemy ships before they could decide to fight or run. But, as the wavering lines of FTL gave way to normal space, she realised she was too late. The enemy ships were already making transit into GS-3532. The last one vanished before she could even *begin* to issue interception orders.

Irritating, she thought. Destroying a mere handful of ships wouldn't slow the Tokomak down for a second, but it might have worked in the Galactic Alliance's favour later on. *We'll just have to cope.*

"Detail another squadron to cover the gravity point, with orders to harass the enemy if they appear," she ordered, instead. The minelayers would be on their way from Apsidal as soon as she sent the order. They'd give the enemy a few nasty moments before they were brushed aside. "And take us straight to the planet."

"Aye, Admiral."

The population of Mokpo, she noted, didn't seem to believe that the human starships were coming in peace. Hundreds of freighters were scattering in all directions, dropping into FTL and running into interstellar space. She felt a moment of sympathy for the aliens who'd had their lives disrupted, even though they were the enemy. She'd heard enough stories about just how unforgiving the interstellar combines could be—they embodied every stereotype of the black-hearted capitalist—to know that those freighter crews were going to have a very hard time. They might never be able to get their cargoes to their destinations before the penalty clauses in their contracts wiped them out. She wondered, with a flicker of amusement, just how many of them might take their ships and join the Galactic Alliance, if they were asked. Even a handful of additional freighters would be very helpful. But she couldn't afford to make the offer now.

"Admiral, the planetary defences are coming online," Yolanda said. "They're deploying gunboats and armed shuttles."

They must have stripped the cupboard bare to try to hold the gravity point, Hoshiko thought, relieved. Intelligence had been vague on just how strong the defences actually were. *Or they decided it would be better to rely on fixed defences...*

"Target their orbital industries," she ordered. There was no point in battling the orbital defences, let alone the ground-based PDCs. She would have nothing to gain and a great deal to lose. "Fire on my command."

"Aye, Admiral," Yolanda said. "Weapons locked."

Hoshiko took a breath. She'd considered, briefly, trying to take the planet's industries and putting them to work. Mokpo didn't have the vast industries of Apsidal, but they weren't anything to sneer at either. Every little helped. But she knew, all too well, that she couldn't hope to hold the system when the Tokomak came knocking. Better to smash them now, before they could be turned against her, then give the enemy another advantage. The Tokomak already had too many advantages.

The enemy gunboats swooped into attack formation, their weapons tearing through space and slamming into her shields. Her ships returned fire, picking off the gunboats with terrifying ease. The enemy pilots clearly hadn't had any time to practice. They'd probably never done anything more challenging than customs and patrol work for the last thousand years. Mokpo—and Apsidal—had been too heavily defended for pirates or rebels to challenge the *status quo*. They'd allowed themselves to go slack...

"Fire," she ordered.

Defiant shuddered as she unleashed a barrage of missiles, plunging down towards the planet below. The other ships followed suit, their missiles flashing past the remaining gunboats and heading towards their targets. Hoshiko watched, grimly, as the enemy point defence attempted to sweep the missiles out of space, but there were too many missiles. One by one, the giant orbital industries began to die. Pieces of debris flew in all directions, some heading into outer space and others falling down to the planet itself. Hoshiko hoped, desperately, that anything large enough to do real damage when it hit the surface would be picked off by the PDCs before it was too late.

"All targets destroyed, Admiral," Yolanda said.

We just wrecked the work of hundreds of years, Hoshiko thought. *And we did it in bare seconds.*

She dismissed the thought, angrily. There had been no choice. The human race was already on the brink. Allowing the enemy to keep and use a sizable chunk of its industrial base would just make the odds against humanity even steeper. There was no time for sentiment or guilt, let alone room for negotiation. The Tokomak intended to exterminate mankind. She was authorised to do whatever it took to stop them.

"Take the fleet back to the gravity point," she ordered. Things had been a *great* deal simpler when she'd been fighting the Druavroks. There weren't any enemy forces waiting for her in Apsidal, she thought, just paperwork and endless discussions with the provisional government. "We'll sit on top of it until reinforcements arrive."

"Aye, Admiral," Yolanda said.

"And send a signal to the LinkShip, once we arrive," Hoshiko added. There was no point in sending the signal now. The fleet would outrace the message on the way back to the gravity point. "She is to come through the gravity point at once."

"Aye, Admiral."

Hoshiko leaned back in her chair, suddenly feeling very tired. The brief engagement had been very satisfactory—and she'd send ships further up the chain to Winglet once Mokpo was secure—but she was all too aware of just how *little* damage they'd done, compared to the sheer might the Tokomak could bring to bear against humanity. Their industrial base was still intact. The capture of Apsidal and the destruction she'd wreaked at Mokpo had barely taken out a percentage point of a percentage point. Given time, the Tokomak would simply crush the human race under a tidal wave of production. No, humanity had to go on the offensive.

She keyed her console, bringing up the starchart. The Tokomak had a cluster of stars in the centre of the known galaxy, stars that were almost completely theirs. Even the other Galactics tended not to visit. And humanity would have to invade those stars if they wanted to win the war. There was no other way to win. Hoshiko knew, from history, that her ancestors had won great victories in the Second World War. But they hadn't been able to destroy their enemy's industrial base…

…And so they'd been ground to powder.

Lying to their people, even to their own government, probably didn't help either, she thought, sourly. *At least we don't have that problem.*

She studied the starchart for a long time, considering options. Humanity would *have* to go on the offensive, sooner rather than later. And humanity couldn't do it alone. They'd be fighting a war on an unimaginable scale. No wonder the Tokomak had built and deployed such huge fleets. Hoshiko had been born in space and even *she* had problems grasping the sheer immensity of the war. It was truly the war to end all wars.

Hah, she thought, as the gravity point blinked into existence on the display. A handful of reinforcements had already arrived. *There's never been any such thing.*

Her mind raced. Perhaps, once they'd smashed the enemy fleet, they could ravage the nearby sectors or push directly into Tokomak space. Her orders didn't include any suggestions that she should take the war to the enemy, but…she might never have a better chance to actually *win*. Or even to land a knock-out punch. If they could raid their cluster, they could devastate the enemy industries. They might even be able to convince the Tokomak to come to the negotiating table.

If they can be convinced to take us seriously, she reminded herself. The Tokomak had a towering superiority complex—and the hell of it was that they deserved to think highly of themselves. They'd built a star-spanning civilisation while humanity had been crawling in the mud. *We're a very young race to them.*

Yolanda interrupted her thoughts. "Admiral, the LinkShip just transited the gravity point," she said. "The pilot is hailing you."

"Put her through," Hoshiko ordered. She waited until the image blinked into existence, then leaned forward. "Captain Hameeda. I trust you had a pleasant rest?"

"I slept, Admiral," Hameeda said. She didn't *look* very rested. The briefing notes had suggested that part of her would *always* remain awake. "Is it time to proceed to N-Gann?"

"Yes," Hoshiko said, putting her doubts aside. It was a risk, but she needed as much warning as possible before the enemy fleet arrived. And the LinkShip was the best scout under her command. "Go there, watch the enemy, run back here when they start to move."

"Understood," Hameeda said. She sounded confident, at least. "I won't let you down."

CHAPTER FIFTEEN

N-Gann had been a dead world when the Tokomak discovered it, hanging on the end of a gravity point chain like a piece of rotting fruit. It wouldn't have been considered useful, certainly not to a race with access to most of the riches of the known galaxy, if it hadn't been lucky enough to be located near to a handful of very important and wealthy worlds that might have developed...*ideas*...if they hadn't been carefully watched. N-Gann had been converted into a naval base and industrial node and, over a thousand years, it had grown into an important and wealthy world in its own right. It even had a massive planetary ring of its own.

And facilities to support a major fleet deployment, Empress Neola thought. She sat in her command chair and studied the display, watching her ships as they were replenished for the next stage of their voyage. *We don't have to worry about bringing supplies all the way from the homeworld.*

It was, she had to admit, an awesome sight. The N-Gann Ring was impressive, but so were the thousands of starships holding station near the planet. It had been hard—almost impossible—for the planet to supply them all, despite the warnings. But N-Gann was steadily converting its industrial base to support a truly massive fleet. There would be a price to pay for that, Neola knew, but the bill wouldn't come due for years. By then, she would have exterminated the human race, crushed any of the servile races that dared to raise a hand against their masters and taught the other

Galactics that there was a *reason* the Tokomak ruled the known universe. No one would dare question ever again.

As long as I get the fleet to Earth, she reminded herself. The galling part was that the deployment wouldn't take anything like so long if the gravity points weren't bottlenecks. She couldn't speed up the transits any further without risking absolute disaster. *But once we get there, we can destroy the humans and end the war.*

She looked up as an aide hurried over to her. It was bad news. She could see it in the young male's eyes, the fear of giving his superior something they wouldn't want to hear warring with the fear of not doing his job. She held out a hand for the datapad before he could say a word, took it and scanned it quickly. The humans had attacked Apsidal. The humans had attacked and *taken* Apsidal. She had to smile, coldly, at just how badly the messenger was trembling. The idea of a younger race attacking a major world was unthinkable.

But not to me, Neola thought. She'd learnt hard lessons in the Battle of Earth. The human creatures were revoltingly ingenious. Apparently, they'd spent centuries considering space tactics before they'd even made it into space…no, they *hadn't* made it into space. They'd stolen the technology off someone else. *I planned for this, did I not?*

She tapped the messenger's bowed head. He flinched, as if he'd been expecting a blow.

"Inform my senior staff that there will be a conference in two hours," she said. "Go."

The messenger turned and walked away, his stance suggesting that he wanted to run for his life. Neola waved her hand in irritation. The gerontocrats probably *would* have killed the messenger for bringing them bad news—or at least destroyed his career—but *she* wasn't going to do that, not when she *needed* to hear bad news. She turned her attention back to the datapad and reread the brief report. The humans had attacked through the gravity point, demonstrating a new weapon in the process, and then taken the planet and the remaining gravity points. And it looked as if they'd brought a major fleet of their own.

Good, Neola thought. *The more ships I destroy here, the fewer I'll have to face at Earth.*

She tapped her console, bringing up the starchart. She'd expected *some* response to the fleet, assuming the humans knew she was on her way. An invasion of Apsidal was a logical response. Indeed, she could admire the cleverness and daring of the move. The humans would bleed her fleet white if she mounted a conventional attack through the gravity point herself. She had plenty of expendable units, but...she didn't want to waste them. Fortunately, there was another option.

"Divert a courier boat to contact Task Force Gamma," she ordered. "I want them to be ready to move in two weeks."

She studied the starchart for a long moment, then started snapping out more orders. The fleet was ready to proceed to Winglet. It was going to be difficult to get through the gravity points to Mokpo, let alone Apsidal itself, but she had vastly superior firepower. She doubted the enemy would risk making a stand anywhere short of Apsidal itself. As long as they held Apsidal, they could force her to call off the campaign or take the *very* long way to Earth; if they lost Apsidal, they'd have to either retake the system, whatever the cost, or resign themselves to eventual defeat. She could pin them in place, then crush them when her surprise went into play.

The humans might see it coming, she mused. One thing she'd learnt was that the humans were cunning enough to anticipate what *she* might do and plan countermeasures. But she'd worked hard to ensure that there were *no* countermeasures. *And yet, there's nothing they can do to stop it.*

She keyed her console, bringing up the latest readiness reports. The fleet would be departing in an hour or so, travelling directly to the nearest star. And then...the humans would see them coming, of course, but they wouldn't see the real threat. She wondered, idly, just how they'd feel when they finally saw it. She'd taken a leaf out of their books and turned it against them.

It doesn't matter what they think, she told herself, stiffly. *All that matters is that they die.*

...

Hameeda had thought that Apsidal had been a big system, with hundreds of thousands of starships coming and going, but N-Gann managed to be bigger. The single gravity point was surrounded by hundreds of ships, yet there were many—many—more surrounding the planet itself. N-Gann wasn't anything like as heavily populated as Apsidal—Hameeda's sensors insisted that the planet's atmosphere was pure poison—but it was clearly significant.

And yet, the planet was almost dwarfed by the enemy fleet.

Hameeda could barely keep her awareness off the enemy ships as the LinkShip drifted into the system. There were thousands upon thousands of warships, ranging from giant battleships to tiny destroyers and gunboats; there was enough firepower, right in front of her, to devastate the Solar Union from one end to the other. And the enemy fleet was slowly coming to life. Her sensors noted drives and weapons systems coming online, while merchant shipping was steadily directed away from the giant formation. She'd seen the simulations, she'd watched as Admiral Stuart's fleet left Earth, but she still couldn't grasp the sheer size of the enemy fleet. Her sensors couldn't even give her an accurate ship count, not without going a lot closer. There were so many ships that their energy signatures were starting to blur together.

A flicker of fear ran down her spine as the datanet analysed the raw data, trying to tease out hard information from the blur. There were so many ships that they could mount a conventional assault on Apsidal, pushing through the gravity point one by one, and *win*. And they had a giant support base, only a few days behind them. They could be churning out assault pods already, preparing to tip the odds back in their direction. She dreaded to think what would happen if the Tokomak started mass-production of assault pods of their own.

This could get really bad, she thought, numbly. She'd thought she'd grasped the size and power of the Galactics, but now...now she was starting to realise she hadn't had a clue. A race that controlled nearly a third of the galaxy, directly or indirectly, wouldn't deploy fleets of a *mere* few hundred ships. Hell, Admiral Stuart's fleet numbered nearly two thousand ships. *This could get very—very—bad.*

She forced her awareness away from the fleet and studied the planet itself, trusting in the analysis subroutines to alert her to anything important. It wasn't something she would have trusted a standard RI—or even an AI—to handle, but the LinkShip datanet had a combination of high-speed processing power and an almost human intuition. The scientists had told her that it would learn from her, and eventually embrace her mental engram for itself, yet she hadn't really understood that either. Perhaps no one understood it. The LinkShip was both part of her and yet separate from her.

Perhaps it's just a suit of clothes, she thought. She giggled at the thought of putting the LinkShip on as easily as she donned a shipsuit, then forced herself to concentrate. *We don't have much time before their fleet leaves.*

N-Gann was, if anything, even more heavily defended than Apsidal. She could see a dozen battlestations on this side of the planet alone, protecting a formidable industrial base. Worse, it had a planetary-scale forcefield. The entire *planet* was wrapped in a bubble of energy. It wasn't something she'd seen before—her records noted that planetary forcefields were actually relatively rare, even for the Galactics—but it was there. Invading the planet would be an utter nightmare.

We could slam rocks into the shield, she thought, *but that would devastate the planet too.*

Her analysis subroutines failed to come up with anything better. A planet could supply enough power—and mount enough backup shield generators—to make it impossible for a heavy bombardment to crack the shield. The fleet could bang away at the planet for weeks without doing any significant damage. She could see a way for *her* to get under the shield—it wouldn't be that hard, if she was careful—but what then?

She swept her awareness over the planet, looking for something—anything—that might be helpful. But nothing came to mind. N-Gann appeared to be nothing more than a giant industrial node, shipping complex and warehouse. She guessed there were shore leave facilities somewhere on the planet, perhaps near the lone orbital tower, but they were of no concern to her. There was no way she could land on the planet, claiming to be an innocent spacer. Her stealth mode wouldn't stand up to such close inspection.

Nothing, she thought, finally. She remembered some of the weirder ideas for future weapons and smiled. *What we really need is a supernova bomb.*

She shook her head as she took the LinkShip back towards the edge of the system. The enemy fleet was coming to life now, its first units moving with ponderous speed as they settled into formation. They were surprisingly elegant, for such huge ships; she would have admired their station-keeping if she hadn't known their exercises were designed more for show than anything else. The Tokomak had chosen to look good rather than be good. Hell, they hadn't *had* to be good. She hoped that attitude hadn't changed too much.

But it had, if her analysis subroutines were correct. The Tokomak were sweeping space for possible threats—she put a little extra room between her and the enemy fleet—their sensors displaying a considerable improvement over the recordings from five years ago. Their gunboats, too, were patrolling in a manner that was almost human. Hameeda's lips quirked as she thought about how some of *their* old sweats must have reacted to their flight paths. If a human who was a mere seventy years old had problems adapting to modern technology, how much worse must it be for an aged Tokomak?

They've probably improved their missiles too, she thought. *They might even have hammers.*

She sighed, inwardly. There was nothing more to be gained, as far as she could tell, by prowling around the enemy system. She didn't dare go any closer to the fleet, or to the planet itself, and yet there was nothing else of interest in the remainder of the system. None of the other planets appeared to be inhabited, as far as her sensors could tell. Normally, she would have surveyed them anyway, just to be sure, but the enemy fleet was on its way. She didn't need a complex analysis program to tell that it was heading for Winglet. The enemy CO must have learnt that Apsidal had been attacked.

They won't want to give Admiral Stuart time to dig in, Hameeda thought. The Tokomak had pioneered the technique of prefabricating fortresses for hasty assembly, but they took longer than the human engineers to put them together. *And they won't realise just how much she* has *dug in already.*

Rotating the LinkShip, she sped past the alien fleet—taking one final look at the starships as she passed—and then dropped into FTL. Sweat was dripping down her forehead as she removed the helmet, her uniform so drenched that she started to strip it off in the command room before walking down to take a shower. The flight to Winglet wouldn't take *her* more than a couple of days, but it would take much longer for an entire fleet. She doubted the enemy fleet would reach Winglet in less than five days.

And we'll be ready for them, Hameeda thought. She'd heard that Admiral Stuart had decided against placing any ships or fixed defences in Winglet, but GS-3532 was another story. A handful of minefields would probably be more than enough to slow the enemy down, at least for a few minutes. They'd certainly have to brace themselves before pushing more ships through the gravity point. *They won't know what hit them.*

Smiling, she had a quick shower and headed for bed. She didn't feel that tired—she thought it was a sign that she was getting used to the connection—but she knew she had to get some rest while she could. There would be no time for sleep once the shooting started. Admiral Stuart hadn't told her what she actually wanted from the LinkShip, once the shit *really* hit the fan, but Hameeda was sure there would be *something*. The LinkShip had more than proved its worth.

She'll want me to raid the enemy rear, she thought, as she closed her eyes. *Or something that will give the enemy a real fright.*

On that thought, she drifted off to sleep.

. . .

It was impossible, even for a trained spacer, to pick out one star from the unblinking array of lights glowing in the inky darkness of space and say, with confidence, that it was a particular star. Neola didn't *know* the star she was looking at was their destination—or if the dim star ahead of her was actually Sol—but it didn't matter. They were in the right general area and *that* was all that mattered.

She stood in the observation blister, watching as ship after ship—so close that they were visible to the naked eye—fell into place, allowing the formation to take shape and form. It still awed her to know that so much firepower was under her command, even though failure would be utterly disastrous for her. Her rivals wouldn't hesitate to remove her if they thought they could get away with it. And yet, it would be worse for the entire Tokomak race. If they failed so badly, if they let a younger race beat them, the other junior races would rise up in revolt. And some of the Galactics might join them.

A servant brought her a glass of *Hyacinth* wine and she sipped it, savouring the taste. It had been reserved for the gerontocrats, once upon a time, but no longer. She could drink it now, if she wished, although she thought it was just a little *too* strong. The gerontocrats had been old, of course. They'd probably thought it was too weak.

She smiled at the thought, then sobered. She'd been a spacer for long enough to know, from records if not experience, that trying to be clever in wartime was a good way to lose. There were too many things that could go wrong with her plan, although—in some ways—that was an advantage.

The humans might consider the possibility of her trying to be clever, but they wouldn't take it very seriously. They might not even take more than basic precautions...

And even if they do, they don't have many options, she reminded herself. The humans had done well, in taking Apsidal, but they'd trapped themselves too. They were committed to a fixed defence of a star system very far from their homeworld. *It isn't as if they can just flee back home.*

She sighed, feeling the weight of command settling around her shoulders. She ruled, now. She ruled an empire larger than anything a mere *human* could hope to comprehend, an empire that looked solid, from the outside, but was actually terrifyingly fragile. The empire was held together by the threat of force, not force itself. She knew, all too well, just what would happen if half the empire revolted. There were already entire sectors that had effectively slipped out of their control. How long would it be before the remainder of the empire was torn apart?

We have to win, she told herself, as the fleet readied itself for the jump into FTL. *Whatever the cost, whatever the pain, we have to win.*

CHAPTER SIXTEEN

"Well," Hoshiko said. "That's a *lot* of ships."

"A *lot* of ships," Commodore Yu said. He rubbed the back of his neck. "I'd have said a *fucking* lot of ships, myself. Have we ever seen so many ships that we couldn't get an accurate count?"

Hoshiko shook her head, wordlessly. The LinkShip had returned to Mokpo, bringing with it the first images of the oncoming juggernaut. She'd thought her fleet was large, when she'd set out from Sol, but the Tokomak fleet dwarfed her command. In a straight fight, even with her tech advantages, she'd lose. The only thing slowing them down was the need to pass through each gravity point one by one, causing considerable delay. Her most conservative calculations insisted that the Tokomak would need months—practically a year—to reach Sol.

But when they do, they'll sweep across the system like locusts and destroy everything we've built, she thought. It wouldn't be long before the Tokomak reached Winglet, if they hadn't reached Winglet and GS-3532 already. They could cross the gulf of space between N-Gann and Winglet in FTL. *We have to stop them here.*

She turned her attention to the long-range sensors. Traffic in and out of Apsidal had fallen off sharply over the last two weeks, even though she'd made it clear that civilian traffic would still be permitted to pass through the gravity points after a brief inspection. Rumours were already spreading widely, if her intelligence officers were to be believed. Some interstellar corporations were waiting for the Tokomak to regain the system before they started to send ships through the gravity points again; others, more fatalistic, were simply hanging back until Armageddon had come and gone. The handful of convoys that had passed through the gravity points had been operated by combines that simply couldn't afford to wait for the situation to resolve itself.

"I assume we'll be meeting them here," Commodore Abdul said, his words breaking into her thoughts. His holographic image looked pensive as he stroked his goatee. "We can give them one hell of a bloody nose."

"We'll be harassing them from the moment they show themselves in GS-3532," Hoshiko said, keeping her doubts to herself. It was quite possible that the fast formations she'd dispatched to GS-3532 were already under fire. She wouldn't know until the courier boats reported back. "And we'll keep bleeding them until they attack us here, in force."

"We'll just be nibbling at their flanks," Commodore Hassan pointed out. "We're not going to inflict much, if any, damage."

"No," Hoshiko agreed. "But we can put them on notice that they're no longer the unchallenged masters of the universe. Their servants will take note."

She allowed her face to darken at the thought. The Tokomak had been masters of the known universe for so long that the other races, even the Galactics, seemed to instinctively defer to them. There was no real difference between their dominance and playground politics, where a bully might cow his classmates without ever having to actually *do* anything. And yet, if the human race showed that the Tokomak could be challenged—that they could be *beaten*—who knew *what* it would unleash? The Russian Emperor Nicholas II hadn't known what would happen when his regime lost its aura of invincibility. Hoshiko suspected the Tokomak didn't know either.

And a number of their ships are crewed by their servant races, she thought, grimly. *We might just convince the bastards to turn on their masters.*

She cleared her throat. "We'll deploy additional squadrons and minefields to the gravity points here," she said. "Mokpo itself can be ignored, for the moment"—the planet had refused all calls to surrender or join the Galactic Alliance—"and dealt with after the Tokomak have been stopped. And then...we wait. They'll have to come to us."

"Yes, Admiral," Yu said. "We *could* take the entire fleet to GS-3532."

"And then get in trouble when we try to fall back," Commodore Hassan countered. "Even with a five-second transit delay, the odds of an interpenetration event are terrifyingly high."

"Particularly if we're trying to get thousands of ships through the gravity point while under enemy fire," Hoshiko agreed. She didn't envy the Tokomak. They had ships to waste...and, by all the gods, they were going to waste a *lot* of them. "Better to fight the main engagement here, where we have layer upon layer of fixed defences."

She allowed her eyes to sweep the room—and the assembly of holograms. "I'll be returning to Apsidal this afternoon," she added. "Commodore Hassan will remain in command at Mokpo. Are there any concerns before we bring this meeting to a close?"

"Merely that we could do with a few more ships," Commodore Hassan said. "Say...a *million* or two."

Hoshiko smiled, humourlessly. "We can hope that the Galactic Alliance comes up with a fleet," she said, although she wasn't convinced that it would ever arrive. The last set of updates had been vague on the fleet's exact arrival date, so vague that she was starting to think that the Galactic Alliance was having second thoughts. They might not have *seen* the enemy fleet, but they certainly knew how many ships their former masters could deploy. "If they manage to dispatch some ships..."

She shook her head. "We won't count on them until they arrive. Are there any other concerns?"

"No, Admiral," Commodore Yu said.

Hoshiko looked from face to face and nodded. "Dismissed," she said. "Good luck to us all."

She watched the holographic images vanish, then turned her attention to the main display. The enemy fleet was clearly visible, falling into formation as it set out from N-Gann. She reminded herself, once again, that the report was several days out of date. They didn't dare assume that the enemy wouldn't make all haste. The Tokomak *had* to know, by now, that she'd taken Apsidal. They'd want to recover the gravity points before she managed to dig in so deeply that even *their* fleet couldn't dig her out.

Tapping her console, she brought up the latest series of reports. Everything was running smoothly, smoothly enough to worry her. The local industries were churning out vast numbers of mines, outdated missiles and other products she could put to use. Indeed, deploying the mines would take longer than producing them. And yet, she knew just how much firepower was bearing down on her. There was a very good chance that all their efforts would simply be swept aside.

But we'll make them bleed, she thought. *Oh yes, we'll make them bleed.*

She looked up at the display again, silently calculating—once again—just how long it would take the enemy fleet to reach Apsidal. Weeks perhaps, if they were lucky. She disliked the idea of just standing still and waiting to be hit—she had always preferred to go on the offensive—but there was no choice. She was in a perfect position to stop the enemy in their tracks. They *had* to come to her.

And yet, their sheer weight of numbers works in their favour, she reminded herself. It was nice to think that the Tokomak would just send their ships through the gravity point, one by one, giving her a chance to wipe out their entire fleet, but she doubted they'd cooperate *that* much. The Tokomak hadn't launched a full-scale gravity point assault in centuries, if the records were to be trusted, yet they presumably hadn't forgotten how to do it. *The lone warrior on a bridge can still be overwhelmed and killed if the enemy just keeps coming at him.*

She contemplated the thought for a moment, then keyed her communicator. "Yolanda? My compliments to Captain Lifar and inform him that we are to return through the gravity point as soon as possible."

"Aye, Admiral," Yolanda said. She sounded tired. The poor girl had been working double shifts as Hoshiko's staff struggled to cope with their ever-expanding responsibilities. "I'll inform him at once."

And then take a rest, Hoshiko thought. She looked up at the display, once again. *We're going to be very busy when that fleet arrives.*

• • •

"This is the weirdest place I've ever visited," Trooper Rowe said, as the team explored yet another sector of the Apsidal Ring. "And I visited the ruins of Dubai."

Captain Martin Luther Douglas shrugged. "Just keep your eyes on the floor," he said, shortly. There *was* something about the immense structure that screwed with their minds, as if there was something fundamentally *wrong* about it. "You'll be fine."

He forced himself to keep his unease under control. The Apsidal Ring was so large that there *shouldn't* be any sense of curvature, let alone anything else that might unsettle his mind. And yet...he shook his head, telling himself that it wasn't a problem. They might as well be on the planet's surface. There were few differences between the interior of the ring and the giant megacities on the planet below.

His sense of unease deepened as they passed through a set of airlocks and into what looked like a giant garden. The Apsidal Ring reminded him of a Stanford Torus Space Colony, although it was on a far greater scale than anything in the Solar System. Perhaps it was *that* that was bothering him, he thought. The Apsidal Ring felt like a Stanford Torus that had been turned inside out to catch the sunlight.

"They've got plants here from across the galaxy," Trooper Singh commented, as they made their way down the nearest path. "Who do you think owns this place?"

"Some rich fucker," Trooper Rowe suggested. "The whole place feels like a gated community to me."

Martin was tempted to agree. The Apsidal Ring was secure—or, at least, it *should* have been secure. Perhaps it *had* been, in the beginning. It was quite easy to imagine mega-rich aliens buying large sections of the ring and turning it into their private kingdom. There were a number of asteroid settlements back home that hosted people who were quite staggeringly rich. Thankfully, they never made a show of flaunting their wealth in front of the poor.

And most of them earned their money, he thought. He'd learned to respect people who'd turned themselves into millionaires, although he'd come to realise that he'd never be wealthy himself. The Solar Union adored self-made men and scorned inherited wealth. *I wonder how many of the aliens earned their cash...*

His communicator buzzed. "Report back to the Command Post," a voice ordered. "I say again, report back to the Command Post."

"Understood," Martin said. The communicators were supposed to be impossible to track or jam, but the sheer size of the ring played merry hell with communications. Martin had never been *sure* that their signals were undetectable, either. "We're on our way."

He took one last look at the garden, wondering what lay behind the distinctly-alien trees in the distance, then led his men back into the ring. There were no signs of any inhabitants in the corridors, but he was sure they were there. The ring was so large that searching *all* of it was an impossible task. Its former masters had installed a tracking and surveillance system that would have made Stalin, Castro and Hammond wet their pants, yet even the aggressively comprehensive network had blindspots. Reading between the lines, Martin had privately concluded that the system had been deliberately weakened in places. The operators probably hadn't wanted *their* illicit activities to be recorded.

A surveillance state benefits two types of people, and those types only, he reminded himself, remembering lessons in History and Moral Philosophy. *First, the shitheads who want to control their populations; second, the grafters who can profit by figuring out how to bend the system to their advantage.*

"Captain Douglas," Major Griffin said, when Martin reached the Command Post. A handful of other officers were taking chairs or pouring themselves coffee. "Do you have any further impressions of the ring?"

"Disturbing, but we'll get used to it," Martin thought. "It feels like...it feels...I don't know how to put it into words."

"You're not the only one," Major Griffin said. "Captain Higgs"—he nodded towards a dark woman in an infantry uniform, sitting on one of the chairs—"was the only one who *did* manage to put it into words. She said it was like being aware, truly aware, that the world was a sphere...and that you might walk off it at any second."

"Yes, sir," Martin said. It wasn't a bad description. "It might have been a mistake to see the ring from the outside. It confuses us."

"It may be a new form of Asteroid Unease," Major Griffin said. He shrugged. "Take a seat, Captain. The briefing is about to begin."

Martin nodded—salutes were forbidden on the Apsidal Ring, even though the Command Post was secure—and took a seat near the front of the room. A couple of other officers sat down next to him, both looking as tired as Martin felt. The Apsidal Ring wore people down, even the ones who'd teleported onto the ring. But then, he supposed it shouldn't have been *that* much of a surprise. He'd had problems coping the first time he'd visited an asteroid colony too.

Colonel Jackson took the stand. "The bad news is that we've sighted the enemy fleet," he said, crisply. "The navy will attempt to slow them down, of course, but the worst-case scenario is that they'll be in Mokpo within two weeks and trying to punch their way to us shortly afterwards. Then... best case, the navy kicks their collective ass and we discover we've wasted the last few weeks here. Worst case...we have to prepare for invasion."

He paused, just long enough to allow his words to sink in. "If the navy loses control of the system, this world *will* be invaded. And if that happens, we *will* have to fight to keep them from recovering the ring's industries. It is our belief that they will attempt to recapture the ring intact. Destroying it would have serious impacts on both the planet and interstellar trade through this sector."

Literally, Martin thought. The Apsidal Ring was *huge*. If it were to be destroyed, if chunks of it were to fall on the planet below, it would render Apsidal uninhabitable. No, the Tokomak would need to fight to recover it. They couldn't threaten orbital bombardment if they'd be shooting themselves in the foot as well. *And we can't threaten to destroy it either.*

"Accordingly, we will be deploying to fight a holding action," Jackson said. "If they land, we will make their lives miserable for as long as possible. The local defence forces, such as they are, will be doing the same on the planet below. However, the *real* action will take place on the ring."

An officer Martin didn't recognise put up his hand. "Are they likely to even *bother* with the planet, sir?"

"We don't know," Jackson said. He adjusted his display, bringing up a holographic image of the planet, the ring and the four orbital towers. "They should, in theory, be able to repair the economic damage simply by recapturing the ring and the uppermost levels of the towers. The planet itself is largely immaterial to them. However, given how many of their people were killed in the uprisings on the surface, they may want revenge."

Martin winced. He'd seen the local defence forces. They might become decent soldiers, given time and better training, but right now they were nothing more than cannon fodder. And the Tokomak wouldn't have to worry about the side effects of bombarding the planet's surface from orbit. Whoever controlled the Apsidal Ring controlled Apsidal itself.

"That would not be surprising," Major Griffin said. "Revenge is a motive that they understand as well as us."

"This raises another point," a female voice said, bluntly. Martin turned his head to see the speaker. Captain Higgs. "If the navy loses control of the system...what then?"

"That depends, very much, on *precisely* what happens," Jackson said. "Ideally, the navy will rally, reassemble its formations and return to liberate the system for a second time. There are contingency plans to do that, if the Tokomak push the fleet away from the gravity point. That said"—he took a visible breath—"there is a good chance that we will be separated from the fleet, and the rest of the Solar Union, for years. We may never be relieved at all."

Martin made a face. "You could just have lied to us, sir."

A chuckle ran through the room. "You know the score," Jackson said, when it had died down. "And you know the odds. There's no point in trying to hide it from you. This could easily turn into a suicide mission."

"But it won't," Major Griffin said. He took the stand. "We have only a short time to deploy, so we're going to proceed as follows. I want…"

Martin listened, silently making notes for his subordinates. It explained, he supposed, why they'd been moved around so much. His team might not be quite *used* to the alien environment, but at least they understood how to operate within it. And, if they were cut off from the rest of the unit, they could harass the enemy on their own. His lips twitched at the thought. It would be like playing a combat simulation in a truly massive environment, with only a handful of players.

Hell, we could run around all year and never run into the other side, he thought, wryly. The Tokomak would have the same problems, only worse. *They* couldn't count on any help from the locals, either. They'd have to do everything themselves. *And they might never run into us too.*

CHAPTER SEVENTEEN

Captain-Commodore Sally Fredrick, SUS *Freeman* had been half-asleep when the alarms started to howl.

She rolled out of bed, cursing her luck. The scouts had made it clear that the Tokomak were moving towards the GS-3532 gravity point—and she hadn't been able to get a scout through the gravity point after they'd secured the far side—but there had been no way to predict when the enemy would mount its offensive. It was sheer bad luck that she'd been sleeping, although it could have been worse. She might have been lost in a VR sim instead.

Which is a court-martial offense, in a combat situation, she thought, as she slapped her control panel with one hand and reached for her trousers with the other. *I'd be in real trouble.*

"Report," she snapped. "What's happening?"

"The enemy started to push through the gravity point," Commander Wiseman said. Her XO sounded revoltingly fresh. "The minefields are engaging now. Captain Hammond has put the Alpha platforms on alert."

"Understood," Sally said. She frantically pulled on her trousers, silently thanking all her ancestors that she hadn't slept naked. "I'll be on the bridge in a moment."

She grabbed her jacket and pulled it on, then ran through the hatch and onto the bridge. The main display was flickering and flaring with light as enemy icons appeared through the gravity point, only to vanish seconds later as the mines took them out. She couldn't help thinking, as she took her chair, that it looked like the Eye of Sauron. The gravity point itself was invisible, at least to the naked eye, but the dying ships were all too clear.

"Inform Captain Hammond that I am assuming command," she said, as she scanned the status reports. Their cloaking fields were holding. The enemy shouldn't have the slightest idea of their presence, let alone their exact location. "And then route control of the Alpha and Beta platforms through us."

"Aye, Captain," Commander Wiseman said. "The platforms are standing by."

"Good," Sally said. "Do *not* release them without my direct command."

She leaned forward, hastily assessing the situation. The minefields were doing better than she'd expected, but the enemy was sweeping them by sheer weight of numbers. It was sickening, in a way. Years ago, human soldiers had driven sheep across minefields to clear them; now, the Tokomak were doing the same...with sentient beings. They were casually expending ships crewed by their servants just to clear the way. The death toll had to be well over ten thousand already.

Sick, she thought. *Did they never think to invent assault pods? Or did they just decide they didn't need to think of a new way through a gravity point?*

"Order two courier boats to head straight back to Apsidal," she said. "They are to alert Admiral Stuart that the enemy offensive has begun."

"Aye, Captain."

A red icon materialised in the gravity point...and remained intact. The enemy ship moved forward a second later, its weapons already spitting fire towards the nearest mines. Sally silently credited the ship's CO with good judgement, even if he *was* on the wrong side. He was sweeping mines that would otherwise have killed his fellows. Two more ships appeared, moments later. They pushed outwards too. Sally gritted her teeth. She'd hoped to keep some of the platforms in reserve, for when the bigger ships started to come through the gravity point, but it was starting to look as if that wasn't going to be possible. The platforms would have to be used before they were wiped out by the advancing alien ships.

"Clear the Alpha platforms to engage," she ordered, shortly. "They may fire at will."

"Aye, Captain."

The first enemy ship vanished from the display. Its fellows followed a moment later, but not quickly enough to keep *more* enemy reinforcements from popping out of the gravity point. Sally scowled, remembering an ancestor who'd faced an entire stream of human wave attacks. The enemy had died in their hundreds, perhaps in their thousands, but they'd eventually punched through when the defenders had run out of bullets. It had been a textbook example of a pyrrhic victory, yet…it had been a victory.

"They're targeting the platforms," Commander Wiseman said. "We're losing them."

"Keep engaging until there are no platforms left," Sally said, curtly.

She reminded herself, sharply, that the automated weapons platforms were completely expendable. They'd bleed the enemy, even though they wouldn't *stop* them. She was grimly aware that the Tokomak hadn't lost more than a tiny fraction of their fleet, but they'd still be weakened. Who knew *what* would happen when they tried to force their way through the Apsidal Point?

There has to be a limit on how many ships they're prepared to lose, she thought. *What would it profit them, to kill every last human and bomb our worlds to rubble, if it weakens them so badly that their enemies tear them to shreds?*

But the enemy ships just kept coming, one by one, systematically clearing the space around the gravity point with their deaths. More and more ships survived for longer, launching probes in all directions even as their sensors drew fire from the stealthed platforms. Sally felt cold, even though she'd *known* she wouldn't be able to stop them. She'd seen the images from N-Gann, she'd watched her intelligence staff try to count the enemy ships, but she hadn't really grasped just *what* was coming her way. The Tokomak could lose thousands of ships and maintain their advance. They *were* maintaining their advance.

"The Alpha and Beta platforms have been destroyed," Commander Wiseman said. "They're locking onto the Delta and Gamma platforms now."

"Order them to engage," Sally said. She didn't hold out much hope—the weapons platforms were only of limited value against ships that *knew* they were there—but at least it would force the Tokomak to be careful. "And the mines?"

"They're obliterating the last of them now," Commander Wiseman said. "They'll be gone soon."

Sally nodded. Minefields were of limited value in space warfare, at least outside a gravity point. There was simply no way to lure the enemy ships onto a minefield without taking the risk of being targeted by one's own mines. Now, she could see another weakness all too clearly. The enemy ships could see—and destroy—the mines before the mines could destroy them.

They didn't cost us much, she reminded herself, dryly. Producing hundreds of thousands of mines was no big deal for a Galactic world like Apsidal. *And they did hurt the enemy.*

She shook her head, slowly. The mines *had* hurt the enemy, but it wasn't enough. They were massing their forces on the gravity point, bringing through larger ships to help them secure the system now the gravity point was clear. They'd start the slow march towards the next gravity point when they felt secure. And then...

"Inform the squadron," she said. "We will engage once they begin their advance."

"Aye, Captain."

...

"They're trying to stop us," her aide said. "Us!"

"Of course," Neola said, dryly. "What did you expect?"

She ignored the younger male's prattling about interstellar treaties as she turned her attention back to the display. She'd hoped he'd be capable of expanding his mind to comprehend that the universe had changed, but apparently not. The treaties about not barricading the gravity points had been ripped up long ago. Besides, why exactly would the humans refrain from defending the gravity points? It was their only way to force her to pay a heavy price for each system she took and they knew it.

And they never signed the treaties in the first place, she thought. *They're certainly not going to honour them.*

"Order the next two squadrons to advance," she said, dismissing the thought. "They are to concentrate on expanding our control of the gravity point instead of heading deeper into the system."

"Yes, Your Excellency," the aide said.

Neola eyed his back nastily—it was clear she was going to need a new aide fairly soon, someone who was capable of learning to *think*—and then silently totted up the losses. Thirty-seven starships, all expendable...it could have been worse. The humans had set traps, but they hadn't backed them up with mobile firepower. Not yet, anyway. That would change as the Tokomak kept forcing their way towards Earth.

The next set of reports flowed into the display. GS-3532 was as worthless as the files said, save for the presence of a second gravity point on the other side of the system primary. It wouldn't be long before fast elements of her fleet took control of the gravity point and prepared for the next offensive. There didn't look to be any real *human* presence within the system, but looks could be deceiving. A fleet twice the size of *hers* could hide within the immensity of an entire star system and remain undetected.

And if they had a fleet that size, with all the firepower that that would imply, the war would be over by now, she thought. *And we would have lost.*

It was a chilling thought. She'd given the Gerontocrats—the *former* Gerontocrats—several good reasons to wage war on humanity, but the *real* reason was the one they'd refused to accept. Humanity had taken the technology they'd stolen and *improved* upon it. How long would it be, she'd asked herself, before the human race invented something that rendered her entire fleet so much scrap metal. The Gerontocrats had refused to even *consider* the possibility, even in the face of indisputable evidence. She, on the other hand, knew better. Giving the humans a chance to invent something *truly* devastating would be the last mistake her people would ever make.

"Continue the offensive," she said, when the aide came scurrying back. "And keep funnelling ships through the gravity point. Once we have enough ships in position, they can secure the second gravity point."

She made a discontented face as the aide bowed and hurried off to do her bidding. There was another gravity point assault to come before the fleet punched its way into Mokpo, then a third assault before they reached Apsidal. The plan had looked perfect, when she'd drawn it up, but now... now she was all too aware of just how many things could go wrong. She'd done her best to minimise the risks, but...she shook her head crossly. A human would take the risk. Of *course* a human would take the risk...

...And she had to take it too.

・・・

"The enemy fleet is deploying now, Captain," Commander Wiseman said. "It won't be long before they go into FTL."

Sally nodded. The enemy were playing it carefully, even though there was no indication that they'd detected her ships. Whoever was in charge on the other side was clearly feeling cautious. But they'd have to move sooner or later, if only to keep her reinforcements from jumping through the other gravity point. The chance to fight a gravity point defence of their own *had* to be tempting.

Although we might have cured them of that impulse, if they saw the assault pods at work, she thought, wryly. *And we probably taught them how to build assault pods of their own too.*

The enemy icons glided forward, their sensors sweeping through space. There were a *lot* of starships, enough ships to pose a very real threat to hundreds of advanced worlds. It was terrifying to realise that they were nothing more than a tiny fragment of the enemy fleet, which was itself a small proportion of the fleets the Tokomak could deploy. She wondered, grimly, just how many of those ancient ships could really be manned, updated and sent to the front. Intelligence had produced a number of possible scenarios, ranging from suggestions that the enemy could deploy all those ships, given time, or that only a small percentage could actually be put back into service. The ships themselves wouldn't have decayed, of course, but the crews were another matter. It was hard enough to crew the Solar Union's fleet. The Tokomak would need *millions* of trained personal to crew *theirs*.

She put the thought aside for later contemplation and considered the situation. There was nothing stopping the enemy from dropping into FTL at any moment and *racing* to the other gravity point. She had a feeling that whoever was in command would want to keep his ships under tight control, but they'd be idiots to throw away the chance to seize the gravity point before human ships started popping out of it. Sally had only a small window of opportunity to hit the enemy ships, but it would only be open while her squadron was too close to the remainder of the enemy fleet for comfort. They were *still* gliding out of the gravity point at a terrifying rate.

"We'll open fire when they reach Point Omega, unless they see us first," she said, looking at the tactical officer's back. "If they do see us, fire at once. Don't wait for orders."

"Aye, Captain," the tactical officer said.

Sally felt the tension start to rise as the enemy ships drew closer. Her cruisers were faster than anything the Tokomak could put into space, at least as far as they knew, but the range was closing rapidly. The Tokomak would get at least *one* shot at her ships, once they knew they were there. And while she had a lot of faith in her point defence, she also knew the Tokomak would be firing thousands of missiles. They might break through her defences by sheer weight of numbers.

And if they see us, they'll get the first shot, she thought. *It could get very bad.*

"They'll be at Point Omega in two minutes," Commander Wiseman said. "Captain?"

"Fire as soon as they reach Point Omega," Sally ordered. "And then bring up our shields and drives."

She braced herself as the final seconds ticked down to zero. The enemy ships were sweeping space thoroughly, with an intensity she had to admire, but—so far—the cloaking devices were holding. They'd get one free shot, assuming the enemy hadn't seen them already and was playing dumb while the range closed. There was too much room for second-guessing herself as the fleet reached Point Omega...

"Firing," the tactical officer said.

Freeman shuddered, violently, as she flushed her external racks, followed rapidly by her internal tubes. Sally smiled, coldly, as the enemy ships appeared to flinch. It was an illusion, she knew from bitter experience, but one she clung to anyway. The enemy ships would have seen the missiles come out of nowhere. She leaned forward, hungrily, as the enemy ships altered course slightly, bringing up their datanets. Did they have time to spin up their stardrives and jump into FTL?

No, she thought, as the enemy ships spat missiles back at her formation. They would have jumped into FTL if they could, rather than wasting time trying to destroy her ships. *They don't have time.*

She allowed herself a cold smile as the missiles plunged into the enemy datanet. The Tokomak had clearly been improving their defences, but they weren't ready for the latest generation of penetrator warheads. A handful were wiped out, blasted by the enemy point defence, but the remainder struck home. Antimatter explosions ripped through shields and destroyed ships, leaving the enemy formation in disarray. It looked as if they could be wiped out at minimal cost...

"Captain, we can take them," the tactical officer said. The enemy missiles were already entering *Freeman's* point defence datanet. "We can finish them off and then..."

"No," Sally said. She understood the impulse. She even *shared* the impulse. But their orders were clear. And she understood the logic behind them too. They simply didn't have the firepower to do more than harass the enemy fleet. "Pull us back; drop into FTL as planned once we're clear."

"Aye, Captain," the tactical officer said.

Sally nodded shortly, watching as the enemy missiles sliced into her point defence network, trying to push their way through. The enemy had *definitely* been caught by surprise or they would have fired more missiles, although they were trying to make up for that now. It didn't *look* as though they'd managed to make any significant improvements in their warheads and penetrator aids, certainly nothing better than what had already been seen...

"ND running into FTL now," the helmsman said. The display blurred, then froze. "Setting course for Point Theta."

Sally nodded. "Tactical? Your analysis?"

"We caught them by surprise," the tactical officer said, studying his console. "They would have fired more missiles at us if they'd realised we were there. That said, their missiles *did* show a certain degree of improvement."

"Really." Sally's eyes narrowed. "Are you sure?"

"Yes, Captain," the tactical officer said. "They didn't fire enough missiles to make it evident, but there was some additional improvement. Their penetrator aids were actually a generation in advance of those we saw during the Battle of Apsidal. I think the same is true of their warheads, although we didn't really get a good look at them. And if these aren't their front-line forces..."

Sally frowned. The Tokomak wouldn't consider their *own* people to be expendable, would they? She doubted that *any* government, human or alien, could survive such an attitude, not when its angry servants commanded starships, missiles and beam arrays. But if they were giving advanced—or at least improved—weapons to their servants, what might their *own* ships be carrying? There was no way to know.

"Add it to the report," she ordered, finally. "We'll send it to the courier boat once we're out of FTL, then we can return to the attack."

And see what else they throw at us, she added, in the privacy of her own mind. *And if we get a look at their advanced weapons now, they won't be a surprise when the fleet encounters them.*

CHAPTER EIGHTEEN

There was surprisingly little debris near the gravity point itself.

Or perhaps, Neola told herself as her flagship moved back into normal space, it wasn't that surprising at all. The layers upon layers of mines the humans had laid to trap her fleet had taken out dozens of ships, some of which had been armed with antimatter weapons. They'd been vaporised by the blasts, but their deaths had served a purpose. The human defences had been cleared with minimal cost. She'd expected far worse.

"Get me a status update," she snapped, glowering at her aide. She really *was* going to have to replace him before the *big* battle. Her staff would have to check the lists of up-and-coming young officers and see if there was one who could think outside the box. "Where are the humans?"

"Slipping in and out of cloak," the aide reported, as the display rapidly updated. "They're engaging us briefly, then retreating back into cloak and vanishing. Long-range sensors insist that there are hundreds of human ships in the system."

"Sensor ghosts," Neola said, dismissively. If there *had* been hundreds of human ships in the system, they'd have inflicted a great deal more damage before they were finally forced to retreat. They certainly didn't gain anything from hiding in cloak when they had the opportunity to weaken her flanks. "There won't be more than a couple of dozen at most."

She turned her attention to the display. GS-3532 was useless—and more useless to the humans than *her*. They couldn't afford to get a sizable number of their ships cut off from the remainder of the Apsidal Chain, not unless she'd vastly underestimated their numbers. The handful of ships that were sniping at her might have orders to go into cloak when she finally secured the system and then attack her supply lines, but even *that* would be risky. Battles had been won or lost before on the presence or absence of a single ship. Would the humans take the chance?

"Concentrate four squadrons of superdreadnaughts," she ordered, shortly. The humans had led her subordinates by the nose—she gave them that much credit—but the game was about to come to a crashing halt. "They are to proceed into FTL and secure the Mokpo Point. The remainder of the fleet will follow when ready."

The aide hurried away to carry out her orders. Neola scowled at his retreating back, then started to consider her next move. She'd known about the problems with using the gravity points for such a large fleet before, of course, and there was no way to avoid them, but the sheer scale of the problems was magnified when the fleet was under fire. She really should have secured the second gravity point immediately—it was only minutes away in FTL—yet she hadn't had the mobile firepower on hand. It wouldn't surprise her if the humans fired their wretched missile pods through the gravity point when her squadrons arrived, catching them by surprise. She had to admit the cursed devices were a neat solution to the problem of assaulting a defended gravity point.

And we never came up with the idea for ourselves, she thought, irritated. In hindsight, it was more of a cultural blindspot than a technological problem. The very concept of a single-use jump drive seemed *wrong*, although she could see some advantages. Her engineers were already working on a design that could be put into production relatively quickly. She might not be able to use them on *this* campaign, but the next...anyone who challenged her people was in for a nasty surprise. *And everyone else will be coming up with their own versions too, now they know it can be done.*

Neola dismissed the thought as the superdreadnaughts jumped into FTL, speeding across the system towards the second gravity point. She tensed, half-expecting a gravity well to appear out of nowhere to yank the superdreadnaughts out of FTL, but nothing happened. She'd drilled her crews to expect to have to fight at any moment, even though everyone had *known* that a starship in FTL was untouchable...right up until the moment she'd flown her first fleet into an utterly inconceivable trap. It had never crossed her mind that they might be yanked back into normal space without even a second's warning.

They showed us what could be done, she reminded herself. *And we have profited from the experience.*

"The superdreadnaughts have reached their target," her aide told her. "And they've returned to normal space."

"And now they're out of contact," Neola said, tightly. She'd ordered her commanders to back off if they ran into overwhelming force, but she knew that not all of them would obey orders. They'd grown up in a universe where *they* were the overwhelming force. Some of them were still in denial. "Bring the remainder of the fleet through the gravity point, then we will proceed to Mokpo."

"As you command, Your Excellency."

...

Sally rubbed the sweat from her forehead as the enemy superdreadnaughts dropped out of FTL, right on the edge of the danger zone. The gravity tides around a gravity point could be dangerously unpredictable and very few spacers would risk coming out of FTL *too* close to the point. She was mildly impressed that the Tokomak had taken the risk. They were normally so safety conscious that they never left home without a map, a compass and a GPS navigator.

And they imposed that view on the rest of the Galactics, she reminded herself. God, the laughter when the penny had finally dropped and the Solar

Union had realised why the Galactics were so blind to the potentials of their technology. *They put so many limitations on their technology for so long that they came to be seen as natural laws.*

"Fire," she ordered, quietly.

The cruiser shuddered as she emptied her missile tubes, launching a devastating salvo towards the enemy ships. Her consorts followed, the missiles linking together into a coordinated swarm as they approached their targets. The enemy ships returned fire immediately, trying to overwhelm her point defence by sheer weight of numbers even as they brought up their own point defence. Sally wanted to retreat at once—there were so many missiles coming at her ships that *some* of them were bound to strike home—but she wanted to see the superdreadnaughts in action. The largest ships the Tokomak had produced, they were normally kept in reserve. It said something about how seriously the Tokomak took the human race, she supposed, that they'd dispatched hundreds of superdreadnaughts to the front.

Her eyes narrowed as the superdreadnaughts launched another massive salvo. That was quick, uncomfortably quick. They didn't seem to mount external racks, as far as her sensors could tell, but they didn't seem to need them. There was a *professionalism* about their conduct that was almost human. She had the nasty feeling that, for the first time, humanity was facing the best the Tokomak could produce.

"Our missiles are entering engagement range," Commander Wiseman said, quietly. "The enemy point defence is opening fire."

Sally nodded, curtly. The enemy point defence didn't seem to be up to human standards, but the superdreadnaughts were putting out so much firepower that it hardly mattered. They weren't making any attempt, as far as she could tell, to figure out the difference between *real* missiles and sensor ghosts. The enemy ships had enough point defence firepower to engage both sets of targets. And she had to admit it was working. Her missiles were amongst the most advanced in the known universe, but the enemy fleet was defending itself rather well.

And their shields are tough too, she noted, as a handful of her missiles slammed home. One superdreadnaught exploded into a ball of plasma, another shuddered and fell out of formation, but the remainder stood up to the antimatter blasts and kept advancing on the gravity point. *And whoever's in command of the formation didn't lose sight of what their* real *objective is.*

The enemy squadron belched yet another salvo of missiles, an instant before the *first* salvo entered point defence range. Sally braced herself as her ships opened fire, slicing dozens—hundreds—of enemy missiles out of space, yet barely making a dent in the sheer weight of enemy fire. A handful of missiles appeared to be modified penetrator aids; others appeared to be completely focused on ECM, blasting out everything from basic radio jamming to EMP pulses. She puzzled over it for a moment, then realised the truth. The Tokomak were attempting to destroy her datanet. They clearly hadn't realised it was impossible.

Yet, Sally reminded herself. She had to admit it was a logical approach. The Tokomak knew that humanity's datanets were better—humanity's RIs were far more capable than anything the Tokomak had produced—and weakening them made sound sense. *They might come up with something new, given time.*

"The enemy missiles are nuclear-tipped," the tactical officer reported, as the swarm entered terminal attack range. "But there are a lot of them."

Sally smiled, despite herself. Clearly, the Tokomak were *still* safety conscious. Nuclear warheads were deadly on a planet's surface, although she'd heard stories of wars where they'd been used in vast numbers, but in space...well, they weren't firecrackers, but they weren't antimatter warheads either. Her ships had a slightly better chance of survival against enemy superdreadnaughts if the latter weren't allowed to carry antimatter warheads. Not, she supposed, that it mattered *that* much. The sheer number of missiles the enemy ships were firing was more than enough to make up for their deficiencies.

"Comms, signal the courier boats," she ordered. "Copy our last records to them, then tell them to jump out now. The Amethyst Contingency is now in effect."

"Aye, Captain," Lieutenant Lafarge said.

Sally nodded. "Order the fleet to pull back and drop into FTL," she added. "It's time to take our leave."

She leaned back in her chair as *Freeman* dropped into FTL, not a moment too soon. The enemy would be frustrated at having wasted so much ammunition, she supposed, although if they had a fleet train and support base comparable to Admiral Stuart's they could probably recover and refurbish most of those missiles. Either they hadn't realised that her ships had also been on the edge of the danger zone or they simply hadn't cared. Probably the latter, she decided. They'd had to drive her away before her second salvo, programmed with all the intelligence gained from the *first*, started to tear into their defences. It was a shame her ships hadn't had the firepower to take advantage of what they'd learned.

"Set course for the RV point," she ordered, once they were clear of the gravity point. The odds of interception were very low. "And prepare to resupply the ships."

"Aye, Captain."

Sally nodded, feeling a cold hand clenching around her heart. They were alone now, until the fleet fought its way back up the chain or they found a way to sneak back to Apsidal. She'd known the mission, when she'd been briefed on it, but now...now it felt real. Admiral Stuart wanted them to hit the enemy supply lines, when the Tokomak started funnelling freighters through the gravity points. It would probably be quite some time before they had to go back into action, unless the situation radically changed. The Tokomak were going to be moving warships through the gravity point for the next few weeks.

And once we run out of supplies, we'll have no choice but to retreat through FTL, she thought. She hadn't liked *that* aspect of the plan. *Odyssey* had made it home, after being cut off by the Harmonies, but she'd been a single ship. Getting twenty-seven starships home was going to be a great deal harder. *Perhaps we should go on the offensive instead.*

She stood. "We did well today," she said. It was true, even though she knew they'd barely slowed the enemy down. "And we showed those bastards that human lives don't come cheap."

Commander Wiseman grinned. "We hurt them," he said. "And even if we lose, we might encourage some of their slaves to rise up and go for their throats."

Sally nodded. She'd heard that there were plans to insert propaganda messages into the galactic news networks, although she hadn't heard anything more concrete than vague rumours. The Galactic datanets were closed systems, incredibly restrictive. A rogue message could be wiped, even from private terminals, before it was seen by more than a handful of people. And if a few of them chose to lash out at their masters, they could be crushed without much effort. The Galactic security forces were incredibly ruthless. Now, with the Tokomak facing their first real challenge for thousands of years, she doubted they'd be *gentle* with any rebel cells.

"We'll see," she said. "Commander Wiseman, you have the bridge."

"Aye, Captain."

. . .

"The enemy missiles were impressive," a researcher commented, his voice echoing through the ship's datanet. "We were lucky they didn't seem to have many of them."

"And that they didn't fire their black hole missiles," another said. "They could have devastated the superdreadnaughts."

Neola listened to the debate with half an ear as her fleet slowly took possession of the gravity point. The human ships had vanished into FTL, which meant they *hadn't* tried to get through the gravity point and escape. No doubt they intended to attack her rear or harass the other worlds within FTL range. She wasn't really concerned. The humans hadn't had anything like enough time to establish a proper supply dump for their ships. Cut off from its supply lines, the enemy squadron would wither on the vine and die. And whatever problems they managed to present in the future would die with them.

She smiled, grimly, as the chatter continued. The researchers were brilliant—she'd picked the smartest scientists she could, the ones who were interested in pushing the limits once again—but they weren't *practical*. How could they be? They'd never flown starships, they'd never been in real combat…they didn't understand the implications of what they were saying. *She* knew that producing black hole missiles wasn't easy. The vast industrial base on Tokomak Prime hadn't been able to produce anything *like* enough missiles for her fleet. It was easy to believe that the humans had the same problem.

And they wouldn't have risked making a stand here, she reminded herself, once again. She could see a couple of alternate ways to reach Apsidal from Winglet. They'd add several weeks and three more gravity points to the journey, but it could be done. *They have to make their stand somewhere they know I have to come to them.*

She cut the datanet connection and studied the display. The humans hadn't launched any counterattacks, not yet, but none of the scoutships she'd sent through the gravity point had returned. She hadn't been surprised. The humans could have layered enough mines over the gravity point to allow someone to walk from one end to the other, although it would be counterproductive. A single interpenetration event would wipe out the entire minefield. And a more *rational* defence would still have been enough to take out her scouts before they could reverse course and retreat.

Perhaps we could build two single-use jump drives, she mused. It seemed a plausible—and practical—idea. *One to get the ship through the gravity point, the other to yank it back before the mines could take it out.*

She reached for her personal datapad and started to make notes. The idea might be impractical—she knew she was no engineer—but it had to be tried. A starship's sensors would be scrambled by the jump, limiting what it could see in the seconds between the first jump and the second, yet... perhaps if she rigged the ship with *more* sensors, they'd see something...

And the researchers will probably try to find a way to tell me it can't be done, she thought, crossly. It was notable that the *humans* hadn't tried to modify their assault pod technology to produce recon probes. If *she* could see how the technology could be modified to launch spies through a gravity point, she was *sure* the humans could see it too. *But it might start the researchers thinking.*

She sent her notes to the researchers, with orders to consider the possibilities, then settled back to wait as her fleet slowly assembled for the next assault. Technically, she could afford to wait before pushing into Mokpo—she was fairly sure the humans couldn't do more than they already had even if she gave them a few extra weeks—but she did have a timetable. She was too experienced an officer to believe that the timetable could, let alone *would*, be followed to the letter, yet all her planning would be wasted if she waited too long. It had been hard enough to put all the pieces in place without giving the game away.

Her aide approached, looking confident. He hadn't realised that he was going to be replaced, then. Neola considered simply informing him herself, but it would be a mistake to let him know until she had a replacement lined up. Besides, she also needed to find a place for him, one that wasn't too dishonourable. His family would be annoyed if she simply fired him.

His voice was very calm. "Your Excellency, the first assault forces are in place. The freighters are also ready."

"Very good," Neola said. The humans would expect the freighters, she was sure. The tactic dated back all the way to the early wars, before FTL had made the Tokomak unquestioned masters of the universe. "Signal the lead forces. They are authorised to begin the attack."

CHAPTER NINETEEN

They're getting better, Hameeda thought. *That isn't good.*

Her intelligence and analysis subroutines picked apart the data from GS-3532 even as the LinkShip maintained station some distance from the gravity point. Two courier boats had made it through the gravity point before the enemy—evidently—had cut off all traffic from GS-3532. They'd sent through a handful of scouts, none of which had survived long enough to report back to their masters, but otherwise the gravity point was quiet. Hameeda doubted that would last for long.

She studied the intelligence reports as she waited. So far, the fears that the Tokomak might have quietly developed a universe-changing superweapon didn't appear to have turned into reality, although she was grimly aware that a superweapon was most effective if it was held back until it could be deployed decisively, with all the bugs worked out. The *Superiority* dilemma affected the Tokomak too. But yet...she scowled as she saw how the enemy had improved everything from missile throw weights to point defence. They might not have produced a game-changer, but they'd certainly started shaking the dust off their shoes.

Then it is all the more important that we continue to push the limits, she thought, and felt the LinkShip hum in response. *We need to build on our advantages before they overwhelm us through sheer weight of numbers.*

A dozen examples ran through her mind as her subroutines assessed the situation. The Germans in World War Two had often had technological superiority over their enemies, but they simply hadn't the numbers to defeat them. Hitler hadn't helped, she supposed—he'd wasted resources on battleships and rockets when they would have been better spent on tanks and aircraft—but Germany had faced severe resource limitations that no amount of fascist propaganda could overcome. And the same could be said for many of the post-Contact wars on Earth. The good guys—or at least the better guys—often hadn't had the numbers to turn their technological superiority into guaranteed victory. And then...

Her awareness snapped back to the gravity point. A freighter—a massive bulk freighter, easily ten kilometres long—materialised in the exact centre of the point. Hameeda blinked in surprise. No civilian shipping had passed through the Winglet Point to GS-3532 once the system had been occupied by the enemy, even though it would give the bastards a chance to spy on the defences. The Tokomak had been more interested in throwing warships through the point than allowing civilian craft to pass through. And yet...

The freighter twinkled...and exploded. A blinding white light filled her awareness, pain surging through her nervous system a second before the automated limiters cut in. Hameeda felt her hands scrabbling at her helmet as she fought to control herself, panic yammering at the back of her mind. Her eyes felt as if someone had stabbed daggers through her eyeballs and deep into her brain. The sensation was so acute that she was half-convinced she was dead—or dying. Her body had been thoroughly enhanced, in all kinds of ways, but she couldn't survive a knife in the brain. She was dead...

No, she told herself firmly, as her implants took control. *I'm not dead.*

She felt numb, oddly disconnected from the world. She'd *hated* the emergency system when it had been tested, even though she knew why it existed. She felt as if a pane of glass hung between her and the world, as if whatever was happening on the other side wasn't truly *real*, as if it was no more than a television program. And yet, she *knew* it was real. She took a long breath, steadying herself, then reached out through her implants. The LinkShip was hurting, but it was intact.

And the enemy are flooding through the gravity point, she thought, as her mind slowly cleared. Her internal clock told her that she'd only been stunned for five minutes, but it had been more than long enough for the situation to change dramatically. The Tokomak were sending a steady stream of light units through the gravity point, ignoring the handful of surviving defenders. *What did they do?*

Her subroutines provided an answer. They hadn't invented a new superweapon. Instead, they'd dug up a very old one. They'd taken a freighter, crammed her to the gunnels with antimatter, and sent her through the gravity point. It didn't matter, from their point of view, if the freighter struck a mine or survived. All that mattered was that the containment fields would fail and the antimatter would explode. Given the sheer *size* of the blast, it had to have been a *lot* of antimatter. The blast had wiped out the entire minefield and most of the automated defences.

Clever, she thought, sourly. *And unanticipated.*

She ran a handful of simulations as she steered away from the gravity point. If the Tokomak repeated the tactic when they attacked Apsidal... no, they *would* repeat the tactic when they attacked Apsidal. They wouldn't have wasted so much antimatter on Mokpo if supplies were limited. She had a feeling they'd pour a stream of disposable freighters through the gravity point, clearing more and more of the automated defences with every blast. The fortresses and starships would be safer—their crews wouldn't be tied to neural nets—but they'd still be weakened. It was, she had to admit, a very neat tactic.

The Tokomak kept coming, steadily expanding their control over the gravity point. They didn't seem to be in any hurry to secure the Apsidal Point or Mokpo itself. But then, they didn't *need* to do more. There was no hope of keeping the combat reports from getting back to Apsidal, not when sensors right across the system would have picked up the antimatter blast. It made her wonder if they *wanted* to intimidate the defenders…or if they had something else in mind. Did they have a shortage of antimatter after all? No, her logic held. They wouldn't have wasted the antimatter if they didn't have it to spare.

She kept a wary eye on them as the first superdreadnaughts began to slide out of the gravity point, one by one. The reports from the previous engagement made it clear that the superdreadnaughts were tough customers, even if they lacked some of humanity's technology. It was enough to make her wonder if the Solar Union's concentration on cruisers had been a mistake. Sure, a human cruiser could go toe-to-toe with an alien battleship, but it lacked the sheer weight of fire a superdreadnaught could produce. But superdreadnaughts took longer to build, even with the latest technology. The Solar Union simply couldn't have produced enough of them to make a difference.

And now they're heading straight for the gravity point, she noted, as the superdreadnaughts bunched up into a tight formation. It looked as if they expected to be attacked at any moment. There *were* raiders, waiting for them, but they couldn't do more than irritate the enemy ships. *It won't be long before they slam the door closed.*

The LinkShip spun around, then raced away from the gravity point. Hameeda was tempted to buzz right through the enemy formation, to test her stealth systems against the best the Tokomak could offer, but she knew it would be incredibly dangerous. And foolish, too. The Tokomak could *not* be allowed a close look at her, not until she could bring her full weight to bear. Instead, she circled the superdreadnaughts at a respectful distance—their sensors didn't even notice her, as far as she could tell—and dropped into FTL, heading straight towards the gravity point. Hopefully, she'd be able to nip through it before the enemy took up position to intercept stray human ships.

And if they get there first, I'll just have to blow through them, she thought. Ideally, she could sneak through the defences—she'd done it before—but there were too many unknown factors for her to be sanguine about the risk. If the Tokomak had figured out that *someone* could sneak through the gravity points...she shook her head. Unless they'd invented a completely new drive technology, or improved the one they had, there was no way they'd beat her to the gravity point. *And then...*

She winced, inwardly. Admiral Stuart was *not* going to be happy when she read the report.

Thankfully, she's not in the habit of shooting the messenger, Hameeda thought. *But this time she may make an exception.*

...

"The antimatter blast worked, Your Excellency," the aide said. "We cleared their defences."

"Perhaps," Neola said. She wanted to *believe* that the antimatter explosion had wiped out the enemy defences, but she knew better. The humans hadn't bothered to put up a serious fight for Mokpo, even though a handful of starships were sniping at her ships as they advanced into the system. A better-organised defence might have cost her dearly. "But we don't know for sure."

She contemplated the situation for a long moment. There *hadn't* been any fortresses on the gravity point, although the reports from Apsidal had made it clear that the humans were putting together prefabricated fortresses with terrifying speed. The fortresses would have survived the blast, even if their shields had been down. And they *wouldn't* have been down, not when the humans *knew* she'd just captured the last system. They would have been ready and waiting for her. No, she hadn't smashed a major defence system. She'd just killed a few thousand mines.

"Dispatch additional superdreadnaught squadrons to the gravity point," she ordered. The gravity point *had* to be secured. "And then order the flag squadrons to prepare to advance on the planet."

A stream of reports from her covert observers flowed into her terminal as the fleet prepared for its next move. Mokpo hadn't been formally occupied by the humans, but that hadn't stopped rebel factions from making an appearance. Large parts of the planet had fallen out of the planetary government's control, although—so far—they'd managed to keep the rebels from contacting the human fleet and requesting help. Neola made a face as the remainder of her flag squadrons signalled that they were ready to advance. The rebels would have to be...dealt with.

"Order the flag squadrons to advance on the planet," she said, coldly. "The remainder of the fleet is to continue preparing for the coming engagement."

"Yes, Your Excellency," the aide said.

The fleet slipped into FTL. Neola waited, bracing herself against the inevitable moment the fleet dropped *out* of FTL. If the humans had baited a trap...she told herself, once again, that the humans were not *gods*. They were good, both technologically-adept and imaginative when it came to *using* their technology, but they couldn't predict everything she'd do. They certainly hadn't tried to set up a gravity trap in Mokpo. And even if they *had*, she had enough firepower to blast her way *out* of it.

She smiled, grimly, as Mokpo appeared on the display. It was a thoroughly ugly world, its only real assets—the orbital industrials—smashed by the human fleet. A series of messages from the planetary government popped up in front of her, but she ignored them. They were too independent for her tastes. It was time they learned—it was time everyone learned—that rebellion would be severely punished.

"Contact the planetary government," she ordered, curtly. "Demand that they send us a list of places controlled by the rebels."

"Yes, Your Excellency," the aide said. There was a pause. "Ah...Your Excellency...they want to talk to you in person."

"Repeat our demand," Neola said. She wasn't going to waste her time with a planetary government that couldn't keep control of its own territory. Apsidal's government, at least, had the excuse of being invaded. "And inform them that, if they fail to answer, our bombardment will be indiscriminate."

"Yes, Your Excellency," the aide said. "They're sending the details now. And they want to lodge a formal protest."

"Do they now," Neola said. That planetary government would have to go. It wasn't as if she had any need to coddle them. "Show me the targets."

The display changed, showing a handful of red spots on the planetary map. There were more than Neola had feared, even though she'd read the reports. Clearly, the planetary government was incompetent beyond belief. Why hadn't they crushed the rebels with overwhelming force? It was obvious the humans weren't going to intervene. They could have knocked out the planetary government by now if they'd wanted.

"Target the rebel positions with KEWs," she ordered, as the squadrons slipped into orbit. "I want maximum punishment. No one within the affected areas is to walk out alive."

The aide hesitated. "Your Excellency…"

Neola felt her temper rise. "Yes?"

"Your Excellency, the affected areas are amongst some of the most productive sectors of the planet," the aide said. "We will be killing their workforce…"

"Yes," Neola said. She supposed it was a good thought, if one couldn't think beyond one's nose. "And their workforce has risen up against them. They cannot be put back to work."

She snorted at the thought. Generations of servants from a hundred different races had never questioned their place in galactic society. They'd been raised from the mud and brought to the stars and all they had to do, in exchange, was serve their masters. But *these* servants had dared to challenge their masters instead. They could *not* be allowed to live. And their deaths would serve as an example to anyone else who dared challenge the natural order.

"Yes, Your Excellency," the aide said. At least he had enough sense not to question her further. "The weapons have been targeted."

"Then fire," Neola ordered.

The superdreadnaught shivered, gently, as she unleashed a spread of KEWs. They appeared on the display a second later, falling down through the planet's atmosphere like a stream of shooting stars. But the rebels would have no warning, no chance to escape or take cover, before they were wiped off the planet. The icons vanished one by one, strike reports blinking up in their place...it was easy to forget, at times, that each icon represented a thunderous impact. The icons were bloodless, nothing more than images in a holographic display, but hundreds of thousands of rebels had simply been smashed flat by the blasts. The property damage would be immense. Mokpo would need years to repair everything it had lost because of the war. By then, the planetary government would have put its house in order.

And if it hasn't managed to convince the servants to obey orders and remain loyal, I'll put a governor in instead, she thought. *The planet will remain under our control.*

She looked up at the aide. "Detach one squadron of destroyers to provide fire support to loyalist forces as they reoccupy the rebel territories," she said. She doubted there would be any real resistance, now the bombardment had smashed the rebels flat, but it was well to be careful. "And inform the planetary government that I expect them to keep their planet under firm control in future."

Her lips curved into a sneer. "The remainder of the flag squadrons are to proceed to the gravity point," she added. "And when we're ready to move, we will move."

• • •

"Those...those murdering bastards!"

"Quiet," Lieutenant Quinn Davao hissed. She understood Lieutenant Brock's feelings all too well—she shared them—but there was no time to allow their emotions to get in the way of professionalism. "Do we...do we have a count on how many KEWs were fired?"

And how many people were murdered, she added silently, as Brock bent over his console, his expression dark and thunderous. There were only two of them in the tiny picket and, right now, it felt as if their ship was too small for comfort. *How many people did the bastards just kill?*

"They fired over two *thousand* mid-sized KEWs," Brock said, finally.

His voice was calmer now, although Quinn could hear the anger behind it. Brock's family had spent the last fifty years working with aliens and he had long since abandoned any concept of humanity being different—or superior—to its neighbours. Aliens were people, as far as he was concerned. She had the feeling he'd join the Inclusionists when he left the navy, if he ever did. They made such a good team that the navy would do everything in its power to keep them.

"Shit," Quinn said.

"It's hard to be sure, but I'd say they killed upwards of two *billion*," Brock added. "The direct death toll is going to be huge, Quinn, and the indirect death toll might be larger still. Just firing so many KEWs into the atmosphere alone will be shitty…"

"Yeah," Quinn agreed. Blowing so much dust into the atmosphere would play merry hell with the weather. She didn't think there would be enough dust to trigger a genuine nuclear winter, but she might be wrong. "And there's nothing we can do about it."

She keyed her console, sending a report to the watching destroyer. It looked as if they wouldn't be able to get a report back to Apsidal, not since the enemy had secured the gravity point, but who knew? She'd heard rumours that there was a way to get a cloaked ship through a gravity point. Perhaps the rumours were actually true. But then, she'd *also* heard rumours about a plan to build a real-life Death Star.

"I know," Brock said. He pounded his console with his meaty fist, then turned his attention to monitoring the passive sensors. "They wanted to send a message. I'd say they succeeded."

"It isn't over yet," Quinn reminded him. "And we will make them pay for what they've done."

CHAPTER TWENTY

Hoshiko had seen the interior of the LinkShip before, when she'd visited via holographic projection, but there was something different about seeing it in person. It was...odd, a strange cross between a *bona fide* warship and a luxury liner. The design made sense, she supposed, even though it grated on her sensibilities. Captain Hameeda would be living on her ship for the rest of her life.

"Welcome onboard, Admiral," Hameeda said, as Hoshiko stepped into the bridge. "Thank you for coming in person."

"You're welcome," Hoshiko said. "I must confess I was fascinated with the concept behind your ship."

She gave the bridge a quick glance—apart from the command chair, with the neural helmet, it was practically an empty chamber—and then focused on Hameeda. The LinkShip pilot looked better than the last time—she certainly didn't look *quite* so worn down—but she also looked... sloppy, as if she'd forgotten how to dress. Hoshiko remembered the First Midshipman, on her middy cruise, and smiled. Midshipman Hedrick would have blown a fuse if *she'd* dressed so poorly. Hoshiko would have been doing press-ups for the rest of her projected lifespan.

"It does seem to be working as planned, now I've worked out the teething problems," Hameeda said. She stood beside her chair, one hand resting on the chair's shoulder. "But I don't think that was what you came to discuss."

"No," Hoshiko said. "I didn't like your report."

A flicker of...*something* passed across Hameeda's face. "I don't like it either, Admiral," she said. "The Tokomak produced a hammer out of the past."

"It was certainly something we should have anticipated," Hoshiko agreed, sourly. There would be hard words exchanged at the Admiralty when the news got home. "That said, we can cope with it. Any further antimatter explosions will take out the mines, but little else."

"Yes, Admiral," Hameeda said. "My simulations agree on that point."

"And we believed that the mines wouldn't be *that* effective in any case," Hoshiko continued, wondering just who she was trying to convince. She'd always expected to lose Mokpo, but losing it so *quickly* had been a nasty surprise. Thankfully, no one else had seen the enemy attack coming either. "Do you think you can return to Mokpo?"

Hameeda's tinted face seemed to darken. "...Perhaps," she said, after a moment. "But the enemy will certainly throw a comprehensive sensor web around the gravity point. We *could* take a leaf out of *their* book and send a freighter, crammed with antimatter, through the gravity point first..."

"We don't have enough antimatter," Hoshiko said. She'd already considered something similar. "Apsidal simply cannot produce it in sufficient quantities."

"That's...unfortunate," Hameeda said. "I could try, Admiral, but the odds of success are quite low. These days, the merest gravitational flicker is enough to alert the enemy."

"As they may know we have a way of sneaking through gravity points," Hoshiko said. It was a frustrating thought. "Do you have any alternatives?"

"Nothing, save for travelling to Mokpo in FTL," Hameeda said. "But that would take months."

"Yes," Hoshiko said. She looked at the blank bulkheads, wishing for a display. Hameeda didn't need one, of course. Her neural link provided her with all the information she could possibly require. "And by the time you got back, the situation will have resolved itself."

She sighed, suddenly all-too-aware of how her ancestors must have felt when they'd grappled with the fog of war. The enemy fleet was on the other side of the gravity point, plotting its offensive…and while she knew the offensive would come, she didn't know *when* it would come. Her best estimates were nothing more than estimates. Hell, in *their* shoes, she might ram a suicidal freighter though the gravity point every few days before beginning the main offensive. Or simply launch raid after raid to keep the defenders on edge. Her crews were highly-trained, and their bodies had been enhanced, but they couldn't stay alert forever. A smart enemy might delay the *real* offensive long enough to wear down her crews.

And we can't take the offensive ourselves, she thought. *We don't have enough assault pods to justify expending them in futile raids.*

"We'll just have to wait, Admiral," Hameeda said. She waved a hand towards the hatch. "Can I offer you some coffee? Or tea? I have genuine tea from Earth."

Hoshiko raised her eyebrows. "Did they give you *real* imported tea?"

"I had to purchase it myself," Hameeda said. She walked towards the hatch, which opened as she approached. "They gave me tea from the habitats, Admiral, but it doesn't have quite the same taste."

"My grandmother said the same," Hoshiko remembered. "She would always import food from Japan, and later from the Edo Cluster, rather than use a food processor or cook with home-grown ingredients. She insisted that the latter just didn't have the same taste."

"My mother did that too," Hameeda said. She glanced back, a faint smile on her face, as they entered the kitchen. It was impossible to think of the luxury compartment as a galley. "I could never tell the difference myself and…"

Her voice tailed off. Hoshiko understood. The Solar Union had always discouraged looking back at Earth, even though it was far from illegal. But then, most of the original settlers—and the ones who'd formed the government—had been determined to put Earth and its ramshackle decline into chaos behind them. There was no room for regrets, they'd said; an immigrant could only be loyal to his new home. Hoshiko had always thought that a little hypocritical, even though she had no love for those who wanted to look back to Earth. The founders hadn't hesitated to set up cantons based on earthly societies.

But a person can leave a canton, if he finds it oppressive, she thought. She had no idea why anyone would want to remain in a canton that shunned advanced technology, or expected men and women to follow clearly-defined gender roles, but at least the inhabitants had made the choice to stay. *Earth didn't let anyone leave their past behind.*

Hameeda made tea with casual skill. Hoshiko watched, silently admiring her devotion to producing the perfect cup of tea. Most people took their tea or coffee from food processors, rather than bothering to make it themselves. It was one of the reasons, she supposed, that *real* teashops and restaurants did a roaring trade. People wanted home-cooked food, but simply didn't have the time to make it themselves. Or the skills, perhaps. Hoshiko's grandmother had tried to teach her, but Hoshiko hadn't wanted to learn. It had all seemed so…irrelevant.

She took the cup Hameeda gave her and had a sip. "Perfect," she said, sincerely. "It's good."

Hameeda gave her a small smile. "My mother would be pleased," she said. "She always told me that the secret to being a good cook lay in attention to detail."

"My grandmother said the same," Hoshiko said. "That, and getting the right ingredients."

She wondered, suddenly, if Mariko Stuart had been a little homesick. She'd spent most of her life in America—and then the Solar Union—rather than her native Japan. But then, her memories of her home country would have been more than a little rose-tinted. Hoshiko was much younger and even *she* had trouble remembering that her childhood hadn't always been idyllic. The family asteroid had had its dangers as well as its pleasures.

They sat for a long moment in companionable silence, sipping their drinks. Hoshiko was enjoying the chance to relax, even though she knew the alert sirens might start howling at any moment. She couldn't stay for long. Her most pessimistic estimates indicated that it might be nothing more than a matter of hours before the enemy attack began. It was coming, she knew with a grim certainty that defied all contradiction. The Tokomak could no more leave her entrenched than they could abandon their jihad against the human race.

"I feel I could do more, now," Hameeda said, as she put her empty cup down on the table. "I think I understand what this ship can do."

"I'm not going to throw you away," Hoshiko said, firmly. The LinkShip was tough, but not tough enough to take on an entire enemy fleet. "And we're still trying to decide how to use you for more than scouting and spying missions."

Hameeda smiled. "I sent your staff a list of possible options."

"Half of which are insanely dangerous," Hoshiko said. "We will find you something to do, don't worry."

She smiled at Hameeda's crestfallen expression. She understood the urge to get out and prove oneself—it was why she'd climbed up the tallest tree on the asteroid when she'd been five years old—but she also had no intention of wasting an irreplaceable asset. The last she'd heard, the NGW program had decided to wait for Hameeda's full report before deciding if they wanted to produce a fleet of LinkShips. The cynic in her wondered if the real problem was the high cost of the program or the prospect of one or more of the pilots going mad.

"Thank you, Admiral," Hameeda said. She picked up the teapot. "More tea?"

"No, thank you," Hoshiko said. She stood. "I really should be getting back to my ship."

Hameeda smiled, rather wanly. "You're welcome anytime, Admiral."

Hoshiko kept her face carefully blank. She was Hameeda's superior officer, not her friend...and yet, Hameeda seemed to be hinting that she was desperate for company. Perhaps it would be best if she assigned a commando team to the LinkShip for a few weeks...one of the planned missions, after all, involved inserting commandos onto an enemy world. It would give Hameeda some company without suggesting that she was being indulged—or monitored.

Although she'd be a fool to assume that she wasn't being monitored, Hoshiko reminded herself. The project director's briefing notes had stated that practically everything on the LinkShip was being recorded for later study, just to allow the psychologists a chance to assess the impact of a permanent neural link on a human pilot. *I wonder what everyone will make of the files.*

She shook her head in irritation. Privacy was rare on a starship, certainly on a warship, but it still galled her to think that Hameeda would have *no* privacy. Even *prisoners* had more privacy. Hameeda had signed up for the program, in full knowledge of what would happen if she was accepted, but still...it was an unpleasant thought. Perhaps she'd suggest that the monitors be taken out, eventually. Or Hameeda might fly away from the Solar Union, preventing the monitors from ever uploading their files to the datanet...

"I'll teleport you back to your ship," Hameeda said. "The LinkShip can handle a place-to-place teleport without a pad."

Hoshiko grinned. "I thought that was forbidden."

"Not forbidden," Hameeda said. "Just taboo. And this ship *does* have enough processing power to make it work without any more risk than the average teleport."

"I know," Hoshiko said. She considered it, briefly. The longer the teleport, the greater the number of signal buffers, the higher the chance of an error that would fatally compromise the matter stream and kill her. She might as well step into a vaporisation chamber. It wouldn't need to be a *big* error either. And yet, it would show trust. "Do it, please."

The world dissolved into golden light, then reformed. Hoshiko had to smile as she looked around. She'd been teleported straight back into her cabin. Hameeda would have had to send the signal all the way to *Defiant*, then convince the cruiser to allow the teleport pattern to reform in the cabin instead of on a teleport pad. Even with her access codes, and Hoshiko's permission, it was an impressive feat. She glanced down at herself, just to make sure that everything was in place, then snorted. The old stories about teleporting mishaps where someone ended up with their partner's eyes or crossed with an insect were nothing more than old wives' tales. It was far more likely that a glitch in the matter stream would reduce her to dust.

Her communicator bleeped. "Admiral," Yolanda said. "There is an update from the planet for you."

"Understood," Hoshiko said. She brushed down her uniform. "I'm on my way."

. . .

Hoshiko had laid a minor bet with herself that the enemy offensive would begin within a week of the fall of Mokpo, which would give them more than enough time to bring a massive amount of firepower to bear on the gravity point. And yet, as the days slowly turned into a week, no enemy attack materialised. She watched the gravity point constantly, ready for anything…but nothing happened. Her crews were starting to feel the stress too. The waiting was getting them down.

She paced the decks of her cruiser, inspected the fortresses and discussed contingency plans with her officers that had already been discussed several times before, wishing—deep inside—that *something* would happen. Boredom was not something she handled well, certainly not when she had no one to turn to for advice or comfort. She almost wished she'd found *some* kind of companion, someone she could talk to without crossing rank boundaries in a manner that would harm both of their careers. Perhaps she *should* have pressed for a diplomat to be assigned to the fleet, rather than assuming that they'd be doing nothing apart from fighting to hold the system while grinding the alien fleet into powder. It might have been a mistake.

It will just have to be endured, she told herself, firmly. *And everyone else will have to endure it too.*

She put her crews through a number of simulations, ranging from a mass transit of enemy superdreadnaughts to a steady series of attacks that wore the defences down, asking—time and time again—what the enemy would do when the shit hit the fan. What the hell were they doing? They were going to attack...they *had* to attack. She could understand why they'd want to build up their reserves first—their fleet had to be spread out across several star systems—but delay would still cost them dearly. There had been dozens of freighters passing through the system in the last few hours alone, all of which had been denied transit. The Tokomak couldn't leave Apsidal alone indefinitely, could they? They had to recover the gravity point nexus before a large chunk of the interstellar economy fell apart.

Unless they want to blame us for the chaos, she thought. *That does make a certain kind of sense.*

She prowled the decks, attended meetings and projected a veneer of confidence whenever she encountered a reporter. They'd grown very persistent in trying to set up interviews—clearly, they'd grown bored of filing stories about the liberation of Apsidal—and she was running out of excuses. It grated on her, more than she cared to admit. The Admiralty would not be pleased if she managed to avoid *all* interviews. Citizens might have a right to privacy, but not military officers. And yet, she couldn't allow herself to get distracted. She'd stayed away from VR sims for the same reason.

"I think the crews just want the waiting to end," Commodore Yu observed, ten days after the fall of Mokpo. "The Tokomak are taking their sweet time."

Hoshiko nodded, savagely. Doctrine—Galactic doctrine—insisted that a thrust down a gravity point chain had to be pushed as far as possible. Giving the enemy time to dig in was almost always a mistake, although she had to admit that assault pods might have evened the odds somewhat.

Perhaps *that* was the delay. The Tokomak fabricators at N-Gann were rushing their own version of the assault pod into mass production. She supposed that made sense. The Tokomak hadn't seemed to care how many ships they threw into the fire, but even *they* had to have limits.

"Or they want to be sure they can take advantage of a crack in our defences," she said, although she knew the defences past the gravity point were tissue-thin. There were no really powerful defences until Varner itself, a mere fifty light years from Sol. "And they might be bringing up their fleet train."

"Or they're planning something clever," Commodore Yu said. He rubbed his forehead, testily. "Frankly, Admiral, something is going to blow. There have already been a string of incidents on the lower decks."

"It will all be over soon, one way or the other," Hoshiko said. The Tokomak *couldn't* delay forever. Even if they didn't realise the threat posed by human technology—and the prospect of the human race coming up with a game-changer—they couldn't take the risk of looking weak. Too many of their subject races hated and feared them for *that*. "They will come—and we will smash them."

"Yes, Admiral," Commodore Yu said. "We do have enough firepower to give them a very hard time, at a place of our choosing. And if we stop them dead, the entire galaxy will see that they can be beaten."

Hoshiko nodded. *Some* of the freighters that had passed through the system were spies, she was certain, although there had been no solid proof. The Admiralty was keen to make it clear that *humanity* wouldn't do anything to impede interstellar shipping. Quite the opposite, in fact. The Galactic Alliance would banish all the regulations and tech restrictions that had blighted commerce under the Tokomak. It would, she'd been assured, get the interstellar shipping community on their side.

Alarms started to ring. Hoshiko stood, grabbing her communicator. "Report!"

"A handful of ships just transited the gravity point," Yolanda said, crisply. The alarms grew louder. "It's begun."

CHAPTER TWENTY-ONE

"The first wave of ships has been deployed," the aide said. "They're jumping now."

Neola nodded, impatiently. It had taken longer than she'd wanted to prepare her forces for the decisive engagement, although she knew the delay might have worked in her favour. The timing was a little off, but she hadn't expected perfection in any case. Only a fool would try to carry out a complex plan on an interstellar scale and expect the timing to work just right.

"Very good," she said. The gravity point looked dull on the display. And yet, on the other side, antimatter explosions were devastating the first layers of fixed defences. She could barely imagine the sheer scale of the forces she'd unleashed. And yet...they weren't enough to win, not on their own. "Ready the second wave to jump."

She leaned back in her chair, knowing that—whatever happened—it was going to cost her badly. The humans had had plenty of time, if the reports were to be believed, to establish a formidable defence. Some of her analysts believed the enemy fortresses didn't exist, that they were nothing more than sensor ghosts, but Neola wasn't so confident. The humans had adopted a defensive posture that made no sense, unless one assumed the fortresses were real.

And we'll find out if they're real or not when they open fire, she thought. If Tokomak-designed fortresses possessed awesome firepower, she had no doubt that human-designed fortresses would do the same. *They'll either tear our ships to pieces or do nothing.*

"The second wave is ready, Your Excellency." Her aide looked up from his console. "Your orders?"

Neola smiled, coldly. "Send them through."

. . .

"They must be mad," Yolanda breathed, as forty enemy ships materialised in the middle of the gravity point. A handful interpenetrated and vanished in colossal explosions, but the remainder hastily oriented themselves as the nearest mines streaked towards them. "They practically committed suicide."

"They're expendable," Hoshiko said, coolly. It was stunning to her too, but she didn't want to show it. Her ancestors had crashed planes into ships in a desperate attempt to stave off inevitable defeat, yet they'd never expended so many ships so casually. It was a grim reminder, if she'd needed one, that the Tokomak had literally *millions* of ships and sepoys they could expend in their wars. "And they're burning their way through our defences."

She watched, grimly, as the enemy ships opened fire on the mines. There were too many mines for them to kill before it was too late, but it hardly mattered. The next wave of enemy ships would face fewer mines and the wave following *that* would face fewer still. And then the real offensive would begin, once the enemy had cleared a space to deploy. She knew she couldn't allow them the chance to start sending through battleships and superdreadnaughts.

Although, if they send them through one by one, we could blow them away piecemeal, she thought. *And we have enough missiles to end them all before running out of ammunition.*

The last of the enemy icons vanished. There was a long pause, then another set of red icons materialised in the display. Hoshiko sensed, more than heard, a wave of dismay rippling through the CIC. It was like playing a combat simulator where the enemy had unlimited resources and absolutely no hesitation in unleashing a massive human wave attack, climbing atop their own bodies to get at their targets. The Tokomak just kept coming.

No, she reminded herself. *There are no Tokomak on those ships. Just... expendable servants.*

She cursed under her breath as the enemy ships managed to unleash a salvo of missiles before they were wiped out. None of them posed a real threat—it looked as if the enemy ships hadn't had time to do any targeting before they opened fire—but they were a problem. The seeker heads would lock onto *something*, distracting her gunners from their work. *And* the missiles seemed to be standard-issue, utterly unimproved. Further proof, if she'd needed it, that the Tokomak considered the first waves to be completely expendable.

"Admiral," Yolanda said. "Commodore Yu is requesting permission to unleash the alpha platforms."

"Denied," Hoshiko said, curtly. She understood Yu's concerns, but they hadn't run out of mines yet. "Order him to keep holding them in reserve."

Another wave of enemy ships appeared on the display. One of them, incredibly unlucky even by the standards of a simultaneous transit, crashed into one of the previous wave of ships and both ships vanished from the display in a tearing explosion. Hoshiko hoped, as the mines swooped towards their new targets, that the blast had disrupted the enemy sensors. The mines were designed to be stealthy, but they weren't cloaked.

A pity the plan for self-replicating mines never got off the television screen, she thought, sourly. *It would make the gravity point impregnable.*

Her lips twitched. The Solar Union had access to nearly a century of science-fiction writers speculating about what humans could do with advanced technology, long before the technology had been captured from the Horde, but not all of the ideas had proven feasible. Yet. There was an insane lunatic who thought it would be possible to build a Death Star, although Hoshiko suspected it would be a giant waste of resources. Why would anyone build a giant space station that could be destroyed by a single starfighter pilot? It was only a matter of time before someone figured out how to build *starfighters.*

"The enemy ships are opening fire," Yolanda said. "They're targeting the alpha platforms."

"Raise Commodore Yu," Hoshiko said. The enemy had forced her hand, damn them. "He is to clear the targeted alpha platforms to engage the enemy."

She sucked in her breath as a handful of platforms died, a moment before their comrades opened fire. The Tokomak tactics were unbelievably ruthless—she couldn't imagine *humans* putting up with masters who were prepared to throw them into the fire in vast numbers just to gain a brief tactical advantage—but she had to admit they were working. Her defence plans were still workable, as far as she could tell, yet it was only a matter of time before the Tokomak cleared enough space to bring in the bigger ships. Her only real edge was that, so far, the Tokomak didn't know how much damaged they'd done.

Although they will have a very good idea, she admitted to herself. *And it won't be long before one of their ships survives long enough to cycle their jump drive and return to Mokpo.*

The fire and fury surrounding the gravity point steadily grew worse. Dozens of ships appeared, time and time again, some surviving long enough to orientate themselves and open fire. The minefields were nearly gone, save for a handful of mines at the very edge of the engagement zone; the automated platforms were taking a beating, even though she was trying to conserve as many of them as possible. It wouldn't be long before she would have to authorise the fortresses to open fire, keeping her fleet in reserve. And that would wear her defences down too.

At least we haven't lost anyone, she thought. The enemy was tearing her automated defences apart, but they hadn't managed to touch her manned facilities. *No human has died yet.*

Another wave of enemy ships appeared, then doubled. Hoshiko blinked in surprise. A handful of ships had interpenetrated and vanished, of course, but...for a moment, she couldn't understand what she was seeing. Had two groups of ships made transit within seconds? Had the enemy messed up the timing? Or...a quarter of the newcomers simply vanished. It took her a moment to realise that they'd jumped *back* through the gravity point.

Her terminal bleeped. "Admiral, this is Hoskins in Analysis."

"Go ahead," Hoshiko said.

"Our preliminary analysis suggests that there were two ships, physically linked together," Hoskins said. "The first one jumped through the gravity point, taking the second ship with it; the second ship jumped back, as soon as it had a chance to evaluate the situation. There'd be no risk of interpenetration because the ships were effectively one ship."

"And they did it dozens of times," Hoshiko said. "Damn it."

She bit down the urge to curse out loud as she realised the enemy had managed to get a message back through the gravity point. It was a neat trick. Simple, effective...and completely unexpected. No one had thought about sending two ships through at once, not in thousands of years...not unless the Tokomak had come up with the tactic, then kept it in reserve until it was needed. Whoever was on the other side was definitely no slouch.

"And that means we can expect further attacks, targeted against our weak points," she said, after a moment. "Can you see any way to counter the tactic?"

"No, Admiral," Hoskins admitted. "The second ship wouldn't have to wait to recycle its jump drive. We simply couldn't kill them all before it was too late."

Hoshiko nodded and closed the connection, then looked at Yolanda. "Contact the minelayers," she said. She was all-too-aware that she was sending a number of men—and aliens—to their deaths. "Tell them to start deploying additional mines."

"Aye, Admiral."

• • •

Neola allowed herself a cold smile as the first reports—the first *true* reports—flowed into her display. The expendable ships had done better than she'd expected, clearing layer after layer of mines and weakening the enemy's automated defences. They hadn't touched the fortresses, but she hadn't expected them to get anywhere *near* the heavier defences. There was no way to know—for the moment—if the fortresses were truly real.

But we have to assume they're real, she reminded herself.

"Order the next waves to continue the offensive," she said, calmly. "And ready the main assault elements to jump once the gravity point is clear."

"Yes, Your Excellency."

• • •

Space around the gravity point boiled and seethed in a constant wave of explosions as ships erupted into existence, launched their missiles and died in a blaze of glory. Hoshiko nodded to herself at the grim confirmation that the enemy had *indeed* managed to get a message back through the gravity point, as if she'd doubted it. Their targeting wasn't perfect, but it was vastly superior to their earlier attempts. They'd done most of the programming before their jump into the fire.

"They're targeting the fortresses," Yolanda observed. "But with only a handful of missiles."

Hoshiko frowned. The enemy didn't seem to have *hammers*...and without hammers, a lone missile or two was not going to take out a fortress. Even an antimatter-tipped missile wouldn't be enough to do real harm. They wouldn't even get through the point defence network. It made no sense.

"Order the missiles taken out as soon as possible," she ordered. She was jumpy, but the enemy *had* shown a disconcerting degree of imagination. Who knew what *else* they might come up with? "The minelayers?"

"Being engaged," Yolanda said. "The enemy isn't giving us the time to replenish the minefields."

Which isn't really a surprise, Hoshiko told herself, tiredly. *They've already expended a great deal of energy in clearing it.*

She watched the missiles die, one by one. They were antimatter-tipped, the deadly payloads detonating as their containment fields failed, but there was nothing particularly special about them. They wouldn't have done real damage even if they'd been allowed to strike the protective shields. The enemy would need to fire a great many more missiles to make a real impact.

It struck her suddenly. She smiled, shaking her head in disbelief. The Tokomak didn't think the fortresses were *real*! Of *course* they didn't. They hadn't bothered to develop any concept of prefabricated fortresses, let alone dragging the components along and assembling them on the spot in record time. The enemy CO might simply have assumed that the fortresses were ECM buoys, configured to look like fortresses. He'd fired the missiles to test the theory. And he'd learnt that at least *some* of the fortresses were real.

We should have layered deception decoys everywhere, Hoshiko thought. The Tokomak wouldn't have believed that the human race could have assembled hundreds of fortresses, ringing the gravity point in an impregnable sphere, but they wouldn't know which fortresses were real either. *That would have wasted a lot of their missiles.*

She grinned at the thought, then sobered as she looked at the display. The enemy ships were still dying, but her automated platforms were nearly gone and the minefields were a distant memory. A handful of enemy freighters materialised and began a charge towards the nearest fortress, only to explode with terrifying force when they were hit. There was no way the enemy was going to get a suicidal freighter, crammed with antimatter, close to a fortress, but the sheer size of the blasts was bad enough. Her sensors and communications networks were taking a beating. If the designers hadn't put so much redundancy into the datanets, it was quite likely that a few of them would have collapsed by now.

They're slowly pushing us back, she thought. *And there's nothing we can do about it yet.*

She contemplated her options as the never-ending flood of starships seemed to pause. The human fleet was holding back, but she could take her ships forward and engage the attackers directly. That would make it harder for the enemy to repeat some of their tricks, although it would also give the bastards a chance to hit her ships with a suicide freighter. Or she could just rely on the fortresses to handle the enemy ships. They'd been designed to seal off the gravity point, even if they had to take a beating in the process. She wondered, absently, if the Tokomak realised that the Solar Union had based its fortresses on their designs. There weren't *that* many improvements. They'd done a very good job.

"Admiral," Yolanda said. "An enemy ship just made it into FTL."

Hoshiko looked up, sharply. "It made it?"

"Yes, Admiral," Yolanda said. She nodded to a blinking light on the display. "She's already well past interception range."

"Interesting," Hoshiko mused. Going into FTL so close to a gravity point was dangerous. It wasn't something she would have expected from the Tokomak, although it was quite likely that the ship was crewed by one of their servant races. And yet…where was it going? The nearest enemy naval base was seventy light years away. "Keep an eye on her."

"She'll be outside sensor range in sixty minutes," Yolanda warned. "We'll lose track of her then."

"Understood," Hoshiko said. Another wave of enemy ships appeared on the display, spitting missiles in all directions. This time, they survived long enough to start enfolding the gravity point. "We'll worry about her later. Concentrate on the main threat."

She leaned back in her chair, taking a breath as more and more enemy ships flickered into existence. The attack seemed to be slowing down, as if the Tokomak had finally gotten sick of throwing so many of their servants into the fire. They were staggering the transits now, sending the ships in groups of three rather than twelve. It improved their odds of survival considerably, at least until they reached their destination. Their datanets barely had time to come up before human missiles started screeching in for the kill.

Maybe the bastards are getting sick of the slaughter, she thought, although she didn't really believe it. Her forces might have killed hundreds of thousands—perhaps millions—of servants, but it was a mere drop in the ocean. The Tokomak had *trillions* of servants from nearly a hundred different races. Everyone she'd killed was nothing more than a rounding error. *Or maybe they're planning something really bad.*

"Order the replenishment crews to start pushing the next set of platforms forward," she said, as space fell quiet. "We need to rebuild as fast as possible."

"Aye, Admiral," Yolanda said.

Hoshiko nodded. She'd killed hundreds of ships—it said something about the sheer scale of the forces unleashed that no one had an accurate count of how many enemy ships had been blown to atoms—but she knew she'd barely scratched the enemy fleet. If they were holding back, they were planning something. And that meant...what? She wanted to think they might be dealing with a mutiny, but she doubted it. She knew enough about how the Galactics kept their servants under control to suspect that mutiny simply wasn't possible.

And yet, they built a towering interstellar civilisation, she thought. Slave societies on Earth had invariably stagnated and collapsed. The Tokomak had stagnated, to some extent, but they hadn't collapsed. Instead, they were facing a major war that could inspire their servants to rise up in revolt. *Will they be able to keep their empire together long enough to beat us?*

A new wave of red icons appeared on the display, followed by two more. The enemy warships slid away from the gravity point, firing their missiles in all directions. A stream of smaller targets followed, launching away from the warships and heading out into space. Gunboats, Hoshiko realised. The enemy had turned their smaller warships into makeshift carriers. It was proof, she supposed, that the gunboats couldn't transit on their own. They were too small to carry a Tokomak-designed jump drive.

They'll have to slim the drive down, she thought. *Or cut out everything else, including life support, to give the gunboat the ability to jump.*

Yolanda sucked in her breath as a larger red icon materialised. "Admiral…"

"I saw," Hoshiko said, as the enemy battleship belched its first salvo of missiles. She'd been wrong. The Tokomak offensive had entered the next stage. "The big boys have arrived."

CHAPTER TWENTY-TWO

Commodore Yu paced his command deck, trying not to let the worry show on his face as the second enemy battleship materialised beside the first. They were already moving away from the gravity point, clearing the way for two more to follow in quick succession. The contemplative part of his mind admired the sheer nerve of the enemy officers in cutting the transit time down to a minimum; the more practical side of his mind cursed how rapidly the enemy firepower was multiplying. Their battleships were already launching massive salvos towards the fortresses.

"Contact all fortresses," he ordered. He didn't have to consult with Admiral Stuart. They'd already planned the battle. "They are authorised to fire at will. I say again, fire at will."

Fortress-One—no one had bothered to give the prefabricated fortress an actual *name*—barely shifted under his feet as it unleashed a massive salvo of its own. It was a far more stable launching platform than any starship, even though it was also a sitting duck. Yu was all too aware that his command could *not* jump into FTL if it was facing destruction, something the enemy would know too. The fortress's only *real* advantage was that the mass saved on starship drives had been spent on weapons, ammunition storage chambers and shield generators. It would take one hell of a beating to knock his fortress's shields down and, even then, the hull was incredibly tough. Fortress-One was designed to keep fighting even as she was battered into rubble.

The enemy missiles roared towards his point defence envelope. He watched them on the display, silently noting the text boxes that warned of missile improvements and a dozen different factors that proved they were facing the Tokomak, rather than their servants. Yu thought he would have spotted it even without the reports from the analysts. The missiles seemed to have a command network an order of magnitude more capable than anything else they'd seen so far. And they'd targeted his fortress.

His eyes narrowed. Did the enemy *know* they'd targeted the command fortress? Or was it merely a coincidence? There was no visible difference between Fortress-One and the remainder of the fortresses, nothing to suggest that it might be *special*. The command network consisted of tight-beam lasers...and, even if the enemy *had* managed to read the messages, they were repeated so often that it would be hard to tell where they'd actually originated. Hell, Yu knew his subordinates on the other fortresses would take command if Yu was killed or put out of contact. The enemy wouldn't gain anything if they took Yu out of commission.

Apart from a destroyed fortress, he thought, wryly. *That will give them an edge, even if Captain Hastert takes command at once.*

He frowned as the enemy missiles entered his engagement envelope. They weren't as sneaky as their human counterparts—and some of them were following a ballistic trajectory, making them easy prey—but they had some advantages of their own. A couple exploded with terrifying force when they were taken out, proving that they were antimatter-tipped; their deaths took out several of their comrades, threatening to trigger a chain reaction that would wipe out the remainder of the salvo. But the remainder just kept coming.

"Two of the enemy battleships have been destroyed," his tactical officer reported. "But they're still coming."

Yu nodded, stiffly. "Then we'll keep destroying them," he said. "They have to run out of missiles at some point, don't they?"

He frowned as a trio of freighters appeared on the gravity point. Were they loaded with antimatter? They *couldn't* be loaded with antimatter. The enemy battleships were sitting on the gravity point, firing in all directions. An antimatter explosion now would be a colossal own goal. The Tokomak might not give a damn about their servants, to the point where they were prepared to send them to their deaths in their millions, but surely they'd be a little more worried about their own people. And then the display blossomed with red icons.

"Gunboats," the tactical officer said. "*Hundreds* of gunboats."

"I see," Yu said. Gunboats were rare in fleet engagements—they were too small to defend themselves and too large to evade—but he could see some uses for the little craft. They could enhance the enemy point defence, if they wished, or harass the fortresses. He hoped they'd chose the latter. They'd be irritating, but they'd also be easy to kill. "Target them when they enter engagement range."

The steady flood of battleships showed no sign of letting up, even though the fortresses had more than enough combined firepower to keep them pinned on the gravity point. They belched wave after wave of missiles towards the fortresses, some of which inevitably got through the point defence and slammed home. Yu kept his face immobile as the damage reports steadily got grimmer and grimmer, although—so far—his damage control teams seemed to be keeping it under control. The real danger lay in simply shooting his magazines dry. He had thousands of missiles in each of his fortresses, but the enemy fleet was soaking them up with terrifying speed. It was easy to believe that he'd kill one enemy ship with each of his missiles, then watch helplessly as yet another enemy ship advanced on his position after he'd fired his last missile.

He gritted his teeth as his fortress shuddered under yet another impact. The aliens just kept coming, trampling on their own dead to get at him. He'd considered the defences impregnable, when he'd helped design them. They'd *all* considered the defences impregnable. It had been easy to understand why the wars had gone on for so long, before the Tokomak had invented FTL. Getting through a gravity point was incredibly costly. It was more surprising that the first Galactics hadn't realised they couldn't kill each other and decided to come to terms centuries before the Tokomak had turned the universe upside down.

"Sir, they're concentrating their fire on our forward shields," the tactical officer said, urgently. "They're trying to punch through the shield hexagon."

"Rotate the inner shields to compensate" Yu ordered. "And then bring up the reserve shield generators."

And hope we can stand up to the battering long enough to win, he added, silently. Another battleship made transit through the gravity point, a handful of destroyers following through on her tail. *This could get really bad.*

・・・

"The enemy fortresses are *all* real," the aide said. He sounded astonished as he accessed the latest reports. "Your Excellency..."

"I can see that," Neola said, keeping one eye on the timer. The enemy had done a remarkable job of preparing their defences, even though they'd faced severe limitations. She had to admit she was tempted to keep some humans around, if she could ensure they were kept under proper control. Their skills could be put to good use as she brought the known galaxy back under Tokomak rule. "Continue funnelling battleships through the gravity point."

She watched, coolly, as yet another battleship entered the gravity point and vanished. The battleships were far less expendable than the smaller ships, but they had to be risked at some point. She would have preferred to send in the superdreadnaughts, yet she simply didn't have enough of them to risk heavy losses. There were too many factions, even amongst the Galactics, who'd turn on the Tokomak if they thought their masters looked weak.

And we're not going to win the war simply by winning this battle, she thought, as she checked the reports. *We're still going to have to push on to Earth.*

Another report popped up in front of her. An enemy fortress had been destroyed. It looked to have been a lucky hit, a brief shield failure when one of her missiles had been in the perfect place to take advantage of it, but it had hurt the enemy. They'd be shocked to realise just how much of their firepower they'd just lost. Indeed, they'd have to bring their fleet forward to compensate for the disaster...

And that, she told herself, would be playing right into her hands.

• • •

"Fortress-Seventeen has been destroyed," Yolanda reported. "The crew had no time to reach the escape pods."

Hoshiko cursed. "Hoskins? What happened?"

"As near as we can tell," the analyst said over the intercom, "the enemy got lucky. Their missile went off too close to the fortress's missile elevators, destroying the warhead containment chambers. And the antimatter went boom."

"Shit," Hoshiko said. The fortresses were tough, but there were limits. No one could *really* prepare for an antimatter explosion *inside* a fortress. "If the enemy got lucky..."

"They may try to do it deliberately next time," Hoskins warned. "And we *have* to move missiles from the magazines to the tubes."

Commodore Yu can worry about that, Hoshiko thought. It was his job. She wouldn't peer over his shoulder without *very* good reason. *We have other problems.*

She studied the display, keeping her face under tight control. A cluster of red icons was sitting on top of the gravity point, just far enough from the gravitational nexus to be fairly sure they weren't going to interpenetrate with a new arrival. The Tokomak had managed to establish enough of a datanet, despite her best efforts, to ensure a degree of continuity as older ships were destroyed and newer ships arrived. Their missiles were seeking out their targets with lethal efficiency, while their gunboats were trying to shoot down human missiles that might otherwise hit the battleships. And the steady stream of warships was slowly starting to grow faster. It was only a matter of time before they started to send through the superdreadnaughts.

A blue icon flickered on the edge of the display. She glanced at it, then snorted in irritation. An interstellar convoy in FTL, one that hadn't heard that Apsidal was closed to shipping. They were in for a surprise when they arrived at the gravity point. She wondered if they'd stick around to see who won or simply turn around and flee back into FTL. They weren't the only freighters heading to Apsidal too. Anyone unlucky enough to be in transit when the shit hit the fan might not have *heard* that it had hit the fan.

Poor bastards, she thought, although she wasn't entirely averse to an audience. The Tokomak had already taken heavy losses, including forty battleships. Their fleet was vast, but it wouldn't suffice to keep their empire under control if *everyone* rose up against them in one vast wave of hatred. *I wonder how many of the Galactics wish they had a chance to send observers to this fight.*

She dismissed the freighters and turned her attention to the gravity point. Losing one of the fortresses was a serious matter, particularly as her remaining fortresses were also taking a beating. In theory, they had enough firepower to hold the line; in practice, she wasn't so sure. It might be time to order her ships to advance and blow the battleships off the gravity point. If nothing else, it would give her ships a breathing space. Her crews would probably kill for a chance to rest. The battle hadn't lasted more than a few hours, but it felt as if they'd been fighting for *days*.

"Signal the fleet," she ordered. "The battleline will prepare to advance to engage the enemy."

"Aye, Admiral," Yolanda said, as another wave of red icons popped into existence. "The fleet is responding now."

The enemy CO must be feeling the heat, Hoshiko thought. Two of the newcomers interpenetrated and died, but the remainder—all destroyers—hurried forward to take up positions between the battleships and their enemies. *How many of his people can he throw into the fire before they throw* him *into the fire?*

"The fleet is ready," Yolanda said. "Admiral?"

"The battleline will advance to Point Horn"—Hoshiko tapped a place on her console, marking it on the display—"and engage the enemy."

Defiant quivered under her feet, as if she was eager to come to grips with her foe. Hoshiko sat back on her chair, watching grimly as the fleet slowly advanced. The sheer volume of firepower they could put out would blow the enemy battleships to vapour, allowing her to regain undisputed control of the gravity point and putting the enemy advance back for hours. Days, perhaps. The enemy CO had spent her ships like water. It was hard to believe that even the Tokomak had an *unlimited* supply of ships, no matter who was crewing them. The Tokomak had built their fleet up over centuries. How quickly could they replace what they'd lost?

We don't have a hope of out-producing them, Hoshiko reminded herself. She'd seen too many facts and figures to doubt it. Even if the Tokomak *never* improved their weapons, let alone anything else, they'd still have an edge. Humanity could only win by outthinking them, by coming up with completely new concepts. *They don't seem to have come up with anything genuinely new for centuries.*

She braced herself as the fleet slowly advanced on the gravity point, allowing the range to close before opening fire. The enemy battleships *must* have seen them coming, but they continued to pound on the fortresses rather than the fleet. Hoshiko suspected that was a mistake on their part, although she understood the logic. The fortresses would have to be destroyed if the enemy wanted to take the system, but humanity's starships were far more important in the long run. A dozen fortresses could easily be left to wither on the vine once Sol and the Solar Navy had been destroyed. It was surprisingly short-term thinking for the Tokomak.

A human might become so fixated on the short-term that he would ignore the long-term, she thought. Hitler had become so focused on Stalingrad that it had cost him the war. *Would a Tokomak feel the same way? Or would he be aware that this system, as important as it is, isn't the be-all and end-all of existence?*

"Prepare to fire," she ordered, putting her thoughts aside. Her hand came down on the console. "Fire!"

Defiant shuddered as she unleashed a full broadside. The other ships followed suit, pumping thousands of missiles towards their target. An enemy battleship popped into existence on the gravity point, its crew no doubt utterly stunned to see the wave of destruction advancing towards them. Hoshiko fought down a very unprofessional urge to giggle. The enemy ship would barely have time to get a salvo of missiles off before it was smashed to dust.

"Two of the enemy battleships jumped out," Yolanda reported. "The remainder are powering up their drives. And their gunboats are charging the missile swarm."

Too late, Hoshiko thought, vindictively. The enemy ships didn't seem to have made any serious preparations to retreat—absently, she wondered if the ships that *had* escaped had better commanders—until it was far too late. *You won't escape me now.*

She watched, feeling cold hatred flourishing in her heart, as the tidal wave of missiles burst through the gunboat formation and fell on their targets. The Tokomak fought desperately, their point defence datanets weaving their ships together into a single entity that didn't waste so much as a single plasma bolt, but it wasn't enough. Antimatter explosions peppered their formation; knocking down their shields, exploding against their hulls and vaporising their ships. The entire enemy formation died within seconds.

"Hold the fleet here," Hoshiko ordered, as silence fell over the battlefield. The remaining enemy gunboats were charging her ships, but none of them had a hope of hurting her. Her ships picked them off, one by one, as they entered engagement range. "Order the minelayers to return to their work."

She stared at the silent gravity point, wondering when the next enemy ship would make the jump. It wouldn't be long, she was sure. The Tokomak knew better than to give their enemy a chance to rest and recuperate, even if they were feeling the pressure themselves. And they *shouldn't* be feeling any real pressure. *Their* ships were sitting on the far side of a gravity point, completely safe. They *knew* they were safe.

And I need to teach them that that isn't true, she thought. The Tokomak would need to keep their fleet close to the gravity point. They'd be within range of her assault pods. *That might weaken their will to continue the war.*

She looked at Yolanda. "Order the fleet to prepare to deploy assault pods," she said. "And contact the LinkShip. I'll require her to scout the gravity point."

"Aye, Admiral," Yolanda said. She paused. "It will take two minutes to flush the assault pods into space."

"Understood," Hoshiko said. There was no point in urging everyone to hurry. Her crews would move as fast as they could. "It will take the enemy some time to decide what to do anyway."

She forced herself to think. What would *she* do? She'd want to call off the assault altogether, but she doubted the Tokomak considered it an option. They *needed* to smash their way into Apsidal to reach Earth, unless they wanted to dispatch a fleet on a five-year mission through FTL. There were probably ways to cut the journey time down, she thought, but it would still be a major commitment. They'd be putting a vast number of ships out of commission for years. And that would weaken them at the worst possible moment. They might reason that their only *real* hope was to continue the offensive, whatever the cost...

An alarm howled. She looked up at the display and stared in horror. Red icons. Dozens—no, *hundreds*—materialising behind the fleet. Her mouth fell open in shock. They couldn't be real. They just couldn't be real. The Tokomak could *not* have put a fleet in position to attack her from the rear.

But they had.

CHAPTER TWENTY-THREE

For a long moment, Hameeda's mind simply refused to accept what she was seeing.

It was impossible. There was no way the Tokomak could have slipped so many ships into position to attack the fleet from the rear without *someone* noticing. Their stealth technology was nowhere *near* good enough to avoid fluctuations as they crept through a gravity point. And yet, her sensors were not having flights of fancy. The Tokomak had somehow put an entire fleet in a place that allowed them to pin the humans against the gravity point. They'd turned the entire battlefield upside down.

The freighters, she thought numbly, as her awareness expanded sharply. The enemy ships were belching missiles, aimed directly at the human fleet. Alerts flashed up as her sensors picked up a handful of hammers amongst the swarm. *They literally towed the ships into attack position and we never even saw them coming.*

She dismissed the thought for the inevitable post-battle assessment and recrimination session, assuming it ever happened, and turned her attention to survival. Her subroutines raced through a number of simulations at terrifying speed, adjusting the odds as her sensors picked up the first wave of graviton pulses. The Tokomak had no intention of allowing the human ships to move away from the gravity point, slip into FTL and run for their lives. No, they were trapping the human ships in space and setting them up for a pounding. And there was barely any time to retreat.

Shit, she thought. Whatever happened, the human ships were going to take a beating. The trap had been turned on its head. *What do we do now?*

...

A long time ago, when she'd been a little girl, Hoshiko's father had told her that she spent too much time plotting what she'd do to her opponents—on the gaming board, in the VR world, on the playing fields—and not enough time contemplating what they could and *would* do to her. Aggression was a useful skill, if handled properly, but it wasn't invincible. An enemy who refused to allow himself to be bullied into making mistakes—or herself assuming she was unstoppable simply because she'd moved first—would be able to take advantage of the inevitable problems with her strategy and turn it against her.

And now the Tokomak—the *Tokomak*—had done it to her.

She ignored the startled panic over the communications channels, the alarm running through the CIC, as she forced herself to think. The enemy had clearly outthought her. They'd either had a plan to mass a fleet near Apsidal or hastily put one together when they'd realised a large human fleet was on its way. Probably the latter, she suspected. The timing had been good, but far from perfect. They could have drawn ships from a dozen minor fleet bases and combined them into a major force.

Think, she told herself. *There's always a way out.*

But she couldn't see it. The enemy were deploying gravity-well generators of their own—a human trick they'd copied—and her fleet was effectively trapped in normal space. She could turn and run, abandoning the fortresses, but she'd still be trapped in a missile duel with an enemy fleet that was perfectly capable of doing immense damage before she finally outran it and escaped. Or she could charge the enemy fleet, knowing that it would hurt her badly and perhaps even cost humanity its chance to win the war. Or…nothing else came to mind. It was only a matter of time before the alien fleet resumed its attack through the gravity point, catching her on both sides…

…The gravity point.

Her mind raced. What if they went *through* the gravity point? They'd lose the fortresses and probably quite a number of ships, depending on what they encountered on the far side, but the main body of the fleet might survive. And then…they'd be cut off from Sol, yet they might just manage to break back through the gravity point and retake Apsidal. It was a desperate plan, the sort of scheme that would probably have gotten her kicked out of the academy, but she couldn't think of anything better. She *had* to preserve her fleet.

"Prepare the assault pods for immediate launch," she ordered, sharply. "And then inform Commodore Yu that he needs to prepare the Omega Contingency. And then…"

She shook her head. "No, I'll tell him myself," she added. There was a very good chance that Yu and most of his crews wouldn't survive the next few hours. She owed it to herself to speak to him personally. "Tell the LinkShip to execute the assault pod scenario on my command."

"Aye, Admiral."

Hoshiko nodded. There was no denying the fact that her plan had failed spectacularly. Her fleet—and the landing force on Apsidal—was going to pay a major price for her failure. But if she could preserve the warships, she might just be able to turn the situation on its head once again. Might.

"Tell the remainder of the fleet train to launch a courier boat back to Sol, then go dark," Hoshiko added. "If they don't hear from us in a month, they are to return to Sol by the fastest possible route."

"Aye, Admiral." Yolanda looked pale, but composed. "Commodore Yu is on the line for you."

"Put him through," Hoshiko said. "And then start launching the assault pods."

• • •

Hameeda couldn't help feeling nervous as she approached the gravity point, trying not to think about the prospect of an enemy battleship materialising right on top of her. The LinkShip's subroutines insisted that the odds were very low, but they were astronomically greater than they'd be anywhere else. She was mildly surprised the enemy hadn't already resumed their attack through the gravity point. Had they screwed up the timing? Or were they too busy licking their wounds?

They probably planned to catch us while their battleships held the gravity point, she thought, as she triggered her jump drive. The universe seemed to blink. *Instead, we defeated one threat before the other could arrive.*

Mokpo appeared in front of her, the sheer bulk of the enemy fleet slamming into her awareness with all the subtly of a charging elephant. There were hundreds of superdreadnaughts and battleships, each one large enough to smash the LinkShip out of existence and never even notice what it had done. And they were slowly moving towards the gravity point, flanked by a swarm of destroyers and cruisers. Ice seemed to congeal around her heart. For the first time, she wondered if they might lose the battle.

She concentrated on preparing targeting solutions, ready for the assault pods. Admiral Stuart wouldn't delay launching them, would she? But it still felt like hours before the wave of assault pods transited the gravity point. Hameeda ignored the flashes of energy as a dozen of them interpenetrated and died, focusing instead on providing targeting data to the pods before the gunboats could kill them.

A moment later, the pods opened fire.

• • •

Neola blinked in surprise. She'd started to think that something had gone very wrong with the timing, judging by the failure of the reserve fleet to make its appearance before her battleships were driven back through the gravity point or destroyed, but there was something desperate about the human tactic. They'd thrown hundreds of assault pods and thousands of missiles through the gravity point, as if...as if they wanted to drive her back.

Careful, she warned herself, as a tidal wave of missiles roared towards her ships. She didn't dare fall into the trap of believing what she *wanted* to believe. *They might be trying to drive us back instead.*

"Deploy the next wave of dual-jumpers," she ordered, leaving point defence in the hands of her more capable subordinates. "I want to know what's on the other side of the gravity point!"

...

"The fortresses are engaging the alien fleet," Yolanda reported. "But the fleet is continuing to fire on us."

"Unsurprising," Hoshiko said. A missile crashed against *Defiant's* shields, sending a shockwave through the entire ship. "They want to smash the fleet first."

The LinkShip popped back into existence on the display. "I'm getting a feed from her sensors," Yolanda reported. "The assault pods deployed as planned."

"Then order the fleet to start jumping, as planned," Hoshiko said. "And pray."

She gritted her teeth. Sending so many ships through a gravity point in a tight stream practically *guaranteed* at least one collision. She'd seen too many enemy ships interpenetrate to have any doubt about the results. And yet, she simply couldn't see any alternative. The enemy fleet was inflicting considerable damage on her fleet. The only way to break out was to do something insane.

They say a retreat under fire is the most dangerous manoeuvre in the tactical manual, she thought, as the first elements moved up to the gravity point and vanished. *But what about a tactical retreat when you have to get your men through a rabbit hole, also while under fire?*

She pushed the thought aside and concentrated on her ships as they moved towards the gravity well. The enemy didn't seem to have realised what they were doing—there were so many ECM decoys going online that they were having trouble telling the real ships from the fakes—but it was only a matter of time. God alone knew what was happening on the far side, in Mokpo. If the enemy CO reacted quickly, he could slam the door closed and sentence her fleet to inevitable destruction.

"Fortress Seven was struck by a hammer," Yolanda reported. "Major damage, all sectors."

"Try to beam the crew off," Hoshiko ordered, although she suspected it would be completely futile. There was so much electromagnetic distortion in the combat zone that a teleporter matter stream was likely to be completely disrupted. The crews would be better off taking to the lifepods. She hoped the Tokomak would take prisoners. "And then..."

She cursed under her breath. There were so many automated weapons platforms and ECM buoys in the vicinity that it was quite possible that the lifepods would be mistaken for mines and blown out of space. The Tokomak wouldn't have to have a 'take no prisoners' policy to accidentally slaughter helpless victims. Merely being paranoid about human tricks would be more than enough.

The ship shuddered, again. "They're targeting us, Admiral," Yolanda said. "I think they know we're leaving."

"It looks that way," Hoshiko agreed. "Let's just hope we can keep the fleet together until we get through the gravity point."

. . .

Neola resisted the urge to unleash a string of blistering curses as her fleet reeled under the impact of enemy missiles. The—she couldn't think of a word unpleasant enough to describe the confoundedly innovative race and their new weapons—had somehow targeted her ships, even though their assault pods should still have been scrambled by the jump through the gravity point. And her fleet had taken a beating. Dozens of ships had been destroyed, hundreds had been crippled...she had plenty more, she knew, but her losses were becoming worrying. It was not to be borne.

Her eyes narrowed as the first human ships started to advance through the gravity point. It was incredible! They were going on the offensive... wait. She looked closer, feeling her heart start to race as she realised the human ships were actually pulling *away* from her warships and heading into deep space. An entire stream of starships...

"They're running," she said. Understanding clicked. The timing hadn't been *too* badly off, then. The reserve fleet had arrived, as planned, and trapped the human ships. And the humans were fleeing *through* the gravity point. It was madness, but it might just give them a chance to survive. "Order the fleet to advance. We'll slam the door closed, once and for all."

. . .

Hoshiko had always been told that a naval officer, particularly one with her heritage, shouldn't leave her people behind to die. It gnawed at her, as *Defiant* passed through the gravity point, that she *had* left too many people behind. Commodore Yu and his crews had known the risks, they'd all volunteered *knowing* the risks...and yet, she felt as if she'd betrayed them. She *had* betrayed them.

The display filled up rapidly. Hoshiko sucked in her breath as, for the first time, she saw the full might of the alien fleet. It was immense. It looked as if the vast number of losses had barely even *weakened* the fleet. And it was advancing right towards the gravity point. She didn't dare let it get too close.

"Launch one barrage," she ordered, as tactical combat groups were hastily reorganised. Her order of battle was an absolute mess. The neatly-organised squadrons were a thing of the past. She silently blessed her commanders and crewmen for training so hard. Throwing together a combat group on the fly would be difficult, but doable. "And then set course for RV Point Orange. We'll jump into FTL as soon as the fleet clears the gravity point."

The latest update—a constant liturgy of disaster—scrolled up in front of her, but she ignored it as her fleet unleashed a barrage of missiles. A handful of ships were still popping through the gravity point, bringing with them the final messages from the fortresses. She felt another pang of guilt. She'd given Commodore Yu the authority to surrender, if he felt it wise, but there was no way to know how the Tokomak would react. They certainly wouldn't be pleased if Yu refused to allow human technology to fall into their hands. *That* was something that might anger them to the point they slaughtered all of the remaining humans without further delay.

"The fleet is clearing the edge of the gravity field," Yolanda reported. "But there are elements that will not be able to jump for several minutes."

"Order them to prepare for evacuation," Hoshiko said. Her missiles were striking home, roaring through the enemy defences to slam against their targets, but it wasn't enough. She'd been cut off from her supplies too. The weapons she had with her were the only ones she'd have until she fought her way back into Apsidal or died. "We can't afford a delay."

She looked at the enemy fleet. What would it do? Try to chase down her fleet? It had the firepower and numbers to do it, if its CINC wished. Or…secure Apsidal? It would be the smart move. Did they have enough ships to do both?

Yolanda's voice broke into her thoughts. "Admiral, the fleet is ready to drop into FTL."

Hoshiko took a breath. "Then take us into FTL," she ordered. "And hope they don't follow us."

...

"The enemy has jumped into FTL," the aide reported. "Shall we pursue?"

Neola fought down her delight and considered it. Giving chase, running the wretched fleet down, was a very tempting thought. She certainly had enough ships to keep advancing her combat elements forward while keeping track of the enemy fleet's location. But the human fleet was cut off from its base, in a sector where it could expect little in the way of sympathy and nothing in the way of actual *help*. The only place the humans could get supplies was N-Gann and the base was practically impregnable. No, they'd wither and die on the vine.

"No," she said. "We'll take the fleet to Apsidal instead."

...

"Fortress-Two has taken heavy damage, sir," Commander Ella reported. "Fortress-Nine has been effectively destroyed."

Commodore Yu nodded, feeling nothing but cold hatred for the aliens. They'd mouse-trapped the human fleet—somehow—and he and his men were going to die. There was no way out. The contingency plans had never considered that the aliens would somehow manage to get a fleet on the wrong side of the gravity point, but he had known there was a chance that his fortresses would have to be abandoned. He didn't blame Admiral Stuart. The fleet—and the fleet train—was far more important than the fortresses.

I knew the job was dangerous when I took it, he thought, wryly.

"Continue firing," he ordered, shortly. "Throw everything at them."

"Aye, sir," Ella said. "Including the kitchen sink?"

Yu grinned, despite himself. "Why not?"

He sobered as he watched the next wave of enemy ships popping out of the gravity point. The fleet must have escaped, then. He hoped it had escaped, even though he knew he would never know. The aliens were pushing the offensive, steadily wearing down his defences and punching missiles through his shields…

"Incoming hammers!" Ella's voice was filled with alarm. "They're targeting us!"

"Deploy countermeasures," Yu snapped. He had to hand it to the Tokomak. Their countermeasures were crude, but they were better than their human counterparts. "And then…"

"Too late, sir," Ella said, grimly. The enemy hammers were coming in too fast to be stopped. "Incoming!"

"Abandon the station," Yu ordered, sharply. "I say again…"

• • •

"The enemy fortresses have been destroyed," the aide said. He slapped his chest in glee. "The gravity point is clear."

Neola smiled. She'd won. The greatest space battle for a thousand years and she'd won. It was *her* victory. None of her rivals would ever be able to take it from her. People would be studying the battle for centuries, learning from her success…and her enemy's mistakes. It was definitely *her* victory. She was so pleased she couldn't even bring herself to be annoyed at her aide. Maybe she'd keep him around after all.

"Very good," she said. Apsidal appeared to have been cleansed of the human infection, but she knew that was an illusion. Their remaining ships had either slipped into cloak or fled into FTL. "Order the fleet to advance towards the planet. It's time to take it back."

CHAPTER TWENTY-FOUR

"The fleet is gone?"

"For the moment, we have to assume the worst," Martin said, as the squad took up positions near the massive spacedock. "Major Griffin knew little more than anyone else."

He gritted his teeth. The fleet was gone, fleeing through the gravity point to escape certain destruction. *Yolanda* was with them...he hoped. He didn't want to think of her being dead instead, her body reduced to free-floating atoms in space. It was a horrible thought. He pushed it away, savagely. The Tokomak were on their way. It wouldn't be long until the marines were engaged.

The spaceport was...odd. It felt more like a planetside spaceport than a space-based facility, although there was no air outside the Apsidal Ring. And yet, freighters could land on the ring—dock with the ring—and unload their cargos as casually as if they'd landed on a planetary surface. The giant hangars, set within the ring, allowed freighters to be maintained and, perhaps, warships to be concealed. Martin couldn't help wondering if the Tokomak had missed a trick there. They could have hidden hundreds of starships inside the ring and the invaders wouldn't have known until it was far too late.

But the ring would draw fire, if they turned it into a naval base, he reminded himself. *And if chunks of it broke up and started to fall on the planet below, it would be disastrous.*

He felt a flicker of awe as he accessed his implants and contemplated the spaceport through the embedded sensor network. It was immense, far larger than the giant spaceport he'd seen on Mars, a network of docking ports, warehouses, personal quarters and hotels for wealthy travellers. A visitor to Apsidal could spend his entire stay in the spaceport and miss nothing, apparently, although that struck him as stupid. Why bother travelling hundreds of light-years just to stay in a spaceport? But then, the Galactics never seemed to realise that planets were *big*. The human spaceborn had the same problem.

Which is stupid, Martin thought. *Earth is more than just religious fanatics, corrupt governments and millions of people too cowardly to breathe free.*

The enemy shuttles came into view, firing decoys as they dropped down fast towards the spaceport. They were unchallenged, but their pilots were taking no chances. Martin nodded in approval, even though he knew he'd be fighting and killing some of the aliens in a few hours. The Tokomak soldiers weren't taking anything for granted. They *knew* the Apsidal Ring was infested with humans and rebels. And the lack of any attempt to stop them from landing probably worried them. Martin knew there were times when *he* was happier taking incoming fire than waiting for the other shoe to drop.

He smiled, grimly, as the shuttles grounded themselves in the warehouses, rather than the docking ports. It was good thinking on their part, he noted; he'd have been suspicious of the docking ports himself, even though he happened to know they hadn't been sabotaged. Instead, the Tokomak flowed out and into their warehouse, their weapons at the ready. Their bodies moved oddly—he felt a shiver running down his spine as his mind fought to accept their mere existence—but there was nothing wrong with their technique. A little unpractised, perhaps...

"They're not Tokomak," Sergeant Howe subvocalised. "I don't know what they are, but they're not Tokomak."

Martin blinked in surprise, then nodded. The Tokomak wouldn't want to waste thousands of lives—thousands of their *own* lives—on the Apsidal Ring, not when they had millions of servants to throw into the fire. He studied the suited figures for a long moment, wondering just which species they actually were. One of the ones that wanted to get out from under the Tokomak? Or one of the servant races that regarded them as gods? But there was no way to know, at least for the moment. The invaders wore black armour that covered their bodies from head to toe.

"They're going to be moving through the warehouse," he said, as he checked his terminal. A pair of sensors had dropped out of the network, their final reports suggesting that they'd been destroyed. The Tokomak would presumably not be keen on their servants destroying their population control systems, but as long as they didn't actually *command* the network it was nothing more than a liability. "We'll meet them as planned."

He checked his rifle as they waited, watching a handful of additional sensors go off the air. They'd been warned that the Tokomak wouldn't let them keep the network—that it would be destroyed if there was a chance the enemy would regain control—but it still felt as if he'd been struck blind. Martin kicked himself, mentally. He'd been trained to fight in the fog of war. It was really too much to expect the enemy to put up beacons and IFF signals to make them easier to identify and kill.

Fighting on Earth taught us some bad habits, he thought, crossly. The insurgents and terrorist shitheads they'd faced on Earth had *never* realised just how good the Solar Union's surveillance systems really were. Martin had had no trouble identifying and isolating his targets, from terrorist masterminds to the thugs who enforced religious laws on entire communities. *The Tokomak have far more understanding of what we can do than any of our human foes.*

"Here they come," Sergeant Howe muttered.

"Take your places," Martin ordered. "And prepare to bug out."

The Tokomak infantry appeared at the far end of the giant warehouse, advancing forward with the familiar mixture of determination and squeamishness of untried troops. One group advanced forwards while the other provided cover, then held in place to allow the other group to leapfrog to the next position. Martin felt an odd sense of kinship, even though the aliens were as alien as could be. No, that wasn't entirely true. The Tokomak and the other Galactics weren't *that* alien, not compared to some of the non-humanoid races. Their thinking wasn't too different from humanity's. And the soldiers in front of him were *very* familiar.

They advanced forward, picking their way through the maze of giant storage boxes as if they expected to be jumped at any moment. Martin didn't blame them for being nervous. The rebel factions on the planet below expected precisely *no* mercy from their former masters, not if they managed to retake the Apsidal Ring. They'd probably planned on the assumption that every last inch of the Apsidal Ring would be turned into a booby-trapped nightmare to rival Fallujah, Tripoli or Beijing. The absence of any visible threat would probably unnerve them more. But then, the ring *was* huge. Billions of aliens could be lurking further along the torus and the invaders would never know.

Martin tapped his terminal, once, as the aliens reached the centre of the room. The IED detonated violently, blowing a dozen alien troopers into atoms. Their body armour was *good*, he noted, as his men opened fire. The IED hadn't taken out more than a handful of the invaders, even though several more had been caught in the blast. They were injured, but alive.

The remaining aliens hit the deck, then returned fire with a savage intensity. Martin took cover, noting that the alien weapons didn't seem to be particularly advanced compared to the samples captured during the Battle of Earth. Perhaps the Tokomak had not seen fit to give their sepoys their best weapons. Or, perhaps more likely, they'd seen no need to issue advanced weapons to alien troopers they considered expendable. It didn't make any difference, Martin thought. Their plasma blasts were burning through the human position at a terrifying rate.

He unhooked a grenade from his belt, counted to two and hurled it into the enemy position. Two of his men followed suit, setting off a series of plasma explosions that silenced the enemy weapons for a few seconds. Martin covered his eyes, despite his implants, from the blaze of white light, then sounded the retreat. The platoon crawled backwards with only minimal grumbling, leaving a handful of traps in their wake. Martin understood the desire to just stay where they were and keep shooting, but real life wasn't a video game. The enemy would bring their immense firepower to bear on his position and that would be disastrous.

We don't want to die so early in the game, he thought, as they entered an access shaft and slid down to the next level. Behind him, he heard an explosion. One or more of the booby traps had been tripped. *They might risk firing on us from orbit if they knew we were so close to the ring's outer shell.*

He tapped out a message to Major Griffin, then uploaded it to the ring's communications network. Relying on the network was a risk, no matter what the WebHeads and AIs said about how easy it was to hack Galactic computers, yet it was safer than sending microburst transmissions from place to place. The engineers swore blind that the Tokomak wouldn't be able to localise a microburst transmitter—not in time to do any good, in any case—but Martin found it impossible to take that for granted. Even a rough location would be enough for a killshot if the Tokomak decided to unleash some of their nastier weapons. An old-style MOAB blockbuster would kill them all without damaging the ring.

They passed through an airlock, then paused to assess the situation. The enemy troops were spreading out to secure the spaceport—*all* of the spaceports—before they started to drive on the control centres. It wasn't a bad tactic, he supposed, although *he* would have preferred to capture the control centres before they could be destroyed. But then, the human troops *had* had plenty of time to destroy the entire ring. The Tokomak might see little point in hurrying.

"They're moving to secure the transit tubes too," Sergeant Howe observed. "They may think they can use them to outflank us."

Martin nodded. The vactrains themselves—trains that moved at awesome speeds through the transit tubes—had been shut down, but the tubes themselves could be used to move soldiers and shuttles through the ring. He wondered, idly, if they'd have the nerve to fly a shuttle through the tubes. It would give them a chance to bring considerable firepower to bear on the human positions, if they were willing to take the risk. *He* might have tried it, if he'd been attacking the enemy...

"There are other units in place to counter that possibility," he said, as another explosion echoed in the distance. The enemy would have problems getting out of the transit tubes, unless they used the stations...and *that* would force them to emerge at an easily-predictable location. "Right now, we have to make them pay."

He tensed as he heard a rattling sound in the distance. The aliens were advancing forward again, flooding troops down the corridors. He checked their position, then motioned for his men to take cover behind the airlock. The control system was already disabled. There was no way to open the hatch, save by brute force. He wondered, as he took up position himself, if the Tokomak would have the patience to cut the hatch open or if they'd simply blow it to pieces. It would be a difficult task. The interior airlock wasn't particularly inferior to a docking port. Whoever had designed the ring had been *very* careful.

Which is good, Martin thought. His lips twitched in cold amusement. *It's good that they did that.*

A dull *thud* echoed through the chamber. Martin had a second to realise that the enemy's *first* attempt to break down the door had failed before there was a second, much larger explosion. The airlock hatch shuddered, then fell inwards and crashed to the ground. A team of enemy soldiers emerged from the smoke, their weapons sweeping for trouble. Martin gave them a handful of seconds to relax, then barked a command. His men opened fire with savage intensity. Five aliens fell dead at once.

"Grenade," Sergeant Howe shouted. "Get down!"

Martin ducked, sharply, as the alien grenades exploded. They seemed to be conventional HE, rather than plasma charges, but there were a lot of them. He tossed back a grenade of his own, then snapped out the command to retreat as it detonated. The alien advance seemed to slow, just long enough for the marines to beat feet down the corridor to the next prepared ambush site. He wondered how long it would take the aliens to reach them or if they'd concentrate on securing the spaceport rather than chasing a small human unit into a potential trap.

We'll see, he thought. He checked the updates, then smiled. The aliens hadn't been stopped—no one had seriously expected them to be stopped—but they had taken a beating. It might just slow them down for a while. *And that will buy time for the fleet to return.*

. . .

"They're definitely forcing their way into the transit tubes, Major," MCCLELLAN said. The AI didn't sound alarmed, although—as a third-gen AI—MCCLELLAN had emotional as well as conversational overlays. "They've already taken out the sensors."

Major Griffin nodded, curtly. "I take it they haven't managed to hack the control system yet?"

"No," MCCLELLAN said. "I can keep them out for the moment."

"Good," Major Griffin said. "Inform me if that changes."

He turned his attention to the terminal and studied the developing situation. MCCLELLAN was not a battlefield commander—he'd thought, at first, that the AI's name was a joke—but there were few humans who matched its capabilities for absorbing and analysing vast amounts of information. Indeed, like its namesake, MCCLELLAN was a genius at logistical planning and operations. Griffin and his superiors didn't have to work through a vast logistics staff to get things done. They could simply order the AI to handle it.

But that will change, Griffin thought. *We're going to have to leave the control rooms soon.*

There was no denying it. The enemy were pushing their offensive hard, now they'd secured the spaceports. They'd taken some losses—and some of their probes had been wiped out completely—but they were still coming, climbing over the bodies of their own dead. It angered Griffin, in some ways, to see how casual the enemy commanders were with the lives of their men. He'd been a professional soldier long enough to know that lives should *never* be spent freely.

"They're attempting to hack the network," MCCLELLAN said, suddenly. "I'm countering them, for the moment, but they're using a brute-force attack keyed to hardwired control functions. I can't keep them out forever."

"Then keep them out as long as you can," Griffin ordered. "Can you maintain a link if we disengage the physical connection?"

"Yes, but not for long," MCCLELLAN informed him. "And their sensors may be able to track me. I may have to go dark."

"They'll be here in an hour, unless they slow down," Griffin said. He'd prepared a number of possible escape routes, all of which led into a maze of corridors, transit tubes and maintenance depots. The Tokomak would have problems sealing off *all* the possible ways to leave the control centre, unless they chose to devote most of their manpower to occupying chokepoints. "We'll leave in forty minutes, unless the situation changes radically."

"It might," MCCLELLAN said. "I've lost the active sensors on the ring's surface, sir, but the passive sensors are reporting a new wave of shuttles. My best estimate is that the enemy intends to land another twenty thousand men."

Griffin smiled. Twenty thousand men was nothing to laugh at, not when they might *all* be advancing on his position, but the sheer *size* of the ring would be too much for them. Twenty thousand men would vanish without trace in a single sector, let alone the whole ring. And yet, as long as the enemy held the right places, they could safely ignore the remainder of the ring until the war was over. He wondered, morbidly, if they'd start venting chunks of the structure. It would be one way to cleanse the ring of unwanted life forms. And the Tokomak were certainly ruthless enough.

"We'll deal with them when we see them," he said. "Have you managed to make contact with any fleet elements?"

"No, Major," MCCLELLAN said. "The skies appear to be uniformly hostile."

"Then we'd better prepare for a long war," Griffin said. There was no point in dwelling on the very real possibility that the war would continue until all of them were dead. He glanced at the terminal, then nodded to himself. "Inform the troops, please. We're shutting this command centre down and evacuating in forty minutes."

"Yes, sir," MCCLELLAN said.

Griffin watched his men hastily pack up the handful of supplies and equipment they'd moved into the command centre, then emplace demolition charges around the chamber. They wouldn't do *that* much damage, he knew, but they'd slow the enemy down while they searched for replacement consoles and supplies. Hopefully, they'd class the whole affair as human incompetence...and ignore the cluster of viruses and malware inserted into the computers network. The ring was going to have real problems until the Tokomak could clear out the infection, which wouldn't be easy. Their reluctance to use AI was going to bite them in the rear.

"The enemy have made a breakthrough," MCCLELLAN reported. The terminal flashed red, indicating that a delaying team had been wiped out. There were no details, but they weren't needed. "They'll be here sooner than expected."

"Then we go now," Griffin said. He raised his voice. "Set the charges to detonate in ten minutes, then *run*."

CHAPTER TWENTY-FIVE

Hoshiko sat in her cabin, staring at her sword.

It was an antique *katana*, she'd been told. Her grandmother had brought it from Japan when she'd moved to America, but its history stretched back into the mists of time. Noble warriors had worn the sword when they went into battle, although she wasn't sure how many of the stories she really believed. And yet, it had clearly meant something to her grandmother. Hoshiko had only been given the sword after she saw combat for the first time. She'd been told to keep it with her, despite the risk of losing it. She had to pass it down to her children when they too saw the elephant.

And yet, she thought she understood—now—why so many of her grandmother's people had committed suicide, rather than face up to their failures. It must have seemed impossible, in such a prideful culture, to admit that one had screwed up. She'd found it hard to admit her own errors too, even when she'd gone to the academy. But now...she hadn't just made a fool of herself. Her mistakes had cost her fleet badly. It was tempting, very tempting, to just commit *seppuku* to atone for her mistakes.

And that would mean leaving everyone else in the lurch, she thought, feeling a flash of contempt for her ancestors. How many of them had chickened out of facing up to their mistakes by taking their own lives? How many of them had given up when they could still be redeemed? And how many of them had left the blow to fall on others when it should have been rightfully theirs? Hoshiko had never let her brothers be blamed for *her* misbehaviour, back on the family asteroid. *I owe it to my crews to get them out of this mess.*

In hindsight, the mistake was all too clear. She'd watched hundreds of freighters entering and leaving Apsidal during the occupation. It had been just...background noise. And, when the system was under heavy attack, she'd ignored the convoy approaching the gravity point until it was far too late. If she'd suspected the truth, if she'd taken a handful of precautions, she could have kept the enemy trap from snapping closed. But who would have dreamed of such a plan? Coordinating an offensive on an interstellar scale was incredibly difficult. The KISS principle was the founding platform of interstellar warfare doctrine.

They have enough ships to make it work, she thought, sourly. In hindsight, the timing might have been a little off. If the second fleet had arrived sooner, her fleet would have been trapped between two fires. *The only thing that saved the fleet was enemy incompetence.*

She pinched herself, hard. The enemy had *not* been incompetent. They'd tried something that shouldn't have worked at all and come *very* close to pulling it off. A little more luck and her fleet would have been destroyed. *She* would have been killed, her crew would have been killed... and the road to Sol would lie open. She'd underestimated her enemy and paid a steep price for it. If nothing else, she should have realised that the Tokomak would try to copy everything they'd seen. Knowing that something was possible was half the battle.

Her intercom bleeped. "Admiral," Yolanda said. "The commanding officers are ready for the conference."

"Are they?" Hoshiko fought down her irritation. She'd already faced one attempt to remove her from command, back in the Martina Sector. *That* had been a close-run thing and she hadn't screwed up anything *like* so badly. "Do you have a comprehensive set of reports?"

"Yes, Admiral," Yolanda said. "Do you want me to forward them to you, or present them at the conference?"

My ancestors would close their eyes and ears to bad news, Hoshiko thought. *And they would take refuge in a fantasy world.*

She wondered, wryly, just how many of her civilian ancestors had believed the lies they were told. American carriers were being sunk in their hundreds, but the ships were being sunk closer and closer to Japan with each battle. Midway, Guadalcanal, the Philippines, Guam, Leyte Gulf, Iwo Jima, Okinawa...anyone who looked at a map, if maps had been available in Imperial Japan, would have known that the Americans were closing in. Perhaps the propaganda had also backfired. The Americans were taking staggering losses and they were *still* advancing.

"You can present them," she said. It was no favour, but no one would blame Yolanda for Hoshiko's mistakes. "I'm on my way."

She walked into the washroom and splashed water on her face before inspecting herself in the mirror. Her face looked grim, but otherwise composed. She wondered, morbidly, if some of her commanding officers had *expected* her to commit suicide. They knew that she'd gotten them out of the mess, but only after she'd gotten them *into* the mess...she shook her head, brushed back her hair and headed for the hatch. It was time to plan their next step.

The conference room was brimming with holograms, overlapping in a manner she had come to detest, but she couldn't help noticing just how *few* holograms there were. There should have been more, a lot more. But Commodore Yu and his subordinates were dead, along with dozens—hundreds—of *her* subordinates. She took a long breath as she sensed the despondency pervading the compartment. The Solar Navy had lost battles before, but never on such a scale. And the route to Earth lay open.

"Attention on deck," Captain Lifar said.

Hoshiko took a moment to survey the holograms as they turned to look at her. They looked grim, but not angry...not yet. She wondered how long it would be until they started to blame her for the disaster. The plan had been her brainchild, even though hundreds of staffers had worked on it. She had been the one who'd authorised the final version, she'd been the commanding officer...the buck stopped with her. And yet, she didn't have *time* to fight for her command. The situation was dire.

"We lost a battle," she said, crisply. There was no point in pretending otherwise. They were competent military officers, not reporters or civilians. "And we took a beating. Yolanda?"

Yolanda stepped forward, her hands clasped behind her back. She was the lowest-ranking officer present, but her stance showed no awareness of it. Her face was calm and composed as she spoke. Hoshiko wished that some of her other officers could borrow that calm.

"We managed to get four hundred and seventy ships through the gravity point and into deep space," Yolanda said. "The remaining warships that were near the gravity point must be presumed destroyed, although they *may* have managed to escape and link up with the fleet train. It is certain that none of the fortresses remain in our hands. We cannot tell if they were captured or simply destroyed."

She paused to let her words sink in, then continued. "The supply situation is dire," she added, slowly. "Seventeen ships are deemed beyond repair, at least without supplies we don't have. The remainder are terrifyingly short on ammunition. We must assume that the enemy is capable of keeping us from returning through the gravity point to link up with the fleet train."

"They don't have prefabricated fortresses," a captain grumbled.

"They have enough ships to hold a gravity point against us," Hoshiko said, flatly. Her ships had only a handful of assault pods left. The Tokomak would *love* a chance to force her into a conventional gravity point assault. It would end very badly. "Getting back through the gravity point is not an option."

"We can strip the disabled ships of supplies and weapons," Yolanda said, "and transfer missiles around the fleet to ensure that the modern ships have full loads, but we'd be pushing the limits as far as they will go. In short, we have enough ammunition for one fairly short engagement and that will be that. A long engagement will leave us without *any* missiles to shoot at the enemy."

And we'd be shot to pieces while we closed the range so we could bring our energy weapons to bear, Hoshiko thought. She'd known the situation was bad, but it was clearly worse than she'd thought. *The Tokomak would love that too.*

"We need options," she said. *Asking* her subordinates for ideas, particularly in a public forum, would make her look weak or indecisive, but she was past caring. "We need to find a way to flip the situation before they secure their supply lines and start the advance on Earth."

"We could block their supply lines," Captain Pringle said. "We have enough firepower to tear any convoy to shreds."

"Or we could punch our way through to GS-3532," Captain Leedey offered. "And then we sit on the gravity points, blowing them away as they come through."

"And then they will simply overwhelm us, as they did in Apsidal," Captain Nolan sneered, rudely. "Or outflank us by going through GS-3531 and GS-3530."

"Do you have a better idea?" Captain Leedey glowered at Captain Nolen. "Or are you just talking bullshit?"

Hoshiko slapped the table. "We are in a bad situation," she said, sharply. "We are *not* going to start fighting amongst ourselves."

"We could take the supplies," Commodore Ross suggested. "It isn't a long flight to Palladio, Admiral. That world could probably supply us with everything we need."

"And I'm sure that world will be heavily defended too," Captain Nolan said. "*Could* we take everything as easily as you suggest?"

"And would they have everything we need?" Captain Thaddeus looked grim. "Their missiles will need to be modified before they can be fired from our tubes."

"The modifications aren't hard to make," Commodore Ross reminded him. "Come to think of it, we could modify the tubes instead. They were designed for hasty modification if necessary."

"And then what?" Captain Nolen said. "Do we return to Apsidal? *Can* we return to Apsidal? Or do we play *The Lost Fleet* and run rampant in their rear for a few months until they gather the force to tear us to shreds? Or…"

Hoshiko gritted her teeth as an argument threatened to break out. The hell of it was that the doubters had a point. They *were* cut off from Sol. Even if they set off immediately in FTL, heading directly for Sol or for the nearest gravity point that led in the right general direction, it would be months before they reached home. In the meantime, the Tokomak could funnel ships and men down the Apsidal Chain and turn the Solar System into a burned-out cinder. She had no doubt they'd do it. Her long-range sensors had detected signs of intensive bombardment on Mokpo. And then…

The fleet cannot endure forever, she thought. Her cruisers were designed for long-term missions, but there were limits. *We'll be worn down in time, even if the enemy doesn't manage to catch us. And then our ships will start to fail.*

Her mind raced. There had to be a solution, something so unconventional that the Tokomak wouldn't see it coming. And yet…what? The LinkShip could get back through the Apsidal Point without being detected, but then…what? Try to sneak elements of the fleet train through the point, gambling that the Tokomak wouldn't insist on inspecting and searching the fleet? *She* would insist on searching every starship that passed through the point, even if it imposed immense delays on interstellar shipping. The Tokomak wouldn't miss that trick, not when control of the gravity points underpinned their empire. That, and a network of naval bases in prime position to control the core sectors…

A thought struck her. What if…what if the fleet went to N-Gann?

On the face of it, the idea was insane. The Tokomak base was heavily defended. If she'd had any doubts about that, they'd faded when she'd seen the LinkShip's reports. And yet, the sheer level of defences around the base was more than enough to convince the enemy CO that she wouldn't risk attacking N-Gann. It would come right out of left field.

Obviously, she thought. *They'd assume that we'd be smashed flat if we did.*

And yet...there *was* a flaw in the defences. Not a big one, perhaps, but one that could be exploited. Capturing N-Gann—or even devastating the facilities—would put the enemy schedule back *years*. The Tokomak hadn't paid anything like as much attention to their fleet train as the Solar Union, but why *should* they have? They had a massive network of bases they could call on for support. Excitement ran through her as she realised the plan might just work. If nothing else, she'd force the enemy to dance to *her* tune for a change.

"We need to move," she said. "And we need to hit the enemy in a place they won't expect."

She outlined her plan, careful to keep the details a little vague. Her staff would have to go over the plan—and all the intelligence reports—in cynical detail, just to make sure that they didn't overlook any obvious weaknesses. But...she thought it would work. If they could take and hold N-Gann, the Tokomak fleet would have to reverse course and recover their base or risk running out of supplies. And even if they merely did immense damage to the base, it might be worthwhile in the long term. A delay worked in humanity's favour.

"They'd have to expect us to go for the base," Captain Nolen said. "It's the highest-priority target in the sector."

"I thought that was Apsidal," Captain Leedey jibed. "Admiral... can we take N-Gann? Or will we just bleed ourselves white against the base's defences?"

"I think we can take the planet," Hoshiko said. "At the very least, we can lay siege to it."

She tapped the table before another argument could break out. "Let us be brutally honest," she said. "We cannot fight our way back to Apsidal. Raiding the remainder of the sector will be easy pickings, for a time, but there is very little worth the effort of stealing. And our raids will *not* do humanity's image any good. The Tokomak will portray us as pirates and they'll be right."

"The ignorant sheeple on their worlds already *think* we're ravening monsters who somehow pose an immense threat without posing any sort of threat at all," Captain Nolen pointed out, dryly. "That sort of double-thinking is quite common amongst the Galactics."

"The spacers have more awareness of reality," Captain Marin said. "And it is *their* support we need."

"Quite," Hoshiko said. "And, quite apart from all that, we cannot get back to Sol."

She allowed her voice to harden. "We took a beating," she said. "Yes, we were outthought and defeated. But that is not an excuse to stop fighting. You *know* what will happen if—when—the enemy fleet reaches Sol. Our entire system will be destroyed. And while there are a few colony ships heading as far from Sol as they can, there is no guarantee that any of those seeds will grow into a new Solar Union. The Tokomak have got to be stopped.

"We will head for Falladine in two hours. That will allow us to reach Galan—hopefully without being intercepted—and make the crossing to N-Gann. My staff will work out a plan to either take the planet, or lay siege to it. And we will put that plan into action. Unless, of course, any of you have a better idea."

There was a long moment of silence. Hoshiko almost regretted it. She had no compunctions about using a good idea, even if someone else had thought of it. If she'd missed something, if there had been an easy way out of the trap, she would have recommended whoever thought of it for promotion and medals. But there was nothing. They had one desperate plan—and nothing else.

"Dismissed," she said, finally. "And, if any of you have time to pray, please ask God for His help."

She watched the holograms vanish, then looked at Yolanda. "Get Operations to start work on planning," she said. "If there are any major flaws in the concept, I want to know about them before we reach our destination."

"Aye, Admiral," Yolanda said. She looked tired, now the holograms were gone; tired and stressed. "I'll get right on it."

Hoshiko eyed her for a long moment. "Get some sleep afterwards," she ordered, although she doubted it was a kindness. Yolanda's partner was on Apsidal. He might easily be dead by now. "I'll see you in the morning."

She watched Yolanda go, then keyed her console. "Get me Captain Hameeda."

Hameeda appeared in front of her. Hoshiko's eyes narrowed, just for a second. Hameeda seemed to have regressed, even though she'd done well—very well—during the savage engagement. A few more LinkShips might have made a *real* difference. But then, a few hundred more cruisers would have made a difference too.

"Admiral," she said. "What can I do for you?"

"We're going to N-Gann," Hoshiko said. She pushed her doubts aside. "And I have a very specific task for you—two tasks, really."

Hameeda looked brighter. "Are they dangerous?"

"Very," Hoshiko said. "The first is relatively simple. I want you to survey Mokpo, then move up the chain to Winglet and cross the interstellar void to meet us at Galan. We need to know what the enemy is doing."

"Aye, Admiral," Hameeda said. She sounded a little bored. There was little chance of being intercepted in Mokpo as long as she was careful. "And the other?"

Hoshiko allowed her smile to widen. "Now, *that* is the really interesting task..."

CHAPTER TWENTY-SIX

"Your Excellency," Representative Kumar said. "You are...rather young."

"And you lost control of your entire planet," Neola said, trying to keep the snarl out of her voice. Kumar was clearly too stupid to remember what she'd done to the Gerontocrats, let alone realise that she could do the same to him. "You'd be dead now, if the humans hadn't kept you alive."

She turned her attention to the planetary display, ignoring the wretched elder's babbling. He was old enough to be her great-great-grandfather, yet he had none of the wisdom her honoured elder had displayed. Kumar certainly didn't have the self-awareness to realise that he really *did* have the humans to thank for his survival. The mobs roaming the planet's surface, now the human forces had transferred themselves to the ring, were slaughtering every last Galactic they could find. And there was very little she could do about it.

"Your task is to put your system back into operation as fast as possible," she said, without looking at him. In the old days, it would have been an unpardonable insult. But, in the old days, seniority alone determined promotion. "Can you handle it?"

"Once those vermin are removed, I can handle it," Kumar said. "But the council demands that you provide support..."

Neola turned, slowly. "Demands?"

Kumar seemed to hesitate, just for a moment, as he finally realised what sort of dangerous waters he'd sailed into. But he was too stupid to close his mouth and let the matter go.

"My family—and the other families—own property on the surface that must be recaptured," Kumar said. "You must devote troops to…"

Neola snapped her fingers. Two guards hurried over.

"Remove this idiot to the cells," she ordered, sharply. "He'll be going back to the retirement camp."

She ignored Kumar's protests, then his shouts, as she turned her attention back to the display. The planet itself was worthless, particularly with the population in revolt. She had few qualms about bombarding the world into dust and ash, and then bringing in a replacement population, but she didn't want to risk damaging the ring. It was the key to the planet's rebirth. No, the ring had to be retaken piece by piece. And it was a *very* slow operation.

But it has to be done, she thought. *We have to rebuild the sector's economy.*

She sighed, inwardly. She'd won the greatest battle for a thousand years, but she still had to cope with the aftermath. Her fleet was being repaired and readied for the drive on Earth, if she decided to continue the offensive. She really needed Apsidal up and running, both as an economic hub and a supply base for her fleet. She'd already sent messengers back to N-Gann with orders to forward the supplies to Apsidal. But would the ring be ready to support her fleet?

We're going to need to build up a whole new fleet train, she reflected. In hindsight, they'd grown too comfortable with their network of naval bases. *And then we're going to have to expand the network towards the rim.*

Her lips quirked. She'd won. Her problems were the problems of victory. The enemy commander, on the other hand, had lost. Who knew how *she* was feeling?

. . .

The chamber was shrouded in darkness, despite the presence of a single light-globe high overhead. Martin crept forward, moving between the stacked boxes until he could see the small alien team clearly. They seemed to be moving supplies from the spaceport down to the transit tubes, now they'd been opened and pressed into service. The semi-darkness didn't seem to bother them. He suspected that they'd either been enhanced, like the marines, or naturally happened to have better eyesight than humans. There were some races that were practically nocturnal.

And they're alone, he told himself. The Tokomak had searched the area thoroughly, then redeployed their hunter-killer squads to search the other sectors. *Unless they're bait in a trap.*

He tensed, then slowly drew his knife from his belt. It felt *right* in his hand, although his instructor had told him that bringing a knife to a gunfight was always a mistake. He glanced back to make sure his team were ready, then threw himself forward. The alien he'd targeted barely had a moment to react before Martin wrapped his left arm around him and sliced his throat wide open. There was a gurgling sound as the alien collapsed to its knees. Martin allowed himself a moment of relief—no one had been *entirely* sure the monofilament blades would cut through the alien armour—then checked the others. All five aliens had been killed before they'd managed to get a shot off.

"Check the doors," he subvocalised, as he rolled the dead alien over and struggled with its helmet. It was a blank mask, stripped of all individuality; it was nothing like the fearsome helmets he'd worn during his service. He pulled at it for several seconds before finally figuring out how to pull it free. The alien face stared up at him. "Shit."

The alien was...very alien. It's face—he had no idea if he was looking at a male, a female, or a weird and wonderful alien gender—was covered in brown prickles, rather like a small hedgehog. The eyes were dark pools, without any visible iris; he wondered, suddenly, if his sense the aliens might be nocturnal was correct. Human pupils tended to expand to catch the light in darkness.

"A Hatchet," Sergeant Howe said. "That's as close as we can get to pronouncing their name, sir. They're known for being a warrior species."

Martin shrugged. The Hatchets—or whatever they really called themselves—were good, but not invincible. His marines had cost them dearly already and there would be more to come, as the fighting continued to expand. It was interesting to know just *which* species they were fighting, but he had no idea if the information had any practical value. Perhaps they could use stun-grenades or flash-bangs to disorientate the enemy. If they were nocturnal, they might be blinded by a sudden flash of light.

"Sir," Trooper Paris hissed. "I hear trouble."

"Time to go," Martin said. The temptation to stay and fight was almost overwhelming, but they were in the middle of enemy territory. Merely getting in had been a difficult task. They might kill the first responders—they *would* kill the first responders—but they'd be caught and killed by the rest. "Let's move."

He kept a wary eye out for danger as they made their way back to the garbage tubes. He'd disliked the idea of crawling through waste, back during basic training, but now he'd come to terms with the idea. It wasn't as if he'd expected to be clean and tidy when he'd joined the marines. If he'd wanted comfortable beds and easy duties, he would have joined the Solar Navy. Or the Solar Guard. Besides, the Tokomak might not realise just how easy the waste pipes were to navigate. They were taller than the average human. They might see the waste pipes as being too small to use effectively.

Though they do have smaller species under their command, he thought, as he clambered through the hatch, slamming it shut behind him. His mask, thankfully, kept him from the worst of the smell. *They should at least consider the possibility.*

He dismissed the thought as they made their way through the pipe. The entire system had been shut down for the last week, leaving most of the waste trapped in the pipes. He didn't envy the poor slobs who'd have to clean up the mess, once the occupation force got around to restarting the system. They'd have a nightmare on their hands. He wondered, grimly, if the Tokomak were hoping to force the insurgents to surrender by systematically weakening the life support systems. The ring was huge, far larger than a conventional asteroid habitat, but there were limits. Its environment was very far from natural. It wouldn't take *too* much to push it over the edge.

"That girl isn't going to look twice at me," Trooper Rowe complained. "I *stink*."

"So, no change there," Trooper Paris said. "Perhaps you should date Alice instead. I happen to know she has no nose."

Rowe snorted. "And how does she *smell*?"

"*Terrible*," three voices said, at once.

"It's nothing a good shower won't cure," Martin said, tetchily. *His* girlfriend was somewhere on the other side of the gravity point, he hoped. "Or you can take a wash in the pond up ahead."

Rowe shot him a mock-betrayed look. "Very funny, sir," he said. "It's true, then. Senior officers get their sense of humour surgically removed when they get promoted."

"Not removed, just twisted," Martin said. He grinned. "For example, a junior soldier looks very funny when he jumps into a pool of clear liquid and discovers, too late, that it's alien piss."

"Hah," Rowe said. "I..."

The roof fell in, just behind them. Martin leapt forward instinctively, unslinging his rifle as he heard the sound of armoured boots clattering into the pipes. He spun around, opening fire as the aliens brought up their own weapons. A dozen aliens died, but more were coming all the time. They'd tracked the patrol and mounted a surprise attack of their own.

Clever bastards, Martin thought, as he felt the ground beneath his feet begin to shift. The ring's main supports were very strong, practically indestructible, but its interior was nothing of the sort. They might be about to fall down to the next level. Anyone who lived there was in for a nasty surprise. *A million tons of alien piss and shit are about to land on their heads.*

He threw a grenade up into the alien position, then snapped out a command. "Fall back."

The team moved, laying down covering fire as they ran. Martin saw odd-coloured flames dancing among the alien wastes, as if they were on the verge of exploding. Gunpowder had originally come from shithouses, if he recalled correctly. Was something going to blow? A grenade exploded, further down the tube. Were the aliens trying to cut them off? Or...

"Contact ahead," Howe snapped. "Sir, we're cut off!"

"Blow a hole in the ground," Martin ordered. The pipe was already weakening. A good explosion might allow them to jump down to the next level. The aliens had already done it, damn it. Why couldn't he? "Now!"

"Fire in the hole," Sergeant Howe barked. "Brace for..."

Martin looked away as the shaped charge detonated. The pipe base seemed to waver, then collapse in on itself like a whirlpool of destruction. Liquid—he didn't want to think what—spilled through the hole, heading downwards. Martin snapped orders, throwing a pair of grenades back at the aliens as the humans headed down to the next level. The shock of the explosion weakened the pipe still further, forcing him to jump in a hurry. Liquid waste pooled around his ankles as he landed in a heap. There was no time to brush it off.

"Harper's snapped his leg, sir," Rowe said. "I'll carry him."

"Give your grenades to me," Martin said, ignoring Harper's protests. No one doubted that Harper was a tough guy, but there was no time for pride. Better the indignity of being carried than either slowing the rest of the troop down or being left behind. "I'll cover you."

"Yes, sir," Harper managed. He was breathing hard, his face pale and sweaty despite his combat implants. The damage had to be worse than it looked. "I can still hold a pistol..."

"If we need you to," Martin said, as the small troop hurried away from the aliens. "But, for the moment, concentrate on remaining quiet."

The sound of crashing debris and alien shouts echoed all around them, but there was no sign of any immediate pursuit. He allowed himself a moment of relief. The aliens must have put the plan together on the fly, as soon as they'd realised how the humans planned to escape, without substantial forces in reserve. It was a grim reminder that the aliens were better soldiers than he cared to admit. They might have been killed if the aliens had had more time to set the trap.

He glanced at Harper's leg as he started to feel they'd broken contact successfully. It wouldn't be hard to repair the damage normally, not in a regular medical centre. Harper had broken bones during training—they'd *all* broken bones during training—and he'd been up on his feet again within the hour. But now, with most of their medical facilities with the fleet?

Hopefully, the medics can fix it themselves, he thought, as they turned down another corridor and out of the area the Tokomak had occupied. *And if they can't...*

He shook his head. He was sure it wasn't going to come to that. And if it did...

We knew the job was dangerous when we took it, he told himself. *Harper might just have to sit on the sidelines for a few weeks.*

It was nearly an hour before they reached the base camp, hidden deep within the maintenance tunnels between levels. Major Griffin had set it up carefully, then used his AI to erase all mention of the tunnels from the ring's command network. It wasn't perfect, Martin thought, but even if the aliens realised the tunnels were there...they'd still have literally thousands of miles of tunnel to search if they wanted to find the base. He nodded politely to the soldiers on guard, then helped Rowe to carry Harper over to the medics.

"He'll be fine," the medic assured him. "It just might take a little longer to get him ready to go back to the fight."

Harper coughed, weakly. "How much longer?"

"A few days," the medic said. "You can lie on your backside until then, surely."

"Definitely not," Harper said. He looked at Martin. "Sir, I..."

"Do as you're told," Martin said. "And that's an order."

A young infantryman hurried over to him. "Sir, Major Griffin wants to see you."

Martin nodded, spoke briefly to Sergeant Howe, then hurried after the infantryman. Major Griffin had set up his office in what Martin privately thought had once been a janitor's closet, although there was no way to know what the empty room had been intended for before it had been pressed into service. Perhaps it had been a prison cell. It was certainly bland enough to serve as a jail.

"Martin," Major Griffin said. "I hear you ran into a little trouble?"

"Just a little," Martin said. He ran through the full story. "Sir, these guys are fucking *good*."

"They must have gotten lucky," Major Griffin mused. "It was dangerous letting you have a free shot at their workers. Still..."

He shrugged. "We'll just keep sniping at them," he said. "And when the fleet returns, we can take the offensive back to them."

"Yes, sir," Martin said. "And what if the fleet does not return?"

"The bastards need this ring," Major Griffin said. "And I intend to keep it from them as long as possible."

...

General Wooleen had one great advantage, as far as Neola was concerned. He was young, a mere two hundred years old. Old enough to have some real experience, young enough to be a little more flexible than the deadwood that had infested the army's high command...and, she admitted privately, attractive enough that she would consider taking him as a consort after the war was over. And yet, he wasn't telling her what she wanted to hear.

Which is his job, she reminded herself, sharply. *I need to know the truth, not what they think I want to hear.*

"The ring is simply vast," Wooleen said, flatly. "Your Excellency, it will take years to secure it with the present level of force."

"We need that ring," Neola told him. "Is there any way to speed up the process?"

"Not unless you want to negotiate with them," Wooleen said. "Your Excellency, we are fighting a war on...well, what is effectively an interstellar scale. We simply don't have the manpower to drive them out of the ring, or even to keep them from hitting us and then running away."

"Vent the ring," Neola suggested. Kumar would complain, but Kumar wouldn't be a factor ever again. He was waiting for his free trip to the retirement home. "Blow the atmosphere into space."

"That's not technically possible," Wooleen said. "The ring was designed to make it impossible for someone to vent the atmosphere. And most of the safety systems are automatic. We'd have to tear open hundreds of compartments ourselves to vent the atmosphere. It would take longer than we have."

Neola cursed. In theory, she had all the time in the universe. In practice, she was racing against a clock...a clock she couldn't even *see*. How long would it take the humans to come up with something *new*? Something that would turn her entire fleet into scrap metal? Or...something that would let them win the war in a single blow? She knew there was room for technological development and improvement. They were locked in a race, a race she didn't dare lose. She wanted to press on to Earth—and leave the human invaders and their fleet to wither on the vine—but she needed to keep her supply lines open. There was no way she could sustain an offensive without them.

"Then concentrate on securing the outer layers of the ring," Neola said. They could bring in extra troops as the new conscripts were trained. Perhaps they could even turn the ring into a training base. "But hurry, General. Time is not on our side."

"No," the General agreed. "It never was."

CHAPTER TWENTY-SEVEN

Hameeda was feeling...out of sorts as she flew the LinkShip back to Mokpo.

She'd grown used to her own company. The LinkShip didn't need a crew and there was nothing, save perhaps for companionship, that she couldn't get from the datanet. But Admiral Stuart had attached a pair of observers to her ship when she'd given Hameeda her final orders. It felt... *strange* to have company. It felt as if she'd been alone for years. But Admiral Stuart hadn't given her a choice.

She scowled to herself. The awareness subroutines were keeping track of her guests and, the moment she thought of them, they snapped into her awareness too. Jeannette O'Neil was sitting in front of a terminal, playing *Sonic the Hedgehog*; Shaun Conner was sleeping, tossing and turning in his bed. Hameeda reminded herself, stiffly, that she was supposed to grant her guests a certain degree of privacy, although there was no such thing on the LinkShip. The monitors were everywhere. She could hear a whispered comment from the other end of the ship.

You're being stupid, she told herself, pulling her thoughts away from her guests. It wasn't easy. The neural net was designed to provide her whatever information she wanted, as if she was a WebHead browsing the datanet by following random links. It reacted to her merest whim. *You don't need to worry about them.*

She turned her attention to the Mokpo System as she crossed the system limits and headed towards the gravity point. The researchers *claimed* they'd found a way to peer out of FTL, but—so far—it remained purely theoretical. She could see the gravity shadows cast by the star and its family of planets, yet there was no way to see anything smaller. Even the gravity point was invisible to her. The tight knot of gravimetric forces wouldn't be visible until she was a great deal closer.

And there's no way to know what we'll encounter, she reminded herself. The Tokomak *shouldn't* be able to see her coming—there was no sign that they'd figured out that there *was* a way to travel through FTL without being detected—but she had to be careful. *They'll have put a strong guard on the gravity point.*

She cleared her throat, opening the intercom. "Your attention please," she said. Her awareness snapped back to her guests. "We will be dropping out of FTL in thirty minutes. I suggest you prepare for the mission."

Conner threw himself out of bed and grabbed for his clothes. Hameeda smirked, despite herself. Conner clearly hadn't realised that it made no difference if he was dressed or not, not on the LinkShip. But then, there *was* a human crew now. Getting dressed was common decency. She watched him for a moment, then turned her attention to Jeannette. The woman was already shutting down her terminal and heading for the hatch. It opened as she approached, letting her into the corridor. She entered the command centre moments later.

"I could get used to this," Jeanette said. "This ship is like a hotel."

Hameeda gritted her teeth. She was *good* at multitasking—it was one of the skills she'd developed during training—but she still found it hard to deal with having someone in the command centre, sitting right next to her, while her mind was lost in the datanet. It felt as if she was trapped between two worlds, rather than being free to give her attention to just one.

"Take the consoles in the emergency control room," she grunted. Her awareness was threatening to split. "I'll feed the sensor reports to you."

"I have orders to stay in the control room during the flight," Jeanette pointed out. "I..."

"That's an order," Hameeda said, a little more harshly than she'd intended. "Right now, you're a distraction. Go."

Or I'll teleport you back into your cabin and lock the door, she added, silently. Internal teleports were tricky, but the LinkShip could handle them. It would be difficult to explain, when she rejoined the fleet...no, it wouldn't be. She was the ship's commanding officer. A refusal to obey orders while the ship was underway was a court-martial offense. Technically, she had the legal right to *shoot* Jeanette for disobeying orders. *Although...has it ever been done?*

She watched Jeanette leave, her body language suggesting she was pissed. Hameeda scowled at her back, then turned her attention to the sensor feed. The seconds were ticking away rapidly now, warning her that she'd be dropping out of FTL in moments. She barely noticed Conner joining Jeanette in the emergency control room, barely heard Jeanette grumbling to her friend about Hameeda. The only concern was leaving FTL without being detected.

Space lurched around the LinkShip as the FTL drive disengaged. Hameeda braced herself, ready to fight or run. The odds against dropping out of FTL in weapons range of an enemy ship were very low, but improbable things had happened before. She let out a tight breath as her awareness filled with raw data. A handful of ships were making their way from gravity point to gravity point, but apart from them there was little more activity in the once-active system. Mokpo really had taken a beating.

We smashed their space-based industries, she thought, *and then the Tokomak hammered the planet's surface too.*

She directed her sensors to send a live feed to Jeanette and Conner, then turned her attention to the gravity point. The LinkShip glided forward, hidden behind its cloaking field. She frowned, despite herself, as the sheer scale of the enemy defences came into view. There were no fortresses, not entirely to her surprise, but a hundred heavy ships sat on the gravity point and another hundred, carefully held in reserve, squatted nearby. It looked as if someone was trying to come up with a doctrine to counter assault pods, she decided, although it hardly mattered. There wasn't anyone on the far side who was going to throw an attack through the gravity point. The steady stream of warships making the journey from N-Gann to link up with the enemy fleet was grim proof that they held both sides of the gravity point.

"They're deploying gunboats," Jeanette said. It was easier to deal with her when she wasn't in the control room. "Can you sneak through the gravity point?"

"I doubt it," Hameeda admitted, reluctantly. The enemy had blanketed the gravity point in active sensors. Her subroutines gave her barely even odds of making it through without being detected. And, if she assumed that the other side was equally covered, the odds fell rapidly. Her cloaking device wouldn't fluctuate on transit, unlike a regular warship, but the slightest electronic leakage would be more than enough to reveal her presence. "The risk of being detected is too high."

"Then we have to check out the GS-3532 Point," Conner said. He sounded marginally more practical than Jeanette, although he'd treated the trip as a chance to catch up with his sleep more than anything else. "Can you take us there?"

"Already on the way," Hameeda said. She swung the LinkShip away from the gravity point, carefully keeping her distance from the enemy ships. Admiral Stuart's fleet could take them, she was sure, but they were only a tripwire for the forces on the far side. A shiver ran down her spine as she realised what that meant. A tripwire consisting of over two hundred ships...it was incredible. "We'll be there in a few hours."

Jeanette looked up, sharply. "You don't intend to go into FTL?"

"We have orders to survey the system," Hameeda said, as the LinkShip rapidly picked up speed. They were moving incredibly fast, yet compared to a ship in FTL they might as well be crawling. "And we might as well do that while we head to the gravity point."

She ignored Jeanette's complaint and turned her attention to her long-range sensors. There was no hint of any of the observation ships that had been left behind, although that was meaningless. They were designed to avoid detection, even by her. She hoped that meant they were keeping an eye on the enemy, rather than having been hunted down and destroyed by prowling Tokomak warships. A star system was an immense hiding place, but a careless scout might well be located and destroyed...

Worry about yourself, she thought, as they made their slow way towards the gravity point. *You don't want to be caught on the hop.*

The gravity point slowly came into view. It was largely undefended, save for a handful of destroyers that prowled the outer edge of the gravity point. Hameeda eyed them suspiciously, wondering why the enemy hadn't deployed more warships to cover the point, then decided it probably didn't matter. There was no *point* in retaking the gravity point unless one could either retake Apsidal or hit N-Gann. No doubt the enemy CINC would be delighted if Admiral Stuart wasted her strength trying to cut the supply lines. There were too many other ways to reach Mokpo for the scheme to have any long-term effect.

"We can get through," she said. "It shouldn't be too hard."

Conner frowned. "They're probing the gravity point pretty hard," he said. "Are you sure?"

"Yes," Hameeda said, irked. She *was* a commanding officer, damn it. Her formal rank was *captain*. And she was a real captain, not some REMF who delighted in the title without ever having set foot on a ship. He didn't have to doubt her so openly. "Here we go..."

She opened her awareness wide, just to be sure there weren't any surprises waiting for her, then slid forward. The enemy ships didn't notice her as they circled the gravity point, their sensor sweeps running in predicable patterns. They had to be reservists, she decided, or perhaps they simply hadn't seen any action. Predictability was death. The Tokomak really should have learned that lesson by now.

The LinkShip glided onto the gravity point and triggered the jump drive. Hameeda braced herself, again, as the universe seemed to sneeze… and then opened her awareness as soon as they were on the far side. A handful of warships were maintaining formation above the gravity point—her perceptions insisted they were *above* her, although it was largely meaningless in space—but no other ships were visible near the gravity point. She smiled grimly, then moved the LinkShip into space. The enemy ships showed no sign they knew she was there.

"That's a large convoy," Jeanette said, as new ships flashed into Hameeda's awareness. "Do you think the holdouts are still here?"

"I hope so," Hameeda said. She studied the convoy through her sensors. Two hundred freighters and nearly fifty escort ships, dropping out of FTL with a precision she could only admire. She felt a flash of humourless amusement. For a race that was supposed to have largely ignored the concept of a fleet train, the Tokomak were clearly fast learners. But then, those supplies wouldn't walk to the front under their own power. "They wouldn't need so much covering fire if they didn't fear attack."

"They could be concerned about pirates," Conner said.

"Pirates would be deterred by a handful of warships," Hameeda said. Pirates—and scavenger races—tended to be reluctant to pick fights unless the odds were heavily stacked in their favour. Besides, piracy was rarely a problem this close to the core worlds. "No, they're concerned about our raiders."

She kept moving away from the gravity point, avoiding the newcomers as she spread her awareness as far as it would go. GS-3532 was as empty as she remembered. There was nothing to suggest where the cut-off forces might be lurking, although she had a feeling they might be near the Winglet Point. It would be their best chance to strike a blow before the enemy was ready to repel them. She steered the LinkShip towards the second gravity point, keeping a wary eye on her sensors. There might be a *lot* of enemy ships lurking near the point.

Conner yawned. "Can I go back to bed, mummy?"

"You haven't finished your homework," Hameeda said, amused. She took one last look at the enemy ships, then dropped into FTL. "You can rest when this is over."

"Hah," Conner said. "It will never be over."

Jeanette shot him an odd look. "Why not?"

"We can win this battle—no, this *campaign*," Conner said. "And yet, it won't be the *last* campaign. We could be fighting this war for years."

"And, every year, we'll have better and better weapons," Hameeda said. "We might find ourselves with weapons that can blow their entire navy away with a single shot."

She smiled at the thought, although she knew they couldn't *count* on a technological breakthrough. Her subroutines had attempted to predict the course of the war, but none of their answers had been particularly good. It depended on the underlying assumptions fed into the systems. Would the Galactics remain united in the face of military defeat? Would the middle-class races take advantage of the opportunity to rise against their masters? Or…there were simulations where humanity romped to victory and simulations where the only humans left were the ones who'd fled the galaxy completely. There were simply too many variables for anyone to make an accurate prediction.

And yes, we might invent something tomorrow that will turn the whole universe upside down, she thought. *Or they might invent it.*

It was a galling thought, she considered, but one that had to be faced. They'd gone into the campaign with the belief that the human race would always have an edge in imagination, but events had proved them wrong. The Tokomak might be ancient, and they might have a superiority complex that put anything humanity had evolved to shame, yet they were clearly far from stupid. They'd learned from their experiences and kicked humanity's ass.

"The war will not go on forever," Jeanette said. Hameeda hastily dragged her attention back to her two guests. "And what will you do afterwards?"

Hameeda took a moment to review the conversation. Jeanette had been talking about their lives after the war...

"I'll think of something," she said. "Perhaps I'll go exploring."

She told them both to concentrate as the LinkShip dropped out of FTL on top of the Winglet Point. Five enemy ships lingered near the gravity point, but otherwise it was completely undefended. Hameeda hesitated, reminded herself that the enemy had little to gain by turning the system into a strongpoint and steered through the gravity point. The universe disappeared...and reappeared, bringing with it a small fleet of enemy ships. Hameeda tensed, expecting to come under fire at any moment. It felt as if she'd walked right into a trap...

"Hang on," she said, as she realised the enemy ships were scanning the gravity point. "We might have to run."

Alerts flashed up in front of her. The enemy had *seen* her! She threw caution to the winds and gunned her drives, flashing away from the gravity point as the enemy ships opened fire with savage intensity. She threw the LinkShip through a series of evasive manoeuvres as she hurled her ship towards the edge of the gravity point, then slammed the LinkShip into FTL as soon as she was clear. There was a point—long enough to feel like an eternity—when she feared she'd activated the drive too early, or the enemy were trying to trap her in normal space, before they jumped into FTL. She let out a sigh of relief. That had been far too close.

"That could have been worse," she said, as she disengaged the neural helmet and stood on wobbly legs. She'd been sitting for too long, at least partly to avoid her guests. "We're setting course for Galan now."

She straightened her uniform, then walked down the corridor to the kitchen to pour herself a cup of tea. The other two could join her or not, as they liked. Her hands shook as she poured water into the teapot, then searched for a cup and saucer. That had *definitely* been way too close. The only reason she knew it wasn't a deliberate ambush was that they hadn't been ready for the LinkShip. They'd probably assumed the stay-behind forces would be making the jump.

"That was very well done," Conner said, as he stepped into the kitchen. "We collected a great deal of valuable data."

"But not enough," Hameeda said. "I have a feeling we'll be heading to N-Gann in the near future."

"Probably," Conner said. "Do *you* think the Admiral's plan will work?"

Hameeda shrugged. The simulations, like every other simulation she'd run, couldn't give her a clear answer. Admiral Stuart's plan was risky, but so was every other option. And at least she'd have the chance to back off if it was clear the whole plan had gone to hell.

She took a sip of her tea and studied Conner, instead. He was reasonably handsome, reasonably clean...she could take him to bed, if she wished. She would be surprised if he declined. Or Jeanette...no, she'd always found it harder to maintain relationships with other women. The touch of misanthropy in her, the distaste for long-term companionship that had made her an ideal candidate for the program, also made it hard to form emotional connections. A man would understand a no-strings relationship. A woman might not.

And I don't like her anyway, she thought. Jeanette was pretty, but abrasive. She and Hameeda had more in common than either one would care to admit. *I don't want to go to bed with her.*

She smiled at the thought, then looked at Conner. A mischievous glint entered her eye as she met his. "Would you like to go to bed with me?"

Conner stared at her, shocked. Such a blunt invitation...it had to have surprised him. The Solar Union took an open attitude to sex, but it was rare for anyone—male or female—to be prepositioned so openly. And...

"Ah, yes," he stammered. "I..."

Hameeda smiled again, then held out her hand. "Come on," she said. "The bed is waiting."

CHAPTER TWENTY-EIGHT

I must be out of my mind, Martin thought, as he scrambled up the shaft. *What was I drinking when I thought up this idea?*

He forced himself to keep moving, even though it felt as though the walls were gradually closing in. The shaft might have been designed for creatures that were larger than humans—the shaft was actually wider than some of the tubes he'd used during basic training—but there was something *wrong* about the dimensions. The ladder shifting ominously under his weight—and that of the three men following him—didn't help. He had the nasty feeling they were going to fall to their deaths long before they reached the top.

Don't think about it, he told himself sharply, as he kept heading up the ladder. They were deep in enemy territory now, far too close to their garrisons for comfort. The scale of the ring would make it difficult for the Tokomak to guard everywhere, but they could have scattered hundreds of sensors around the ring. The team didn't dare talk amongst themselves, let alone use even a single microburst transmitter. *Just keep going.*

It felt like hours before the top of the shaft finally came into view. He crawled out and slumped on the deck for a moment before staggering to his feet and looking around. The shaft terminated in a repair shack, mounted on the outer edge of the ring. He peered through a tiny porthole, feeling his senses reel as—once again—his mind struggled to grasp the sheer scale of the ring. It looked immensely huge and yet—somehow—tiny at the same time. He looked down at the ground as Sergeant Howe emerged from the tube, carrying the HVM launcher slung over one shoulder. It was easier to think of the ring's surface as just another patch of flatland. It was just too huge for the curve to be noticeable.

He'd expected, even though he'd known better, that the outer edge of the ring would be smooth. Instead, it looked like a deeply-weird city. Giant constructions rose up, poking towards the stars, yet there was something...*unfinished* about them, as if a child had built the whole city out of building blocks. No one moved on the ring's surface, save for a pair of shuttles taking off from the distant spaceport. The whole complex was just *eerie*.

He checked his suit's life support, making sure he could survive in vacuum, then signalled for Trooper Rowe to open the hatch. The Galactics didn't seem to have bothered with any real precautions, certainly nothing to keep the outer hatch from opening while the inner hatch was open too. It struck him as careless, quite out of character for the Tokomak. But then, the maintenance shaft was part of a complex that could be easily sealed off from the rest of the ring. A slow leak would prove more dangerous in the long run, he thought, than leaving both hatches open...

Bracing himself, he opened the outer hatch and stepped out. The gravity field was weak outside the ring itself, but strong enough to hold him down as long as he didn't do anything stupid like jumping for joy. He glanced up at the unblinking stars, wondering which of them were starships holding position high above the planet, then forced himself to take a step forward. It felt strange, reminding him—again—of his basic training. Zero-g operations had defeated men he'd been *sure* would graduate as marines. He swallowed hard, then pushed himself onwards. He'd get used to it.

The exterior of the ring seemed dead—and yet alive—as he strode into the city-like construction. He felt as if he was an ant crawling over something unimaginably vast, an explorer entering a lost city for the first time.

Giant machines moved in incomprehensible patterns, while others—older and smaller—remained utterly unmoving. A construction the size of a skyscraper on Earth towered over him as he passed, only the lack of windows convincing him that it *wasn't* a skyscraper. Surely, even *aliens* would want to see the stars.

A shuttle flew overhead. He tensed, sure they'd been spotted, but the shuttle flew away before they could hide or try to shoot it down. There was a brief pause to exchange hand signals, then they continued their march towards the spaceport. It felt like hours before it finally came into view. Martin stared at it, feeling—once again—a strong sense of unreality. The spaceport was huge, yet...yet it looked more like a model than a *real* construction. He could see hundreds of freighters, ranging from small transports to giant bulk carriers, docked along the ring. As he watched, another bulk carrier appeared out of the inky darkness above and dropped down towards the spaceport. It moved with all the grace of a thrown brick, but somehow managed to land neatly beside the docking port. Martin was almost impressed. No one in their right mind would try to land a ship *that* size on a planetary surface.

His eyes swept the scene. Dozens of automated robots were moving around, unloading sealed crates and transporting them into the ring. Larger vehicles were helping to move freighters, as aircraft would be moved around an airfield on Earth; Martin watched, impressed despite himself, as a mid-sized freighter was moved into a hangar elevator and taken underground. It sank into the ring and vanished.

He glanced back at Howe, then motioned for him to set up the HVM launcher. Normally, it wouldn't be used to engage anything larger than a shuttle, but the ring's spaceport was a special case. Starship shields would normally be able to shrug off a HVM—it wasn't as if they carried antimatter warheads—yet they weren't *allowed* to use their shields close to the ring. Martin suspected the spaceport's defences—which had been destroyed during the first invasion—were configured to vaporise a freighter that lost control, rather than risk having it crash into the spaceport. There was a *reason* most races declined to risk having large ships land on their planets.

Ready, Howe signalled.

Wait for it, Martin signalled back. They wanted a *good* target, something big enough to do real damage, but not big enough to shrug off the HVM even without shields. A warship would barely notice the impact. *We'll get our chance.*

He peered into space, allowing his suit's sensors to pick out a multitude of possible targets overhead. The bulk carrier was big enough to do damage, but there were too many redundancies built into her drive systems for her to be an easy target; the light freighter would be an easy target, yet she wouldn't do enough damage to make the effort worthwhile. He forced himself to wait, despite the risk of being spotted, until a mid-sized freighter drifted into view. *That* would make an ideal target.

Fire when ready, he signalled.

Howe took aim, then fired. The HVM streaked across the spaceport and slammed into the freighter's drive section. Its drive field staggered, then collapsed completely. Gravity asserted itself a second later, yanking the freighter down to the ring. Martin ducked as the enemy ship smashed into a bulk freighter, which exploded with staggering force. The entire ring seemed to quiver under his feet as a series of secondary explosions swept the spaceport clear. He doubted the blasts would damage the structural integrity of the ring itself—it was a very solid piece of work—but they would do a hell of a lot of damage.

He looked up. The spaceport had been devastated. A handful of ships were streaming oxygen or superheated plasma, while a chain of explosions was shattering the lower levels and hopefully killing the enemy logistics staff. Martin would have preferred to kill the enemy's front-line combat soldiers, but he understood the logic. The Tokomak would have problems coordinating their offensive further into the ring if their logistics staff were killed. *They* didn't use AIs to do the hard work…

This way, he signalled. The enemy had been shocked, but it wouldn't be long before they got suited up and gave chase. *Hurry.*

He allowed himself a tight smile as they hurried back into the city, trying to make it to the maintenance shaft. The Tokomak didn't seem to have considered the possibility of someone going *outside* the ring to attack them, but they knew now. *And* they'd be able to use it for themselves, once they worked out what had happened. They might drop troops into the rebel-held sections of the ring in a bid to catch them by surprise.

We hit them, they hit us, he thought. The Tokomak were supposed to have unlimited manpower reserves, but there was no way they could bring their *entire* reserves to bear on the ring. *And we keep killing them until they kill us.*

It wasn't a pleasant thought, but it had to be faced. They'd been trapped on the ring for nearly three weeks, sniping at the enemy whenever they got the chance. Major Griffin might talk a good game—and he had enough logistics capability to keep his troops armed and mobile—yet the engagement couldn't go on forever. Oh, in *theory* it could—the ring was immense, large enough to hide a *dozen* armies—but in practice, Martin knew they were getting ground down. They couldn't keep the engagement going indefinitely.

We might have to, he told himself. *What happens if the fleet never returns?*

They reached the repair shack and checked it carefully, then clambered down the shaft. It didn't *look* as though the enemy had realised what had happened—or maybe they simply hadn't had a QRF at the ready—but there was no way to be sure. They'd pulled off quite a few ambushes before. Who knew what was about to happen?

No one, Martin thought, as they passed through a pair of airlocks. *No one knows what is about to happen.*

• • •

"So," the Empress said. "What happened?"

General Wooleen was not having a good day. Spacers—even a spacer as smart as the *Empress*—simply didn't grasp the complexities of planetside warfare. Space warfare was relatively simple, as long as both sides had relatively even technology; planetside warfare was frighteningly complex. General Wooleen was one of the youngest and most adaptable officers to gain power under the old regime and yet even *he* knew that success was never guaranteed. He'd have suspected that the only reason he'd been promoted was so that his superiors would have a scapegoat, except he doubted the old buzzards had possessed the imagination to think they'd *need* one. No doubt they were wishing they'd cracked down harder on imaginative subordinates now.

"They sneaked an attack close to Spaceport Two, Your Excellency," he said. It had taken his officers some time to realise what had actually happened. They'd assumed that the whole disaster had been an accident—or a long-range shot from an enemy starship—before they'd put the pieces together and figured out the truth. "They were lucky enough to hit one of the ammunition freighters."

The Empress looked thoroughly displeased. Even in the holographic display, she was a terrifying figure. General Wooleen tried hard to keep his face expressionless. The whole concept of revolt against one's elders had been unthinkable until the Empress had simply launched a coup. No one had tried to stop her because what she'd done had been literally inconceivable, at least until she'd done it. Now...now General Wooleen couldn't help wondering what would happen if the *Empress* saw him as a threat.

"This will put us behind schedule," she said. "How *badly* will it put us behind schedule?"

"Weeks, if not months," General Wooleen said. There was no point in trying to lie. The Empress was not some elderly idiot who couldn't tell the difference between a setback and a catastrophe. "We simply cannot sustain the offensive in that sector without the spaceport, Your Excellency, and we cannot rebuild in a hurry. The damage is simply too great. Worse, we must also guard the other spaceports. They may be targeted too. The enemy has hit on a way to hurt us at little cost."

"I see," the Empress said.

"I've started rerouting supplies, for the moment," General Wooleen said. "It should impede their attempts to take advantage of the chaos they've caused. But...we have to be careful for the next few weeks. Our incursions into the ring will have to slow."

"No," the Empress said. "*Vent* the ring."

General Wooleen frowned. "That's technologically impossible," he said. They'd had that discussion already. "There's no way to vent the entire ring."

The Empress's face darkened. "Keep our troops in suits," she said. "As they go further into the unsecured sectors, have them open airlocks and vent the air. Tear the airlocks open so they can't be sealed. We'll vent the entire ring piece by piece until they surrender."

"That will kill everyone on the ring," General Wooleen protested.

"Everyone who isn't wearing a suit," the Empress corrected. "Do it."

General Wooleen hesitated. The *humans* would probably survive. His forces had captured samples of their combat armour. It was certainly capable of keeping its wearer alive in an airless environment. And his forces were protected too. But everyone else? There were millions of aliens on the ring. The Empress had just sentenced them all to death.

"They may surrender, once they realise what we're doing," he said, finally. "But venting the entire ring will take years."

"Then get started now," the Empress said. "We have *got* to regain control of the trade routes, General. They're our path to Earth."

...

If she was forced to be honest, Shelia Frankenberg had never liked aliens. There was something about them that bothered her, even though she'd grown up in a universe where humanity was very far from alone. It wasn't something she could put into words, either; she didn't hate aliens, she didn't fear them...she simply didn't *like* them. Her head found it hard to accept that the aliens were living creatures in their own right. It was a joke, she'd thought when she'd received the assignment, that she'd been posted to Civil Affairs. How was *she* meant to cope with *aliens*?

And yet, she had to admit that she was finding it a more interesting task than she'd expected. The aliens were aliens...and yet, they had points in common with humans. Younger males and females who wanted to fight, older mothers and fathers who feared for their lives...children who needed medical help and mothers desperate to do whatever it took to *get* that help. Aliens might be alien—there was a species that was composed of intelligent males and unintelligent females and another that was precisely the opposite—but they were very human too. It was odd to reflect that the differences might be a matter of culture as much as biology.

She looked around the refugee camp, feeling a grim sense of satisfaction at just how well things were working out. The aliens had been moved from the upper levels when the invasion began, the military-age aliens joining the various militias while everyone else hid in the lower levels. It was a fantastic logistical challenge—the aliens had hundreds of dietary requirements that she found it nearly impossible to meet—but they'd made it. The aliens would be safe...

The floor vibrated under her feet. She tensed. They should be quite some distance from the front lines, let alone the nearest invader base, but the Tokomak had developed a habit of throwing thrusting attacks down the corridors at random over the last few days. Another distant explosion shook the complex, followed by a faint hiss. She frowned, wondering just what was happening. And then a third explosion echoed down the corridor.

Alerts flashed up in front of her eyes as she grabbed for her mask. They were blowing the airlocks, smashing their way down to the refugee camp. The atmosphere was already starting to stream out of the ring, wind brushing against her skin as it rushed towards the breach. She stared in horror, then started to bark orders at the refugees. There was another airlock, further into the ring. They had to get out before it sealed itself, automatically. There was no way they could open it once it had closed.

The air pressure dropped rapidly. She breathed through her mask, but she could see aliens, young and old, suddenly gasping for breath. There simply weren't enough masks for *all* of them. Her staff pushed the aliens towards the hatch, but it was already too late. She saw an alien toddler, a child who'd only taken his first steps a day or two ago, totter to the floor and die. His mother screamed for help, but there was nothing anyone could do. Shelia's mask refused to come free, even when she pulled at it. It wasn't designed to be easy to remove.

They're killing everyone, she thought, as she pushed and prodded the handful of survivors towards the hatch. It was already closing, crushing a pair of aliens as it slammed closed. A moment later, even the survivors began to die. All she could do was watch in horror as they breathed their last. *They killed everyone.*

She keyed her terminal, trying to send a report. But the cold was already seeping into her fingers. The chamber was in vacuum. She knew she needed a spacesuit—even a shipsuit would do—but she didn't have one. There weren't any within the chamber...

I'm sorry, she thought. She was too realistic to hold out any hope for survival. She was going to die here. *I'm sorry...*

CHAPTER TWENTY-NINE

"So, the enemy is concentrating on rushing supplies to Apsidal," Hoshiko said. She looked at the two intelligence officers, who had arrived in person, and Captain Hameeda's holographic image. "Have they made any attempt to fortify any of the systems between Apsidal and Winglet?"

"No, Admiral," Conner said. "They've deployed warships, but no fixed defences."

"Yet," Jeanette added. "They could lay vast minefields too."

"Which we would have no trouble sweeping away," Conner said.

Hoshiko held up a hand. "Captain Hameeda, conduct a final survey of N-Gann," she ordered, briskly. "I'll be moving the fleet to a point just outside detection range. You can link up with us there, then prepare for your role in our offensive."

"Aye, Admiral," Hameeda said. "I can depart immediately."

Without your guests, Hoshiko added. *But I need to debrief them both before deciding if I want them to stay on your ship.*

"We'll see you in a couple of days," she said, out loud. "And *don't* get spotted."

"Aye, Admiral." Hameeda held her hand up in salute. "Be seeing you."

Her image vanished. Hoshiko let out a breath, then looked at Jeanette. "Your report?"

"Captain Hameeda was not best pleased by our presence, at least at first," Jeanette said, bluntly. "She was...she reacted more like a person might to an unwanted houseguest, rather than a pair of fellow naval officers. I think she found it easier to deal with us—me, at least—over the intercom. She was polite enough, but her body language made it clear that she didn't want us there."

"She found it easier to deal with *you* over the intercom?" Hoshiko leaned forward. "Can you clarify that for me?"

Jeanette smiled, thinly. "Shaun took her to bed."

Conner coloured. "She took *me* to bed," he said. "We had about four days together during the flight from Winglet to Galen."

Hoshiko cocked her head. "And how *was* it?"

Jeanette snickered. Conner's blush deepened. "It was...fairly normal, if that's what you're asking," he said. "She didn't seem to want anything more than a brief sexual relationship, Admiral. I think she was merely satisfying her hormones rather than looking for a long-term partner. She... treated me more like a sex robot than an actual person."

"I'm sure you enjoyed yourself," Jeanette said.

Conner glared at her. "I did," he said. "But that isn't the point."

"And what *is* the point?" Jeanette asked. "Were you planning to spend the rest of your days on her ship? Or...or what?"

"Enough," Hoshiko said. The conversation was strikingly inappropriate, but it was one she had to have. "What is your assessment of her mental condition?"

Jeanette and Conner looked at each other, then came to an unspoken agreement that Conner should speak first. "Overall, I'd say she was fairly stable...just distant. I think she has a lot more in common with a merchant spacer, rather than a military officer; she's quite aware, on a very basic level, that everyone who enters her life will do so on a temporary basis. I don't think she feels she *needs* a strong connection with anyone else."

"But a merchant spacer would still have a crew," Hoshiko pointed out.

"Yes, Admiral," Conner said. "But anyone from outside the group would be a transient, by the nature of things. Unless the spacer actually got married."

Jeanette leaned forward. "She's very capable and very competent," she said. "At the same time, she's also abrasive and not—in my opinion—a good team player. That said, given the shortage of people *willing* to bond with a LinkShip, we may have to take what we can get. I don't know if she has quite realised just how long she's going to be bonded to that ship."

Hoshiko leaned forward. "And do you think she knew that you had orders to assess her mental state?"

"We were unable to add anything to the reconnaissance mission," Conner said. "Yes, Admiral. I'd say she knows what you had in mind."

"Unless she thought the Admiral was providing her with a sex robot," Jeanette teased.

Hoshiko slapped the table. "I want a full report by the end of the day," she said, feeling her temper snap. "Do you have any other observations—*serious* observations—that I should consider now."

"I don't believe that her sanity is starting to slip, Admiral," Jeanette said, finally. "However, her naval discipline *is* starting to slip. Talking to her, Admiral…half the time I feel like I'm talking to a civilian pretending to be a military officer. That's not uncommon in places where discipline has become lax, Admiral, but it's worrying on a front-line starship."

"She has no one to practice on," Hoshiko mused. God knew *she* hadn't been as disciplined as she should have been when *she* was a junior officer. The family name had gotten her out of more scrapes than she cared to admit. "I see your point."

She studied her hands for a long moment, then looked up. "Dismissed," she said. "I'll read your reports later."

The two intelligence officers hurried out the hatch. Hoshiko shook her head slowly, wondering if she'd done the right thing. Hameeda *had* needed some form of human contact, although it was evident that she'd needed it more than Hoshiko—or Hameeda herself—had realised. Jeanette might be as abrasive as Hameeda herself, but she wasn't a poor judge of character. Hameeda's naval discipline had been steadily wearing down.

But she really doesn't have anyone to practice on, Hoshiko thought. *No one will kick her ass or issue demerits if she slips up.*

The buzzer rang. "Open."

She looked up as Yolanda stepped into the room. "Admiral?"

"Yes," Hoshiko said, resisting the urge to point out that Yolanda could *see* her clearly. Who *else* would be in the compartment? "Is the fleet ready to move?"

"Yes, Admiral," Yolanda said. "We've redistributed the weapons loads to make sure that everyone has enough ammunition for the engagement."

"Good," Hoshiko said, although she knew they didn't have anything *like* enough ammunition for a long engagement. "And the plan?"

"The tactical plan has been uploaded to the datanet," Yolanda said. "Some officers thought you were being too careful, but others thought you weren't being careful enough."

"Success has a thousand mothers," Hoshiko misquoted. "Failure, that ugly little child, is a bastard orphan."

She shrugged and brought up the last set of images from N-Gann. They were out of date by nearly six weeks, but she doubted the situation would have changed *that* much. The fixed defences were unlikely to have been improved, not when the local industrial base was churning out supplies to support the fleet. But a conventional attack against N-Gann would end badly even if her fleet was at full strength. It was the kind of system that could be put under siege, but probably not captured by a single blow.

Either that piece of military wisdom dies today, she thought grimly, *or I condemn my fleet to utter destruction.*

"If we knew what the enemy was doing..."

She shook her head. She *knew*, in general terms, *precisely* what the enemy was doing. The Tokomak were moving vast quantities of supplies to Apsidal, preparing for a thrust into the Galactic Alliance's heartland. She had no doubts about what would happen if the Tokomak arrived in strength. A number of races would immediately prostrate themselves before their former masters, begging for a mercy that would never come, while others would fight to the death. The Tokomak might just ignore them and drive on Sol. Once the Solar Union was gone, the rest of the Galactic Alliance was doomed.

Which means we must not fail here, she thought, as she stood. *We must not fail.*

"Ready the fleet," she ordered, leading the way into the CIC. "We will depart for Point Tabasco at once."

And hope they're not watching for us, she added, silently. She'd tried to think of a way to get the fleet to N-Gann without being detected, but nothing had come to mind. They simply didn't have enough freighters to tow the fleet into attack range. Besides, the Tokomak would probably be suspicious if they saw a hundred freighters heading towards the planet. *Why not? They did it to us, after we did it to them.*

She took her chair and watched as her staff put the giant fleet into motion. They moved with purpose, yet there was a...*despondency* around them that worried her. The human fleet wasn't used to defeat, certainly not on such a scale. They'd been outthought and outfought and only sheer luck had saved the fleet from certain destruction. And even so, they were trapped on the wrong side of a heavily-defended gravity point. Hoshiko knew they had also been given a chance to tip the scales back, in the other direction, but not everyone agreed with her. She'd been lucky not to be challenged by her officers.

And I might be, if this fails, she thought. *And if there's anyone left to do the challenging.*

"Admiral," Yolanda said. "The fleet is ready to depart."

"Then give the order," Hoshiko said. "Jump."

• • •

Is it too much to ask, Hameeda asked herself, *for some consistency?*

She smiled at the thought, even though it wasn't particularly amusing. She'd been unhappy to have guests on her ship, and she'd been relieved to teleport them to *Defiant*, but now she *missed* them? Or Conner, at least. The nights they'd spent together had been wonderful, even though she *knew* they couldn't last. Conner was hardly likely to *want* to be permanently assigned to her ship, even if it meant sharing her bed.

And we'd probably get in trouble for dereliction of duty, Hameeda thought. Rank wasn't *that* important on a small ship, as long as everyone knew the chain of command was still there, but dereliction of duty was a serious matter. *Jeanette would rat us out to her superiors if we spent too long in bed together. I should probably have invested in the sexbot.*

She snorted to herself as she pulled the neural helmet over her head. She could afford a sexbot, and no one would object if she had it transferred to her ship, but it wouldn't be *real*. It wouldn't be a living breathing human. God knew there was a stigma attached to *using* sexbots, male or female, yet...she dismissed the thought as the LinkShip entered the N-Gann System. She'd think about it later. Right now, it was time to make war.

Or at least to survey the system, she thought, as she dropped out of FTL near N-Gann itself and headed towards the planet. *The Admiral will be making war.*

The system seemed smaller, somehow, as she opened her awareness wide. There were still vast numbers of freighters moving around, some heading into interstellar space and others heading towards the planet, but the immense war fleet she'd seen the last time she'd visited was gone. Of course...it had flown to Apsidal and invaded the system. Her sensors noted several squadrons of capital ships maintaining position near N-Gann, but they were clearly only a supplement to the vast planetary defences. N-Gann had never been a particularly inhabitable world. The Tokomak had taken advantage of the lack of an indigenous population to raise some really *scary* defences.

But they do have a weak point, she thought, as she surveyed the planet. *It just isn't one that would be immediately obvious.*

She glided slowly around N-Gann, noting the presence of nine battlestations orbiting underneath the ring. The Tokomak had taken a considerable risk emplacing them in low orbit, even though they had the technology to prevent disaster. She wondered if it was a sign of their arrogance, and their belief that the universe would bow to them, or a sign that they hadn't thought through what they were doing. Or both. She shrugged and directed her attention towards the vast orbital warehouses. It was hard to believe that they represented only a tiny fraction of the system's warehousing capability.

Whatever else you can say for the Tokomak, she reminded herself once again, *they simply don't think small.*

A convoy of freighters was rising slowly up towards her. She moved the LinkShip out of the way, watching as the freighters set course for Winglet and jumped into FTL. N-Gann's authorised emergence and departure zones seemed to be quite some distance from the planet, although she supposed *that* wasn't a surprise. Anything that dropped out of hyperspace too close to the gravity shadow risked crashing into the planet—or, worse, it might be an enemy ship on a suicide run. It wasn't as if they were heading towards a gravity point.

They'll see the fleet coming, she thought, as she swept the planet one final time. *And what will they do then?*

She shrugged. Admiral Stuart was *counting* on the fleet being detected. Hameeda wasn't sure how she felt about *that*, but she knew the fleet couldn't remain undetected whatever happened. Hopefully, the enemy would take the bait and not realise where the *real* threat lay... hopefully. The Tokomak had shown too great a capacity for innovation over the last few weeks for anyone's peace of mind. She carefully glided the LinkShip away from the planet, then surveyed the remainder of the system with her passive sensors. The Tokomak had expanded the defences around the gravity point, but not the gas giant. It made her wonder precisely what they had in mind.

They're probably worried about a stab in the back, she thought. There were two major species within jumping range of N-Gann. Both of them were supposed to be Tokomak loyalists, but their loyalty couldn't be taken for granted. Who knew *what* they'd do if the empire looked weak? *They have to consider the worst even as they prepare for their drive on Earth.*

The LinkShip fell back into FTL and rocketed away from N-Gann. Hameeda sat back in her chair, waiting until she was *sure* she was clear to remove her helmet. The automated systems *might* be able to cope with a gravity well in her path, if the enemy had managed to get a sniff of her presence and sound the alarm, but she didn't want to put them to the test. Instead, she waited until she was beyond the system limits. It was only a few minutes to get out of range.

A shame the rest of the fleet can't move so quickly, she thought. *We'd be on top of them before they had a chance to get ready.*

She kept a wary eye on her sensors as the timer ticked down to zero. In theory, Admiral Stuart's fleet should be well outside sensor range. In practice…it wouldn't be *that* hard for the Tokomak to set up a network of pickets watching for intruders to ensure that the defenders got some early warning. There was simply no way to know. A scoutship might have already seen Admiral Stuart and rushed to N-Gann with a warning. And if *that* happened, N-Gann would have already started preparing to meet the offensive.

The LinkShip returned to normal space. Her awareness was suddenly full of starships, alarm bells ringing in her head until her sensors confirmed that they were friendly. Admiral Stuart's fleet looked powerful, to the naked eye, but her sensors could pick out their weaknesses. They'd been in a major engagement and they simply hadn't had anything like enough time to make more than basic repairs. She suspected that some of the officers had fudged their readiness reports a little. Being sent out of the combat zone was bad enough, but having to leave when one was on the wrong side of a defended gravity point was worse.

Admiral Stuart's image appeared in front of her. "Captain."

"Admiral," Hameeda said. "I'm transmitting the data to you now."

"Very good," Admiral Stuart said. She sounded distracted by a far greater thought. "And are you ready to carry out your part of the operation?"

"Yes, Admiral." Hameeda couldn't help a thrill of excitement. This was *real* flying, the kind of precision operations the LinkShips had been designed to do. "I am ready."

"Then prepare to depart," Admiral Stuart said. "We will be leaving in thirty minutes."

"Aye, Admiral."

. . .

Hoshiko ignored the babbling from her intelligence staff as she surveyed the raw data, concentrating on the defences around N-Gann itself. The Tokomak had, arguably, overdone it, although by conventional standards the planet was effectively impregnable. Hoshiko could wreak havoc on the cloudscoops and anything else outside the planetary defence shield, but there was no way she could touch N-Gann itself. And yet, she had an ace up her sleeve. It was one she knew the Tokomak would never anticipate.

"They can shield the whole planet," Yolanda breathed.

"We knew that," Hoshiko reminded her, dryly. "And that gives us an edge."

She keyed her intercom, opening a channel to the fleet. "All hands, this is Admiral Stuart," she said. She wished, suddenly, that she'd taken the time to write a better speech. Or crib one from someone with more time on their hands. "I don't think I need to tell you what is at stake, here. The survival of our entire civilisation depends on us. If we fail to stop them, our parents, our siblings, our *people* will die. Their defence rests in our hands. And we will not let them down.

"They gave us a battering. Yes, they did. There's no point in trying to hide from the truth. But today, we give *them* a battering. Today, we show them that this war will be long, hard and ultimately a disaster for their tottering empire. Today, we show them what humans can do."

She closed the channel. "Signal the fleet," she ordered, quietly. "Prepare to jump."

CHAPTER THIRTY

Admiral Valadon was having a good war.

In truth, he'd expected to be relieved of his command as soon as he'd realised just *who* had overthrown the government back home. He had, after all, been one of the officers who'd denied Viceroy Neola's request for accelerated promotion, something that he'd been *sure* would come back to bite him now Viceroy Neola was *Empress* Neola. And he was easily five hundred years older than her. He might not have been one of the ruling circle, with the power to promote or demote at will, but she had no reason to think he was reliable either.

And yet, she'd left him in his post.

It wasn't entirely a blessing, he had to admit. He'd had to prepare N-Gann to receive a fleet an order of magnitude larger than any that had been deployed for nearly a thousand years, then support the fleet as it moved up the chain towards Apsidal—and Earth. His logistics staff had been working triple shifts, shuttling supplies from the nearest systems to the ring's giant warehouses and then either transferring them to the navel warships or loading them onto freighters for transport to Apsidal. It was an incredibly complex task, one that had been harder than anyone—perhaps including the empress—had anticipated. They'd come closer to failing than he cared to admit. But they'd succeeded.

He stood on his command deck, studying the latest series of reports from the front. The fleet had conquered Apsidal, but the human invaders—and their allies—were refusing to surrender and submit to Tokomak rule. Instead, they were fighting back with a savagery unseen since the early wars around the gravity points. Admiral Valadon had been ordered to keep running supplies—and troops—up the chain to the occupied world, while simultaneously assisting the fleet in turning Apsidal into a forward base and preparing for the drive on Earth. It was a major headache, he had to admit, but they were winning. They had all the time in the universe.

His aide hurried up to him. "Admiral, the latest set of conscript barracks are ready."

"Very good," Admiral Valadon said. He contemplated the details for a long moment, then shrugged. "Have the next set of conscripts detailed to those barracks for basic training."

"Aye, Admiral."

"And keep them under tight security," Admiral Valadon added. "We don't want them trying to escape."

He snorted at the thought. The servant races had been getting uppity recently, as rumours of vast defeats and embarrassing setbacks made their way from world to world. None of the rumour-mongers seemed to care that losing a few hundred ships would barely scratch the surface of the vast reserves the Tokomak could deploy, or that those few hundred ships had weakened an enemy fleet that simply couldn't afford losses. No, they were spreading discontent and causing trouble. It was quite likely that some of the conscripts, plucked from their world to serve their masters, were already infected. Some of them might even do something stupid.

At least we'll weed the idiots out, Admiral Valadon thought, with a flicker of cold amusement. A group of escaped convicts could hide for years, on a normal world, but N-Gann's atmosphere was poisonous to humanoid life. No known race could live on the surface without protection. *Anyone who goes out the airlock without a suit will be dead very quickly.*

He sobered as he contemplated the problems facing the armed forces. It normally wasn't necessary to invade a world, to put boots on the ground, in order to control it. A single orbital bombardment platform was normally enough to convince the locals to behave. But the Apsidal Ring wasn't the only place that would need to be occupied in order to put it to use. The Tokomak would need to conscript, train and deploy *millions* of soldiers in order to control the rebellious worlds. Earth itself would be a nightmare, unless the empress pressed ahead with her stated goal of destroying the entire planet. Admiral Valadon wasn't so sure that was a good idea—humans had been a useful race, in the past, and they might be useful again once they had been beaten into submission—but he knew better than to challenge the empress openly. She could have him sent to the retirement world with a wave of her hand.

It wasn't a pleasant thought. Empress Neola hadn't killed the gerontocrats. Instead, she'd sent them to luxury retirement worlds where their every whims were met, save one. They had no power outside the planetary atmosphere, no ability to steer the course of the entire galaxy...they were utterly irrelevant. He'd wondered, when he'd heard about the coup, why the empress simply hadn't killed them, but he knew now. They were utterly powerless, as powerless as *she* had been when she'd been a young officer, staring defeat and disaster in the face. Admiral Valadon would sooner die than embrace helplessness. It would keep him loyal in a manner...

"Admiral," the tracking officer said. "Long-range sensors are picking up a multitude of ships heading towards N-Gann."

Admiral Valadon gave him a sharp look. "A convoy?"

"No, Admiral," the tracking officer said. "Our computers call it an enemy fleet."

"Show me," Admiral Valadon said, striding over to the console. "Put them on the main display."

His eyes narrowed as the display updated. The incoming ships were clearly visible, flying in close formation to make it difficult for his sensors to tease out just how *many* ships were about to land on his head. And yet, by gravimetric emissions, there couldn't be more than five hundred ships at the most. It was consistent with the reports from Apsidal. The enemy fleet had fled to Mokpo, then jumped into FTL. No one had expected the humans to head for N-Gann, of all places, but it was well within their capabilities. Judging by the timing, they'd headed *straight* for N-Gann.

"Bring the orbital defences to combat readiness, then prepare to activate the shield," he ordered. The enemy fleet was coming in fast. They'd be dropping out of FTL in barely thirty minutes, assuming they were heading for N-Gann itself. A fleet that size could cause real trouble if it decided to ravage the remainder of the system instead. "Order the freighters to get under the planetary shield or head out to a safe distance."

Admiral Valadon hesitated, considering his next move. The humans could do a great deal of damage, true, but there was no way they could *take* the system. And most of the damage they *could* do would be very limited. He could have new cloudscoops built from scratch long before the sudden shortage of HE3 began to bite. His giant orbital industries would not be seriously threatened. He didn't *have* to scream for help.

But he knew his duty. "Send a courier boat to Apsidal," he added. By the time it *reached* Apsidal, the engagement would probably be over... unless, of course, the humans decided to lay siege to the system. "Inform them that we are about to come under attack."

He smiled, coldly. The humans *couldn't* crack his defences. And, if they decided to lay siege to his planet, the main fleet would return and catch their fleet between two fires. It could shorten the war...

...And that, he knew, was an outcome that would definitely please Empress Neola.

• • •

"Twenty minutes to arrival, Admiral," Yolanda said. "All ships report that they are at full combat readiness."

"With a certain degree of fudging," Hoshiko said, dryly.

Her lips quirked. There were readiness reports that seemed to have been written with a civilian eye in mind, as if the commanding officers who'd written them didn't seem to believe that their readers would notice the tactical omissions, skewed viewpoints and outright lies. Normally, she would have called up the commanding officers in question for the express purpose of ripping their heads off, both for trying to misrepresent the truth *and* for taking damaged ships into combat. But now, when she was risking everything on a desperate gamble, she needed every ship she could field. A handful of ships, even *damaged* ships, might make the difference between success and failure.

She sat in her command chair, concentrating on projecting calm composure to the rest of the compartment. Her staff knew the odds, they knew just how much could go wrong...they knew that, if the plan failed, the fleet would have no choice but to turn and flee. And yet, they were handling their duties with a calmness Hoshiko had to admire. They'd seen the elephant. Combat was no longer a mystery. They thought they could handle anything.

It had been easier, she thought, in the Martina Sector. There, she'd known that a defeat—even the total destruction of her squadron—would not have materially affected the balance of power. The Solar Union would have mourned her loss—she was morbidly sure that the analysts, armchair admirals and historians would have taken to their keyboards to condemn her in no uncertain terms—but it wouldn't have died with her. Now, losing the fleet could prove disastrous. She'd allowed herself to be outthought and outfought. She didn't dare let that happen again.

"Five minutes to arrival," Yolanda said. "Admiral?"

"Deploy as planned," Hoshiko said. She knew the importance of being flexible, but there was no point in changing things now. She'd adjust her plans if they jumped into N-Gann and discovered that the enemy had rushed their fleet back from Apsidal, yet she wouldn't *know* she needed to make adjustments until she saw the fleet. "And prepare to engage the enemy."

THE LONG-RANGE WAR

The timer ticked down to zero. Hoshiko braced herself as the display blanked, then rapidly started to fill with green, blue and red icons. N-Gann was directly in front of them, wrapped in a haze that signified a full-scale planetary shield. She couldn't help a flicker of admiration for the alien engineers, even though the planet-sized forcefield was an attacker's worst nightmare. N-Gann had more than enough power plants and shield generators, lining the ring—to make it impossible to batter down the shield. Her fleet could expend every missile it carried, from antimatter warheads to kinetic projectiles, and the field would remain intact. It was no surprise that the Tokomak felt confident in their rear-area security. N-Gann was practically impregnable.

Maybe we should have built a Death Star after all, she thought. She smiled, despite the situation. *It isn't as if the Tokomak have starfighter pilots who are strong in the Force.*

"Admiral, their warships are holding position above the shield," Yolanda reported. "They're recalling their freighters *through* the shield or sending them into deep space."

Hoshiko nodded. The enemy was opening gaps in the shield, very brief gaps, just long enough to allow freighters to make it down to the ring. It was an impressive display of control, she admitted sourly. They'd emplaced more than enough shield generators to allow them to manipulate the forcefield in any way they pleased. They might even be able to expand it to the point where they could swat her ships, if she was fool enough to take them so close to the planet. Humanity could duplicate the trick, but there was no point. It would take decades to fortify Earth to the point where it could support its own planetary shield.

And this is a relatively minor fleet base, she thought, feeling cold. *What's it going to be like if we have to hit one of their main worlds?*

"Let them get a good look at us," she ordered, quietly. "Can you confirm the location of their main shield generators and command posts?"

"Yes, Admiral," Yolanda said. The display focused on the planetary ring. "I believe I've spotted the main locations."

Hoshiko's eyes narrowed. "Forward the data to the LinkShip, then hold us here," she ordered. "And order the LinkShip to jump."

• • •

"They're remaining out of range," the aide reported.

Admiral Valadon nodded, curtly. The human fleet was impressive, particularly for a race that had only been in space for sixty years, but it didn't have the firepower to crack the planetary shield. Unless, of course, it had some weapons system the revoltingly ingenious humans had invented and carefully kept under wraps until they needed it…he shook his head, irritated at the mere thought. They would have deployed any superweapons during the Battle of Apsidal.

"We wait," he said. It wasn't particularly heroic, but his objective was to preserve the fleet base…*not* to grind down the human fleet. He could wait patiently, under the shield, for the empress to return with her fleet. "Order the warships to hold position."

"Aye, Admiral," the aide said. He broke off, suddenly. "Admiral, something's happening!"

• • •

Hameeda silently counted down the last few seconds as the LinkShip started to shake violently. She was brushing against N-Gann's gravity shadow, a problem made worse by the presence of the N-Gann Ring and its forcefield. Most gravity shadows were easy to predict and avoid, even when one was trying to drop out of FTL as close to the planet as possible, but N-Gann's was dangerously unpredictable. The mission was far riskier than she'd realised when she'd received her orders.

A moment longer, she told herself, as the shaking grew worse. The LinkShip couldn't plunge through the planet itself—that would be certain death—but it *could* come out of FTL within the gravity shadow, if she was careful. *A moment longer...*

The LinkShip crashed back into normal space. Alarms howled at the back of her mind, but she ignored them as she opened her awareness as wide as she could. The enemy forcefield was a clear and present danger, *above* her. She laughed out loud as she realised she'd made it. She'd come out of FTL *underneath* the field. The LinkShip veered from side to side as she gunned the drives, hastily deploying a whole string of ECM drones. There was no hope of remaining undetected. Her return to normal space had been so violent that they *had* to have seen her.

But they couldn't have expected me, she thought, as she roared towards her targets. *No normal starship could survive a jump into a planet's gravity shadow.*

Her awareness filled with enemy ships and installations. A giant battlestation, its weapons already turning to target her, and a command node on the N-Gann Ring itself. Her sensors picked out the shield generators, noting how they worked together to keep the forcefield active. The Tokomak were masters of redundancy, often taking it to an extreme, but this time they'd outdone themselves. There were so many shield generators along the Ring that, for the first time, she doubted her success. She had to take out hundreds of them in order to make an impact. Fortunately, there was a simpler option.

The enemy opened fire. Hameeda grinned, throwing the LinkShip into a series of evasive manoeuvres as space filled with phaser beams, plasma fire and short-range countermissiles that tended to be sucked towards the drones. She selected her targets a moment later and fired, unleashing the hammers that had been fitted to her hull. The LinkShip seemed to move more freely, as soon as the hammers were gone. She knew it was an illusion—it wasn't as if they were flying through an atmosphere—but it couldn't be denied.

Target the other shield generators, she ordered, swooping along the ring and triggering burst after burst of phaser fire. The enemy would find it harder to target her, unless they wanted to risk damaging the ring themselves. It was probably designed to soak up a great deal of damage, like the previous ring, but there were limits. *Don't give them a chance to lock onto us.*

The first hammer struck home, smashing an orbital battlestation into a cloud of debris that expanded outwards in all directions. Two more struck the main shield generators on the ring itself, smashing through the outer hulls and tearing through the interior. Hameeda had a weird mental image of a donut with a single bite taken out of it, a moment of whimsy that nearly got her killed. The enemy were firing desperately now as their forcefield flickered and started to fail. A fourth hammer slammed into the main power generators and destroyed them. The entire ring seemed to convulse under the force of the impact.

Ignore the gunboats, she ordered, as she kept targeting the shield generators. The ring was too big to be destroyed easily, even by a hammer missile, but the damage was mounting up rapidly. Her analysis subroutines insisted that the enemy power network was failing, suggesting that it was only a matter of time until the forcefield collapsed completely. *Take out as many shield generators as possible.*

A second enemy battlestation died. Hameeda barely noted its passing, although her subroutines suggested that the enemy had been unwilling or unable to unleash any anti-hammer countermeasures. They'd be reluctant to deploy antimatter warheads in orbit, even though N-Gann was nowhere near the galaxy's premiere vacation spot. She concentrated on the shield generators, sweeping along the ring as fast as she dared. The enemy were definitely panicking now. Their forcefield was dying...

...And then it snapped out of existence. The planet was defenceless.

Hameeda laughed—the mission had been a complete success—and then threw the LinkShip into FTL. There was no point in remaining so close to the enemy defences any longer, not when the mission had been completed. The remainder of the operation was in Admiral Stuart's hands. The impregnable world was suddenly very pregnable. Admiral Stuart's plan had definitely been a complete success...

...And, as far as she was concerned, the LinkShip had been a complete success too.

CHAPTER THIRTY-ONE

"Impossible," Admiral Valadon breathed.

He was too stunned to care that his staff could hear him, although he was dimly aware that they were just as shocked. Everyone had *known* that the planetary shield was utterly impregnable. He could have held N-Gann against a fleet large enough to daunt even the Tokomak. And yet, the humans had somehow jumped *below* the shield and taken out the entire network of shield generators. The generators that hadn't been destroyed directly had been crippled when the power network surged or simply deprived of power.

"Order the fleet to prepare to engage," he managed, as he struggled to reassess the situation and come up with a plan. None of his contingency plans had included losing the shield and two of his battlestations. The ring itself was in serious danger. "And send an update to Apsidal. Inform them...inform them that we are on the verge of losing the system."

He gritted his teeth in bitter frustration. The planetary defences were tough, even without the forcefield, but they weren't tough *enough*. There was no way he could keep the enemy fleet from devastating the planet's orbital industries. He snapped out orders, telling the industrial workers to evacuate their locations at once, even though he knew it was futile. The humans would bombard the planet as a matter of course. There was no longer any safe space on the planet's surface. And the conscripts might start getting restless.

The Empress is going to retire me for this, he thought, glumly. It wasn't *fair*. He'd done everything right and he'd *still* lost. Who could have predicted that the humans would find a way to jump *under* the shield? It should have been impossible. *I'll spend the rest of my days in a retirement home.*

"Admiral," his aide said. "The human fleet is moving to engage the defence force."

Admiral Valadon barely cared. His remaining life expectancy was over seven hundred years. And he was going to spend the rest of them in a prison. A nice prison, perhaps, but still a prison.

"Admiral?"

"Order the fleet to engage the enemy," Admiral Valadon said, sharply. He knew his duty, damn it. He'd keep going until the battle was over. "And keep evacuating the orbital stations."

"Aye, Admiral."

. . .

"The LinkShip succeeded, Admiral," Yolanda said. "The planetary shield is down."

"I saw," Hoshiko said. "Order the fleet to engage the enemy."

She studied the cluster of red icons on the display, wondering if the enemy fleet would turn and run. It would be the *smart* choice, even though it wouldn't be particularly brave. Maybe they'd fire a shot or two for the honour of the flag before dropping into FTL and running to link up with the main fleet. It wasn't as if they had a chance against her. She outnumbered and outgunned the enemy ships. And they *had* to know it.

"We will open fire at Point Alpha," she ordered, tapping commands into her console. "And if they decide to run, let them go."

The enemy fleet did not appear to be commanded by a tactical mastermind, she decided as the two fleets converged. They formed into a simple blocking formation, drawing a line in space and daring her to cross. Hoshiko snorted, torn between relief, suspicion and a hint of pity for the alien crews. Either they had something *really* nasty up their sleeves, which seemed unlikely, or their commanding officer was going to get them killed for nothing. It didn't even look as though they were preparing to jump out and run. *She* wouldn't have blamed a CO for retreating in the face of overwhelming firepower.

"They're targeting us, Admiral," Yolanda said. "They've locked on."

Hoshiko shrugged. She wasn't trying to hide. She would have been more surprised if the Tokomak *hadn't* managed to lock their weapons on her hulls. Still, she couldn't help a flicker of disapproval as the display sparkled with red icons. The Tokomak had fired too early, if they wanted to defeat her fleet. She had all the time in the world to configure her point defence to wipe out the missile swarm.

"Hold fire," she ordered, calmly. "We will fire at Point Alpha."

She tensed, despite herself, as the enemy missiles roared into engagement range. They looked to be unmodified, the kind of missiles the Tokomak had considered perfectly adequate until they'd gone to war with the Solar Union. She was surprised N-Gann didn't have more modern weapons, although it made a certain kind of sense. The enemy fleet would probably have absorbed most of the new production, leaving nothing for the rearguard. And besides, refitting the ships and fortresses to fire modern missiles would have been a pain in the butt. Perhaps they'd just earmarked it as something to do later and simply ran out of time.

Or maybe they didn't realise that we would strike at N-Gann, Hoshiko thought. The Tokomak wouldn't have been wrong. It had never been part of *her* plan, at least not originally. *And when we found ourselves on the wrong side of the gravity point, it was too late for them to upgrade their weapons and defences.*

Her lips thinned as the enemy missiles evaporated against her defences. Her point defence crews, from the humans on the command decks to the RIs that handled the actual *work*, had plenty of experience dealing with more modern weapons. The Tokomak simply didn't have the weight of numbers to make up for their weaknesses. In their place, she would have retreated into FTL or sought to combine her firepower with the planet's defences. Instead, they looked reluctant to do anything that could be taken as an admission of failure...

If the definition of insanity is doing the same thing over and over again and expecting a different result each time, she thought as she watched the enemy unleash another salvo of missiles, *then the Tokomak are definitely insane.*

"Admiral," Yolanda said. "We have reached Point Alpha."

"Fire," Hoshiko ordered, quietly.

Defiant shuddered as she opened fire. Hoshiko tensed, telling herself—again and again—that she wouldn't need to expend more missiles. The enemy fleet was small, too small to be a serious threat unless it linked up with the remainder of their fleet. And yet, it could soak up enough of her missiles to cripple her. She had no idea what she'd do if her fleet was effectively unarmed. Try to sneak back to Earth? It would take months, if not years, and by then Sol might have been swept clean of life. What would she do *then*?

She watched, grimly, as the enemy formation struggled to beat off her offensive. Their point defence was better than she'd expected, although there didn't seem to be any significant improvements in hardware. *That* was a good thing, she supposed, even though it showed that the Tokomak were taking training seriously once again. She wondered how their new government had managed to convince its military to run unscripted exercises. The Tokomak planners had *always* known what both sides would do, right down to how many missiles would be fired and who'd actually *win*. There would have been no surprises to *really* test their mettle. But now...

Not enough, she thought, vindictively. Her missiles were slipping through the enemy defences and slamming into their shields. *Nowhere near enough training to save their lives.*

The enemy formation came apart, a handful of ships jumping into FTL while their comrades—suddenly thrown back on their own resources—struggled to survive. They didn't stand a chance. One by one, they died; Hoshiko considered, briefly, asking them to surrender, but she didn't dare risk introducing random factors. Given time, who *knew* what they'd do?

"The enemy fleet has been destroyed, save for a handful of runaways," Yolanda reported, shortly. "They're heading out of the system at speed."

"Smart," Hoshiko muttered. She wondered, absently, just what sort of reception awaited the runaway ships. Would their commanders be rewarded for recognising the hopelessness of their position? Or would they be put in front of a court-martial and shot for desertion in the face of the enemy? "Bring the fleet around. We will advance on the planet as soon as we are ready."

She checked the reports and nodded to herself, silently relieved that they hadn't expended *too* many missiles during the brief engagement. The fleet could still take—or devastate—the planet, then...well, it depended. She had a whole string of contingency plans, ranging from detailed operational outlines her staff had put together to vague concepts that might—*might*—prove feasible if the stars were right. But it depended on the outcome of *this* engagement. If she fired too many missiles, or lost too many ships, the whole gamble might prove utterly disastrous.

"The fleet's reporting, Admiral," Yolanda said. "We are ready to advance."

"Then advance," Hoshiko ordered. "And signal the planet. Inform them that we will accept surrender, if they refrain from damaging the planetary infrastructure."

"Aye, Admiral," Yolanda said.

Hoshiko settled back into her chair and waited. The Tokomak rarely bothered to accept surrenders, except in very rare circumstances. And they had such a superiority complex that it was quite possible they'd sooner die than surrender to a race that hadn't even been in space for a hundred years. And *that*, of course, assumed that they trusted their human captors to keep the terms of their surrender. There were factions on Earth that Hoshiko would sooner die fighting, even if the battle was hopeless, then let them take her alive. The Tokomak might feel the same way too.

"No response, Admiral," Yolanda said.

"Repeat the signal," Hoshiko ordered. "And target their battlestations with hammers."

She heard a gasp running through the chamber. It was *dangerous* to use hammers so close to a planetary surface, even a world as inhospitable as N-Gann. Normally, Hoshiko would have held back from using such weapons, but now she had no choice. She didn't dare get into a missile duel with the orbital fortresses. They were too heavily armed and defended for her to destroy without massive losses. And even if their weapons were outdated, there were an awful lot of them.

"Repeating now," Yolanda said.

Hoshiko asked herself, grimly, just what *she'd* do if she was on the other side. She might surrender, knowing that she would be assured of good treatment, but…that would mean allowing a sizable industrial base to fall into enemy hands. And yet, the Tokomak fleet wasn't *that* far away. They could dispatch most of their ships back to N-Gann to crush the human fleet before she had a chance to put the industrial base to good use. It was quite possible they'd calculate that surrender was actually their *best* option. She would either have to destroy the industrial facilities, thus rendering them useless to her as well as the enemy, or allow herself to be pinned down.

And they'd destroy me if I let myself be pinned to a single world, Hoshiko thought. In a conventional war, without the planetary shield, N-Gann was indefensible. *And yet, I need supplies from the planetary industries.*

"Still no response, Admiral," Yolanda said.

Hoshiko gritted her teeth. "Take us into attack range," she ordered. A full-scale engagement would destroy most of the orbital nodes she wanted to capture, even if she didn't *intend* to do it. It was frustrating, but there might be no choice. She couldn't leave N-Gann in her rear if she couldn't convince it to surrender. "Prepare to engage."

...

"The humans are demanding our surrender, again," the aide said. "Admiral?"

Admiral Valadon forced himself to think. N-Gann was doomed. Either the humans occupied the planet—or at least the high orbitals—or they devastated the system from end to end. And his career was doomed with it. There was no way to escape blame for the debacle. The Empress would want a scapegoat and he'd be perfect for the role.

He cursed under his breath. The thought of surrender was anathema. There were dark rumours that *some* of the ships that had attacked Earth had surrendered, although officially the stories had been denied time and time again. No Tokomak ship had surrendered for nearly a thousand years. He couldn't remember the last time a *planet* had surrendered. It might have been far more than a mere *thousand* years ago.

But if we do surrender, he asked himself, *what then?*

If the humans kept their word, he thought, they might have some problems. They couldn't hope to transport all the prisoners from N-Gann to another world, even assuming they had a place to put prisoners in the first place. Whatever POW camps they'd set up on Apsidal were lost to them now. And the Empress would return, soon enough, with her fleet. It was quite possible that the humans would see their prisoners liberated when they were chased from the system. The workers could go back to work immediately.

But what if they *didn't* keep their word?

It was a chilling thought. Everyone knew, the humans most of all, that this was a war of extermination. Sure, the Empress *might* keep a few humans alive—for their imaginations as much as their skills—but the majority of the human race would be wiped out. Why should they *not* slaughter prisoners? It wasn't as if they had any motive to treat their prisoners well when they had no reason to expect anything better from their enemies. In hindsight, it might have been a mistake to treat the younger races as inferiors. They might not be amongst the elder races, but didn't they deserve a little respect?

But it's too late now to offer them the respect they deserve, he thought. It was an insight he wouldn't have had if he hadn't been soundly beaten by overwhelming force. *We have alienated too many of the younger races to expect mercy.*

"Contact the humans," he ordered, quietly. "Inform them that we wish to discuss the terms of our surrender."

His staff recoiled in shock. He didn't blame them. The thought of surrendering to an upstart race was horrific. And yet, they had no choice. They *had* to surrender. Their surrender might serve a greater purpose than dying in futile combat.

"Aye, Admiral," his aide said. "I'll make contact now."

A human face appeared in the display. It—he couldn't tell if the human was male or female -- was strikingly ugly, even by their standards. The black mass on its head was unthinkably awful to the bald Tokomak. And the lack of open respect was shocking. This was a being who had no regard for the Galactics. He found it hard to grasp, even as he understood it. The human and its entire race had been sentenced to death.

"I greet you," he said. There *was* a procedure for talking to equals. He'd use it, although he had a feeling the humans wouldn't realise how they were being honoured. "In the name of..."

"My terms are quite simple," the human said, cutting him off. Admiral Valadon recoiled in shock. He had never—*never*—been interrupted by someone from a younger race, not even once. "You will stand down your weapons and defensive systems at once. The freighters in orbit will shut down their drives and wait to be boarded. Your forces will return to their barracks and wait for transfer to POW camps. You will make no attempt to destroy your industrial facilities, wipe your computers cores or do anything else that will render the facilities unusable. My people will secure the ring, the industrial nodes and your surviving orbital defences. Any resistance will be met with deadly force."

There was a pause. Admiral Valadon was too stunned to speak.

"If you accept and honour these terms, you have our word that you and your people will be treated according to the Galactic Conventions," the human continued. Left unmentioned was the simple fact that hardly anyone took the Conventions seriously, even the Tokomak who'd written them. "You will be treated well and returned to your people, either as part of a prisoner exchange or simply handed back once hostilities are over. Those of you who cause trouble, however, will be summarily dealt with. There will be no further warnings."

Admiral Valadon felt as if he'd been punched in the belly. His race had ruled the galaxy for so long that *everyone* deferred to them. To be contradicted by one of the lesser races was bad enough, but to be dictated to… it was worse. And yet, he knew his position was hopeless. If he fought, he died. He would die for nothing.

"We accept your terms," he said, ignoring his staff's shock. There was no time to explain his reasoning. They'd just have to accept it. He wondered, morbidly, if one of them would try to remove him from command and keep fighting. The wretched precedent had been set. "You may land your troops whenever you wish."

He closed the channel, then looked at his staff. "Dispatch a final courier boat to Apsidal, then stand down all weapons and defences," he ordered, quietly. It didn't look as if they were going to mutiny, but it was well to make it clear that the surrender was *not* the end of everything. "This is a shameful day"—*and I will be blamed for it*, he added silently—"but the Empress will avenge us."

"Aye, Admiral," his aide said. He didn't sound convinced—in fact, he was pushing the limits when it came to speaking to an elder—but at least he was obeying orders. "I'm sure she will."

Yes, Admiral Valadon thought. His career might be over, even if the humans kept their word, but the war was *far* from over. *She'll be back here sooner than the humans think.*

CHAPTER THIRTY-TWO

"So far, Admiral, they have offered no resistance," Colonel Jenison said. She was a tall woman, her body so muscular that Hoshiko found her a little unnerving. The skinhead haircut didn't help. "We have secured the orbital defences and the industrial nodes without problems."

"Very good," Hoshiko said. In one sense, it was a very small victory. She'd destroyed more tonnage during the battle at Apsidal, which she'd lost. But, in another, it would shake the very foundations of the galaxy. Her analysts hadn't been able to locate another example of a Tokomak naval base being captured. Their enemies would take note. "And the warehouses?"

"They're crammed with supplies," Major Harkin said. "We have more missiles and suchlike than we can hope to use. However..."

"Most of them are outdated," Hoshiko finished. "And not all of them will fit in our tubes."

"No, Admiral," Harkin confirmed. "We designed our tubes to fire a number of different missiles, but there are limits. Some of the larger enemy missiles would force us to retool our systems completely to fire them, which would render them useless when we link up with the fleet train and try to stock up on *our* missiles. The tubes would have to be retooled *again*."

"I think we can cope with that," Hoshiko said, dryly. "Did we happen to capture any external tubes?"

"Yes, Admiral," Harkin said. "They have an immense stockpile of missile pods. Most of them are outdated, but they can still be used."

"They'll have to be used," Hoshiko said. She allowed herself a tight smile. The victory had opened up a whole set of options, now she was sitting atop the enemy supply line. "And the freighters?"

"A handful of crewmen sabotaged their ships," Harkin said. "They're currently in uncomfortable accommodations. The remainder of the freighters are intact, but their cargoes are not all useful. We captured quite a bit of farming equipment."

"It might come in handy, if we have to flee to another world," Hoshiko said. "Very well, Major. You can proceed with Plan David."

"Understood, Admiral," Harkin said. "I have complete call on the fleet's engineering crews?"

"All of them," Hoshiko confirmed. The captains would shout bloody murder—*she* would have shouted bloody murder when *she'd* been a captain—but she'd overrule them. Her most optimistic projections insisted that they had less than three weeks before the enemy fleet arrived, with blood in its eye. "Get those ships and pods up and running, whatever it takes."

"Aye, Admiral," Harkin said. He hesitated, then leaned forward. "I could move faster if I pressed some of the aliens into service…"

"Dangerous," Colonel Jenison warned. "What happens if one of them manages to trigger a warhead?"

Hoshiko made a face. On one hand, using alien labour would speed things up; on the other, it would create an unacceptable security risk. They didn't dare take the chance.

"No," she said, flatly. "Stick with human labour."

"As you wish, Admiral," Harkin said. "That said, we may not be able to get *everything* ready before the show starts."

"Or even evacuate the ring completely," Colonel Jenison added. "Admiral, there are a *lot* of people on the ring."

"I know," Hoshiko said. "Do what you can."

She dismissed them both, then returned to studying the reports from the survey teams. They *had* captured a great prize, with enough supplies to keep the fleet going for years, although she knew they wouldn't be allowed to keep it for long. The enemy CINC would *have* to double back and chase Hoshiko and her ships away from N-Gann before it was too late. They couldn't allow her to block their supply lines indefinitely. Her lips twitched at the thought. Perhaps, if the Tokomak had been less dependent on their supply lines, they could have stabbed at Sol anyway.

Unless they already set out, she thought, grimly. It was the nightmare scenario. The enemy fleet might have already set out for Sol, unaware that she'd closed their supply lines behind them. They might never realise that something had changed until it was too late. She'd run the simulations over and over again, telling herself that the enemy *needed* those supply lines, but there was no way to be *sure*. *They might just trade N-Gann for Sol*.

Her intercom bleeped. "Admiral," Yolanda said. "Analyst Robin Craig has requested a meeting."

Hoshiko's eyes narrowed thoughtfully. Robin Craig was an xenospecialist, specialising in the Tokomak. She'd been one of the team assigned to study the captured battlestations and, if they were inclined to cooperate, interrogate the prisoners. What did *she* want? Hoshiko was tempted to deny the request, to tell Robin that she should go through proper channels, but it might be something important. And besides, it would keep her mind off fretting about the future.

"Send her in," she ordered. "I'll give her twenty minutes."

She looked up as Robin Craig entered the suite. The young woman looked *young*, barely old enough to drive an aircar or fly a spacecraft. Hoshiko resisted the urge to make a snide remark about youngsters who didn't think about how they presented themselves to others. Sure, a young woman *could* lock her apparent age at eighteen, but a hint of maturity was often useful in ensuring that one was taken seriously. Robin looked more like a teenager who refused to grow up rather than a naval officer in her own right.

But then, there are lots of weirdoes in intelligence, she thought. *And anyone who tries to think like an alien is bound to be a little insane.*

"Admiral," Robin said. She sounded over-excited. "I was conducting an interrogation and…"

"Calm down," Hoshiko said, amused. "And then start from the beginning."

Robin flushed bright red, but managed to start again. "I had the chance to speak to some of the senior officers on the station…ah, the *alien* officers," she said. "They were quite informative about some details. I don't think they realised how much I could learn from their words."

"I see," Hoshiko said, resisting the urge to ask how much *she* could learn from Robin's words. "And what did they tell you?"

"There was a coup," Robin said. "Ah…the commander of the fleet that attacked Earth overthrew the government and took power. She's now their *de facto* monarch, dictator in all but name."

Perhaps we shouldn't have let her escape, Hoshiko thought. She shook her head. The enemy commander had thought fast and escaped before she could be killed. No one had anticipated her somehow taking control of her government, not least her former masters themselves. *We created a rod for our back there.*

"I see," she said, again. "What does this mean for us?"

"The Tokomak are gearing up for full-scale war," Robin said. "They're bringing the reserve online, they're training up new spacers, they're even conscripting the junior races into their war effort. One of my…subjects insisted that they were even offering political concessions to the Galactics, in exchange for their support. We may be facing a far bigger threat than we'd assumed."

"Duly noted," Hoshiko said, dryly. At some point, it hardly mattered. The threat was already overwhelmingly large. The Tokomak alone were a deadly threat. If the tech balance ever equalised, the human race was screwed. "Did they have anything *useful* to say?"

"Apparently, some of the middle and lower races are restless," Robin said. "But, so far, that restlessness has not materialised in any useful way."

"See if you can think of a way of turning it into something useful," Hoshiko said. A thought struck her. "How many members of the subject species do we have on N-Gann?"

"Millions," Robin said. "Some are guest-workers, some are conscripts, some are outright slaves...a handful own their own freighters, but the remainder are pretty much contract workers of one form or another. I believe they're restless, Admiral. I just don't know if any of them can do anything useful."

"Unfortunately true," Hoshiko agreed. There was no point in trying to set up an insurgency on N-Gann. The planet's environment made it impossible. Any invading force merely needed to puncture the domes to win. "Still, it might be interesting to consider what we can do with them."

"They could go home," Robin suggested. "And tell their people what happened here."

"Maybe," Hoshiko said. It wasn't as if they were short of freighters. She could put a few of them aside for prospective subversives. But the odds of the whole effort amounting to anything were very low. "Or maybe they'd just be rounded up and fed into the death chambers."

She dismissed the thought with a shrug. Her staff would have to consider the matter, then put forward proposals. Hoshiko had no qualms about supporting an insurgency, particularly one that would tie down enemy forces, but she knew it would be hard for an insurgency to gain any real traction. The Tokomak would simply smash the insurgents from orbit if they showed themselves too openly. No, any widespread rebellion was doomed. She doubted they'd even slow the Tokomak down for more than a few days.

"Yes, Admiral," Robin said. "It *might* be possible to make inroads into the Tokomak themselves. A handful of officers have expressed interest in defecting."

Hoshiko's eyes narrowed. *The Tokomak wouldn't do that*, she thought, *unless they genuinely believed there was no hope of rescue—or victory.* And yet, the Tokomak had been absolute masters of the universe for so long that she doubted their faith in themselves would be shaken so quickly. They were probably already coming up with rationalisations for their defeat, starting with her superior numbers and firepower. Their population, back home, would probably not even *notice*. What was the loss of a few dozen ships and a single naval base when there were *hundreds of thousands* of ships and *hundreds* of naval bases?

Ah, but this one is in the right position, she thought, wryly. *They cannot let us keep it.*

"See what you can do with them," she ordered. She would make sure that any defector was thoroughly checked, of course, but...who knew what they could do with a defector's willing cooperation? Someone who might even be able to speak to his fellows...had they merely captured a Tokyo Rose? Or someone a great deal more influential? "And send me a full report on their current government."

She watched Robin walk through the hatch, then considered what she'd been told. It had been a long time since she'd taken History and Moral Philosophy, but her tutors had made it clear that many of the *advantages* of a dictatorship simply didn't last very long. A dictator *could* cut through the red tape and remove worthless bureaucrats, giving the impression of efficiency, yet no one mind—human or alien—could hope to keep track of all the details necessary to keep society functioning. And the devil was in the details.

And that assumes that the dictator is not in it for his own personal glory, she reminded herself, dryly. *When he is, he puts his own safety and security ahead of his people.*

It was tempting to believe that the Tokomak government would simply collapse under the harsh weight of reality. She certainly *wanted* to believe it. Human history suggested that the dictatorship, however disguised, could not last forever. And the *Empress* had set a precedent that every ambitious officer on Tokomak Prime could hardly fail to note. But there was no way she could *count* on it. Or have any idea when it would happen. The government merely had to last long enough to win the war and crush the human race. After that...it didn't matter. Humanity would be dead.

She spent the next few hours touring her flagship, listening to an endless series of reports and updates on the frantic defence planning. She would have liked to go over to the enemy base herself, or even set foot on the ring, but she knew her security team would have had fits. If the last update from Apsidal was to be believed—and she didn't think the Tokomak had had time to fake anything—the human forces were still fighting hard. There was no reason any surviving enemy forces on the ring couldn't do the same. She was a little surprised by how quickly they'd surrendered.

Which doesn't mean they all surrendered, Hoshiko reminded herself. Her ancestors had often refused to surrender, even when they were ordered to do so. Some of them had held out for years before they were finally rounded up and returned home. *They might be hiding until we lower our guard.*

Her communicator pinged. "Admiral, we managed to hack their command network," Yolanda said. "The techs swear blind that it should be possible to duplicate the feat, even when they're fighting back."

"Very good," Hoshiko said. She turned and started to walk back to the CIC. "How far can we go?"

"It depends," Yolanda said. "The techs weren't entirely clear."

Hoshiko sighed, inwardly. If she had a credit for every wondrous idea that had worked perfectly under controlled conditions, but not in the heat of an unpredictable battle, she'd be the richest woman in the Solar Union. The idea was brilliant, she had to admit, and it would come in handy if—when—the enemy attacked the system, yet there was no way she could depend on it. The Tokomak weren't *stupid*. They understood their weaknesses as well as their strengths.

But it doesn't matter, she thought. *If it works, it works; if it fails, I can back off and retreat into FTL.*

"Tell them I want to read a full report by the end of the day," she said. "And I want the idea tested under combat conditions—or as close as we can come to them."

Her lips thinned as she walked into the CIC. The display was clear, save for a handful of freighters heading in from deep space. None of them *looked* to be coming from Winglet, but she wasn't about to dismiss them as harmless. She'd learnt *that* lesson the hard way. Her ships would fire—automatically—on any freighter that dropped out of FTL too close for comfort. She wouldn't let them fool her again.

Her eyes swept over the planetary display, then she turned to Yolanda. "Call the LinkShip," she ordered. "Inform Captain Hameeda that I want a word."

"Aye, Admiral."

. . .

Hameeda had been worried, more worried than she cared to admit, about her FTL drive system. The stardrive *had* managed to jump her into FTL, when she'd outstayed her welcome near N-Gann, but it had been damaged by the jump *to* N-Gann. She'd been lucky to escape, she knew. If the designers hadn't built so many redundancies into the system, she would have had to flee in normal space.

But at least the self-repair units can handle the damage, she thought. She hadn't been looking forward to calling an outside engineer. The LinkShip might well be impossible to repair, at least until they met up with the fleet train again. *I should be back at full efficiency within a couple of days.*

She closed her eyes, accessing the reports from her analysis subroutines. The brief engagement had been brilliant, from the point of view of the ship's designers, although it had also shown a handful of weaknesses. In hindsight, if she'd been armed with hammers right from the start, she could have done a great deal more damage. But then, she'd have to tear out half her lower hull to make room for the missiles and their launch tubes.

How long would it be, she asked herself, before they started turning cruisers into LinkShips? Or would that be considered a step too far?

An alert flickered through the neural net. Admiral Stuart was calling. Hameeda felt a pang of disappointment—she'd hoped that Conner would call, although she knew it was unlikely—and allowed the call through. The Admiral's image materialised in front of her.

"Captain," Admiral Stuart said. "Congratulations on your victory."

"Thank you, Admiral," Hameeda said. "And congratulations on yours."

"I couldn't have done it without you." Admiral Stuart smiled. It was oddly endearing. "And now we've congratulated each other, how is your ship?"

"Intact," Hameeda said. "My FTL drive should be fully repaired in a couple of days, but I'd prefer to take her back to the shop for some work. It's the first time the self-repair functions have been really tested."

"They'd be useful on other ships," Admiral Stuart observed. "Or do they have hidden flaws?"

Hameeda smiled. "They're better at fixing solid-state drives than the bigger, more modular units, Admiral. The designers traded an FTL drive that cannot be fixed easily for greater efficiency. But if the drive was kayoed, I'd be in deep shit."

"I can't argue that," Admiral Stuart said. "Would you care to repeat your mission?"

"Yes, Admiral," Hameeda said. "I won't deny it was chancy, and that it could have gone badly wrong, but it was the sort of mission this ship was *designed* to do. We have to use advanced tech as a force-multiplier and…"

"I believe I put that argument forward myself," Admiral Stuart said, dryly. "Do you have any concerns?"

"Only the unpredictable nature of the gravity shadow," Hameeda told her. "The next LinkShip might slam straight into the planet itself and vanish. There's always going to be an element of chance in such missions. I think I pushed my luck about as far as it would go."

"I see," Admiral Stuart said. Her lips curved into an expression Hameeda couldn't help thinking was a little predatory. "Your next mission will *not* involve flying straight into a planet."

"I'm glad to hear it," Hameeda said, feeling a shiver running down her spine. "What *does* it involve?"

Admiral Stuart told her.

CHAPTER THIRTY-THREE

It was a major frustration, Empress Neola decided, that there were relatively few fleet bases—and none of them particularly large—between Apsidal and Earth. She could dispatch a raiding force to Sol, if she wished, and rely on freighters to support it, but there was no way she could send an entire fleet until she'd built up her logistics base. Recapturing Apsidal was a good start, yet she needed an entire string of bases leading all the way to Varner. And she doubted the humans would let her assemble a base in peace.

She scowled in frustration as she sat in her office and read the latest set of reports from Apsidal. The fighting was still going on, with no end in sight. There *would* be an end eventually, of that she was sure, but when? The gerontocrats had had an advantage, she conceded sourly. They could afford to wait years, if not decades, for their operations to pan out. *She didn't have anything like that long.*

The intercom bleeped. "Your Excellency?"

Neola looked up. "Yes?"

"A courier boat just entered the system through the Mokpo Point," her aide said. "N-Gann is under attack."

"What?" Neola shook her head, dismissing her surprise. "The human fleet?"

"Yes," her aide said. "We're downloading the recordings now."

"Put them through to my console," Neola ordered, putting the report aside. N-Gann was under attack? That was unexpected, although welcome. If the humans wanted to bleed their fleet white while grinding through the planet's defences, who was *she* to stop them? N-Gann was heavily defended. "They may be trying to trick us."

Her mind raced. She'd expected the humans to try to cut her supply lines, perhaps in GS-3532 or Winglet, but N-Gann? A chill ran through her body as she realised it made no sense, as far as she could tell. The humans had nothing to gain and a great deal to lose by laying siege to N-Gann. It was embarrassing for her, true, but hardly fatal. The planet and its immense halo of orbital industries were protected by a massive planetary defensive shield powerful enough to resist even *her* fleet. N-Gann could afford to wait out any attacker.

She brought up the starchart, considering her options. The humans *could*—and presumably would—cut her supply lines, simply by sitting on top of the gravity points in N-Gann and destroying anything that came through. It would be some time before Neola's officers on Tokomak Prime realised that N-Gann had turned into a black hole for starships, let alone tried to do something about it. And what *could* they do? Neola had already rounded up every active starship short of the capital fleet itself. They'd need time to organise a counteroffensive and dispatch it down the gravity point chain.

We'll have to go back, Neola thought. She wasn't as angry about it as her subordinates might have expected. They couldn't press on to Earth until Apsidal was secured. She could afford to double back and take out the human fleet. If nothing else, they'd be forced to expand ammunition and fuel they couldn't afford to waste. *And then they'll have no choice, but to retreat into interstellar space.*

She was midway through drawing up a preliminary outline for her staff to turn into a detailed operational plan when the door buzzer rang. Neola frowned, then keyed the switch to open the hatch. Her aide stepped in, looking terrified. Neola's eyes narrowed sharply. They'd been getting on better, now he'd finally managed to demonstrate a genuine degree of competence. But...if he was terrified, what had happened? A presentiment of disaster ran through her. Perhaps, just perhaps, the humans had invented something that turned everything she knew about space combat on its head.

"Your Excellency," her aide said. "I..."

"Spit it out," Neola snapped, impatiently. It was bad news. Of *course* it was bad news. "Tell me what has happened!"

"N-Gann," her aide said. "N-Gann has fallen!"

For a moment, Neola could only stare at the younger male. N-Gann had fallen? N-Gann could *not* have fallen. The humans didn't have the weapons or technology to knock down the shield and seize control of the high orbitals. N-Gann could not have fallen. She would sooner have believed in an alien fleet appearing out of nowhere and laying waste to Tokomak Prime than the human refugees taking N-Gann. Their fleet simply didn't have the firepower to take the world...

She found her voice. "What happened?"

Her aide flinched at her tone, as if she'd physically struck him. "They... they found a way to bring down the shield," he managed. "And then it was just a matter of time."

Impossible, Neola thought. The humans *didn't* have a weapon that could bring down the shield. Even a hammer wouldn't be able to punch through the forcefield. If they'd had such a weapon, they'd have used it before they were pressed against the wall. *They couldn't have taken down the shield.*

"Put the records on the display," she ordered, savagely. "Now."

Her mind raced as she tried to grapple with the universe being turned upside down. She understood, now, why the gerontocrats had found it so hard to believe *her* report. They simply hadn't been able to comprehend a younger race—an *absurdly* younger race—beating a fleet of fifty battleships and escorts. Now, Neola could barely comprehend N-Gann falling to the human fleet. It shouldn't have happened.

It could be a trick, she thought. *But my staff would have already verified the authorisation codes.*

She took a deep breath, controlling her temper as the recording started to play. The human fleet arrived in N-Gann and deployed for battle, then...a human ship appeared *under* the forcefield. She thought, just for a moment, that the humans had sneaked the ship into position before the planetary forcefield had been raised, but the sensor records were clear on that point. The enemy ship had dropped out of FTL *under* the planetary shield. It should have been impossible.

Not as impossible as we'd thought, she told herself, firmly. The Tokomak had never tried to find ways to drop out of FTL within a planet's gravity shadow. It had seemed too risky to try, particularly as the slightest mistake would crash the starship into the planet's gravity well. No one would ever know what had happened to the ship. *The humans clearly found some way to do it.*

She contemplated the possibilities for a long moment, none of them good. The Tokomak had prided themselves on their unquestioned mastery of gravimetric technology, but it was clear that the humans had jumped ahead. Who knew what *else* they might discover? The Tokomak had thought they'd discovered everything, but...she shook her head, angrily. That assumption had clearly been wrong. Who knew what the humans would discover next?

"Inform General Wooleen that I wish to speak with him immediately," she said, stiffly. "And prepare the fleet for immediate departure."

"Your Excellency?"

"We cannot leave them in place," Neola snapped. "They're not only sitting across our supply lines, they have control of the planet's industries and warehouses. Given time, they can replenish everything they've lost. Go."

The aide scurried away, leaving Neola to her thoughts. There was no way to know if the *humans* knew what they'd done, but *she* knew. They'd done a great deal worse than merely cutting her off from her supply lines. They'd cut her off from her government. How long would it be, she asked herself, before one of her more ambitious officers decided to make a bid for power? She doubted it would be very long. She'd encouraged too many young officers to think they could jump right to the top.

And that wasn't the only major problem, Neola considered, as she mulled the possible implications. N-Gann led directly to a number of important worlds, some of which were on the verge of revolt. If N-Gann had fallen—if the populations found out that N-Gann had fallen—they might rise up against their masters. And even if they didn't, the human fleet was large enough to move from system to system, leaving a trail of devastation in its wake. That would weaken her too, when the implications became clear. It was quite likely she'd have to return to Tokomak Prime to deal with troubles at home.

She bit down a curse that damned the humans to the seven hells. She'd had no choice, but to take command of the fleet personally. There was no way she could put that much power in anyone else's hands. A competent officer would be a threat, an incompetent officer would get himself killed and his ships destroyed. No, she'd had no choice. And yet, she was now thousands of light years from home. She needed to be back there to keep the situation under control.

It wasn't a complete disaster, she told herself firmly. Cold logic insisted that N-Gann was a very minor fleet base, compared to the giant industrial facilities surrounding the original core worlds. The empire would barely notice its loss. And yet, its fall was going to have massive repercussions. The Tokomak no longer looked invincible. There was no way they could avoid unrest, not now. She had no doubt the Galactics would start reconsidering their stance as soon as they realised what had happened.

The situation is not under control, she thought, as General Wooleen's image appeared in front of her. *But it isn't a complete disaster either.*

"Your Excellency," General Wooleen said. He sounded calm and composed. "You wished to speak with me?"

"N-Gann has fallen," Neola said, flatly. "That is a major short-term problem."

General Wooleen looked irked. "We were training conscripts on N-Gann," he said. "I assume they won't be coming here?"

"No," Neola said. The conscripts would be executed, when N-Gann was recovered. Who knew what bad habits they would have picked up from the human occupiers? "It may be some time before you receive *any* reinforcements."

"That isn't good," General Wooleen told her. "The enemy is *still* fighting hard, despite our new policy of venting the ring as we proceed."

The humans have masks and spacesuits, Neola thought. *They can keep going even as their allies die.*

She dismissed the thought with a shrug. "It is vitally important that you take control of the ring as quickly as possible," she said, "but I have to return to N-Gann. I cannot leave the enemy in possession of the system."

General Wooleen looked pained, but understanding. Neola had no trouble guessing what he was thinking. If there were rogue human ships watching the system from a distance, hidden under a cloaking field, she'd be giving them a chance to strike the ring. They wouldn't have any particular reluctance to bombard General Wooleen's positions, would they? They'd been quite willing to damage the N-Gann Ring despite the risk of accidentally rendering the planet uninhabitable. Who knew what they'd do if—when—she pulled out of the system?

But N-Gann was uninhabitable anyway, she thought, grimly. *Would they really be willing to wipe out billions of innocent lives?*

"We will endeavour to have the ring in our possession by the time you return," General Wooleen said. "And I look forward to receiving supplies and reinforcements."

Neola looked at the display. The humans had had nearly two weeks to search the N-Gann Ring, remove whatever they wanted to use and prime the rest for destruction. She had no doubt they'd destroy anything they couldn't use. And *that* meant that it would take a *long* time to rebuild her supply lines. Even if the human fleet was wiped out, even if she didn't lose a single ship in the engagement, there was no way she could resume the drive on Earth in a hurry. No, the humans had scored a major victory. They'd bought time for their researchers to invent something new and for their industrial base to start putting it into mass production. And there was nothing she could do about it.

"You'll have them as soon as I can send them to you," she said, although she knew it might be a while. "Do whatever you see fit to secure the ring."

General Wooleen looked amused. "Short of bargaining with the rebels, I assume?"

Neola gave him a sharp look. There was nothing to be gained by bargaining with rebels, save—perhaps—for future trouble. The rebels couldn't speak for the entire planet, let alone the sector. And besides, granting any sort of legitimacy to one rebel group would encourage others. She could see certain advantages in making tactical agreements, even if she had no intention of *keeping* them, but the long-term effects would be bad. They would certainly undermine her standing with the interstellar combines.

"Take the ring, General," she ordered. "And destroy anyone who stands in your way."

She closed the connection, took a moment to centre herself and then strode through the hatch and onto the CIC. The fleet was slowly coming to life, hundreds of ships checking in as the news spread from ship to ship. Neola hoped it wouldn't cause a panic. They might be cut off from their supply lines, but they had more than enough firepower to recover N-Gann and reopen the links to the core worlds. Her crews would understand that, she thought. She made a mental note to make sure that her commanding officers explained it to them.

And we were riding high after our first major battle, she thought. *Being defeated, simply by having our supply lines cut, is going to hurt.*

"Your Excellency," her aide said. "The fleet will be ready to depart in two hours."

"Very good," Neola said. Compared to just how long it had taken her *first* major command to prepare to depart, it was *fantastic*. She wondered, idly, just how long it took the humans to get a fleet underway. "Have you forwarded the data to the analysis decks?"

"Yes, Your Excellency," the aide said. "They haven't been able to shed any light on just *how* the human ship was able to jump under the shield."

Of course not, Neola thought. *That would be too easy.*

She sat down and keyed her consoles, running the record again and again. Could the humans have set out to *trick* the defenders into believing that they'd jumped under the shield? It was possible, although unlikely. The humans couldn't have sneaked into low orbit unless they'd somehow managed to design an improved cloaking device. She wouldn't dismiss the possibility out of hand, even though it seemed improbable. N-Gann had been surrounded by layer upon layer of active sensors. If the humans had a cloaking device that could stand up to such scrutiny, they would have been using it everywhere.

"Your Excellency," the aide said. "The fleet is ready to depart."

"Then take us out of orbit," Neola said. "And straight to the gravity point."

She studied the display for a long moment, silently calculating the timing. There was no way to avoid the simple fact that it would take at least two weeks to *reach* N-Gann. The humans would have plenty of time to destroy everything they couldn't take with them, if they didn't think they could hold N-Gann against her fleet. She had no idea which way they'd jump, either. If they'd had enough time to repair the shield generators and start the orbital nodes churning out weapons and defences, they might just manage to turn N-Gann into a powerful fortress. And *that* would open the core worlds to attack.

The core worlds are heavily defended, she told herself, firmly. *They cannot turn the base into a significant threat.*

The fleet slowly approached the gravity point, the first elements slipping through and vanishing from the display. Neola tensed, despite herself. There was no reason to believe that Mokpo had been attacked, or even that there was a significant enemy presence within the system, but she felt unnerved. The human attack on N-Gann had taken her by surprise. There was no way they *should* have been able to take the fleet base and turn it against her...

And that makes our deployment predictable, she thought. The humans *had* to know she couldn't leave them in place. At best, she would arrive to find a devastated world; at worst, she would encounter an impregnable fortress. The human fleet could simply hide under the planetary shield as it prepared for war. *They know we're coming.*

Her eyes narrowed. Perhaps the humans *would* hide under the forcefield. It would be frustrating, but it wouldn't be a complete disaster. Indeed, she could see some advantages to the whole affair. The human fleet could be bottled up indefinitely while she redeployed her ships to hit Earth and destroy their Galactic Alliance. Given time, she could even mass the firepower necessary to crack the shield and smash the fleet once and for all. She doubted the humans would let her manoeuvre them into such a position, but...they might have no other choice. Her fleet outgunned theirs by a considerable margin.

And they didn't do themselves any favours by shooting missiles at the planetary defence force, she thought. *They must be on the verge of shooting themselves dry.*

"The scouts have returned, Your Excellency," her aide said. "Mokpo is secure."

"Then take us through," Neola said. She allowed herself a moment of relief. "And then set course for the next gravity point."

Her lips curved into a cold smile. She had more than enough time to study the records, to draw up contingency plans, to decide how to proceed...she could do it. Losing N-Gann had been a setback, she conceded, but it was hardly a disaster. And the war was far from over.

We will win this, she thought. *And the humans will be utterly destroyed.*

CHAPTER THIRTY-FOUR

"The map says this is meant to be a garden, sir," Trooper Rowe said. "Did we get lost?"

Martin snorted, remembering all the jokes about junior officers who tried to read maps. It was hard to get lost in the ring, despite its immense size. His suit's navigational systems had little difficulty keeping him firmly localised, even when he went crawling up the ventilation shafts. They'd passed through a set of airlocks into what was, effectively, a gated community for rich Galactics. The anthill-like house they'd walked past as they made their way towards the garden had been the alien equivalent of a mansion. And the garden…

He felt a pang at the sight before him, even though he'd never been a big gardening fan. The Galactics had turned their private estate into a botanic garden, but the plants and trees were dead, slain by the invaders. They'd breached the upper levels and vented the atmosphere, condemning any unprotected individuals within the sector to death. Martin shivered as they slipped into the dead treeline, relying on their battlesuits to hide them from any enemy sensors. They'd discovered an alien family that had been killed by exposure when they'd searched one of the nearby houses.

"I think they'll be coming down the road," he said, motioning for his men to take up positions within the dead growth. "Get ready."

He settled down to wait, his suit scanning the airwaves for enemy transmissions. He'd seen gated communities before, back when he'd been a young man on Earth, but the sheer *size* of the Galactic residence dwarfed the upper-class communities in Chicago. It had taken him years to understand just how thoroughly the Earth aristocrats—in all, but name—and their hangers-on had screwed the poorer communities. The Galactics didn't even try to hide behind absurd buzzwords that they'd be hard-pressed to define, if challenged. They seemed to think that their dominance was a law of nature.

An alert flashed up in front of him, suggesting that alien forces were quite close. Martin tensed, scanning the roadway. The garden—and the network of gated communities—would make ideal supply lines for the invaders, if they pushed their way down the road before the defenders could get in place to stop them. Martin was surprised they hadn't forced their way into the gated communities weeks ago, back when they'd first landed. Colonel Chang had speculated that the alien aristocrats had tried to keep their private communities out of the fighting, even though they'd already been lost. If that was true, and Martin had no trouble believing it, they'd clearly lost power. The enemy were working hard to open up new supply lines.

And kill everyone they come across, he thought, grimly. The bastards had just kept opening airlock after airlock, steadily venting the entire ring. It wouldn't be long until they exterminated every last living thing, from the defenders and alien rebels to people who were just trying to stay out of the fighting. *They're growing more ruthless.*

His eyes narrowed as the lead enemy vehicle came into view, its turrets traversing from side to side as its crew scanned for hostiles. The boxy vehicle looked crude, for something the Galactics had produced, but it was effective. He knew from grim experience that the main guns could blast through solid armour, while the soldiers concealed in the back would be protected from incoming fire while they readied themselves for combat.

There was a certain simplicity about the design that he found admirable. It made him wonder if the Galactics had *really* invented it for themselves.

They probably had someone with real experience do the designing, he thought, as several more vehicles came into view. *There are no bells and whistles on those vehicles.*

"Take aim," he hissed. "Fire on my command."

He mentally checked the escape plan as he targeted the lead vehicle, bracing himself for the coming engagement. The plan was relatively simple, but there was no way to know how the enemy would react. They might flinch back, giving his team a chance to escape, or they might charge forward recklessly. Martin hoped it would be the former, but feared it would be the latter. Other teams had set up ambushes to teach the invaders not to chase them too boldly, but he hadn't had the manpower to set up a second line of traps. They had to get out before the enemy decided what to do and did it.

"Fire," he snapped.

The HVM shot from the launch tube and slammed into the lead vehicle, punching through the armour and detonating inside the hull. Martin felt a flicker of pity for anyone *inside* the vehicle, then turned and started crawling towards the escape route. He heard two more explosions behind him, followed by a string of blistering curses. Trooper Hawthorne had missed his target. He'd be the target of a great deal of ribbing when the marines got back to base.

He heard a whining sound behind him, followed by a wave of plasma fire that blasted over his head. The dead trees exploded, pieces of debris flying in all directions. He expected them to catch fire, but they didn't. *Of course not,* he recalled as he kept moving. Fire couldn't burn when there was no oxygen. He glanced back, just in time to see one of the surviving vehicles unloading its complement of armoured troopers. Martin unhooked a grenade from his belt and hurled it towards the aliens, then kept moving. That should slow pursuit long enough for them to escape.

"They're having problems keeping up with us," Sergeant Howe said, as they reached the hatch. "Shall we go?"

Martin frowned. The invaders were normally more aggressive than *that*. Normally, it took longer to convince them that they didn't *want* to pursue the humans as they fled. Was there an ambush down below? But, as they scrambled down the shaft to a transit tube and hurried along it, no ambush materialised. The enemy seemed suddenly reluctant to continue the fight.

Maybe we hurt them worse than we thought, Martin contemplated, as they passed a checkpoint and entered the safe zone. *Or maybe they're thinking twice about trying to take the entire ring.*

"Ah, Captain," Captain Patterson said. "Major Griffin wants you and all other officers in the briefing room."

"Yes, sir," Martin said. He resisted the urge to roll his eyes. The briefing room was nothing more than a large alien compartment that had been pressed into service. But then, that was true of every hidden base. There was no point in trying to establish a proper garrison when the base might be overrun at any moment. "I'm on my way."

He strode into the briefing room, poured himself a cup of coffee and took a seat. His fellow officers looked tired and worn, some of them thoroughly unkempt. Martin rubbed the stubble on his jaw, silently thanking God that Yolanda liked him clean-shaven. He had resisted the suggestion that he shouldn't grow stubble at all—it was a simple medical procedure—but he had had its growth retarded. The others, it seemed, hadn't thought to have it done until it was too late. Some of them had full-grown beards.

But at least we're still fighting, he thought. He'd known commanding officers who'd throw a fit if one of their subordinates grew stubble, but he'd never wanted to go into battle behind them. *They haven't whipped us yet.*

"There have been some interesting developments," Major Griffin said, as he stood at the front of the room. He didn't have a podium, but he didn't need it. His voice was loud enough to be heard at the far side of the room. "The first one is that the enemy fleet has been withdrawn."

An officer stuck up a hand. "Withdrawn, sir? They're not heading towards Sol?"

Major Griffin didn't look unhappy at the interruption. "We still have links to stealthed recon platforms," he said. "They confirm that the enemy fleet proceeded through the Mokpo Point, not the Garza Point. It's hard to be entirely sure, of course, but intelligence believes the fleet has done something that has forced the enemy to respond. We don't know what."

Hit their supply lines, Martin guessed. Yolanda was out there, somewhere. He hoped she was still alive. *Or...or what?*

"The enemy is no longer in control of the high orbitals," Major Griffin said. "They *have* left a handful of warships behind, presumably to provide orbital fire support, but the majority of their fleet has departed. That gives us an opportunity to go on the offensive."

"Unless it's a trap," Captain Yates said. "They might be ready for us."

"They *were* showing a marked sensitivity to losses," Martin said, remembering how the aliens had practically let his team go. "They may think they won't get any reinforcements in a hurry."

"Either way, it could easily be a trap," Yates insisted. "They might want to lure us up from the depths."

"They still can't bombard the ring," Captain Thompson offered. "We could inflict some *serious* pain."

"At a cost," Yates said. "We could win the tactical engagement, sir, but lose the war."

"We are aware of the risks," Major Griffin said. "But it is our belief that we have to go on the offensive. If the enemy loses here, as well as wherever the fleet hit them, their morale will be weakened."

Assuming the Tokomak care about morale, Martin thought. *So far, they've been happy to keep funnelling people into the tunnels to die.*

He listened, keeping his face an expressionless mask, as Major Griffin outlined the operational plan. It was relatively simple, although in war the simplest things were often the hardest. The aliens wouldn't see them coming, he thought...in hindsight, perhaps it had been a mistake to attack the spaceport. Intelligence had insisted that the Tokomak, embarrassed by their mistake, had started to patrol the spaceports thoroughly. They even had troops patrolling the outer edge of the ring itself. Martin doubted that even the legendary Pathfinders could get though the defences without tripping the alarms.

Too many things could go wrong, he thought. *But yeah, we have to go on the offensive.*

Major Griffin threw the plan open for discussion. Yates put his doubts aside and offered a number of suggestions, while Thompson had a couple of suggestions of his own. Martin couldn't think of any, although he suspected he'd have some later, once he'd had a chance to read the reports and consider the possibilities. There was nothing *subtle* about the plan, nothing that might catch the aliens by surprise. And yet…they couldn't be expecting the humans to go on the offensive. They had to think that there was nothing for the human troops to gain by striking directly at the alien occupiers.

"It should work," he said, finally. "When are we going on the offensive?"

"Two weeks," Major Griffin said. He sounded pained. "I'd prefer to take the offensive sooner, but…it depends on just how much of our firepower can be concentrated and deployed. We spread ourselves out for a reason."

"Yes, sir," Yates said. "What about the alien rebels? Do we ask them to assist?"

"That might be dangerous," Thompson pointed out. "They might betray us."

"They wouldn't betray us to their enemies," Captain Nasser insisted. "They know we're their only hope of freedom."

"There were collaborators everywhere," Thompson said. "All it takes is one spy in the right place and our plans will end up in the gutter…"

"We will inform them when the balloon goes up," Major Griffin said. "Even if they don't have spies amongst them, they will be using the planetary network to communicate. The enemy *cannot* be allowed to get wind of what we're doing."

"No, sir," Martin agreed. "And besides, the rebels are seriously undisciplined."

There was a low murmur of agreement. No one doubted that the rebels were brave, or that they were prepared to fight against immense odds, but they all knew that the alien rebels were not good soldiers. They could delay the enemy, perhaps even stop them for a while, yet…it wouldn't be long until they were pushed aside or simply destroyed. And their tendency to put revenge ahead of reason, and looting ahead of winning, made them liabilities on the battlefield. The rebels had already given the enemy propaganda specialists all the atrocities they could possibly want. It wouldn't take long for the enemy media to convert a handful of deaths into planet-wide slaughter.

And there's no one to present a counter-story, he thought. *The Tokomak will control the narrative from beginning to end.*

He snorted. OCS had covered the many different ways that wars could be steered by the media, and public opinion, even in the Solar Union. The old sweats claimed that Martin and *his* generation had it lucky. *Their* reporters had practically been enemy combatants, taking the enemy's lies for gospel truth while assuming that every word from a military spokesman was a flat-out lie. Martin wasn't sure he believed *all* the stories, but OCS *had* confirmed that the media had a major influence on how a war might develop. The only upside to the whole situation, as far as he could tell, was that everyone *knew* the Tokomak media wasn't free. It was just possible that no one would pay attention to horror stories about human atrocities.

It isn't as if anyone paid any attention to the media on Earth, he thought, sourly. *Everyone knew the media lied about everything, no matter what it claimed.*

"I want to be ready to move in two weeks," Major Griffin said. "Make sure your troops understand that this is to be carried out in total secrecy. I do *not* want to have to call off the operation because someone decided to blunder and tell the enemy we're coming. Clear?"

As crystal, Martin thought.

He stood when they were dismissed, walking out of the chamber and heading down the corridor to the barracks. They were makeshift too—the marines had spread out a handful of bedrolls on the hard metal deck—but he knew better than to complain. A night in a foxhole would be far less comfortable. His men were, wisely, already catching up with their sleep. Who knew when they'd have a chance to sleep again?

Sergeant Howe met him as he stepped into the barracks. "Sir?"

"We're going on the offensive," Martin said. He wasn't entirely sure he liked the idea, particularly given the number of question marks hanging over the exact location of the enemy fleet, but he had to admit that he was tired of constantly being on the defensive. "And we're going to give them one hell of a bloody nose."

...

There was very little *new* about the human strategy, General Wooleen decided, although their approach to military tactics was often disturbingly innovative. They seemed bent on steadily wearing down his men by a combination of hit-and-run attacks and a handful of ambushes, the latter designed more to kill or injure his men than shove them back into space. General Wooleen had hundreds of thousands of troops under his command, most of which were rated as expendable, but the steady drain in lives and treasure was appalling. It didn't help that he couldn't repressurise the sections of the ring he'd secured. The Empress had been most clear that he was *not* to allow the enemy to sneak back and retake their positions.

And now the fleet had departed.

On the face of it, General Wooleen knew, his forces were not significantly hampered by the fleet's absence. He couldn't call down KEW strikes on the ring, not without risking utter disaster. And yet, he knew the enemy could hardly have failed to notice the fleet turning and leaving the system.

What would they do, if they knew the fleet was gone? And, perhaps more importantly, how long would it be before he received reinforcements?

The Empress wanted him to secure the ring. And he'd promised her he would. But...the more he looked at it, the more he wondered if securing the ring was even possible. He simply didn't have enough troops to press the attack, let alone keep smashing down airlocks and venting entire sections. The engineers who'd built the ring had done a very good job. It would take years to vent it *all*...

...And the humans would keep fighting anyway.

He sighed as, for the first time, he realised that the Empress had made a mistake. Apsidal was not *that* important. They could turn one of the other planets into a supply base, if they wished, or even start building a full-fledged fleet train. But the Empress was determined to recover Apsidal, just to teach the rebels a lesson. She was in danger of losing sight of her primary objective as she grappled with her secondary ones.

And there's no hope of talking her out of it, General Wooleen thought. He knew better than to assume that the Empress would listen. She'd already rejected a handful of practical solutions that would have saved them so much trouble. Merely coming to terms with the rebels, and treating them as trustees, would make it impossible for the humans to continue the fight. But it was not to be. *All we can do is keep fighting.*

He tapped his console, calling up a map. His forces had seized vast amounts of territory, but—compared to the sheer immensity of the ring—it was tiny. And his control was more tenuous than he cared to admit. There was no way he could put a guard on *every* access tunnel or maintenance shaft within the occupied zone. The humans could get quite close to his main bases at any point, if they wished. And there was nothing he could do about it.

Except keep fighting, he told himself. *And hope for the best.*

CHAPTER THIRTY-FIVE

As a general rule, Neola disliked second-guessing herself. Agonising over a plan was quite understandable, but once that plan was underway—and her plan *was* underway—there was nothing to be gained by fretting. She'd committed herself to recapturing N-Gann ten days ago and there was no point in worrying about it. There was certainly no way she could change her mind. And yet, that worried her more than she cared to admit. Her movements were depressingly predictable.

They know what I have to do, she thought. *And that means they have a chance to prepare for me.*

Neola asked herself, time and time again, what *she'd* do in their place. And the answer depended upon too many variables that were outside her control. Devastate the entire planet? Turn it into a fortress? Destroy the ring, cloudscoops and everything else that might be useful in the future? Or…what? Set sail into deep space or set up an ambush?

She studied the display, silently counting down the hours until the fleet dropped out of FTL and engaged the enemy. Not, she knew, that they could *count* on staying in FTL until they reached the emergence point. The humans had yanked her *last* fleet out of FTL and battered it to near-uselessness, something she'd *known* was impossible at the time. Now…now she had to assume the worst. The humans knew she was coming—their long-range sensors would be picking her up—and they'd be ready for her. Unless they'd simply fled...

Her teeth widened into a snarl. The humans had held the system for nearly a month. They'd had more than enough time to do everything from stripping the defences bare to raiding further towards the core. Her empire might be tottering, her people utterly confused...her admirals moving to take power for themselves. She had no way to know what she'd find when she entered the system and dropped out of FTL. She'd seriously considered seizing the gravity point first, just to discover what was happening on the far side. Only the grim awareness that the enemy might force her to lay siege to N-Gann had convinced her to focus on the planet first.

"Your Excellency," her aide said. "The analysts have sent you a report."

And they sent it via you, instead of directly to me, Neola thought. *It must be bad news.*

She keyed her console, bringing up the report. It *was* bad news. The analysts believed that the wretched humans were breaking the taboos surrounding the development of any sort of artificial intelligence, to the point where they *might* be able to bring a ship out of FTL far closer to a planet than anyone else. Biological minds—and automated systems—couldn't handle the sort of fine gravimetric control required to handle the gravity tides. Indeed, the report went on to say, the humans might have worked a degree of AI into their point defence systems too. They were simply too good to be basic automated targeting systems.

That wasn't good news, Neola knew. The humans—like the other younger races—had no idea why their elders and betters had installed the taboo in the first place. It had probably never occurred to them that there might be a good reason behind it. Neola was far too young to recall the nightmare that a handful of scientists had unleashed, when they'd developed the first true AI, but she'd heard the stories. AI was just too dangerous to be unleashed. And who knew how far the humans had gone?

They'll destroy themselves, if we don't destroy them first, she thought. In hindsight, maybe it had been a mistake not to explain the reasoning behind the ban. But projecting an image of the Tokomak as all-knowing entities had been deemed more important than admitting to their failures. *And they might take the rest of the galaxy with them.*

She put the report aside for later contemplation, even though every instinct was crying out for her to do something—anything—about the human developments. There was nothing she *could* do. The humans could not be stopped until she managed to get a fleet to Earth and *that* had been put back a year or two, perhaps longer. She needed to reopen her supply lines, push onwards to Earth and then destroy the human race once and for all.

"Your Excellency," her aide said. "We will reach the emergence point in thirty minutes."

Neola nodded. There was no point in issuing further orders. Her ships had gone to battle stations an hour ago. It would put a great deal of wear and tear on the equipment, to say nothing of the crews themselves, but at least the humans wouldn't catch her by surprise. Her ships had orders to open fire if they found themselves yanked out of FTL. The humans would be the ones who got the surprise.

Unless they have something else up their sleeves, she thought, eying the display. There had been no time to scout the system, even if she'd thought she would have been able to get a scout in and out without being detected. *Who knows what's waiting for us?*

She leaned back in her chair. There was no point in fretting about that either. She'd drawn up a whole string of contingency plans, from finding that the humans had abandoned the system to discovering that they'd repaired the planetary shield and were now hiding underneath it. *That* would be a surprise, she'd thought. If the humans could jump under the shield, why couldn't the Tokomak figure out how the trick was done and duplicate it? The humans might not expect the taboo against AI to remain in place if it was suddenly vitally important to put AI to work.

But it will, she thought. *The consequences of undoing the ban will be too dangerous.*

"Contact all ships," she ordered. If she was lucky, the humans would make a fight of it. They might think they could get away with a barrage of missiles and then a crash-jump into FTL, but they were in for a surprise. And if she could destroy their fleet, the war would be within shouting distance of being won. "Prepare to engage the enemy."

. . .

Hoshiko stirred as her intercom bleeped, loudly. Sitting upright in bed, she reached for the terminal and slapped it with one hand. She'd thought she wouldn't be able to get some rest, but she'd fallen asleep almost as soon as her head had hit the pillow. And Yolanda wouldn't have interrupted her unless it was urgent.

"Report," she said.

"Long-range sensors have detected the enemy fleet," Yolanda said. "They're on a least-time course from Winglet. Projections say they'll be within the system in two hours."

"Time enough to finish the game and beat the Spanish too," Hoshiko quoted. She wasn't sure if Sir Francis Drake had *actually* said those words or not, but they fitted. "Bring the fleet to yellow alert, then pass the warning to the folks on the planet. They can take the remaining freighters and go."

"Aye, Admiral," Yolanda said.

Hoshiko closed the connection, then swung her legs over the side and stood. There was no point in trying to go back to sleep now. Her steward had already arrived, carrying a tray of coffee and biscuits. Hoshiko nodded her thanks, drank the coffee as quickly as she could and hurried into the shower. She wanted to be fresh for when the enemy arrived.

And if they decide to drop out of FTL too soon, they may see my trap before the jaws slam closed, she thought. She'd spent a great deal of time trying to deduce where and when the enemy would drop out of FTL, but she'd had to concede that it was impossible. Too much depended on precisely what the alien CINC—the Empress herself, if Admiral Valadon was to be believed—knew about what had happened at N-Gann. *She may assume that I've turned the planet into a fortress.*

It was a tempting thought, but—by the most optimistic estimate—it would take months to repair the planetary shield. Too many generators had been destroyed or disabled during the first engagement. She had repair crews drawing up plans, when they weren't busy doing more important tasks, but it was very much a fifth-order priority right now. She'd consider turning N-Gann into an advance base if she managed to stop the alien fleet.

She washed herself thoroughly, dried her body with a towel and pulled on her uniform before stepping back into her cabin. Her steward had already put a tray of bacon, eggs and bread on her desk, waiting for her. Hoshiko felt a flicker of guilt—her crews wouldn't have anything like as good a meal—before she sat down and started to eat. There was nothing to be gained by starving herself. Besides, her subordinates knew to make sure their crews had plenty to eat before a battle. It was unlikely they'd have time to fill up during the engagement.

Her terminal bleeped, showing a cluster of enemy icons racing towards the system. Hoshiko felt cold, even though nothing on the display really surprised her. The Tokomak had massed five starships for every one of hers, enough firepower to do a great deal of damage to her fleet even with her tech advantage. And her ships simply didn't have enough missiles left to go toe-to-toe with the aliens.

They don't know that, she thought. *And they don't know what else is waiting for them here.*

She studied the reports as she finished her breakfast, then rose and strode into the CIC. Her staff were already working hard, trying to tease out exact numbers of ships from the haze on the display. The Tokomak were flying in close formation, the same trick Hoshiko herself had used to conceal her full strength. Not, she supposed, that it mattered. She knew there were at least two thousand starships bearing down on her. And there could easily be more.

"Yolanda." Hoshiko sat down. "Status report?"

"Force Able is in position, all ships report ready," Yolanda said. "Force Baker and Force Charlie are moving into position now. They should be in place before the enemy arrive."

"Let us hope so," Hoshiko said. She had a feeling she knew where the enemy would choose to emerge—she suspected that the alien empress would want to be close to N-Gann, but not too close—yet there was no way to be sure. The aliens wouldn't take the bait if they got a sniff of Force Baker or Force Charlie before it was too late. "Are we ready to retreat?"

"Yes, Admiral," Yolanda said. She hadn't been too happy when *that* part of the plan had been discussed—nor had anyone else—but there was no alternative. The fleet could *not* afford a long engagement. Better to give the enemy a bloody nose and retreat than fly too close to the guns and get torn to shreds. "The FTL drives are already spooling up."

Hoshiko settled back into her chair, forcing herself to wait. The plan had looked good, on paper, but she knew from grim experience that no battle plan ever survived contact with the enemy. The bastard would have plans of his own, her instructors had taught her, and victory would go to the side that adapted first. Hoshiko hadn't been too sure of that—history had taught her that most overwhelming victories came about because one side had overwhelming power—until she'd actually gained some experience. Too many brilliant plans had failed spectacularly when the enemy had counterattacked.

"They'll enter the projected emergence zone in ten minutes," Yolanda said. "But they might sweep onwards to the planet."

"I doubt it," Hoshiko said. The Tokomak Empress might be willing to take risks—Hoshiko rather admired the alien, although that wouldn't stop Hoshiko from killing the bitch if she had a chance—but some risks were just too close to suicide. An entire fleet, dropping out of FTL on the edge of a gravity shadow...she'd be lucky if she *only* lost a few hundred ships to collisions. "They can't go too close to the planet."

Particularly if they don't know how much work we've done on the defences, she added, silently. *We could have turned the planet into a fortress and they know it.*

She sobered as she watched the timer slowly tick down to zero. There was no way to know just how much the *enemy* knew about her preparations. She'd made sure to keep all ships out of the system—everything that poked its nose through the gravity point had been blown away without hesitation—yet there was no way to be entirely *sure*. She didn't think the Tokomak had a stealth FTL drive yet, but there were plenty of ways to sneak a scoutship or two into the system. Her surprise might not be a surprise at all.

We'll find out soon, she told herself. The plan wasn't as bold or as dashing as the plans she'd devised when she'd been a squadron commander, but it should work. And, even if it didn't, she'd have room to retreat. *The die is cast.*

• • •

The LinkShip hung in the centre of the fleet, waiting.

Hameeda couldn't help feeling a little confined, even though she knew the odds of an accidental collision were very low. It was the downside of her neural link, she suspected; she was intimately aware of the location of each and every starship in the fleet, an awareness that felt curiously oppressive as it pressed down on her. Cold logic told her she was fine, that she was in no danger; emotionally, she felt trapped in a tiny space. She hadn't felt so confined since the first day she'd crawled into a Jefferies Tube as a cadet.

There's nothing to fear, she told herself, although it felt unconvincing. She wanted to gun the engines and move away from the fleet, she wanted to run…alerts flashed up in her neural link as her heart started to pound faster. Hameeda took a deep breath, calming herself as best as she could. *There really is nothing to fear…*

...Except the enemy, her own thoughts answered back. She could see the enemy ships clearly now, even though they were still in FTL. It wouldn't be long before they dropped out of FTL and went on the attack. *We do have them to fear.*

Her lips quirked at the thought. Admiral Stuart had given her some very complex orders, with instructions to carry out as much of them as she could. Hameeda had every intention of carrying out *all* of them, although she knew it might not be possible. Her ship pulsed with anticipation as she readied herself for her mission, despite the risk of a violent death. The enemy might score a direct hit with their energy weapons, or even a lucky shot with a missile, and blow the LinkShip to atoms. She shook her head, dismissing the fear. She'd known the risks when she'd joined the navy. It wasn't as if she'd *had* to join the navy.

Thank God my mother got on that ship, she thought, reflectively. She had no idea what would have happened to her if her mother had stayed on Earth, but she knew it would have been horrific. Earth was a hellhole, even in the halfway decent regions. The Solar Union was far superior. *And now I fight to defend it from alien enemies.*

It was an odd thought. She'd been told, years ago, that people had believed that truly advanced aliens would have outgrown war and conquest by the time they encountered the human race. But the Galactics, thousands of years older than humanity, still invaded worlds, enslaved entire races and generally acted like interstellar conquerors. Perhaps it was a fundamental truth that the universe was red in tooth and claw, that someone could either be strong and secure or weak and *insecure*; perhaps it was a sign that the Galactics, for all their prowess, were simply not advanced *enough*. And even if they had been, could they have remained a healthy society when they ran into new threats? How many human societies had reached the pinnacle of existence, such as it was at the time, and then collapsed when faced with a threat they were unprepared to handle?

Let us hope the Tokomak see us the same way, she thought. It didn't look like it—the Tokomak *had* recognised the threat humanity represented, even if they hadn't managed to crush the human race—but she could hope. *And that we'll be smart enough to avoid creating new enemies.*

The timer ticked down to zero. There was a long pause, just long enough to make Hameeda wonder if Admiral Stuart had been wrong and the Tokomak *were* trying to duplicate her feat of jumping into a gravity shadow, then her awareness filled with deadly red icons. The enemy fleet had arrived. And they looked ready for a fight.

Well, Hameeda thought. A flash of dark amusement ran through her mind. *The band is playing, the stage is set…it's time to see if we can dance.*

CHAPTER THIRTY-SIX

"The enemy fleet has been detected," the aide said, as if Neola couldn't see the display for herself. "They're holding position near the planet."

"Ready to fire a single salvo and run," Neola said. It wasn't a bad tactic, she noted. Indeed, a few years ago, it would have been quite effective. "Angle us towards them, least-time course. Close the range as much as possible."

"Aye, Admiral."

Neola nodded to herself as more and more data flowed into the sensors. It didn't *look* as though N-Gann had been turned into a fortress, suggesting that the enemy didn't have a hope of holding it. She allowed herself a moment of relief—pinning down the enemy fleet would have been costly, even if it would also have had its advantages—as her fleet slowly converged on the enemy position. Their tactics weren't bad, but there was something they hadn't taken into account.

And yet, they should have taken it into account, Neola thought. *Do they think they can jump out of a gravity shadow?*

She shrugged. If the humans *could* escape a gravity shadow, particularly one cast by a gravity generator rather than a planet-sized mass, it was better to find out now than risk being surprised during a more significant engagement. Her imagination was more than up to the task of thinking up interesting ways to use such an ability. Who knew what the *humans* would think up? They seemed to have spent centuries imagining ways to use tech they'd never been able to produce for themselves.

"Activate the gravity generators," she ordered.

Her eyes narrowed as the gravity generators came online, trapping both fleets in normal space. The humans didn't seem inclined to run, even though they could probably have avoided engagement by altering course and simply outrunning her ships. Were they confident they could win a missile duel? Or did they think their point defence was enough to make up for their low magazines? Or...there were simply too many possibilities, none of them good. She reminded herself, sharply, that the humans were not *gods*. They could be beaten. She'd beaten them once already.

"Lock missiles on target," she ordered. If the humans were fool enough to duel with her, so much the better. "And fire!"

Her ship shuddered as she unleashed a massive salvo of missiles. The other superdreadnaughts and battleships followed suit, watching and waiting to see what the humans would do. If they could jump out of a gravity well, they'd do it now. There was nothing to be gained by sticking around and letting her take pot-shots at them. Hell, they'd even cost her a few hundred thousand missiles. But the humans were just sitting there. They weren't even trying to fire back.

Neola frowned. A trick? Human ECM was very good. Had she just expended hundreds of thousands of missiles on a handful of sensor drones? The human fleet might be long gone, leaving only a collection of decoys to make her look foolish in front of the entire galaxy. It might even work in their favour. Neola had no illusions about what would happen if she looked weak or stupid. Her subordinates would start sharpening their knives before plunging them into her back.

And I'll be sent to the retirement home, she thought morbidly. *Unless someone decides to set another precedent by killing me.*

The enemy point defence opened fire, blasting hundreds of missiles out of space. Neola felt a moment of cool relief. The human ships were real...*and* they couldn't jump out of a gravity well. They'd been stupid and they were going to pay the price. Unless...she wasn't sure she believed they *had* been stupid. The humans appeared to have made a number of mistakes, mistakes that no tactician would make. And that meant...what?

"They're cutting down most of our missiles," her aide reported. "Projections indicate that only a few hundred will strike their targets."

"Fire a second salvo," Neola ordered, curtly. The humans would run out of luck, sooner or later. She could afford to smother them in missiles to overwhelm their point defence and smash their ships, one by one. "And then shift to rapid fire."

She frowned as the remaining missiles died, seconds before reaching their targets. The projections had been optimistic. Only a handful of missiles survived long enough to actually strike home, doing little damage. Their targets shrugged off the blows. Perhaps the humans hadn't been quite so stupid after all. They might *survive* a missile duel if her missiles couldn't touch them. But she'd been firing at maximum range. They'd have less time to calculate firing solutions and take down her missiles as the range narrowed.

"Switching to rapid fire," her aide said. He broke off as the display updated. "Your Excellency, the enemy have opened fire."

"Duly noted," Neola said, dryly. The humans hadn't fired anything like as many missiles as she'd expected. Their magazines had to be running dry. She was surprised they hadn't tried to press the captured missiles into service. The captured missiles weren't up to modern standards, but it wasn't as if the humans had a choice. "The point defence will engage the enemy missiles when they enter range."

"Yes, Your Excellency," the aide said.

And then we will put an end to this, Neola thought. She watched her second salvo tear into the human defences. This time, more missiles were breaking through and falling on their targets. The human ships were tough, but not *that* tough. *And then we will drive on Earth.*

...

"Admiral," Yolanda said. "The enemy has switched to rapid fire."

Hoshiko nodded, unsurprised. She'd offered the enemy CO a chance to end the engagement quickly, before superior human technology could come into play. The alien would probably suspect a trap—she'd created a scenario that practically *begged* the aliens to come slaughter their human foes—but they couldn't let the opportunity slide. Normally, she would have switched to rapid fire too; now, she simply couldn't afford it. Her magazines were on the verge of being shot dry.

She gritted her teeth as the alien missiles hurtled into point defence range. There were too many of them for her defences to kill, despite the AIs and RIs handling the defences. A missile slipped through, followed by two more…she cursed as they slammed into a cruiser, their antimatter warheads detonating with terrifying force. Others sneaked through the defences, the damage rapidly mounting up as they struck their targets. She wondered, as the battering match started to grow out of control, if she'd made a mistake. Her fleet could not afford to be battered into uselessness.

"Our missiles are entering their defence perimeter," Yolanda said. "Their point defence is doing well."

"Better than we expected," Hoshiko conceded. The Tokomak seemed to be getting better with every engagement. They'd probably learnt a great deal from the *last* engagement. And the enemy CO didn't seem inclined to make mistakes. The sheer weight of firepower she could bring to bear against her opponents made up for any deficiencies in technology. "Can you locate weak points within their defence?"

"No," Yolanda said. "The analysts are unable to find them."

Too many ships, Hoshiko thought. *They can probably cover themselves even when faced with a serious threat.*

She leaned forward. "Launch the second salvo," she ordered. "And tell the LinkShip to move in afterwards."

"Aye, Admiral."

...

"The enemy are firing a second barrage," the aide reported. "They're targeting the lead ships."

"Good," Neola said. The enemy *should* have been firing a great many *more* missiles. They *had* to be running short. Her point defence had stopped almost all of the first wave of missiles in their tracks. But if the humans had fired a second wave of missiles before the first one had been stopped...she shook her head. It was time to put an end to the affair. "Close the range."

"Yes, Your Excellency," the aide said.

Neola smiled to herself. The humans had overplayed their hand. Their ships were still faster than hers, in and out of FTL, but they no longer had time to reverse course and run for their lives. She'd be on them before they could escape. And then...she'd take damage, of course, but she could replenish her losses before the humans even knew their fleet had been destroyed. The plan hadn't failed, not completely. It had merely been rewritten to accommodate changing circumstances.

Another shudder ran through the giant ship. Neola's smile widened. It wouldn't be long now.

...

Hameeda had to fight to keep her emotions under control as the LinkShip raced forward, protected only by a faint stealth field and the sheer number of missiles heading in the same general direction. Admiral Stuart had deployed hundreds of ECM decoys and penetrator drones to help the missiles break through the enemy point defence, although the vast number of enemy ships tended to even the odds. The Tokomak had enough firepower to engage *every* incoming threat without caring if it was real or not. Hell, they'd learn a great deal simply by noting which target failed to explode.

Space roiled and seethed with energy as antimatter warhead after antimatter warhead detonated uselessly on the edge of the enemy point defence envelope. There were so many missiles that one of them exploding tended to set off a chain reaction that took out a number of others. And yet, it wasn't all bad. The antimatter blasts disrupted enemy sensors, making it harder for them to pick up the next wave of missiles. Or the LinkShip. Hameeda braced herself, then slid through the enemy point defence without being noticed. The enemy had too much else to worry about.

I see you, she thought, as her subroutines hastily dissected the enemy formation. The Tokomak operated a strict hierarchy, with orders coming from the top and being passed down through a network of smaller ships. It was fairly easy for her to locate the command ships, even though they'd made some progress towards concealing them. They probably hadn't expected someone to fly right *into* their formation. *I see you...and I have you.*

She activated both hammers, targeted the command ships and launched the missiles. There was no way to hide their presence, not once the black holes had been unleashed, so she spun the LinkShip into a series of wild evasive manoeuvres. The enemy opened fire a second later, unleashing so many plasma bolts that anything less than a LinkShip *would* have been hit. She ducked and dodged, no longer bothering to hide, as the first hammer punched into a superdreadnaught and vaporised it. The second was nearly at its target when a light cruiser deliberately rammed the missile to save the bigger ship.

Bastard, Hameeda thought, without heat. The explosion had taken out the hammer as well as the enemy ship. *That was a neat trick.*

She corkscrewed through the enemy formation, her sensors picking it apart in a desperate bid to locate the remaining command ships. There were no more hammers, no way of taking the command ships out in a single blow, but the enemy didn't know it. They focused all their attention on her, even as part of their command network started to collapse. She didn't bother to fire back, not with her remaining weapons. They'd write her off as a threat if they thought she didn't carry anything more dangerous than phasers.

At least I made them panic, she told herself. Her awareness was already touching the enemy command network. *And I have one more trick up my sleeve.*

• • •

Impossible, Neola thought, numbly.

She watched the enemy ship flying through her fleet, unable to believe that it could evade the sheer weight of firepower directed against it. It was *tiny*, for all of its potency; the human ship had taken out a superdreadnaught that outmassed it by a several orders of magnitude. *And* it had had a major impact. A number of her ships had fallen out of the point defence network completely. They were already being targeted by enemy missiles.

"Widen the command network," she ordered. She'd never anticipated losing a command ship, not like that. It was sheer dumb luck that *her* ship hadn't been targeted. "And bring all the ships back into the datanet."

She cursed the humans under her breath. Their tactic had been cunning enough to do real damage, although they'd told her a great deal that—she suspected—they hadn't wanted her to know. They only had *one* of the mystery ships or they'd have sent more of them. She didn't want to *think* about how much damage two or *three* of them would have done. Her formation would have shattered if she'd lost more command ships.

That's something we're going to have to fix, she thought. The human datanet was much more flexible. *They'll try and do that to us again.*

"Continue firing," she ordered. The enemy ship was a nuisance, but it appeared to have fired all of its hammers. It would have taken out more command ships if it could. "Destroy the enemy fleet."

• • •

Hameeda allowed herself a tight smile as she feinted at a superdreadnaught, then spun around and dropped out of range when the enemy ship opened fire. The Tokomak seemed almost scared of her, although they hadn't taken their eyes off the prize. She had to dodge instinctively as a wave of missiles shot past her, heading for the human ships. It made her wonder if the aliens would think of trying to use shipkiller missiles to swat her like a bug.

Her awareness expanded rapidly as her sensors picked the enemy command network apart. It was easy, now, to tell which ship was the command ship, although the Tokomak *did* seem to be trying to reorganise their datanet to hide their flagship. Too late, she told herself. They really should have been a little more flexible. Relaying orders from ship to ship wasn't that difficult *and* it would have confused her more than she cared to admit. The plan would have fallen down sharply if she hadn't been able to locate the command vessel.

She swung the LinkShip around and gunned the drives, heading right towards the enemy flagship. It was an immense superdreadnaught, five kilometres long, yet there was nothing to separate it from the other superdreadnaughts. The Tokomak seemed to have settled on a design, then followed it slavishly. She would never have known the superdreadnaught was the flagship if her sensors hadn't picked out the flow of commands into the enemy datanet.

Ready, she told herself, as the timer reached zero. *Now!*

Her awareness lashed out, slamming into the enemy datanet. It resisted, rapidly massing the power to kick her out, but for a few seconds the datanet was completely exposed. And those seconds were quite long enough.

Gotcha, she thought. *And you never even saw me coming!*

• • •

Neola recoiled in surprise as the display went blank. "Report! What happened?"

"The datanet has gone down," her aide said. "I...Your Excellency...the shipboard system is intact, but the fleet datanet is *gone!*"

Neola stared in horror. If the datanet was gone, each and every one of her ships was suddenly isolated. There would be no more combined point defence, no more coordinated missile strikes, no more...she snapped out of her funk. The enemy had revealed a surprise, one that might give them the edge, but she *still* had the numbers. She'd give them a *very* hard time before she was overwhelmed.

"Get it back up," she snapped. If the enemy had managed to hack the datanet, they could have uploaded all sorts of nasty surprises. The shipboard systems couldn't be hacked—they were designed to be impossible to hack—but the datanet itself was a different story. She might link the fleet back together, only to discover that she'd made things worse. "And purge the entire system first!"

"Yes, Your Excellency."

I still have the numbers, Neola told herself, as she snapped commands into the emergency communications network. Her crews were already reacting. *And they cannot get away from me.*

...

"The LinkShip succeeded, Admiral," Yolanda reported. "The enemy fleet has lost its datanet."

Hoshiko leaned forward, watching as the enemy formation came apart. They probably wouldn't collide with each other—that, she suspected, was too much to hope for—but it would take them some time to re-establish their command network. It would be difficult for them to combine a handful of ships together, at least until they set up laser links and started sharing data. Radio signals were too easy to jam.

"Signal Force Baker and Force Charlie," she ordered. "They are to implement Trojan Horse at once."

"Aye, Admiral."

...

Neola gritted her teeth as the display slowly came back to life. Her flagship had no trouble *locating* the other ships, thankfully, but setting up even a basic network was tricky. And she didn't dare reactivate the main network until the system had been thoroughly purged. She briefly considered retreat, even though she still had the edge. Let the humans have their victory. The trick wouldn't work twice. But...she knew what would happen to her if she let the humans go.

"Your Excellency," the aide said. "Long-range sensors are picking up..."

Neola's eyes widened in horror as the display sparkled with hostile icons. A fleet, a human fleet...a fleet that simply couldn't exist. If the humans had so many starships, the war would be within shouting distance of being lost. No, the war *would* have been lost. There was simply no way the Tokomak could beat a foe with both a numerical and a technological advantage...

Sensor ghosts, she thought, grimly. *They have to be nothing more than sensor ghosts.*

And then the human ships opened fire.

CHAPTER THIRTY-SEVEN

"Admiral," Yolanda said. "Force Baker and Force Charlie have opened fire."

And the trap is sprung, Hoshiko thought. The Tokomak formation, suddenly faced with a whole new threat, seemed to be coming apart at the seams. *And now we see just how well the plan stands up to the real world.*

She leaned forward as a torrent of missiles roared towards the enemy fleet. They were *their* missiles, captured from N-Gann, loaded into hastily-refitted freighters and fired in a single massive barrage. The missiles would have no surprises for the Tokomak—technically, they were outdated already—but there were *millions* of them. There was no way the Tokomak point defence could have stopped all of them even if their datanet was at full capacity.

And it isn't, she thought, savagely. *Their ships are alone against the storm.*

Her lips widened into a cruel smile as she contemplated the situation. The Tokomak—normally—would drop into FTL to escape the missiles. But they couldn't. Their gravity wells, the gravity wells they'd deployed to trap the human fleet, held them too. They could turn off the gravity wells—she was surprised they hadn't done it already—but it would take time for the gravity shadow to fade. And by then the onrushing storm would have raged into the teeth of their defences. She allowed herself a moment of pure glee. She'd avenged her earlier defeat a thousand-fold. There was no way—now—the Tokomak would be able to continue the drive on Sol.

"Missiles are entering enemy point defence range," Yolanda reported. "Ah...they're spitting missiles in all directions."

Hoshiko nodded, unsurprised. The freighters had been equipped with ECM, allowing them to pass for human warships, but it wouldn't take long for the Tokomak to realise that the warships simply didn't exist. They'd probably guess the truth when a second salvo failed to materialise, if they hadn't already. Hoshiko wouldn't have needed to retreat from the earlier engagement if she'd had so many ships in reserve. The *smart* thing to do would be to retreat, but...*could* the enemy retreat?

We'll find out, she thought. *It won't be long now.*

. . .

"Incoming missiles," the aide said. "Your Excellency..."

"I can see them, fool," Neola snapped. She'd been tricked. She'd been tricked and her ships and crews were about to pay the price. "Deactivate the gravity generators, then alter course to take us away from the missiles."

"We can't outrun them," the aide protested. "I..."

"Do as you're told," Neola snapped. If the datanet had been working, she could have hastily realigned the fleet to protect as many of her bigger ships as possible. Now...she didn't dare reactivate the datanet until the network had been completely purged. "And continue firing on the human ships!"

Her mind raced as more and more data flowed into the display. The humans had fired *her* missiles at her. The vast stockpiles she'd built up at N-Gann had been turned against her—she silently promised Admiral Valadon a horrific death when she got her hands on him—and there was nothing she could do. Her crews were working frantically, deploying point defence weapons and decoy drones, but it hardly mattered. They could decoy away—or destroy—half the missile swarm and the remainder would do serious damage to her fleet.

And the formation is coming apart, she thought, numbly. *Our coordination is shot to hell.*

The missile barrage tore into her point defence. Neola forced herself to watch as hundreds—thousands—of missiles were vaporised, only for thousands more to keep going. They were nuclear-tipped, not antimatter-tipped, but it hardly mattered. There were just so *many* of them. The warheads slashed towards their targets and struck home, blasting down shields and detonating against hulls. And her fleet started to die.

"Your Excellency," her aide said. "We lost…we lost over two-thirds of the fleet."

Over a thousand ships, Neola thought. No one had taken such losses since the pre-FTL wars around the gravity points. *And many of the remaining ships are heavily damaged.*

She cursed under her breath. The enemy, damn them to the seven hells, had concentrated their missiles on her battleline. Nearly all of her super-dreadnaughts had been destroyed or damaged, along with all of her battleships. The smaller vessels had taken less damage, but they lacked the point defence and heavy armour of her capital ship. It had been sheer luck that the flagship hadn't been destroyed. The enemy would have targeted her personally if they'd identified her command ship.

The battle is lost, she told herself, firmly. The human fleet was already reversing course, preparing to close in for the kill. It could wipe the remaining fleet out without shooting its magazines dry. *I have to recognise that we have lost and react.*

"Take us out of the gravity shadow," she ordered. "Once we're clear, we are to head directly to the gravity point and punch our way through."

"Yes, Your Excellency," the aide said.

Neola forced herself to sit back as the fleet—the *remaining fleet*—picked up speed. The gravity shadow was fading fast, but it would still be several minutes before she dared order the fleet into FTL. *That* would give the enemy more than enough time to land several more blows, each one tearing further into her already-ruined fleet. And then...she had no idea what would happen then. If she died, who would take power back home? And what would they do?

"Detach all ships that are incapable of entering FTL," she ordered, coolly. "They are to form a rearguard and hold the line until the remaining ships have retreated."

"Yes, Your Excellency."

• • •

Hoshiko smiled openly as the first reports started to flow into the display. The enemy formation had been *shattered*. Over a thousand ships had been destroyed, along with their crews; hundreds more had been crippled. Whatever happened, the Tokomak would have real problems deploying another such fleet in a hurry. She'd won plenty of time for Sol to strengthen its defences and look for a technological breakthrough that would render the entire enemy fleet so much scrap metal. Who knew *what* they'd find?

"Admiral, the enemy fleet is deploying a rearguard," Yolanda said. "They're blocking our path to the remaining capital ships."

"Transmit a wide-band demand for their surrender," Hoshiko ordered. The rearguard wouldn't even slow her down. They *had* to know it. "And add an offer to support any of the servant races if they want to rebel."

"Aye, Admiral," Yolanda said.

Hoshiko settled back into her chair. There were only a few moments before the enemy gravity shadows died, allowing their ships to escape into FTL. If she wanted to complete her victory, she had to move now. She had no way to *know* if the servant races wanted to surrender or not, let alone rebel against their masters, but she had to make the offer. She'd seen enough on N-Gann to convince her that the servants *would* rebel, if they thought they could win. The Tokomak were still overwhelmingly powerful, but they couldn't cope with both a full-scale war and hundreds of rebellions in their rear.

"Admiral, a number of ships are dropping out of the enemy formation and lowering their shields," Yolanda said. "They're surrendering!"

"Let us hope so," Hoshiko said. She'd have to make sure the prospective rebels were checked *thoroughly* before they were cleared to join the Galactic Alliance. "Pass the word to the fleet. Those ships are not to be fired upon unless they fire on us first."

"Aye, Admiral."

. . .

For a moment, Neola simply refused to accept what she was seeing. The servant races were surrendering? The servant races were changing sides? It was unthinkable! She could barely comprehend what was happening! And yet, she couldn't deny the truth. Dozens of ships were dropping out of the battleline. They were abandoning her!

"Target the ships that are dropping out of the battleline," she ordered. There was no way she could allow the mutiny to spread. "Prepare to fire!"

"But...Your Excellency, those are *our* ships," her aide protested. "I..."

"They're rebels," Neola snarled at him. "And what happens when they open fire on *us*?"

She forced herself to watch as the mutinous ships writhed under her fire. The human ships were picking up speed, trying to come to the rescue, but it was already too late. She was *not* going to allow the rebels to escape. And yet...a handful of ships dropped into FTL, vanishing from the display. Her sensors showed them racing away from the system, no doubt heading towards a rebellious world. They'd bring nothing, but death. The Tokomak had already scorched a handful of worlds that had resisted them. Now, with the empire tottering, they would do no less. The rebels were doomed.

"Take us into FTL, as planned," she ordered. The gravity shadow was almost gone. "Now!"

The superdreadnaught lurched, violently. For a terrifying moment, Neola thought they'd crashed right into a gravity well before they dropped into FTL, leaving the battlefield far behind. They'd be on top of the gravity point before the humans realised what had happened and gave chase. She hoped she could get the remaining ships through the gravity point before it was too late. Tokomak Prime *had* to be warned, even if it cost her everything. Her people *had* to know that their empire was on the verge of unravelling.

"Dropping out of FTL in ten seconds," the aide said. "Nine...eight..."

The superdreadnaught shuddered again, red icons flaring up on the display, as it dropped out of FTL. A handful of small human ships watched the point, scattering frantically as they realised that her entire fleet—or what was left of it—was heading in their direction. The remaining loyalists followed her out of FTL and through the gravity point. Neola didn't breathe easily until they'd put some distance between themselves and enemy pursuit.

We lost, she thought, shocked. She'd run hundreds of simulations. They'd all agreed that the humans were doomed. But she'd underestimated the humans and it had cost her, badly. The entire fleet, a fleet that had deployed more capital ships than the humans had *starships*, had been smashed. *And what will happen when we get home?*

"Set course for Tokomak Prime," she ordered. She'd have to direct the other fleet bases to deploy a blocking force, if the humans thought they could mount an attack right up the chain towards her homeworld, but she had time. She *thought* she had time. "And then we'll come back."

But she knew, as she rose and walked into her office, that it might be nothing more than mindless bravado.

. . .

There was no suggestion, not in any one of her records, that the Tokomak had ever panicked before. Hameeda had scanned files dating all the way back to the gravity point wars and there was no suggestion the Tokomak had ever reacted badly to defeat. But now...she watched the remaining enemy ships throw their dignity to the winds and plunge into the gravity point as if the hounds of hell itself were after them. The battle ended seconds later.

She pulled the LinkShip away from the point and set course for the fleet, wondering when—if—the Tokomak would return. They still had thousands of starships, although they were going to have problems training the crews without the experienced personnel who'd been killed in the engagement. And yet...they'd lost. They'd lost so badly that their empire would shake and threaten to collapse. It might be years before they rallied the force to resume their drive on Sol.

"This is Hameeda," she said, as she established a link to *Defiant*. "Mission complete."

"Very good, Captain," Admiral Stuart said. "Hold position. I'll have another mission for you soon."

"Aye, Admiral."

• • •

"We fired off nearly all of our remaining missiles, Admiral," Yolanda said. "The fleet is effectively unarmed."

Hoshiko nodded. She'd been tempted to punch through the gravity point and seize the next system, if only to set it up as a firebreak between the Tokomak and N-Gann, but she simply didn't have the firepower. There was no way she could risk exposing her lack of ammunition to the enemy. Better they thought she was turning N-Gann into a fortress than sitting on her ass for want of a few hundred missiles.

"Combat damage?"

"Thirty-seven ships were lost, fourteen took severe damage," Yolanda said. "We were lucky."

"Yeah," Hoshiko agreed. "Detach two squadrons of cruisers to guard N-Gann, at least until the enemy attacks, then inform the remainder of the fleet that we're heading back to Apsidal to link up with the fleet train. We *need* replenishment desperately."

"Aye, Admiral," Yolanda said. "But won't they have left a blocking force in Apsidal?"

"We'll find out," Hoshiko said. *She* would have left a blocking force, if she'd felt she had the ships to spare. But there was no way to know how the enemy CO thought. She might have felt it was better to bring all her firepower to bear against the human fleet and worry about Apsidal later. "What about the rebel ships?"

"They're being cleared now," Yolanda said. "Most of them want to go home and liberate their homeworlds."

Hoshiko shook her head. She understood the impulse, but the largest rebel ship was a light cruiser. The rebels would be blown to atoms when—if—they tried to free their homeworlds from enemy occupation. No, they'd be better off working with her fleet…if, of course, she could convince them that that was actually true. It was quite possible they'd refuse to listen.

"Order them to remain here, for the moment," she said. "And tell them that they can go off on their own, if they wish, but we won't support them."

"Aye, Admiral," Yolanda said.

Hoshiko dismissed her with a nod, then sat down at her desk and closed her eyes. She felt…tired and drained and not even the slightest bit exultant. She'd won a great victory, but it had come at an immense cost. And her fleet was still deep within enemy territory. She needed to take her ships back to Apsidal and replenish her missile magazines before the Tokomak counterattacked.

It should take them years to muster a counterattack, she thought. *But is that actually true?*

She shook her head, slowly. There was no way to know. A massive fleet, fully equal to the one she'd just destroyed, might already be heading towards N-Gann. Or she would have months, if not years, to run rampant through enemy territory before the Tokomak finally gathered the strength to tear her fleet to bits and then turn Sol into a dead system. She thought she understood, now, just how Admiral Yamamoto must have felt. He could sink dozens of American carriers and shoot down hundreds of American planes, but there would always be more to take their place and grind the Japanese to powder. The Tokomak outmassed the human race far more comprehensively than the United States had outmassed Japan.

I won, she told herself. She had won what was, perhaps, the greatest naval victory in recorded history. And yet, it had also been one of the most costly. *But it feels more like a defeat.*

She keyed her terminal, bringing up the list of destroyed ships and killed personnel. It felt wrong, somehow, to admit that she barely recognised any of the names. The fleet was just too large for her to keep track of everyone. And yet, they'd all had lives—they'd lived and loved—until they'd died in combat. She wondered, morbidly, if it had been just as bad for her ancestors. They hadn't known the men who'd died under their command either.

And I'll have to say something about them, when we hold the service, she thought. *But what?*

Her intercom chimed. "Admiral, the fleet is reporting that it is ready to depart," Yolanda said. "We can be in Winglet within a week."

The shortest route back to the fleet train, Hoshiko thought. *Assuming, of course, that the fleet train wasn't destroyed during the first engagement.*

"Good," she said, calmly. There was no point in fretting. If the fleet train had been destroyed—or decided to head back to Sol—she would deal with it later. The real problem, right now, was that her flight plan was predictable...if, of course, the enemy had any ships left to take advantage of it. "Order the fleet to depart."

"Aye, Admiral," Yolanda said. She sounded tired too. "I'll see to it at once."

"And then get some sleep," Hoshiko ordered. "You need it."

"You too, Admiral," Yolanda said. She *had* to be tired. An aide had a duty to point out when an admiral needed sleep, but aides were normally politer than that. "Ah, Admiral..."

"Don't worry about it," Hoshiko said. She'd once tipped a cup of coffee into her commanding officer's lap. It had been an accident, but she'd thought the old man was going to murder her on the spot. "Get some rest, once the fleet is underway."

"Aye, Admiral."

Hoshiko sighed, then stood and headed for bed. Her entire body felt tired. She needed rest, a chance to nap before something else happened. There was little chance of the fleet being intercepted as it made its way to Apsidal, she thought, but she would need to be in peak condition when they forced their way through the Apsidal Point. Who knew *what* would be waiting for them there?

We'll find out, she told herself, as she removed her jacket and trousers. *And we'll deal with it, somehow.*

She climbed into bed and closed her eyes. But it was a long time before sleep overcame her.

CHAPTER THIRTY-EIGHT

"I can see the bastards," Trooper Rowe hissed. "They're taking up position near the transit tubes."

Martin nodded, curtly. The Tokomak hadn't managed to get the transit capsules online—yet—but they *had* been using the tubes to move supplies from place to place. He was mildly surprised they hadn't started using them to push deeper into the ring, although large sections of the network had been booby-trapped. Their bomb-disposal teams were moving as fast as they could, if intelligence was to be believed, but the task was immense. They simply hadn't been able to open up more than a handful of tubes.

He glanced at his timer, watching the final seconds tick down to zero. Major Griffin had put together a good plan, he thought, with plenty of room for improvising—or outright retreat—if things went wrong. Hundreds of small teams were taking up position all along the front, readying themselves for the advance. He smiled grimly, then checked his rifle one final time before the timer bleeped. It was time to advance.

"Go," he subvocalised.

The team moved forward, grenades at the ready. Martin sucked in his breath as he saw the aliens, standing in front of a giant airlock that led to the transit tubes. Sergeant Howe hurled the first grenade, concentrating on taking out the aliens as quickly as possible; Martin hurled his a second later, cursing the enemy armour. It wasn't as flexible as its human counterpart, according to the techies, but it was tough. The aliens barely had a moment to draw their weapons before the grenades detonated, blowing them to bits.

"Incoming, sir," Rowe snapped. "A spider-walker."

"Kill it," Martin snapped. The enemy craft looked like something out of a bad movie—he had no idea what the designers had been thinking, when they'd put the first plans together—but he'd seen the spider-walkers in action. They could be quite dangerous if the drivers knew what they were doing. "And get that airlock open."

A dull explosion shook the chamber as the demolition team blew the airlock wide open. Martin tensed, half-expecting to feel air rushing out of the chamber even though he knew the compartment was vented, then ran forward to peer into the tube. It was empty, save for a handful of magnetic projectors that looked as if they'd been working before the power had been shut down weeks ago. Any transit capsules had been removed by the aliens, he guessed. The giant tube was empty.

"This way," he said, activating his antigravity unit. "Let's fly."

He kept a wary eye out for aliens as he flew down the tube, knowing it was only a matter of time until they were detected. The enemy had probably scattered countless sensors within the tubes, just to keep an eye out for someone trying to turn them into a weapon. He hoped the other attacks, each one targeting a different enemy base along the front line, would be enough to keep the aliens busy. They might not have time to focus on him and his team if they had too many problems elsewhere.

But we're heading right into the central core, he thought, as he took a sharp left and then rocketed up the shaft. *They have to know we're coming.*

He flew around the corner and swore as he saw the alien barricade. A handful of aliens, their weapons already being lifted...he gunned the antigravity unit, flying right towards their position and smashing into the barricade. The aliens fired, but their shots went wild as he tore through their position, his guns firing automatically as they picked out targets and killed them. The remainder of the team followed, pushing onwards over the handful of alien bodies. Their target wasn't that far away.

"They have to know we're coming," Sergeant Howe said. "Sir?"

"Press on," Martin said. He understood the risks, but they could end the battle in a single blow if they captured the alien commander. There was no way the Tokomak and their servants could go underground, not on the ring. Their former servants would hunt them down and kill them. "We have to keep moving."

He sprinted down the tube, relying on the suit to keep him moving. Two more aliens appeared, but both were shot down before they realised they were under attack. Martin barely noticed as he reached the second-to-last transit airlock, the one just below the spaceport itself. His team followed him as he blasted the airlock down, then hurled a string of grenades into the next chamber. There was no time to take prisoners. They had to keep moving.

"This way," he said, as they scrambled into the access tube. "There should be a way up to the lower levels."

He shivered, despite himself. It was easy to forget, at times, that the ring wasn't *just* an unimaginably huge complex. Now...they were under a spaceport, under the heaviest armour mounted on the ring. He knew it was strong. They'd devastated a spaceport further along the ring, but the series of explosions hadn't done anything more than scratch the underlying armour plate. He felt exposed, even though he knew they were relatively safe. But there was no time to worry about it.

The hatch at the top was locked. Martin stuck a demolition charge underneath it, then ducked down as the charge exploded. A handful of aliens staggered backwards in all directions as he burst out of the hatch, his guns already firing. The aliens simply didn't have time to react before they were gunned down. He smiled, tightly. The path to the command centre lay open.

"Trouble, sir," Sergeant Howe said. He was checking his HUD. "They've got a blockade right in our path."

"Shit," Martin said. He'd been wrong. The path to the command centre was closed. "I need options."

"I have one," Trooper Rowe suggested. "But it's risky."

Martin laughed, humourlessly. "What isn't?"

...

"They're attacking in all sectors," a voice said. "I..."

There was a crashing sound, then the voice cut off. General Wooleen swallowed a curse as the entire sector went dark. The humans—and their allies—were attacking with a fury he hadn't seen since his first deployment to a rebellious world. And *there* he'd been able to call on orbital fire support whenever the rebels showed themselves. Here, his soldiers had to grapple with their enemies on even terms.

"They took down a section of the command network," one of his officers reported. "I'm trying to restore a link now."

"Optimism isn't always a virtue," General Wooleen said, dryly. The command network was supposed to be tough. If a section had gone down—and it had—he was fairly sure it meant that the guardpost had been taken out, along with the guards. "Order the next set of guards to prepare to repel attack."

He gritted his teeth as the terminal updated, again. The humans seemed to be throwing in attacks from all directions, without any overall objective. *That* seemed more than a little unlikely, given the human skill at deception. Logically, the humans had an objective in mind, something they considered to be worth the risk of mounting a major offensive. But what? It was hard to believe the humans thought they could take out *all* of his soldiers.

"Barricade 472 has been overrun," another officer called. "The enemy are heading for the spaceport!"

No, General Wooleen thought. *They're heading for here.*

"Tighten the guard around the command centre," he ordered. The humans *couldn't* have any other objective in mind. "And order the engaged units to fall back on my command."

His mind raced. The humans had been trying to divert his attention, but they'd failed. He'd caught their plan before it was too late to stop them. And…there was no way they *could* get into the command centre, unless they wanted to risk using antimatter weapons on the ring. It would be amusing if they did, although he wouldn't live to see the results. Their positions—and their allies—would suffer worst if they set off a chain reaction that destroyed the ring and showered debris on the planet below.

The Empress will not be happy, he thought. *But at least the rebels will have been crushed.*

• • •

"You have got to be shitting me," Martin said sharply, as they made their way into the giant hangar. A freighter sat on a lifting pad, waiting to return to the stars. "You plan to *teleport* into the enemy position?"

"Yes, sir," Rowe said. "Their jammers won't block their *own* teleports."

Martin shook his head in disbelief. Jamming teleporter beams was almost painfully easy for an advanced race. There was a *reason* no one beamed bombs onto enemy starships, even when their shields had been disabled. The teleport jammers ensured the bombs—or boarding parties—never materialised. And yet, he had to admit that Rowe had a point. If nothing else, the Tokomak wouldn't be expecting it.

Of course they won't be expecting it, he thought, as they swept the freighter to make sure it was deserted. *This is nothing more than a fancy way to commit suicide.*

Rowe sat down at the teleport console, looking faintly absurd on a seat designed for an alien who was taller and wider than him, and started to tap on the controls. Martin watched, feeling marginally reassured. The Galactics were safety-conscious to a truly absurd degree. If the teleport beam couldn't get through the jammers, the teleport would simply refuse to activate. And then they'd have to think of something else...

"I've aligned the beam with the jamming signal," Rowe said. "We should be able to teleport behind the lines."

Martin shivered. He'd never really understood how so many of the old sweats could regard the teleporter with fear and loathing, but he thought he understood now. He might well be committing suicide, simply by standing on the pad and triggering the teleport field. And yet, there was no other way into the command post. They didn't dare unleash the kind of firepower that would be necessary to burn through the armour and break into the enemy base.

"Very well," he said. He took his place on the pad, followed by four of his men. Rowe keyed the console, setting a timer, then hurried to join them. "Shall we..."

The world dissolved into golden light. Martin felt uncomfortable, as if insects were crawling over every last atom of his body; he thought, just for a second, that something had gone horribly wrong. And then the golden light faded away, revealing a backroom crammed with alien bedrolls. They'd made it!

"Go," he ordered. "And take prisoners, if possible."

He kicked down the door and charged into the next room. A team of alien REMFs stared at him in horror, clearly unable to comprehend how he and his team had beamed into their sleeping quarters. They certainly *looked* like REMFs, he thought. None of them made any attempt to fight, even though it would have been useless. His men were ready to shoot anyone who resisted in the head.

"Secure them," he snapped. "And then follow me."

. . .

General Wooleen looked up in shock as he heard the sound of someone crashing through the doors and shouting demands for surrender. The humans? How could the humans have broken into his command centre? He checked the display, but the guardposts outside the command post remained resolutely unengaged. The humans had somehow bypassed all the defences and broken into his base. It was impossible.

He drew his sidearm, thinking fast. There was only one way in or out of the complex and, unless he missed his guess, the humans would seal it first. They would need to keep him from bringing in more reinforcements, along with everything else. But...he tried to think of an option as the crashing sound grew louder. He'd have to pass command to his juniors before he was captured.

"Contact Colonel Regan," he said, grimly. "Inform him that he is now in command of the..."

The door exploded inwards. A trio of armoured figures crashed into the room, their weapons already sweeping the room for targets. General Wooleen hesitated, then dropped his sidearm on the floor. There was no point in trying to resist. The terminal bleeped an alert, emergency reports blinking up to warn him that the humans had cracked through two of the guardposts, but it hardly mattered. They'd cracked the command centre itself.

"General," the lead human said. General Wooleen assumed he was the commander, although there was no way to be sure. Technically, a general should only surrender to another general, but he doubted the humans would bother to produce one. Did they even *have* one? He found it hard to care. "Order your forces to stand down and surrender. They will be treated in line with the Conventions..."

General Wooleen frowned. The humans *had* protected some of the planet's former masters from their enemies, but they'd had a large fleet to enforce their will. Now, their fleet was gone and it was only a matter of time until the Empress returned with *her* fleet. And he couldn't issue orders to the system pickets anyway. The most he could do was order his troops to surrender.

He stalled for time. "What guarantees are you prepared to offer?"

"We can take control of the ring and protect your people until our fleet returns," the human said, after a moment. "The locals will not be permitted to kill them."

General Wooleen thought, fast. The Empress would probably expect his soldiers to fight to the last, killing as many humans as they could before they were wiped out. And yet, he doubted they'd kill *many* humans before they were killed themselves. It wouldn't be hard for the humans to turn the ring's systems against its makers, once they regained control of the command networks. His troops, divided and dispirited, would make easy prey. The humans would just have to send in the rebels, then watch as General Wooleen's soldiers were slaughtered.

And they have to help train others, he thought, remembering just how many conscripts had barely been prepared before they'd been issued weapons and told to get to the front. *I can't let them all die.*

He let out a sigh. "Let me have my terminal," he said. "I'll order them to surrender."

The humans watched him carefully as he keyed his console, then issued the orders. It galled him to surrender so tamely, but there was no other choice. The humans had outsmarted him, somehow. He wondered just how they'd managed to get into the command centre. Had they bribed the guards? Or had the guards turned on him? Or...

He shrugged. It didn't matter.

...

"The majority of their troopers have been rounded up," Major Griffin reported, two days later. "But the picket ships have refused to surrender."

"It isn't as if we can get at them," Martin said. The Tokomak had left two squadrons of destroyers behind to monitor the system, but they couldn't bombard the ring and the marines couldn't get to them. The engagement had stalemated. "What do we do now?"

"Now?" Major Griffin shrugged. "We prepare for the *next* conflict."

...

Major Griffin had meant it, Martin decided, over the next two weeks. The marines secured the orbital towers, found accommodation for the hundreds of thousands of prisoners and then threw themselves into preparing for the next engagement. Some of the alien prisoners had proven surprisingly talkative, cheerfully informing their captors that their fleet would return soon enough; others, less inclined to be friendly, merely reminded the humans of their responsibilities under the Conventions. Martin wasn't sure there was any *point* in sticking to the Conventions—it wasn't as if anyone *else* paid attention to them—but Major Griffin had made it clear that the prisoners were to be treated well. If nothing else, he'd said, the Tokomak would be more willing to surrender if they were assured of good treatment.

He was in the command centre when the alarms began to sound. "Sir," Lieutenant Glover snapped. "We have multiple ships transiting the gravity point!"

"You mean they've already transited," Martin reminded him. The speed-of-light delay wasn't something he needed to worry about, normally, but he wasn't ignorant. By the time the planetary sensors had picked the ships up, they'd been in the system for hours. "Alert the CO, then..."

The display updated, rapidly. "They're coming this way," Glover said, as the unknown ships entered FTL. "ETA fifteen minutes."

"Then sound the alert," Martin ordered. If the alien fleet had returned, it wouldn't be long before the humans would have to go back underground. This time, the aliens were going to have an even harder time of it. "And prepare to evacuate this compartment."

He forced himself to relax as Major Griffin strode into the command centre, looking remarkably calm for someone who knew his plans were on the verge of disaster. Martin stood, saluted and briefed his superior quickly, then waited for orders. Major Griffin merely looked at the display, then nodded. The only thing they could do was wait.

"The ships are dropping out of FTL now," Glover reported, as new icons appeared on the near-space display. His voice rose in excitement. "Sir, they're the fleet! They're *our* ships!"

"Thank God," Major Griffin said. "Contact the Admiral, please. I need to have a word with her."

"Yes, sir," Glover said.

We won, Martin thought. On the display, the enemy ships were turning and running for their lives. They weren't even pausing long enough to fire a shot for the honour of the flag. *We fucking won.*

But he knew, as he recognised the flagship's IFF on the display, that the war was very far from over.

CHAPTER THIRTY-NINE

"It's confirmed, Admiral," Yolanda said. "The fleet train remained intact at Garza and is now on its way here."

"Thank God," Hoshiko said. The enemy pickets hadn't realised it, but her ships had been in no state for a fight. "Order them to start replenishing our supplies as soon as they arrive."

She leaned back in her command chair and contemplated the situation. They'd won—and, in doing so, smashed a sizable number of enemy ships. But it was only a tiny percentage of the whole. Given time, the Galactics could assemble a fleet twice the size of the one she'd smashed and send it against N-Gann, then Apsidal. Humanity could still lose the war, if the Tokomak rallied and resumed the offensive. She didn't dare give them the time.

"Contact the senior officers," she said, standing. "Holoconference in ten minutes."

"Aye, Admiral."

Hoshiko rose and walked into her office. Her terminal was blinking, informing her that there were hundreds of reports she had to read, but she ignored them. Her officers would be able to handle most of the problems themselves, without her interference. It was what they were paid to do. She sat down and waited, resting her hands on her lap. One by one, the holographic images materialised. She wished, suddenly, that she could meet her officers in person, but she knew it was impossible. They could be attacked at any moment.

Particularly if the enemy rallies and starts to raid our supply lines, she thought. The Tokomak Empress had options. And she was good enough to *see* those options. *We are sitting on the end of a very long branch and the enemy is going to try to saw us off.*

"We won a great victory," she said, once her officers were assembled. "But the war is far from over."

She leaned forward, willing them to listen to her. "No one ever won a war by sitting on the defensive," she added. "Once we have replenished our supplies, once we have turned N-Gann into a forward base, we have to take the offensive. The Tokomak Empire *cannot* be allowed time to gather its forces and strike back. If we can link up with the rebels, if we can strike deep into their territory, we might win the war."

"Our orders were merely to secure Apsidal," Commodore Jiang pointed out. "Admiral, if we take the war into their territory, we could lose everything."

"We'll lose everything if they muster the force to strike back," Hoshiko countered. The xenospecialists were predicting an enemy civil war, but she didn't dare count on it. "They *cannot* be allowed time to recover."

"We should check with Sol," Commodore Hawking said. "Admiral…"

"There's no time," Commodore Jackson snapped. "By the time we get a message from here to Sol and back, the enemy could have recovered. We have to go on the offensive now."

Hoshiko held up a hand before the debate got out of hand. "We won't be moving immediately," she said. "We have to replenish our supplies and secure our rear. During that time, I want you and your staffs to consider ways of going on the offensive and smashing the Tokomak Empire once and for all. If nothing else, we need to buy time for Sol to improve its defences and produce more ships."

She took a long breath. "I don't pretend it will be easy. There will be much hard fighting ahead. But we cannot sit on our bums and wait for them to hit us. They still outgun us by several orders of magnitude. We *have* to go on the offensive."

"Yes, Admiral," Jackson said. "Dare I assume you have a plan already?"

"The bare bones of one," Hoshiko confirmed. "But we won't be able to go on the offensive for weeks. We'll just have to hope the enemy needs more time to prepare for the next engagement."

"We killed thousands of ships," Jiang observed. "Surely, any *rational* foe would understand that they couldn't continue to soak up such losses indefinitely."

"They have to crush us," Hoshiko said. She looked from face to face. "We're their worst nightmare, ladies and gentlemen. A young race, free of the constraints they imposed on their fellows, with no qualms about pushing technology as far as it will go. They *have* to crush us, simply to keep us from setting a bad example. How many of their servant races have we already influenced to find a way to rebel against their masters?"

"How many of their servants have we condemned to death in hopeless rebellion?" Jiang looked grim. "Admiral, we are taking an immense risk."

"I know," Hoshiko said. "But do we have a choice?"

She met his eyes. "The Tokomak have pronounced a sentence of death on every last man, woman and child, Commodore. The entire human race will be wiped out, if they win the war. We have no choice. We either defeat them, shattering their empire and eliminating the threat, or we die. There are no other alternatives."

"And we will win," Jackson said.

"If we are lucky," Jiang said. "I still think we should check with Sol, though."

"I'll send a courier boat back, as soon as the fleet train has resupplied our ships," Hoshiko said. "But we are on our own out here."

She smiled. "We will go on the offensive," she added. "And their empire will shatter under our blows."

• • •

Martin opened his eyes, feeling—just for a moment—as if he wasn't sure where he was. He was lying on a comfortable bed, the omnipresent hum of the starship's drives pervading every fibre of his being...he smiled, suddenly, as he remembered they were in one of the privacy tubes. Yolanda had met him as soon as he'd boarded *Defiant* and led him straight to the nearest tube, without regard for anything else. Martin suspected that Sergeant Howe would have a few things to say about it, when Martin returned to Marine Country, but it was hard to care. He'd feared the worst when the fleet fled through the gravity point, leaving the marines on their own. Yolanda could have died out there.

He sat up and looked at his partner as she rolled over and yawned. They hadn't been doing much *sleeping*, even though the chronometer on the bulkhead insisted they'd been in the privacy tube for hours. Yolanda would have to go back to her cabin and sleep before the admiral called her back to duty, Martin thought. It wasn't as if she was used to functioning when she was tired.

"It's been too long," he said. "I thought..."

"I was afraid for you too," Yolanda told him. She sat upright, her bare breasts bouncing invitingly. "And we'll be heading further up the chain soon."

Martin tensed. "The fleet will be going on the offensive?"

"That's the plan," Yolanda said. "We can't let the bastards have time to recover."

"Good," Martin grunted. He needed time to recover himself—and reorganise his team, in the wake of the long insurgency—but it wouldn't take long. "And then? What happens afterwards?"

"It depends," Yolanda said. "If we die, we die."

Martin grinned. "And if we don't die?"

"We win," Yolanda said. "Or do you mean what happens to *us*?"

She shrugged. "I want to aim for command myself," she said. "And then you can transfer to my ship."

"If they don't find some other place for me," Martin said. He leaned forward to kiss her. The fleet would be heading onwards soon enough, ensuring he'd have plenty more opportunities to put his life at risk. "We'll see, won't we?"

"Yes," Yolanda said. She kissed him, then stood. "I guess we will."

. . .

"I've already dispatched my final report to Admiral Webster and the NGW project," Hameeda said. "The LinkShip program has been a complete success."

She studied Admiral Stuart as the older woman sipped her tea. Admiral Stuart had insisted on coming in person, rather than sending a holographic image. Hameeda didn't mind, although she rather hoped there would be more to the meeting than simple courtesy. The LinkShip had proved itself. No doubt Admiral Stuart had a whole new task for her.

"So I believe," Admiral Stuart said. "Are you ready to go on the offensive?"

"Yes, Admiral," Hameeda said. She felt a thrill of excitement. "Are we going to hit the enemy?"

"Yes," Admiral Stuart told her. "This is what I want you to do…"

. . .

Neola sat in her cabin, alone.

There was no point, she admitted to herself, in trying to hide from the truth. She'd lost the battle, if not the war. It was quite likely that she would be removed from power when she got home, even though she had done everything in her power to *win*. She'd issued orders to prepare a series of attacks on the enemy lines, sending starships down the chain to N-Gann with orders to raid human shipping, but she knew it wouldn't be enough.

The humans had a window of opportunity to go on the offensive. She was morbidly certain they'd take advantage of it.

But the war isn't over, she thought. Word of the defeat hadn't reached Tokomak Prime, not yet. She'd have a chance to secure her position before the truth sank in. And then…she could rally her forces and go on the offensive again. *We lost a battle, but not the war.*

She sighed, inwardly. It was not a comforting thought. She'd gambled and lost and—even though she knew she could absorb the losses and keep going—she knew there would be consequences. Her enemies would have a chance to remove her, while the humans would have time to prepare an offensive of their own and, perhaps more worryingly, devise newer and better weapons systems. If they came up with something new…

The war is not over, she told herself, firmly. *And we can still win.*

End of Book V.
The Series Will Continue In:
Their Last Full Measure

APPENDIX: A VERY BRIEF RECAP

In the very near future, a handful of military veterans in the USA were abducted by an alien starship. Unluckily for their would-be captors—the Horde, a race of interstellar scavengers—the humans rapidly managed to break free and gain control of the starship. Steve Stuart, a rancher who had been growing more and more disillusioned with the government, saw opportunity—the starship could serve as the base for a new civilisation, the Solar Union.

Despite some small problems with planet-bound governments, the Solarians—as they would eventually be called—started to both recruit settlers for the new state *and* distribute alien-grade technology on Earth. After defeating a series of Horde ships that attempted to recapture their starship and attack Earth, the Solar Union was firmly in place.

This was, of course, unknown to the rest of the galaxy. To them, Earth wasn't even a microstate. This suited the Solarians just fine. Humans could and did travel beyond the solar system—as traders, mercenaries or even simple explorers—but no one wanted to attract the Galactics to Earth. The Solarians were already making improvements to GalTech that could not fail to alarm the major alien powers, particularly the Tokomak.

Fifty years after Contact, the veil of secrecy fell. Humanity's involvement in a series of brushfire wars at the edge of known space could no longer be hidden, nor could elements of advanced technology. In response, the Tokomak dispatched a massive fleet to Sol with the intention of blasting Earth to cinders. Unknown to the Tokomak, the Solar Navy had *just* enough advanced technology to stand off the alien fleet and smash it. The follow-up attacks shattered the Tokomak grip on the nearby sectors, freeing hundreds of planets from their influence. Humanity had suddenly become a major regional power. A number of naval bases were rapidly established, both to extend human influence and protect human trade.

This had unfortunate effects on Earth. The expansion of the Solar Union—and its willingness to insist that anyone who wanted to emigrate *could* emigrate—accidentally accelerated the social decline pervading civilisation. Europe, America and many other countries fell into civil war, something that caused considerable concern in orbit. One faction within the Solar Union wanted to intervene, others—feeling no loyalty to Earth—believed it was better to let Earthers handle their own affairs.

Captain-Commodore Hoshiko Sashimi Stuart—the granddaughter of Steve Stuart—accidentally stepped into a political minefield when she insisted that Earth should be left alone. Her family's political enemies were quick to use it against them. Accordingly, she was placed in command of a cruiser squadron and dispatched to the Martina Sector, where she would be well out of the public eye. However, she rapidly discovered that the Druavroks—a powerful alien race—were bent on a campaign of genocide against their neighbours, including a number of human settlers. Allying herself with other threatened races, Hoshiko led a campaign that broke the Druavroks and laid the groundwork for a human-led federation—a Grand Alliance.

Unfortunately for humanity—and everyone else—the Tokomak had other ideas. Neola, the Tokomak who had commanded the fleet that died at Earth, managed to take control of the Tokomak Empire and prepare her people for a far more serious war. Her first step, after ensuring that the immense fleets were being brought back online, was to attempt to lure a human starship—*Odyssey*—into a trap. Although humanity fell for what was presented, to them, as an olive branch from one of the oldest known races, the crew of *Odyssey* were able to escape the trap and find their way back to the nearest safe port. In their wake, however, an ultimatum was sent. Humanity could surrender...

...Or be mercilessly hunted down and exterminated.

Printed in Great Britain
by Amazon